# BITTERSWEET
## Surrender

# Q.B. TYLER

ISBN-13: 978-1718616806
ISBN-10: 1718616805

This is a work of fiction. Names, characters, businesses, places, events, and incidents are either the products of the author's imagination and used in a fictitious manner Any resemblance to actual persons, living or dead, or actual events is purely coincidental.

Cover Design: Design Honey
Editing: Kristen—Your Editing Lounge
Proofreading: Judy Zweifel at Judy's Proofreading
Interior Formatting: Champagne Book Design

For the women that fell in love with the
original expensive charlatan

# Prologue

WAS A GOOD WIFE.

I was loyal to a fault, playing the perfect, doting wife to a man I married at the naive age of twenty-one, when I viewed the world through those rose-colored glasses they warn you about. I loved him, supported him, and I was undeniably faithful to him.

*I was a good wife.*

Until one day, temptation presented itself in the form of a broken marriage and the beautiful man whose job it was to fix it. I never imagined myself capable of infidelity until the man I married lost all interest in me, just in time for another to take notice.

Now, here I am opening my mind, my heart, and now my body to a man who isn't my husband.

*How did I get here?*

I feel as if I'm having an out-of-body experience, my soul floating above my physical self as I watch myself in complete fascination. I watch as a man shoves me up against the wall of the large corner office on the fourteenth floor of a building on Clinton Street, in Midtown Atlanta. I watch myself wrap my arms and legs around him as his lips find my neck. I hear the clash of our teeth as our mouths ravage each other, our tongues intertwining furiously. His hands move out of my wavy tresses, down my face to grope my breasts. My hands slide down his torso, my fingertips dancing over every hard ridge hidden beneath his cashmere sweater. I watch as I fumble with his pants, desperate to get them down his legs. My body is on fire for his touch. I'm desperate to feel him inside of me, to feel the connection of our bodies becoming one. The arousal pumping through my veins is something I've never experienced. I've never had this kind of passion with anyone.

Not even my husband.

*You may think you know my story, but you have no idea.*

*I was a good wife…until I wasn't.*

# CHAPTER One

*Four Months Ago*

I'M SITTING IN THE WAITING AREA, UNABLE TO KEEP STILL, WHEN a familiar shiver snakes down my spine and I look up just in time to watch *him* emerge from his office. My eyes find his and the boyish smile that crosses his face causes a spike in my heart rate that I can't ignore. I've had a small crush on our therapist ever since my husband and I started seeing him last month, and my infatuation with him seems to strengthen with every session.

Somewhere over six feet tall, Dr. William Montgomery is an enigma. His dark brown hair is short, but with a lusciousness that makes me want to run my hands through it. His sharp jawline is always covered with light stubble that I've spent more time than I care to admit wondering how it would feel between my thighs. His crystal blue eyes are so piercing that I can't hold his gaze for too long without my cheeks heating in response. He's gorgeous, smart, and exudes enough charm to talk a nun out of her panties.

*In short—he's dangerous.*

How he's not married himself, I have no idea. I often wonder how it's possible that he hasn't swept some woman off of her feet with his relationship expertise and those perfect dimples.

"Ms. Pierce?" I stand and wonder if I imagine the look in his eyes. I've never seen him look at me—with such *want.* I shake my head, ridding the thought that this man could possibly be interested in me. *I'm married for God's sake. Why is this thought even crossing my mind?* "Shall we?"

I nod and follow him into his office, unaware that my whole life is about to change in this expensive hour of therapy. I sit in my usual place, the right side of his couch, as my husband, Matthew, always sits on the left. Dr. Montgomery takes his seat, a chair across from us, where he sits as he tries to mediate our bickering. I finger my engagement and wedding rings and look down at my lap.

"You seem nervous," he says, and I look up to see him in his usual chair, his right leg resting on top of his left, ankle crossed over knee. The tip of his pen is resting against his bottom lip, not quite entering his mouth, just enough to catch my attention. He exudes masculinity, sex, and virility in every line of his body and every gesture.

"I–I'm sorry."

"Charlotte, we talked about that," he says. I don't mistake the way my heart skips a beat when my name rolls off his tongue. "Stop apologizing when you haven't done anything wrong."

"Right." I look out the window. A part of me wishes that Matthew was here if only to take the spotlight off of me. *What are we going to talk about for an hour?* "I guess I'm just wondering why I'm here… I mean…why I'm here without Matthew?"

"Mr. Wells was not invited to this session." I drag my gaze away from the window to meet his intense blue eyes. The look he's giving me has so much heat in it, and yet I can't escape the shiver that resonates through me. I want to look away, but I can't. So, we sit, for I don't know how long, staring at each other as I wonder if there is a hidden meaning behind his words.

"Why?" I ask, finally.

"I wanted to get to know you a little better. It's been almost four months since you started coming and I feel that there's something you're holding back. Something you're not sharing. I thought maybe Matthew was the problem. This is a safe space, Charlotte. You can tell me what's wrong."

*A safe space? Does he think Matt is abusive? Matt was a lot of things, but he'd never laid a hand on me.*

"What do you mean? I thought that's what I've been doing for four months. Have you not been paying attention? What have you been writing down this whole time?" I cross my hands and lean forward, eyebrows arched.

*I am so not in the mood for this.*

"There's no room for your attitude in here. You might be able to get away with that with Mr. Wells, but not *now*. Not *today*."

There's something about his tone that causes my heart to beat wildly in my chest. He's never scolded me before and somewhere deep inside of me comes the feeling that I want him to do it again— and again. "What's so special about today?" I ask.

"I want to know why you won't tell me what the real problems in your marriage are."

"I think we've been pretty clear about the problems in our marriage. He doesn't want kids, he doesn't want me to work, and he keeps me locked up in that house." I tick off the reasons on my fingers. "I have to play this role of the doting, trophy wife and I'm sick of it. Ultimately, after five years of marriage, I just don't think he loves me anymore."

*I'm not sure if I love him anymore.*

The words are on the tip of my tongue, but I don't say them aloud.

"The spark is gone." I shrug sadly before a dark chuckle leaves my lips. "Makes me sound like an ungrateful bitch, right? He doesn't hit me, he doesn't cheat on me—to my knowledge—he takes care of me, and I'm complaining that he doesn't…what, fuck me? He doesn't want to go to dinner, or even *have* dinner with me. He forgot my birthday and bought me a house in the Hamptons because you know," I raise my hands before letting them fall in defeat, "what better way to say I'm sorry?" I run a hand through my hair in irritation. "Why am I telling you all of this again? You know all of this. We spent an entire week hashing out that goddamn house and how it so wasn't the fucking point!" My volume has risen steadily as I rant and our eyes meet just as I finish.

"I wasn't aware that you and Mr. Wells weren't *intimate*," Dr. Montgomery says, his hands steepled under his chin, and I swear I hear a growl escape his throat.

"I think we've been fairly clear that we aren't."

"No, it's a topic you both avoid like the plague."

"Well okay…no he doesn't…we don't…" I shrug.

"How long?"

"I don't know?" I let my mind drift back to the last time we had sex. *Whenever it was, it clearly wasn't all that memorable if I can't recall.* "Sometime a few months ago."

"And why is it that you think you don't engage in intercourse regularly?"

"He's busy? He's not into it anymore? He's not into me anymore? Maybe I don't do it for him." I shrug again, knowing full well that Dr. Montgomery isn't going to attend my pity party.

"Charlotte, I find it hard to believe it's you." He rubs a hand over his mouth and I almost convulse when I notice his tongue dart out to wet his lips. I have a vision of him running that tongue over *my* lips, all four of them. It takes everything in me not to moan aloud at the thought. "Have you asked him?"

"I've stopped asking. Whenever I've brought it up, he's brushed me off. He's given me every excuse in the book for why he won't touch me. It's gotten to the point where I think he's not coming to bed until after I'm asleep on purpose." I feel my eyes well up with tears. "Why doesn't he want me?"

I hear the pull of the tissue from the box before I see the white square in front of me. The couch dips next to me and Dr. Montgomery is at my side.

*That's new. He never sits with us. But I guess there's more room without Matthew here.*

"Please don't cry, Charlotte."

"You never call me by my first name," I whisper, the shock taking all the conviction out of my voice.

"You have a beautiful name. A beautiful name for a beautiful woman." He clears his throat and pulls his glasses from his face, tossing them onto the coffee table. "Charlotte, I don't know why your husband treats you the way he does. I watch you two in therapy and frankly…it astonishes me. Why do you stay with him?"

"It was supposed to get better when we found you and started our sessions. I thought it would help. I never wanted to give up on my marriage…it was supposed to be forever."

"But some aren't. You remember I do this for a living."

"We want to try. We were together for three years before we got married and now we've been married for five. That's eight years. I don't want to just give up. How do you start over from that?"

"Staying in a relationship out of some sort of twisted idea of loyalty or co-dependency is not healthy. That's no way to live, and you're still young. You can still meet someone. Someone that makes you happy, that loves you, and takes you out to dinner because he wants to, and not out of some social obligation. Someone who wouldn't dream of forgetting your birthday because he's been planning a surprise for months; a man that makes you come alive in the bedroom. One that spends his days thinking about what he wants to do to you in bed and can't wait for the second he can blow off work to do it. We're all busy, but we have to make time for the things and people that matter. Charlotte, both you and Mr. Wells have forgotten that somewhere along the way."

"I haven't forgotten," I say quickly, and it's true. I am trying my hardest to make this marriage work.

"There are three sides to every story. His side, her side, and the truth. This job allows me to get close to finding out all truths, and the truth is, Ms. Pierce, you and your husband are beating your heads against the wall of this marriage. You are both stubborn in your own ways and unless you *both* make the effort to change what brings you into my office screaming every week, you're only delaying the inevitable."

"A…divorce?" The word tastes harsh and bitter on its way out of my mouth.

"Yes."

"Shouldn't you be diverting us *away* from that?"

"You spend ninety percent of your days arguing. You don't spend any time outside the house together unless it's for appearances, *and* you're not even having sex? You're in the prime of your sexuality. You need to be exploring that regularly. You are too much of a goddess to not be worshipped the way you deserve."

My eyes widen at his choice of words. "Dr. Montgomery…" I shake my head. "I can assure you I'm no goddess. I'm just…Charley. I lost my virginity to Matthew—which you know…" My mind is somewhat scattered over the fact that this beautiful man just called me a goddess. "Maybe he's just bored with me now."

"It's not you…and, Charley?" he asks in obvious reference to the nickname.

I nod. "It's what my family and close friends call me."

He seems confused by my explanation. "But your husband always calls you Charlotte."

I purse my lips slightly. "I know."

He nods as if all of the problems of my marriage can be explained by that simple exchange. "Well," he starts, "as I said, your intimacy problems do not fall on you."

"How do you know?" My eyes find his and search them for any signs of dishonesty in an effort to spare my feelings, but I see nothing.

"I can tell."

"How?"

"Men know." He gives me a shrewd look that makes me want to press him further, but I refrain. I'm silent for a second when he asks, "Did you come?"

My head whips toward his, my cheeks on fire at the three words uttered from that perfect mouth. "What did you say?"

"The last time you and your husband were intimate, did he make you come? Did he take care of your needs? The few times—what—a year that you make love, does he even care about your pleasure?"

"I don't see how that's relevant or any of your business!" I snap, simultaneously trying to channel the lust coursing through me into anger.

"Anything between you and Mr. Wells is my business, Charlotte." It's not lost on me that he continues to call my husband Mr. Wells but now I'm Charlotte. *And Jesus if it doesn't sound good coming from his lips.* I find myself wondering how it would sound while he's coming before I can stop myself. I clench in response to the pornographic thoughts playing through my mind on a loop. "You're blushing," he says, snapping me from my thoughts.

I put my hands to my cheeks in an effort to soothe the fire. "A man other than my husband just asked me about my orgasms. Excuse me if I'm all out of sorts."

"You're thinking about coming," he says and I detect a hint of darkness in his words. "You're thinking about coming *now*."

"You don't know what I'm thinking." I look straight ahead not daring to look at the man next to me who's dangerously close to invading my personal space.

"That is incorrect. I know exactly what you're thinking. Your body betrays you, Charlotte."

*My mind does too. I need to calm down. Deep breaths.* "How…?" *Really, Charley? Don't entertain this erotic type of therapy.*

"Well, for starters, your breathing has changed. Your eyes, which are usually a light brown, are darker, almost mahogany as your pupils have dilated and your thighs are pressed tightly together. Now, tell me, Charlotte, did you come?"

My heart is racing and although I'm a bundle of nerves I try to convince myself that this invasive line of questioning is for professional reasons only. *Nothing more.* Dr. Montgomery is always professional. But I think I would feel more comfortable discussing my sex life if he wasn't close enough to smell the goddamn arousal that is no doubt soaking the satin fabric between my legs.

"No," I say, the air leaving my lungs at the word.

"Does he ever make you come?"

*Not since our second or third year of marriage.* "Sh-shouldn't you be writing this down?"

"I'll remember," he says with such affirmation I feel goose bumps break out all over my skin instantly, my body betraying me further.

"Not…often. It's not exactly his goal when we have sex."

"What is his goal?"

I shoot him a look that says, *"What do you think?"*

"Don't be daft, Doctor."

He looks at me for a beat before leaning against the back of the couch, still eyeing me closely. "When is the last time you had an orgasm?"

I shake my head. "Definitely not your business. That has nothing to do with my marriage."

"And therein lies the problem. Your pleasure, your orgasms, your need for sexual contact, that has *everything* to do with your marriage. One of the things I've learned from this line of work is when couples stop having sex, problems follow. They try to deny it and say it's not about sex or that there are other underlying issues and while there usually are, lack of sex is a fundamental part to the demise of a lot of marriages. As humans we crave intimacy, we crave human contact, and we crave it from the person we signed up with for the *'till death do us part'* pact. So, you sitting here telling me that you coming has nothing to do with your marriage is a problem."

I clear my throat and realize that the walls are closing in. "Water… can I have some water?" I say looking at him.

I need air and he's crowding me. I can't think when he's this close. I'm trying so hard to keep the dirty thoughts of letting him fuck me right on this couch, where I usually sit with my husband, out of my head. But every time he speaks, every time I breathe in his scent, I have a flash of his cock sliding through my folds and I have to resist the moan sitting in the back of my throat.

He gets up and moves to the side of the room where I watch him pouring something. When he returns, he has a glass in each hand. One is water and the other is an amber liquid. He puts both on the table in front of me and I look up. I grab the amber liquid and waft it under my nose before setting it down. "A little early for whiskey, don't you think?" I down the water in one gulp.

"You seemed a little wound up. I thought you could use it to calm your nerves. You're never like this in therapy." He sits back down next to me and I resist the urge to roll my eyes. *You study people's body language; can't you see I need space!?* "Well, no sense in letting this go to waste." He downs the whiskey quickly, as if it were a shot. I stare at him with wide eyes as he swallows the liquid, his Adam's apple bobbing slightly as it slides down his throat.

My eyes drift away from his mouth as I try and put together a sentence. "You're never…usually you sit there." I point at the chair in front of me.

"So, *I* make you nervous, then?"

"Ummm…" I fight the words dying to leave my mouth.

*Yes, you make me nervous because I've been fantasizing about you for months. You make me nervous because I'm sitting here wondering what it would be like to taste your cum.*

"*Why* do I make you nervous? Do I scare you?"

"No."

"Do you think I would hurt you?"

"No."

"Do you trust me?"

I chance a look at him and immediately regret it because I see the mask he's been hiding behind slip for the first time. I haven't been out of the game so long that I don't know when a man wants me. This man *wants* me.

*Your move, Charley. What do you want?*

"Yes," I say letting out a breath. And I wonder what exactly I'm saying yes to.

*His question about whether I trust him, or…something else?*

"This morning," I say before he can respond to my answer. He looks at me confused and I continue, "I made myself come this morning."

He looks me over from head to toe and I'm beginning to see this conversation take a dangerous turn. "How?"

"How did I make myself come?"

He nods, and I can see his resolve weakening.

*But do I want it to? Or do I want him to stay strong. He's my therapist. I'm in marriage counseling.*

"My hand."

His eyes drop to my hands in my lap. "What did you think about?"

*I certainly know what I'll be thinking about the second I get home. Hell, maybe sooner. It wouldn't surprise me if I had my hand inside of my panties the second I get to my car.* "My husband. When the sex was good."

"Don't lie to me," he says immediately.

I furrow my brows. "I'm not!"

"A fantasy is just that, Charlotte, a *fantasy*. It's usually something deliciously forbidden. An act that isn't safe anywhere but within the four corners of your mind. Words you can't even bring yourself to utter out loud. Maybe after you come you feel a moment of clarity before the inevitable shame that comes with your nasty thoughts. But it's there. It's always there, lurking."

"You seem to know a lot about these forbidden fantasies."

"Not until recently."

"Is that so?" I wonder if I might be the star of the dirty thoughts he has while he runs his hand up and down his shaft. The thought does nothing for my racing heart or the ache between my legs. "What do you think about then?"

He shakes his head. "We aren't here to talk about me."

"Tell me."

"No, Charlotte."

"Is it…someone you can't have?" I push further and his eyes narrow at me.

"I can have anyone I want," he tells me and I wonder if I've struck a nerve.

I swallow as I feel the air slowly leaving the room. The tension is so thick you can cut it with a knife. "Not your patients. Legally, you can't have them."

"I'm a marriage counselor. Morally, I can't have them either."

"I know. It makes the fantasy even more sinful." I know I'm playing with fire right now and I wonder if Dr. Montgomery will indulge me in this sexy game of cat and mouse. I don't see myself giving in to the urges but I'm dying to get close. "It's the thrill of the forbidden."

"So, that's what turns you on?"

I look at him and the look he's giving me is unmistakable. *He wants me. Now. But, how bad?*

"Isn't that everyone? The things that make you touch yourself in the middle of the night? The things that send a spike in your heart rate?"

"Some are perfectly happy without the thrill."

"Sounds boring." I shrug.

"Says the woman in a relationship with a man who gives her thrill-less, boring sex."

"He's my husband."

"You keep saying that."

"It's the truth."

"Is it?" My eyes snap to his. *Can he say that?*

"What does that mean?"

"What do you think it means, Charlotte?"

Typical counselor response. I let out a breath and prepare myself for the words dying to leave my mouth. "I think it means you want to fuck me."

He narrows his eyes at me. "Does that thought scare you? Or will that have you touching yourself in the middle of the night?" His breath is on my cheek. I turn to him and our faces are a mere inch apart.

"There's a difference between fantasy and reality. If I cross this line there's no coming back from it."

"Do you want to come back from it?" He leans closer.

"I want the excitement." I can hear my heart pounding. I wet my lips and I watch his eyes drop to the sudden movement.

"And I excite you?" he asks, his eyes still fixated on my lips.

"Fucking my marriage counselor does."

His eyes shoot up to mine. "Just the idea of it?" His breath surrounds me. All I have to do is move a millimeter for our lips to touch. I'm silent. "Tell me I can."

"Can what?"

"Touch you."

"Where?" I ask knowing full well where he means.

"You know where." His voice so low, it sends a shiver through me.

I look down at the growing tent in his pants. "Please."

His hand glides up my thigh and I almost jump through the ceiling at the spark that shoots through me from his fingertips. "Stand up," he says. I swallow before following his directions. He stands as well before walking past me toward the door. I'm shocked when he walks out of it. *Was this a test? Oh my God, what if this was all to see if I'm loyal to Matthew? What if Matthew is here?*

My eyes widen as he walks back through the door, thankfully alone, and the sound of the click as he locks the door resounds off the walls.

"Where did you go?" I ask softly.

"I told my assistant to hold my calls and also that she needed to fetch us some lunch."

"I'm not hungry."

"Neither am I," he says, his eyes darkening. "At least not for food." I swallow as he makes his way back to me. "Would you like to act out one of my fantasies, Ms. Pierce?"

"Oh, now I'm Ms. Pierce?"

"For the sake of this fantasy you are."

"Is that your fantasy? Sex with other men's wives? Your patients?" He stands behind me, drawing his hands up my sides dangerously slow.

"No." His voice sounds like sex and sin, and I feel my legs buckle. "Sex with Matthew Wells' wife is my fantasy."

"So, you have some vendetta against my husband then?"

I feel his hands on the zipper of my pencil skirt, sliding it down. The sound cuts through the air and the tension crackling between us.

"Yes. He has this deliciously sexy wife and he doesn't know what to do with her. It's a waste really. Here's this sexual creature not getting her needs met. He takes you for granted, Charlotte."

"I'm aware."

"Leave him," he says as if the answer is obvious.

"I can't."

"Why?"

"Can you not counsel me…right now?" I say, my skirt now pooled at my feet. He kneels behind me and I feel his breath on my right cheek before I feel his lips. I can't suppress the moan that escapes my lips. It's been so long since lips have touched my skin in this way. *I forgot it could feel like this.* His lips are light, as he trails kisses up till they meet the curve of my ass. He plucks my thong and I yelp as the fabric snaps against the slick flesh between my legs

"I'm not counseling you. As a man who is about to be inside of another man's wife, I want to know what it is about this marriage that keeps you…*trapped* in it. Is it money?" He stands to look at me.

"I don't want to do this now," I say as he begins to unbutton my blouse one at a time. He hums his appreciation when my blouse joins my skirt on the floor. I'm standing before him in a black bra and white panties and he narrows his eyes slightly.

"I would have suspected you'd be the matching-set type, but I like it." He leans forward to place a kiss to the space just between my breasts and begins to pepper kisses down my torso. He stops at the top of my underwear and drags his tongue along the skin. I wonder if he's having second thoughts when he presses his nose to my sex and drags it along the slit, deeply inhaling my scent. I shudder, as I try to make sense of the most erotic moment of my life. I expect him to rip my panties from my body now, but he doesn't. Instead, he rubs his tongue along the satin fabric, penetrating me slightly through my panties. I look down at him as he finally lowers the material down my legs. "Once I have a taste I don't know that I'll be able to stop."

*He's giving you an out, Charlotte. Are you ready to jump down this rabbit hole?* I stare into his gorgeous blue eyes, filled with something that I haven't seen in so long.

*Desire.*

I stare at the face that's only a breath away from the place that has long been neglected of this act of intimacy as I contemplate the decision.

*This is it, Charley. Now or never.*

# CHAPTER

*Two*

THAT WAS FOUR MONTHS AGO. FOUR MONTHS AGO, ON THE first Monday of May, I gave into my primal urges and let my marriage counselor fuck me all over his office. When I left, two and a half hours later, I was sore, sated, and slightly ashamed, but I was blissfully happy and couldn't wait for more. Two days later, he fucked me on his desk just before my session with my husband started.

Two days after that, he personally called Matthew to let him know our session was cancelled, while I sat in his lap.

*Naked.*

Yes, we were playing with fire, and yes, I felt guilty, but I couldn't stop. It felt too good.

*I felt alive.*

Fast forward four months, and I know without a doubt I'm in too deep. I'm falling for one man while I belong to another. The recklessness could end this man's career as well as my marriage.

*Hell, it would end us both.*

He explores my folds with his tongue, bringing me back to the present. He laps up every ounce of arousal that has been forming since I woke up this morning, my body humming with anticipation over seeing him today.

"God, you taste so sweet," he murmurs. His tongue slides through my entrance, fucking me before drawing a path up to my clitoris. He spreads my lips with his fingers as he eats me hungrily, his tongue gliding back and forth across me spreading my arousal.

My hands move to his hair and I relish in the silky feeling under my fingertips. I begin to scratch his scalp and am rewarded with a guttural moan that sends shivers down my spine. His hands grip my thighs harder. "Again," he orders, so I do, which to my excitement only makes him lick more aggressively.

"Fuck," I moan. There's nothing within arm's reach so I do the most cliché thing I can think of. I put my fist to my mouth and bite down hard on it in the effort to quiet the orgasm that is moving through me quick as lightning. "Oh God, Will. I'm right there." My toes curl as I feel every nerve in my body stretch to reach the delicious release that's only a beat away. In an instant, his eyes look up from between my legs to find mine. I'm sitting on his desk as he kneels in front of me, his sincere blue eyes tracing my face. I can't look away, our eyes locked during this intimate moment. I'm at the edge, waiting to jump when he slides two fingers into my dripping pussy and I come completely undone, my legs shaking under the grip of his strong hands, as I roll my hips against his face.

*Holy fuck.*

I feel his tongue flick against my clit one last time and I twitch, slowly pushing his face from my crotch. "Oh my God." I close my eyes, the aftershocks of the most intense orgasm I've ever had still flowing through my body. He drags his lips along my right thigh, kissing and sucking the skin before he stands up to tower over me. I rub my hand along his jaw, feeling the wetness of my arousal on his skin.

"I swear the only time I'm truly at peace is when I'm between your legs." His words are soft, yet they hit me hard. He cups my cheeks and grazes his lips over mine. My eyes flutter closed as the smell of my orgasm on his lips wafts all around me.

His thumb traces my lips and slips it in slightly. I bite down on his finger, relishing in the sensation of him inside my mouth.

*I need another part of him in my mouth.*

"My turn." I wink devilishly as I slide my naked body from his desk and lower myself to my knees. I run my hands up his legs, letting my fingers graze the leather brown belt as I release it from the loops, letting his black slacks fall to his ankles. His cock presses against the fabric, dying to be freed from the confines of his black, Calvin Klein briefs. I slide his underwear down his legs and his powerful erection juts out.

"Touch me, baby," I hear him say, and when I look up his hooded gaze is fixed on me. I lean forward and place my hand at the base of his dick. My tongue darts out to wet my lips and his hand finds my chin, squeezing it gently. I look up at him from where I kneel between his legs, a vast difference from our prior vantage points. "You are so beautiful."

I give him a cheeky grin. "My mouth is a centimeter from your cock; I'll bet you think so." I giggle. He grips my chin harder.

"You *are* beautiful, Charley," he repeats and the way he says it, mixed with the name that my husband refuses to call me—because *Charlotte is so much more effeminate*—makes my heart swell. "God, when you look up at me like that. It takes everything in me not to come on the spot."

I gently tickle the head of his cock with my tongue and he twitches in response, the cum pooling at the tip already. I close my lips around his tip and slide further down until he reaches the back of my throat. I swallow in an attempt to open my throat and push him further and he hardens even more.

"Fucking yes," he hisses through what I assume to be gritted teeth. "Do that again." I do as he says, attempting to swallow his cock whole and his hands find my hair, pulling as much of my hair as he can into a ponytail on the top of my head. I begin to suck his dick faster, as his thrusts meet my face. His body shakes with the force of his impending orgasm when he suddenly pulls from my mouth. He drops from between my lips, a trail of spit connecting my mouth and his dick and I swipe my tongue across my lips effectively breaking the sexy trail. "I want to be inside of you when I come."

He pulls me to my feet and traces my face, his fingers stroking my cheeks just below my eyes. Despite the sexual intensity of the moment, I feel the sincerity radiating off of him as he studies me. *No one has ever looked at me like this. Like I'm the most important person in the world. Hell, Matt doesn't even look at me like I'm the most important person in the room.* He guides me to the couch and lays me on my back, the brown leather couch cooling my heated skin. His hands find my breasts and his thumbs brush over my nipples, the calloused pads causing shivers to run down my spine.

He hovers over me, pressing his face into my neck. I hear the familiar rip of the foil and then he pushes inside of me. "God, you're perfect." In the beginning, the sex was rushed, the passion coursing through our veins made us almost animalistic. This was different. After four months, we'd gone from frenzied fucking to passionate lovemaking. I can feel each ridge of his cock as he fills me completely, the tightness of my vaginal walls making a snug space for his thick member.

His lips find mine as he begins to thrust into me. I taste the sweat from our tryst on his lips and instantly I crave more. I run my tongue over both of them in attempts to collect the moisture and he darts his out to catch mine, drawing it back into his mouth. "You are amazing. I want you every fucking minute," he says between thrusts. "I'm going to come. I need you to get there."

His words have me racing toward my orgasm. My heart pounds wildly in my chest, and I can feel the beat pulse in my sex letting me know that I'm close. "Touch me." His hand finds my clit, and it only takes a few strokes of his finger over the sensitive spot before I explode. The force of my orgasm causing my body to shake with intensity. He must have been holding off because in the midst of my orgasm I feel him swell inside of me and groan.

"Fuck, Will. Oh. My. God," I whimper as I claw at his back,

each word leaving me on its own beat. He fills me fully and my only wish is to feel him skin to skin with no barriers between us.

———

I slide my pumps onto my feet in silence. My eyes find the large clock that hangs in his office, and I fixate on the second hand as it ticks, creating the only noise that can be heard in the quiet room. For the past month or so, I'm quiet whenever this time comes. *The party is over and it's time to go back to my real life. The real life that includes a husband that can't stand me. On top of that is the guilt that plagues my mind for the moments just after our secret meeting comes to an end.*

"Are you ready?" Will asks, his words interrupting my thoughts.

"I guess," I pout as I pull my hair back in a ponytail to hide the post-coital mess it turned into.

"I'll see you on Wednesday?" He lifts my chin so I'll meet his gaze. He rubs his mouth over mine, sliding his tongue through my lips. I nod against him. "Call me later?"

I nod again. "Yes. Maybe around seven?"

"Hey," he shoots me the smile that renders me speechless every time, "chin up." His smile fades as he pulls me into a hug. "Everything is going to be okay, Charley." His lips drag along my forehead as my head bobs up and down. He presses one final kiss to my lips before guiding me to the door.

As always, once I leave his office, the walls come up and I become a completely different person. I sit in the chair and wait for my husband to arrive, his secretary eyeing me the same way she does every time I arrive "early" for my sessions.

"Sorry I'm late." Matthew Wells enters the room, his face buried in his phone just as it always is as he holds an arm to me. I stand and he wraps an arm around me in a half hug, all without taking his eyes from his phone. "Traffic was a nightmare." He finally looks up and I can see the familiar look in his eyes. *Annoyance.*

My husband is tall with a muscular build after spending the better part of his early twenties in the gym. He still goes pretty frequently, since he discovered an affinity for cheeseburgers after one too many late nights in the office. His dark blond hair is always perfectly styled, parted to the side, giving him a sleek look that belongs on the front of a magazine. *It should, he spends more time in the bathroom in the morning than I do.* He has sparkling green eyes, that I used to get lost in, that were the perfect contrast to his tanned skin. He was a perfect visual representation of the *all-American boy.*

The all-American boy and the girl next door. We should have been the perfect couple.

"No worries," I say, forcing a smile onto my lips.

"Shall we?" he asks as he points toward Will's office.

"Go right in, he's expecting you," his secretary offers, giving me a look.

*I feel the judgment coming out of her eyes but I know she wouldn't dare. Will pays her a small fortune.*

*For her talents?*

*For her silence?*

*Probably both.*

"Thank you, Vanessa," I say, and hope she gets the double meaning.

We walk into the office, where I came no less than twenty minutes ago and I see Will sitting at his desk. Immediately, my body reacts. Like Pavlov's dog, I begin to salivate. *Well, my body does. My sex is literally drooling at the sight of him.*

"Ms. Pierce, Mr. Wells. Have a seat. How are you?" he asks as he looks between us, careful not to focus on me for too long.

"Good. Better," Matthew says immediately. "That exercise you gave us last Friday was pretty insightful. Gave me some clarity." I resist the snort that threatens to escape.

Will had given us an assignment where we had to make a list

of all of the things we liked about each other when we first met. We were told to see if those things that made us fall in love in the beginning had changed.

*They had.*

"What did you find?" William asks.

"That Charlotte doesn't look at me the way she used to."

My eyes narrow as I think about the ludicrousness of his statement. "Oh, and you do?"

He rubs his finger over his forehead and I know from years of marriage that he's growing agitated already. "He asked what I found."

"You don't even want to know what I found," I mumble to myself.

"Oh, and what is that?" Matthew asks, taunting me.

"One at a time. Mr. Wells, the rest of your list," Will interjects.

"I also think she's sleeping with someone else."

"What!" I say, both for show and because I want to know what the hell I've done to make him think I'm having an affair.

*What has he noticed? I thought I was covering my tracks. Okay, Charley, stay calm. If you fly off the handle and panic, that is a giant red flag.*

"You're...different."

"How so?"

"Charlotte, I've known you for the better part of a decade. I know you."

"What makes you think this, Mr. Wells?" Will asks and I have to resist the urge to give him a look that says *fix this! Talk him out of it. Do something!*

The irony isn't lost on me that I'm hoping that the man I'm having an affair with can somehow convince my husband that I'm *not* having an affair.

"Little things. It's hard to explain. Things don't bother her. She's been agreeable and she's not initiating sex."

"I got tired of being turned down!" I argue.

"Ms. Pierce," Will says, using his therapist tone, "let him finish."

"You hang out with Lauren and come back home walking like you just got off a horse. I went to Yale, Charlotte. I wasn't born yesterday. And to add insult to injury, you turned me down for sex last week."

"I had a migraine."

"Bullshit," he pauses. "I saw it in the shower," he says casually and I wonder what he's talking about. Matthew and I haven't been in the shower together in forever.

"What?" I try my best to feign innocence even though I know for a fact, my inner thighs are often riddled with Will's hickeys. I just want to know *how* he saw one.

"Last week, when I tried to join you in the shower and you all but pushed me out. I saw the purple on your inner thigh. A hickey. Just a glimpse, but enough to know that I didn't give it to you."

I'm silent. I let Will mark me there because Matthew never goes there. Even if I were to sleep with my husband he never has his face down there where it would be visible. I wonder how I'm going to talk myself out of this hole when Will speaks. "Is this the first you're hearing of this, Ms. Pierce? Your husband's hypothesis?"

The tears flood my eyes as I nod. "Yes."

I see the tissue box in front of me and reach for it, pulling one out and putting it over my eyes to hide from the two men staring at me. *Think, Charley.* "I'm not cheating on you, Matt," I say after a moment. "I don't know what you saw, but it wasn't a hickey."

He eyes me for a moment before looking back to Will. "Fine."

"I think everyone should just take a deep breath. Maybe we need a minute. Ms. Pierce, would you like some water?"

"Yes, please," I say softly. My eyes follow him as he moves through the room and then toward me with a glass of water. "Thank you." I take the water from him, trying to avoid his fingers, knowing that his touch would send a spark through me that I couldn't ignore.

"Mr. Wells," Will begins, "how did you feel when you first suspected that Ms. Pierce had been unfaithful?" I wince at that word. *Unfaithful.*

"I wanted to kill the man who touched her. I'm the only man she's ever been with and to know someone else did…" I can see his jaw tick, and his fist clenches into a ball. "…it drove me crazy. The idea makes me furious. I've never been a jealous person, maybe because she's never given me a reason to be, but I was filled with this jealous rage." He turns to me. "I wanted to fuck you into next week so you remembered who you belonged to but you won't fucking touch me."

*Um, it's you that wouldn't touch me!*

"And I feel like an asshole having to coerce my wife to sleep with me." He shakes his head and my body tenses. "Then I hated you for letting another man touch you."

*Deny it, Charlotte. Maybe at some point I have to tell Matt what I've done, what I've been doing. But today is not that day.*

"I would never want to do anything to jeopardize things between us." I swallow hard trying to get down the bitter pill of lies and betrayal.

"I know, Charlotte, and I know things have been shitty lately. I kept telling myself it would be different once I got promoted, but it's been months and nothing has changed. Our relationship has taken a back seat and I hate myself for it. I wouldn't be totally surprised if you had been unfaithful. I haven't exactly been the perfect husband. I've neglected you. Ignored you. God, when was the last time I've even made you come?" He runs a hand through his hair. His leg is bouncing, and he pulls at his tie, loosening it slightly.

I can't look him in the eye. My brain has re-associated the word "come" with the man in front of me, instead of the man to my side. I let out a deep breath, my eyes finding Will's as Matt continues.

"I want to try and make things right. I mean really try, Charlotte. I love you and I'm sorry…for everything. And maybe you've made a mistake in the past. I don't care. I just want to start fresh. Start new. You and me…like it used to be in the beginning before we got married. Please."

*I've heard all of this before. Last year when I asked for a divorce he'd gotten on his knees and begged me not to leave him. He'd told me things would get better, that he loved me and couldn't be without me. He had promised he would do better, then he recommended counseling, and alas, here we are. I don't buy whatever Matt is selling—the phrase "too little, too late" blaring in my head like a flashing neon sign, but how do I answer this in front of my lover?*

The rest of the hour is tense. I'm a bundle of nerves ready to snap as I actively avoid Will's gaze. Before I know it, the hour is up and Matthew and I are heading toward the door.

"Well, Mr. Wells, Ms. Pierce, you certainly have some things to discuss."

I clear my throat before nodding as I try to push out the nervous energy flowing through me. "Right. Well thank you, Dr. Montgomery," I say, wanting to get out of the room as fast as possible. I know Will well enough to know there was a quick shift in his demeanor the second Matt told me he loved me and wanted to give it a more valiant effort. He became clinical and cold, a vast difference to his usual self.

I'm following Matthew out of the room, when I feel a hand resting on my ass and a gentle squeeze. I gasp quietly so as not to alert the man walking a step ahead of me, and I don't dare look at the one behind me.

"So, I'll see you both on Wednesday?" Will says and I nod, having lost all ability to speak after having my lover grope me literally behind my husband's back. "See you then," he says before heading to his office without another word. Matt reaches for my hand, interlacing our fingers, and in that moment, I know I'm fucked. I'm in a relationship with two men and neither of them are giving me up.

# CHAPTER
## *Three*

I CAN ONLY VAGUELY HEAR THE SOUND OF MY MANOLO BLAHNIKS hitting the pavement in the garage over the roaring thoughts in my head. My mind is completely scattered and I worry I won't be able to complete a sentence if Matt addresses me. When I reach my new Audi Q3—an "I'm sorry" gift from last month after a particularly terrible argument—he opens the car door for me and I look up at him warily, wondering if that whole "I love you, I want to work it out" thing was just a show for our therapist.

"I was going to go to the store. What do you want for dinner?" I ask, thanking my stars that they aligned and allowed us to drive separate cars. It will provide the perfect ruse to go back and talk to Will—and I'm desperate to talk to him, see him, hold him, kiss him. Just that simple squeeze of my butt still has my heart racing.

"How about we go out? We can go to The Grille," Matt counters. The Grille is one of the most well-known restaurants in town, owned by two of our closest friends, Nathan and Bree Cunningham. It was one of those restaurants that required that you know someone to get a table or suffer the month-long waiting list. A place where people went to be seen and Matt always wanted to be seen. We were what some would consider VIP; the restaurant had even named a drink after us. The Wells Manhattan, which is essentially the "Perfect Manhattan" because we're the perfect couple.

*At least we were three years ago.*

"Are we meeting someone there?" I ask, wracking my brain to recall if Matt had mentioned dinner plans for that evening.

"I know we haven't done much lately, just the two of us, but can't a guy take his wife out just to feed her?" His hand still rests on my door. I blink a few times and he must sense my skepticism because he sighs. "There were things we didn't get to in therapy... I thought we could discuss them."

"In public?"

"Our booth is hardly public, Charlotte." He doesn't emphasize the "our" but I can't escape the way the word stands out in my head, and he's right, our usual table is tucked into the corner with no one in close proximity.

I sigh, knowing that I have no real reason as to why I can't share a meal with my husband. "Fine."

He presses a light kiss to my lips before I slide into my car. "I'll see you soon." He smiles at me before he disappears from my sight. I turn around, craning my neck to see if Matthew is still within view of my car. When I've established that he's far enough away I reach for my iPhone. I toss it to the side and reach for my makeup bag to pull out a Blackberry. The cell phone that never leaves my side and if it does it's switched off and safely hidden at the bottom of my purse.

There's only one person that has this number and at this moment I'm desperate to hear his voice. I put the phone to my ear as it rings, my head resting against the steering wheel. I can't fight the tears building in my eyes as I hear the beginning of his voicemail. *"You've reached Dr. William Montgomery—"* I hang up immediately, knowing I wouldn't be able to get through a message without bursting into tears.

*Get ahold of yourself, Charley.*

I type out a text message, in hopes he will see it before I get to the restaurant.

**Me: Matt wants to go to dinner. I might not be able to call you until after 7. Can you talk now?**

I'm pulling out of my parking space when my Blackberry

beeps and I almost hit the car next to me as I reach for it. I have my foot on the break, halfway out of the spot when I see his message.

**Will: On a call. Can't talk now.**

**Me: Call me when you can.**

**Will: Call you? Won't your phone be off soon?**

**Me: I'll leave it on, I just need to hear your voice. Please.**

**Will: Ok.**

I know it's reckless to leave the Blackberry on with the possibility of Matt hearing it, but I also know I need to talk to Will. I need to hear his voice. I need to hear him say that today's session didn't change anything.

*That he still wants me.*

*That this isn't over.*

The thought of ending things with Will leaves me short of breath, and I find myself struggling to catch it. He's angry right now, his simple "ok" proves that, but I can only hope that he doesn't take it out on me.

---

Forty minutes later, Matthew and I are at The Grille, uncorking a bottle of Merlot that we had discovered on a trip to Napa Valley last year. The blend is drier than I like, and yet he insisted on ordering it whenever the opportunity presented itself. *You really need to expand your palate, Charlotte,* he'd told me in front of a group of our friends. I had rolled my eyes to the heavens as I sipped my usual "unrefined" Cabernet Sauvignon. He pours my glass first and slides it across the table toward me.

"Thank you," I say with a small smile. I take a small sip and scrunch my nose.

*Yep, still hate it.*

He pours his before he takes a sip, eyeing me over the top of his glass. "Do you think therapy is working?" he asks finally.

I cinch my brows together wondering where this conversation

is going. I take a long sip of my wine, despite the bitter taste, hoping it will calm my nerves that are still going haywire from therapy. "What do you mean?"

"I mean, are we any better off than we were seven months ago?" He crosses his arms over his chest.

"I think Dr. Montgomery has provided some real insight regarding the problems in our marriage."

*Like we shouldn't be married in the first place.*

He rolls his eyes. "Has he?"

*No.* "I think so?"

I can sense his frustration over the fact that we aren't in agreement. "Nothing has changed in seven months, Charlotte."

"We are communicating more."

He snorts, before taking another sip. "Right."

"I'm certainly happier than I was seven months ago, when I was convinced you'd grown to hate me, and you were only keeping me around as a pawn in your quest for the *American Dream.*"

He frowns. "It doesn't piss me off any less to hear you say that than it did the first time you said it in therapy. I never hated you, Charlotte. I love you more than anything."

I begin to chew on my bottom lip, mirroring the guilt that's currently chewing away at me. "Today is the first day you've expressed any type of feelings toward me in months. You think you would have if Dr. Montgomery hadn't given us that exercise?"

He shrugs. "I don't know, maybe?"

"Maybe? Matt, there are so many problems in our marriage. Problems that we clearly can't work out ourselves. We need help getting to the root of those problems."

*I'm not sure that I'm even buying what I'm trying to sell here, but I don't want to entertain the idea of ending therapy altogether—the idea of ending my time with Will altogether.*

"I can tell you what our problems are. I don't need to keep paying some overly expensive charlatan to tell me that." He holds up his hand, ticking the reasons off his fingers. "You want kids, I'm not ready." He ticks off a finger. "I don't give you enough attention." Another finger. "I don't fuck you enough." Another finger. "Which by the way, nowadays is more on you than it is on me, but I mean, maybe you're getting it somewhere else now," he sneers, and my eyes narrow.

*I knew that wasn't over.*

He ticks off another finger. "We don't spend enough time together…because you know that fancy house you love? It requires *money*, and I work my ass off," he snaps. "Anything else?"

I lean forward, preparing to chastise him for his tantrum. "First off, a difference in opinion regarding children is pretty fucking important, and reason enough for a marriage to end. Secondly, you don't give me *any* attention! 'Enough' implies that you're giving me *something*! I barely exist between the hours of eight a.m. and five p.m. I think I would have to be on fire for you to even take time out of your busy day to check in with me. And then, when you get home? You go straight to your office and stay there, for HOURS. I can't remember the last time we ate a meal together at home. I usually eat by myself the nights we're home and then I go to bed. I feel you come to bed somewhere around midnight and you don't even touch me! You used to spoon me, cuddle me, kiss me, and tell me you love me. You would wake me up in the middle of the night the few times you were working late and make love to me. And now there are times I don't see you again until the following morning and that's IF you even wake me up before you leave. And no, Matthew, we aren't intimate enough. And don't use some bullshit excuse about how last week I didn't want to fuck you in the shower. This is after months and months of you turning me down. Telling me you're too busy. Telling me you're tired. Want to know the last time we had sex, Matt? Five and a half months ago. It's September. The seasons have changed *twice* since then."

"It hasn't been that long—" he interjects.

"Uh uh," I say putting up a finger. "April seventeenth. We had just gotten back from a dinner with your boss. We had too much to drink, and you were on top of the world when we got home. We had sex, you came, I didn't. You fell asleep almost immediately after, I don't blame you, you had just worked an eighty-hour week. But I took a shower and cried for forty-five minutes. *That*, Matthew, is the last time we had sex." I blink a few times, trying to keep the tears threatening to fall at bay. I take another long sip of wine, desperate to feel something—anything other than the dull ache in my heart.

He stares at me for a second before he looks to the basket of bread between us, as if the answers are hidden between the slices of carbohydrates. "That can't be the last time," he whispers.

"It is," I say plainly.

"I remember that night."

"Do you?" I snort. "You were pretty drunk."

"I remember how hot you looked in that red dress. You were the most striking woman in the room. No one could take their eyes off of you. I was so proud to be your husband that night." I guess he realizes his mistake as he corrects himself quickly. "But I'm always proud to be your husband, Charlotte."

I play with my hair, running the ends through my fingertips as I let his words wash over me. "That's why you're proud to be married to me? Because I looked good in front of your boss? Because I make *you* look good?" I feel the angry tears well in my eyes as I stand. "I need a minute. I'll be back."

I don't wait for a response before I rush to the bathroom, where I toss my purse to the side, and slam my hands down on the sink.

*I remember how beautiful you looked in that red dress. I was so proud to be your husband.*

I'm transported back to the last time someone said something similar.

*Will. Last week.*

I had just finished riding him for the past hour, the sweat clinging to our bodies as I collapsed onto his chest. We'd had time to kill before my session, so we had cuddled on his couch underneath a cashmere blanket as the room cooled. We were lazily kissing, our tongues moving slowly against each other when he had pulled away.

"Do you know how amazing you are?" he'd asked. I shook my head, because to be honest, I didn't.

*Despite Will's constant reassurance, I still didn't.*

"You are the most amazing person I've ever met," he had told me as he pushed the still wet hair from my eyes. "I'm so lucky to know you, angel."

*Angel. The name he reserved for certain times when baby didn't feel right. When he needed something—more.*

I'd snorted and turned my head, laying it against his chest, but he'd moved my chin to meet his gaze.

"I'm serious. Anyone would be proud to be your husband. It's a shame that you aren't appreciated or treated the way you deserve." The way he'd looked at me, I almost said the words I'd been thinking for the past few weeks. The three words that would change everything… Or maybe nothing.

*I don't know which scares me more.*

I wipe the tear that trickles down my face as I think about Will's words in comparison to my husband's. Will told me I was a "woman of ethereal beauty." Matt used the word "hot."

I reach for my Blackberry and dial the number I've committed to memory. I don't care that I was supposed to be waiting for his call or that in this moment I was the obsessive, clingy girlfriend, or that my husband is just beyond the four walls of this bathroom.

"Answer the goddamn phone!" I grit to myself as it starts to ring. It goes to voicemail again and I want to scream.

I'm about to press the call button again when the door opens. "Charley?"

Bree Cunningham walks in, and I almost drop my phone. Bree Cunningham is no more than five feet tall, with intense green eyes and blonde hair styled into a sleek bob. "Bree, you scared the shit out of me," I say before sliding my phone as discreetly as I can back into my bag.

"Matt asked me to come check on you, honey, are you okay?" she asks and I nod. Bree and I became fast friends due to the long-standing friendship between our husbands. Matt and Nathan had been friends since childhood, going through adolescence and adulthood side by side.

"I'm fine," I say.

Bree doesn't know all the details but she knows that Matt and I are having issues. We'd had more than a few "girls' days" over the past year where she'd tried to get me to open up and talk to her, assuring me that she was there for me. I don't doubt that she wanted to be there for me. Bree is kind-hearted and doesn't have a mean bone in her body. Even though, she's married to my husband's best friend, I know she cares about me outside of being Matt's wife. That being said, she would be horrified to know this secret I'm hiding. Bree Cunningham can never know what I'm doing behind my husband's back.

"I'm so happy to see you guys here," she smiles, "and in your booth. You had therapy today, right? How did that go?"

Of course, right on cue, I feel my phone start to buzz inside my purse. *Shit.* I desperately want to talk to Will but Bree is making that more than difficult. "It went well. Bree, can you give me a minute? Tell Matt I'll be right out?"

I see the look of hurt flash across her face when I brush her off. "Of course." She smiles before she leaves, and the door has barely closed before the phone is pressed to my ear.

"What's wrong, Charlotte?" he asks as soon as the call connects. I wince, hearing the slight panic in his voice over my calling him.

"Nothing's *wrong.*"

"And yet you called me again. You made me think something was wrong."

"It surely took you long enough to check to see if there was!" I say back.

"I was in the middle of a session, Charlotte. I couldn't just take your call. It was bad enough I checked my phone while he was talking."

I'm silent for a second as I get my thoughts together. "What was *that?*" I ask referring to the earlier session with my husband.

He sighs. "I don't know, Charley. You tell me, he's *your* husband."

I swallow, knowing that was meant to hurt me. *Although it shouldn't. It's the truth, right?*

"Does it change anything?"

"Like what?"

I bite my bottom lip nervously as I prepare to speak the words. "Between you and me?"

"I think I should be asking you that."

I'm silent as I weigh my options. Do I make a valiant effort to fix my marriage? Or continue down this hedonistic path of destruction? One leaves me miserable, the other, happy.

"Will—"

"Charley, I think it would be best if we didn't talk for a few days."

"What?" I say immediately, my body reacting to his words before my brain has even processed them fully. My palms start to sweat, my heart is races, and I begin to shake.

*Is he breaking up with me?*

"You need to take some time. This was a very intense session and you need to figure out if you can still rationalize these choices you're making."

"Rationalize my choices? Don't fucking shrink me right now, William Montgomery. So, help me, I will flip." I didn't want my shrink right now. I wanted the man that was inside me just an hour ago. The man I knew didn't want to let me go for anything.

"I just listened to the husband of the woman I've been sleeping with question her about the affair she's having with me. I knew what I was doing getting involved with someone I'm counseling, but it doesn't mean I'm ready for my life to go up in smoke. Everything I've worked for? If he figures out it's me, we're fucked."

"If he figures out it's you, maybe he'll just leave me."

"Why don't you leave him, Charley?" I'm silent as I usually am when Will asks me this. We've gone over this numerous times and every time he brings it up I feel as chastised as I did when I first told him my reasoning.

*Well, part of the reason.*

My eyes flit to the rings on my finger, remembering how different things were on the day they were slid into place. I was young, my eyes wide and my heart full as I believed that this man who'd saved me from the unthinkable wanted to be with me forever.

*Apparently forever only extended five years.*

We thought we could make it work. We thought we could fix the issues with counseling, but then I started sleeping with another man. And now everything is a mess.

I had told Will all of this. I'd outlined my thoughts as if they were bullet points, giving him thorough and concise reasons why I felt the need to stay in my marriage.

I don't have a job, and the five-year gap in my resume doesn't exactly make me a hot commodity in the job market, especially at twenty-eight. There was a time about a year ago when I'd thought about leaving him, but where would I go? What would I do? The thought had felt scary, and maybe that makes me weak. Thinking I couldn't do it on my own. That a part of me still needed Matthew, but clearly, he felt the same because he begged me to stay to work on things.

*I'd left out the biggest reason though.*

"Exactly," I hear him say, my silence apparently giving him all of the answers he needs. "You don't know what you want. You want me to make you feel good, to put you on this pedestal and worship at your feet because you don't get that shit from your husband. But then you go back to him because he's familiar and there's the security and… I don't know, complacency? I told you this when we first started, you and Wells have this weird sense of co-dependency and loyalty to each other. It's not healthy. You're not happy, Charley. What kind of life is that?"

"Well, I don't see you offering me a better option," I bite out. It's the first time either of us has ever alluded to being *more*. And I'm pissed at myself for bringing it up in a restaurant bathroom while my husband is sixty feet away and Will is sixty thousand feet away.

He's silent. "That's not fair."

"Why isn't it? You're telling me I'm unhappy and I have this horrible life. Why don't you advise me on how to make it better? That is what you've been doing for the last four months, right? Trying to make my life better?"

"You have a lot of nerve, Charlotte. You can't blame me for why your life is the way it isand where are you right now anyway?"

"In the bathroom of The Grille."

He's quiet for a moment. "Did you get those ridiculous drinks?" I know he's referring to the drink named after me and my husband. I remember the first time I told him about *The Wells Manhattan*. He'd snorted and laughed it off but I know somewhere inside of him it stung. I could see the fleeting look of sadness cross his face. It was something so trivial but it reminded him that I belonged to someone else.

"No, we got wine."

"Red or white?"

"Red."

"Red makes you sleepy," he says, and I smile that he knows this little fact about me.

"So?"

"So, you drove there. Are you going to be okay to drive home?"

"After one glass? I think I'll be okay."

"Let me know when you get home."

"I thought you said we shouldn't talk for a few days," I say sadly.

"I still want to know that you're safe." His tone has softened significantly.

"But we can't talk about anything else?"

"Charley…" My name hangs in the air, and I worry about his next words. "Let's just talk Wednesday."

"But, Wednesday?"

"Use tomorrow to think about…everything."

"What am I supposed to be thinking about?"

"If what you're doing is worth risking…"

"Risking what?"

"Everything, Charley! You are risking everything. We both are."

*I am fully aware that this is risky, but it almost sounds like he isn't willing to take those risks anymore.* "Is it worth it to you?"

He doesn't say anything right away and my heart sinks. "If we were on the same page about everything, then yes, but we aren't."

"Yes, we are!" I shout and chastise myself for the volume. *Hopefully no one heard that.*

"No, Charlotte. We are not. You're married. By definition, we are NOT on the same page."

My nostrils flare as I feel the unshed tears brimming under my lids. "Are you breaking up with me?" The words leave my mouth in a rush as the air leaves my lungs, making it harder to breathe.

"I'm saying we should talk on Wednesday."

I let out another breath, trying my best to get control of my breathing, and nod, forgetting that he can't see me. "Okay."

"Be safe, Charley."

I bite the inside of my cheek. This feels like goodbye and I'm praying I can keep the tears at bay until I get home. "You too."

We stay on the phone a good thirty seconds longer, neither of us saying anything when I hear the phone click and the call ends. I swallow hard as I slip the phone back into its hiding spot and stare at myself in the mirror. I look down at my diamond Cartier watch and realize I've been in the bathroom for nearly fifteen minutes.

*Not that I think Matt would even notice.*

"There you are, finally," he says without looking up from his phone as I approach the table. "I have to go into the office."

"What?"

"Something's come up. Patterson doesn't know which fucking way is up. I swear I am sick of putting out his fires," he says. "Bree's here. I figured she'd join you."

"Wait, you're leaving *now*?"

"Yeah, you've been gone for fifteen minutes. You didn't seem too concerned with talking, and I have shit to do. I ordered your favorite, I figured you'd want it. I told them to box mine up and I'll take it with me." He nods at the waiter as he brings over his boxes.

"Mr. Wells, here's your food."

"Thanks, Sergio." He hands him the usual large tip. "Take care of my girl, will you?" I resist the urge to snort. *My girl. Right.*

"Of course, sir. As always."

"I'll see you at home," he says to me, and places a cold kiss on my cheek. Then he's gone. The thought does not escape me that my husband of five years, unlike my lover of four months, wasn't concerned with the red wine affecting my ability to get myself home safely.

# CHAPTER
## Four

B Y THE TIME I OPEN MY EYES TUESDAY MORNING, MATTHEW has already left for work. The sheets beside me are already chilly, indicating his early departure. The weather is rainy and gloomy, a direct reflection of my mood, and it takes everything in me to pull myself out of this empty bed. I make my way down the spiral staircase to prepare my breakfast to eat alone, as usual. Our kitchen is sleek and modern, with stainless steel appliances and marble countertops that borders on the obscenely expensive.

The past four months, Will and I have had our breakfast together most mornings. We talked about anything and everything from current events to movies to how much we miss each other. Sometimes, the conversations took a more sexual turn that always left me sated. But this morning, I sit in silence, forcing down my eggs, not even bothering to taste them, eating just for sustenance. I reach for my phone at least twice but stop myself each time.

*Give him some space.*

*Give you some space.*

I'm fairly certain I've gone an entire day without talking to Matt and was unphased, but with Will I'm climbing the walls over not hearing from him within the first thirty minutes since I woke up.

I wash my single plate before placing it in the dishwasher. I think about braving the elements and going to the mall. *Maybe some new shoes would make me feel better? No, I'm supposed to be thinking about what I want.* I move through the house toward Matt's office, where he spends most of his time. The room is massive and even has a small offset den where Matt has been known to crash after working late. I sit down at his desk and pull out his memo pad, making a mental note to put this through the shredder as soon as I'm done. I write Will on one side and Matthew on the other drawing a line between their two names. *Okay, start with Will.* I don't miss the shiver that runs through me as I think about it.

—

**Will**

-The way he looks at me like I'm the only one that matters.

-Sense of humor

-The sex

-How protective he is

-Extremely intelligent

-How we can talk for hours about anything and the conversation is never boring

-He does what he says he's going to do. (Calls when he says he will.)

-Thoughtful

-Doesn't ignore me

-Most. gorgeous. man. alive.

-Can I mention the sex again?

-Gives the best hugs

-Does he want to let me go?

-Do I want to let him go?

I realize my list is turning into a series of questions I don't have the answers to. I lean back in the chair as I jot down my final bullet point.

-I'm in love with him.

I stare at the words I've written before looking at Matthew's column. I stare at his name longer than I should before I start his list.

—

Matthew

    **-He's my husband.**

    I look at the words and decide to add to it.

    **-He's my husband…so?**

    **-We've been together eight years.**

    **-I lost my virginity to him.**

    **-My first love**

    **-Mom loves him.**

    I think about my mother and the string of men including two stepfathers that she's brought into my life. *I love my mother more than anything but I have the deep-rooted fear of becoming her. On her third marriage, my mother has a habit of flitting from one man to the next. The lack of stability in my formative years is why I crave it so desperately now.*

    *Husbands.*

    *My mother's second husband.*

    I shudder as the darkness creeps into my thoughts.

    **-He knows about Michael.**

    I think about how supportive Matt has always been in this regard. He swore to me he would never let something like that happen to me again and to this day he's kept his word. For a while he had guys on Michael, making it so he never came within a few states of me and my mom. It kept me from looking over my shoulder.

    **-He makes me feel safe.**

    **-The money**—*does this make me a terrible person?*

    I stare at the word for what feels like an eternity, wondering if I really am with Matt for the money. Will has asked me on more than one occasion if that's the case, and every time I deny it. Matt wasn't wealthy in the beginning, and to be honest I loved him more then. He was ambitious, yet humble, something that he seems to lack now. He'd become one of those men, one with ambition fueled by money and power. A man of humility completely forgotten as his bank balance grew.

**-Security, comfort, stability? Being with Will = chaos??**

I circle the word chaos at least five times before I set the pen down. *But what do I actually like about Matthew as a person? Okay, go.*

**-Once upon a time he did make me laugh…harder than anyone.**

**-Good-looking**

**-Intelligent**

I look back and forth between the two columns. Is there anything that he has that Will doesn't? Will doesn't know anything about the skeletons in my closet, the ones that Matthew has been helping me fight for years. *Would Will help me the same way if he knew?* I rub my forehead willing away the headache that I can feel forming behind my eyes. I stare at the sheets as I attempt to commit the lists to memory before I send it through the shredder.

———

I arrive at Will's office at noon and sit in my usual seat and try to busy myself with my phone to avoid Vanessa's judgmental gaze. "Dr. Montgomery is just finishing up a session. It's running a little long," she says.

I look up, giving a simple nod. "Okay."

"Would you like some water or tea?" she asks.

"No, thank you." I smile before turning my gaze back to my phone. I mindlessly delete a slew of emails alerting me about sales, promotions, and new products.

*Do I ever get any emails anymore about anything important? When did this become my life?*

Once upon a time, the ping of an email used to excite me and now I feel a sense of dread as I know it's just another business begging me to buy their product.

I hear a door open and I can't control the physiological reactions to knowing he's near. My skin breaks out in goose bumps, my mouth goes dry, and I feel my heart begin to race. But most importantly, I feel the space between my legs throb with need.

However, nothing could have prepared me for what I see when I look up: a beautiful, blonde woman walks out of his office by herself. Will is a marriage counselor and to my understanding that means that there should be *two* people in that session.

*Unless he's counseling her the same way he counsels me.* The thought causes another physiological reaction—nausea. I let out a long breath.

"Thank you so much for still seeing me, Dr. Montgomery. I'll see you next week," the blonde says.

"You're welcome. Talk to Mr. Goodman about what we discussed and I will be in touch sometime before next week to follow up." *It all seems professional. Of course, we are that way too. Well, we were... I think Vanessa knows we have a different relationship than he does with anyone else that he counsels.* I watch as the woman walks out of the waiting area and then turn my gaze to Will. I know he can see the hurt written all over my face, but his face tells me nothing. *Tell me it's not what I'm thinking,* I plead with my eyes.

"Ms. Pierce, come in."

# CHAPTER
## Five

I FOLLOW HIM THROUGH HIS OFFICE DOORS WITHOUT A WORD. Under normal circumstances, I'd barely be across the threshold before I'd be pressed up against the wall, with his lips covering mine. He would tell me how much he's missed me, how much he's thought about me, how he can't wait to be inside of me, while his hands find their way into my underwear. Today however, he crosses the room immediately and leans against his desk crossing his arms, a defense mechanism I'm all too familiar with. *Does he think he needs to protect himself from me?*

"Are you sleeping with her too?" I ask, all of the air leaving my lungs as I brace myself for the answer.

"You've got a lot of nerve asking me that." On the surface, his eyes are cold and angry, but I can see the hurt lurking beneath the layers as he struggles with the fact that my question insinuates that I don't trust him.

*And yet, he didn't say no.*

I find myself wanting to turn around and run. Run far away from Will, from this room, from this whole situation that is getting more complicated by the day. *Turn around, Charley.* I don't know how long I'm going to hold up without crying as anxiety blooms in my chest. My mind wanders back to that word on my list. *Chaos.* In the midst of all of the chaos, being with Will brings me peace, but I'll be damned if I share him with anyone else. Maybe that makes me a hypocrite, but so be it.

*I'll own it.*

"You haven't answered my question," I bite out as I attempt to turn my sadness into anger.

"Because it's fucking insulting," he says. "And it makes you a hypocrite. You're married, Charlotte."

"So, what, you've been sleeping with women this whole time? These past four months? You know Matthew and I aren't having sex."

He stares at me for a second and I want to smack the smug look off of his face. "So, in an effort to 'repair your marriage,'" he says using his hands to indicate air quotes, "you're telling me you didn't have sex on Monday? Or yesterday?"

It's taking everything out of me to stay strong and not to cry, but his words crush me. *How could he think it would be that easy? After everything that has happened between us, that I could jump back into bed with another man—even if he is my husband.* "You're an asshole."

"You haven't answered my question," he repeats my words back to me.

"Because it's fucking insulting." I do the same. "Are you sleeping with that woman, too? How many of us are you sharing your 'expertise' with? Is there a slew of us? Do all of us get this *special* treatment? Thank God we're using condoms," I snort as I attempt to hide the hurt in my voice.

"Is that what you think?" he yells and my eyes widen. Will never raises his voice. "Is that what you really fucking think?" he repeats as he stalks his way toward me. I take a few steps back and soon I'm against the wall. "You can't actually believe that." His nostrils flare signaling that he's as turned on as I am. I push back against his chest because as turned on as I am, there's no way I'm letting him touch me without answers.

"Will, cut the shit, did you fuck that woman or not?"

He chuckles and I am so angry with how he's acting I could strangle him. "Did you fuck Wells?"

"NO, YOU ASSHOLE. God, and even if I had…you KNEW what you were getting yourself into. You knew I had a husband—"

"You're telling me that you can fuck other people but I can't?"

"It's not the same and you know it!"

"It's a little bit the same," he says, condescendingly and I resist the urge to take off my four-inch heel and haul it at him.

"Answer my fucking question!"

"No, Charlotte. I did *not* fuck Mrs. Goodman. You are the only one of my patients that I'm risking my entire practice for," he says, making his way toward his bar to pour us both a drink. "But let's circle back to what you said—so you're allowed to have sex with Wells, but I can't as a single man, have sex with anyone else? Please explain that logic to me because I fail to see it."

"Don't patronize me," I growl at him. "I never said I was 'allowed' to do anything. And…I'm sorry, I wasn't aware that you were single," I say crossing my arms across my chest. "So, what, because you thought I had sex with Matthew, you were going to have sex with someone else to get back at me? Mature, Will." I reach for the glass that he's poured me and take a sip eyeing him over the glass."

He shakes his head. "You drive me crazy, woman."

"Ditto."

He downs his drink in one gulp, staring at me the entire time. He runs his tongue over his bottom lip to catch a drop of bourbon before moving into my personal space. "But I am fucking crazy about you."

My heart starts to pound in my chest as I feel his lips touch my cheek and move down my neck, setting the skin on fire. "Ditto," I repeat.

"There's no one else, Charley." I clench at his words. I feel his tongue moving back and forth over my pulse point and I convulse, gripping his shoulders just to stay upright. I'm expecting his tongue to find my mouth at any moment so I'm shocked when

I feel him move away from me. I open my eyes and look at him questioningly as he backs away slowly. "You came in here accusing me of sleeping with another patient."

"I thought—"

"I very well know what you thought, Charley. I think it every time you walk out that door with your motherfucking husband," he shouts. "That's the whole point!" I don't say anything because *what can I say?*

"I'm not having sex with him. I haven't...since we started" I say quietly.

"But how long is that going to last?" He walks to his desk and sits down, then pulls off his glasses and tosses them on the desk before rubbing his forehead. He leans back and I can't help but admire how unbelievably gorgeous he looks at the moment. It makes me want to drop to my knees and suck him off under his desk. "How long before Matthew sits you down and says 'we should have sex tonight.'"

"That's not going to happen."

"Oh? You haven't had sex in four months and you think—"

"Five," I interrupt him.

"Okay, you haven't had sex in *five* months and you think he's not eventually going to want to do something about that?"

"What difference does that make? I can say no," I correct myself. "I will say no."

"He already thinks you're cheating on him."

"Sleeping with him won't change that. Why are we even having this conversation?" I move toward him, and perch myself on his desk. I kick my shoes off toward the floor before I let my perfectly painted foot stroke his thigh. "There are so many other things we should be doing," I say, trying to divert the conversation away from my husband.

*Will does have a point. How long can I keep Matt at arm's length and out of my panties?*

"Charley, I think we should stop this."

"Stop what?" My eyes widen. I can't fathom the words he's saying.

"This," he says pointing back and forth between us.

I feel like someone has punched me in the stomach. "You don't mean that."

He narrows his eyes at me. "Don't I? I have to watch you walk out that door every Monday, Wednesday, and Friday. I can only talk to you certain hours of the day. You are MARRIED, Charley. And now your husband suspects you're cheating on him. We can't keep doing this."

I stop my foot from inching toward his crotch and hop off his desk. "I would never… I wouldn't have sex with him while you and I are…" I stomp my foot in frustration over how vulnerable I feel right now. "How dare you do this!" I exclaim and his eyes widen at my outburst. "I know that I am not in the most ideal situation right now. But Jesus Christ, Will, YOU seduced me. You came on to me! You knew what you were doing the second you summoned me here for a 'private session.' And now that you've completely turned my world upside down…completely changed my life—changed *me*, you're out? Fuck you. Fuck you and the morals you've seemed to acquire overnight." I reach down in an effort to snatch my shoes when I'm pushed down and bent over his desk, the cool wood against my cheek.

"You *must* have lost your mind talking to me like that, Charlotte," he growls in my ear.

I feel his foot knock my left foot away from my right separating my legs and I feel his hand wrapping around my thigh underneath the loose-fitting dress that I wore when I thought we'd be at it nonstop for three hours. He wastes no time finding his way into my panties and rubbing. *Hard.*

"I am not out," he says in my ear. He pulls my hair into a makeshift ponytail and pulls hard, hauling me to his chest. He pulls my dress up over my head, my back still to his front and his lips go to my neck as he vigorously continues to finger me. The room is completely silent, the only noises are my moans and the slurping sound of my juices coating his fingers as they move in and out of me. I feel my orgasm nearing and he must as well because he roughly removes his fingers from inside of me. I turn around to look at him.

"What the fuck?"

"Take off your panties," he demands.

"Make me." I put my hands on my hips.

His gaze darkens. "If I have to take them off you, Charlotte… It's going to hurt."

I take a step toward him and finger the lapel on what I know to be a very expensive dress shirt. "I'd like to see you try." I put my hands on his shirt and rip it open, sending the buttons flying in all directions. His eyes shoot fire at me when he pushes me onto the desk, hard.

"Goddammit, Charley. What the fuck?"

His hands find my breasts through my bra. I lean back as I enjoy the feeling when I hear a loud rip. My eyes shoot open and I look down to see my very expensive La Perla bra in two pieces in his hands. "You asshole!" I scream. "That bra was three hundred dollars and it was my favorite!" I push him hard against his chest before I launch myself at him. He catches me in one swoop and my legs wrap around his waist instantly as I kiss him with every feeling I have moving through my body.

*Anger.*

*Fear.*

*Lust.*

His teeth bite down on my bottom lip and I moan at his animalistic behavior as I don't think I've ever been kissed this aggressively. His hands find the back of my head as he continues to lick his way into my mouth, his tongue relentless in its search for mine.

"You are *mine*, Charlotte. If I want to rip your bra in half, I'll rip your bra in fucking half."

"You're buying me a new one."

In this moment, I've realized Will and I will be engaging in a different form of intimacy. *Angry sex.*

"Have your *husband* buy you one," he snaps. "Tell him your marriage counselor ripped it off of you before he fucked you so hard you didn't know your own name," he says before he slams us against the wall. I hear a picture crash to the ground but can't be bothered to inspect the damage.

*I can't see or feel anything but the man holding me up. I don't know anything but him.*

"Hold on, baby," he demands and I obey his command, wrapping my hands around his neck and locking my legs tighter around his waist. *Let's face it; I would do anything he asks in this moment.* He rips my underwear from my body and I moan when I feel the fabric against my clit the moment before it's gone. He presses his body into mine, rubbing his cock against me, his hard member hidden by slacks rubbing against my bare pussy. I hope he has a change of clothes because not only did I destroy his shirt, my arousal is going to be all over the crotch of his pants.

*He'll be able to smell me for the rest of the day.*

He stops moving against me. His body freezes and when I look up into his eyes he's staring straight at me. "You are so beautiful, Charlotte. It almost hurts to look at you. To know that you aren't mine to look at."

His lips are no more than a centimeter from mine allowing me to feel his warm breath on my lips. I run my tongue over my bottom lip, desperate to create some moisture in my mouth as it's run dry over the intensity of this moment. "Will," I breathe out, my emotions getting the better of me, "I know this is difficult—" I start but he interrupts me.

"I want to mark you," he presses his face against my neck and I feel his teeth grazing the skin.

"You know your options," I moan out.

"No," he says. "Somewhere visible."

"Wha-what?"

"I want to leave a bite mark somewhere that he can see. I want him to know that he doesn't own you, Charlotte Pierce. Not anymore. You belong to *me* now," he growls in my ear before he bites down. Normally I would give him an earful for that kind of bullshit but I would be lying if I said his need to possess me didn't turn me on even more.

*Charley, focus, no hickeys, are you insane? Do you want to get caught?*

"Will," I whine hoping I can break him from this possessive trance, "not my neck."

"I need to know that you're mine. I need to see it on you." His voice is hoarse and almost pained as he drags his lips down my neck.

My hands, which should be pushing against his chest to move him away from my neck, drop to his belt. I unbuckle it, sending his pants to the floor. I waste no time reaching inside of his briefs and finding what I'm looking for. I squeeze and he bites down on my neck in response. I yelp and squeeze harder causing him to hiss. "Charley!"

"I'm yours. You can bite me anywhere that isn't visible." I grab his jaw making his eyes lock with mine. "Weren't you just talking about not playing with fire?"

"We both are. This is going to go down in flames, Charlotte. You know that, right?"

His lips are on mine again, biting, kissing, licking. I manage to pull apart for a second. "Don't say that!" I growl before his lips find mine again. I push against his chest hard, angry, at his implication that we are going to get caught. He loses his balance with his pants still around his ankles, and falls backward, taking me with him as we go through his polished wooden coffee table.

"Shit!" I exclaim. "I'm sorry, I'm sorry, I—" My words are silenced by him rolling me over and onto my back.

"Quiet," he grits out. Within seconds, his pants are off and he's sliding his cock through my sex, lubricating his shaft with the juices from my dripping pussy. "You are always so fucking wet. Fuck, Charlotte." He continues to rub his dick against my clit, pushing me closer and closer to the edge without any penetration at all. My clit pulses every time he drags his cock across it and I whimper in response. The tiny nub is getting harder and more sensitive with every brush against me and it makes me blind with lust. Just when I feel myself about to shatter, he stops his assault on the sensitive bundle of nerves and slides his dick inside of me allowing me to feel every ridge of his cock. He lifts one of my legs over his shoulder and I moan when he hits the spot that only he can find.

"Oh my God, Will," I moan, from both the pleasure he's inflicting and the slight rug burn starting to form on my back as I rub against the carpet.

"Tell me how good it feels."

"It feels amazing." I drag my nails down his chest so hard they leave a trail. "If you're going to mark me, I want to do the same."

"You've already marked me." The words hit me as hard as the orgasm that's been building since I walked into this office.

"Fuck," I whimper. "I'm going to come." My eyes flutter shut, the anticipation of my orgasm disallowing me from keeping them open.

"I know, Charley. Give me what I need, baby." I feel the explosion start at the base of my spine and rip through me, shooting out of every extremity. I grip his biceps as he continues to thrust, drawing every ounce of energy out of me through my orgasm. "That's it, you're so beautiful when you come."

I squeeze my eyes shut as the aftershocks roll through me. I'm vaguely aware of him saying that he's going to come when I hear my name. "Charley!" he barks.

"Wh—what!?" I say, my eyes flying open.

"I'm about to come," he says through gritted teeth. "In or out."

"What—you always?" My eyes widen when I realize why he's asking. *He's not wearing a condom*…and just that quick I feel another orgasm brewing. "Kiss me," I say.

"What?"

"Put my leg down and kiss me. Now," I say, wrapping my arms around his neck. He does as I ask and I lock my legs behind him, effectively trapping him inside of me and giving him my answer. He continues to thrust slowly, as his lips move with mine.

"Charley," he whispers as I feel him nearing his finish. I drag my right hand between us and between his legs. "Shit," he groans knowing what my objective is. "Do it. Touch me, baby. You always know how to make me come," he says as he begins to pick up the pace, fucking me relentlessly. "I. Need. You. So. Much," he grunts out with each thrust. "You. Are. Mine." He stares deep into my eyes. I see pure lust lurking behind his piercing gaze but there's something else as well that I can't quite name. I look away in an attempt to gather my scrambled thoughts, so overwhelmed by the intensity behind his blue orbs. I squeeze his balls gently and it causes the man on top of me to explode. "FUCK!" he roars. "Look at me, baby."

Halfway through his orgasm he pulls out of me and the remainder of his cum shoots onto my sex. My eyes pop open and I look down feeling the warm fluids coat my skin. I watch his hands mixing our juices through my sex and I'm so enthralled by the scene unfolding before me that I don't even notice his eyes on me, watching me, studying me. I finally meet his eyes when his index finger, coated with the mixture of our orgasms, comes toward my mouth.

"Suck."

I open my mouth and suck his digit as if it was his cock. "I am going to lick your pussy clean now," he tells me. "So, you don't have to sit through this session, panty-less with my cum inside of you."

"We aren't going to shower?" I raise an eyebrow. We don't every time, but this is definitely one of those times where it will be necessary.

"I don't want you to. I want you to smell like me." I open my mouth to argue that it's a terrible plan when his lips wrap around my nipple, which are always hypersensitive right after I have an orgasm; a fact that I've discovered only recently due to Will's complete exploration of my body. There isn't a part of me that hasn't been touched, kissed, licked or fucked. He bites down gently before he begins to suckle harder. He lets it go with a pop before moving to the other one briefly.

"Do you want to be on top?" he asks and I immediately know what he wants. I nod enthusiastically, before I move out of the way for him to take my place. He's barely on his back before he grabs my hips to straddle his face, opening me up to him completely and submerging his face in my pussy. His tongue is inside of me instantly and it's so deep it's like he's trying to climb inside of me. I reach down to grab his dick, when he grabs my hips, holding me in place.

"But…" I whimper, wanting to take him in my mouth.

"Wait," I hear him growl, his fingers beginning a torturous assault on my clit as his tongue fucks me as if it were his cock, swirling his tongue around my channel. "Fuck, we taste good together."

I hear him slurping and sucking the elixir of our lovemaking out of me, and when I look down at him through my legs, I see the mixture of our cum sliding down his neck. I squeeze my eyes shut trying to ingrain the sexy image into my brain forever.

"Will," I moan. Finally, his tongue finds my clit that is still tingling in response to my earlier orgasm. It only takes a few swipes across the engorged flesh before I'm coming.

"Oh my God!" My eyes squeeze shut as the force of my orgasm takes over. "Right fucking there, I'm there. Fuck, Will!"

I struggle to keep myself upright, my hips pushing back against his face as my hands fall to his torso for balance. I ride out the rest of my orgasm against his mouth as he cleans every ounce of cum out of me. His dick twitches in response to my orgasm and it makes me smile thinking that me coming prompts such a sexy physiological reaction out of him. I want his dick, so I try to move out of his tight hold.

"Will," I whine. "Let me," I say, giggling.

He gives my left ass cheek a hard bite before I feel a slap on the right. "Go for it, baby. It's yours."

I move down his chest rubbing my wet core across his torso before turning around to look at him. He sits up on his elbows to watch me, as always. His cock, painfully hard and waiting for me, is still glistening with my juices and I clench at the taboo feeling of cleaning myself off on him. My eyes lock with his as I move my hand to the base of his cock and run my tongue up his shaft.

"You taste like me," I say with a wicked smirk. His lustful eyes watch me carefully as my lips wrap around his cock. I take him to the back of my throat before I pull back slightly, grazing my teeth slightly over his hard ridges. I repeat the steps over and over until he begins to pulsate in my hand. My other hand massages the balls holding the cum that is ready to explode down my throat. His hand grips my hair as he thrusts upwards to meet my mouth.

"Jesus Christ, Charley. Nobody's ever sucked my dick like you."

I pull back knowing he's seconds from coming and look him square in the eye. "And nobody besides me ever will again." I put his cock back in my mouth and suck hard. I know that this is one of those moments fueled by the forbidden lust coursing through us. I'm not so naive to believe that he'll never have a sexual encounter with another woman. I'm married to another man, and Will and I can't keep doing this forever.

Eventually, this will end and he'll move on. I wince at the thought.

"Fuck," he growls as his cum shoots down my throat fast. "Just you. Only you, baby," I hear him say and I know it's just because he's in the moment but his words send me on a head trip. *Only me?*

———

We're on his couch, the same couch that Matt and I will be sitting on for our session in an hour and a half. Will's head rests in my naked lap, as I stroke his hair.

"I can't believe we broke your table. I'm sorry," I say looking at the destruction.

"Don't worry about it," he chuckles.

"I'll pay for it."

"You certainly will not, Charlotte. It's fine." He moves to sit up and looks me over. "Are you okay though? We went down kind of hard."

"Yeah, you broke my fall," I giggle. "Let me see your back."

"Charley, I'm fine."

"Let me see anyway." He turns around and there's a few scratches, from my nails and possibly from the table. "I don't see any splinters or anything," I kiss his shoulder and rest my head against his back with a sigh. I look at my watch and see the minute hand has moved more than I thought since the last time I looked.

"Time is moving so fast," I say softly. "I need more time." Tears rush to my eyes.

"Shhh," he soothes me. "Don't cry, come here." He pulls me into his lap and kisses me gently. "Was all of that okay? I know I was kind of rough with you."

"I loved it," I say, the tears forgotten. "I want to do that again." I look at his table. "Maybe without the wreckage?"

He smiles. "Deal." He glances down at my center and my eyes widen, wondering if he wants to go again as I take in the slick skin between us. "I'm sorry I didn't use a condom. That was a dick move."

"Yes, it was," I give him a cheeky grin. "But I didn't stop you." I run my hands through his hair. "I mean we aren't sleeping with other people…maybe we can forego the condoms. Since I'm on the pill."

"The pill isn't one hundred percent effective." He raises an eyebrow at me.

"Yes, thank you, Dr. Obvious, I'm aware." He pinches my side in response to my sarcasm.

I'm quiet for a moment before I realize that I need to get all of my thoughts out now. "Is this conversation necessary? I mean… was this the end?"

He furrows his brow. "No, Charley, it wasn't."

Relief floods me instantly. "You can't say things like that. You can't tell me it's over unless it's over," I whisper. "I knew you didn't mean it, but it hurt."

"I shouldn't have said that." He runs a hand through his hair. "I go back and forth between wanting to do the right thing and letting you go and being selfish and keeping you."

"I don't want you to let me go. Please keep me," I whisper and try to ignore the desperation I can hear in my voice.

"For how long?"

I shrug my shoulders. "Forever?"

"But like this? No, Charley. I'm not doing this forever." I'm silent and feel his hands cupping my cheeks. "Earlier, you said that I'd changed…*you*…is that true?" I swallow and nod, words failing me, and I feel his hands wipe my tears before I even realize that I'm crying. "God, Charley. We're not just playing with fire, we're right in the middle of an inferno."

# CHAPTER

*Six*

**A**FTER A SHOWER, A THOROUGH WIPE-DOWN OF HIS OFFICE, and cleaning up the mess from the destroyed coffee table we have about twenty minutes to spare.

"How are you going to explain the table?" I ask as I let the towel fall to the ground. I'd already saturated my body with my Prada body lotion so as not to smell like the sweat, saliva, and cum of William Montgomery.

Will's eyes roam my body before he moves toward me. "What did you ask?" he says, his eyes roaming salaciously over my body.

"Focus!" I giggle. "The table? What are you going to say?"

"If you want me to focus, you should put some clothes on," he retorts as he pushes me against the door. "I'll just say it was time for a new one." His mouth finds my neck.

"Stop, there's no time. And I can't believe you ripped my bra and my panties. You're lucky I can get away with going braless in this dress *and* I brought a jacket."

"Oh," he says before he moves through his office and pulls something out of his closet. "I got you something." He shoots me a sly smile.

My eyebrows cinch together as he brings the Neiman Marcus bag closer and closer. "What is that?"

"Open it." I peek inside and smile when I see the familiar boxes inside. I pull it out of the bag and smile at him. "Is that why you ripped my bra?"

He winks at me before I open it to reveal the most gorgeous

assortment of bras I've ever seen. There are four of them in the box, intricately wrapped in the usual tissue, all my favorite style in various colors. *Including the one he just ripped. My favorite. He bought me these?*

He starts to walk away toward the bathroom. "The other box has the underwear."

"Wait!" I call after him. He turns to look at me and I'm in his arms instantly. "Thank you," I say, kissing him several times all over his face. "Thank you, thank you. This is so thoughtful."

"Well, I figured it's the least I could do if I plan to keep ripping them off of you," he says. I'm still naked and in his arms, and time is running out so I step away quickly, in the attempt to cool my heated skin.

"We don't have a ton of time, but do you want to put it on me?"

He looks at me and then at the bag and chuckles. "You're trying to kill me," he says. He stands behind me as we both stare at them. "Which one?"

"Mmmm, what do you think?"

"That one," he says pointing to a sheer lace, light-pink bra. "And the panties that match."

"Okay." I turn around and hand them to him and he narrows his eyes at me.

"I'm going to get you back for this." He gets on one knee and slides the underwear up my legs around my hips and runs his index finger between the crack of my ass as he adjusts that part of the tiny thong. He puts the bra on me and shoots me a smile. "Turn around." I obey and feel him clasp it behind me. "All done," he says before placing a kiss on my shoulder.

I spin back around and grab my dress, pulling it on over my head. "Thank you, but I don't think I have time to go put this in the car though. Will you hold onto it for me?"

"Of course."

"Rub the panties over your cock before you give them back to me," I tell him and I'm rewarded with a panty-dropping grin.

"You got it."

I'm heading toward the door when an idea hits me. "Will."

"Charley," he says as he puts his glasses back on and I have to resist the urge to pounce on him again. *I should start asking him to leave them on during sex.* The visual sends a shiver through me.

"Matt will be out of town this weekend."

"Charley…"

"What? Are we just never going to be together out there?" I say pointing toward the door to the outside world. "Don't you want to fuck me on a bed?"

He rubs a hand over his jaw. "I'll think about it. You're not going with him?"

"I typically don't, no. Sometimes if Matt wants me to meet a potential client, I'll tag along. But if it's just meetings and all that bullshit? No. If there's one thing worse than being a bored house-wife, it's being a bored housewife trapped in a hotel. I mean if it's New York or Dallas or somewhere in Florida, it's not so bad. But I'm pretty sure Matthew is going to, like, bumblefuck, Oklahoma, or something." I put up a hand. "I'm good."

"Oh, so that's the only reason you don't want to go?" He narrows his eyes at me.

"Maybe I want to stay here with my boyfriend." I shrug and immediately I regret it. *Shit, maybe I shouldn't have said that.*

"Boyfriend?" he asks and I feel the blood rush to my cheeks.

"I mean—I didn't mean—" I trip over my words, as I wonder how he feels about my sudden use of that title. He moves toward me and pulls me to his chest before kissing me deeply. When he pulls away, I'm out of breath.

"Boyfriend." He nods. "I like it. So, this weekend—"

He's interrupted by a beep blaring through the room. "Dr. Montgomery, Mr. Wells has just entered the lobby downstairs."

My eyes widen and I look at him. He strolls to his desk and presses the button for the intercom. "Thank you, Vanessa," he says before he lets the button go, his eyes never leaving mine.

"Are you fucking kidding me?!" My heart begins to race. My breath comes in short spurts as I try to steady myself.

*Vanessa knows.*

*What if she tells Matt?*

"Right, because you really believed Vanessa didn't know." Will rolls his eyes before shooting me a look. "Excuse me if I don't like surprises. Now go. Call me later?"

I look toward the door, knowing what's awaiting me on the other side—judgment. But he's right, it's better if she knows. Besides, she's probably being compensated heavily for keeping this secret. "Yes." I blow him a kiss and then I'm gone.

I shoot Vanessa a small smile as I sit on the love seat of his waiting area and she raises an eyebrow at me.

*Okay, definitely not best friends, got it.*

My thoughts of Vanessa's disapproval are interrupted by my phone ringing and I fumble around in my purse before answering. "Hi, Mom, I can't talk right now. Matthew and I are about to go into therapy." My mother is less than thrilled that we need therapy in the first place, but she is on board with us trying to fix the issues in our marriage. She was ready for grandkids yesterday and believes this might be the ultimate solution.

*Little did she know.*

"Oh, honey, sorry. I forgot it's Wednesday and Matty didn't mention it when I saw him earlier."

My face morphs in confusion. "You saw him?"

"Yes, he came and took me to lunch. We went to that new spot on Cross Street. He mentioned that he'd offered to take you but you said no."

"I didn't say no. I said the menu didn't appeal to me. And he invited me as an afterthought. He was already going with co-workers." *Also, Will and I had a solo appointment the day he asked.* "But wait, you two went?"

"Yes, Charley, they have a molten cake that's to die for."

Matt enters the waiting area and I give him a wave before pointing to my phone. "Mom, can I call you later? We're about to go in."

"Yes, of course. I love you."

"Love you too." I end the call and look at him. "You had lunch with my mother?"

"Yeah, she called the office to see how I was and I was heading out."

I swallow at the simple gesture as I try to ignore the guilt that washes over me. While I was being fucked within an inch of my life by our marriage counselor, my husband was taking my mother to lunch. To make matters worse, my mother adores Matt. Of course, we've talked about the problems in my marriage, but she urges me to try and work through them. She's equally invested in me not becoming a woman of multiple marriages either.

"Hey, you okay?" Matt asks reading my face as if he knows what I'm thinking. *Maybe once upon a time, but as of late, I doubt Matt has any idea the thoughts that go through my brain.*

I don't get a chance to answer before I hear Will's silky voice waft around me. "Mr. Wells, Ms. Pierce," he says and I turn around.

"Hi, Dr. Montgomery." I paint on the smile that is reserved for Will when my husband is around and follow him into his office. Matt takes his usual seat while Will waits for me to sit down before taking his seat across from us. Although it's fleeting, I catch the look in Will's eyes chastising Matt yet again for his lack of chivalry.

"So, Monday's session…we talked about a lot. I advised you

to go home and talk about what was discussed. Did you come up with anything? Resolve anything?"

"Nope, because when I took my wife to dinner to try and open the lines of communication she proceeded to leave me to go to the bathroom for twenty minutes. I took that to mean she didn't want to talk."

"Ms. Pierce?" Will looks at me and I do my best to leave my attitude out of it.

"Yes?"

"Were you avoiding Mr. Wells?"

"No, I wasn't."

"Twenty minutes, Charlotte, really? You don't take that long in the bathroom," he says shaking his head. I scrunch my nose at his childish insinuation regarding my bathroom behaviors.

"I went to the bathroom, Lauren called. I answered."

"And proceeded to talk to her?"

"Yes, she wanted to know how therapy went."

"And so, you discussed it with her, but not with me."

"That's typically how the best friend thing works, Matt. And I talk to Lauren way more than I talk to you, so your point is moot."

"This is the first time I've seen you today, how can you *already* be so pissy with me? Oh, is it that time?" he asks before he adds, "I wouldn't know. It's not like I see your vagina."

I blush bright red. "What the hell? Side note, you've known me for almost ten years and I've been taking the pill for the entire time. How the hell do you not know when it is?" I scoff.

After four months, Will knows when my period is and even plans accordingly when it's that week. He'll order us fried food for lunch and I swear he cleans out the entire stock of *Milky Ways* at any given store. The first time I had one of our sessions while I was on my period, we fucked in the shower. The second time I blew him and by the fourth time he fucked my ass. I hate having sex while it's that time of the month, but I know it's only a matter of time before he breaks me down. I shake my head wanting to end this line of questioning.

"Whatever," I chuckle to myself and see I have the attention of both men. Matt's eyes urge me to continue, taunting me, while Will's try to remain impassive. "Six months ago, you and I went to a party at your boss's house—a cocktail party. About an hour into the party, you disappeared and I couldn't find you for two and a half hours. Only to find out that you, your boss, and a few of the associates had *left*!"

"We weren't supposed to be gone that long. We were just going to get those Cuban cigars from—"

"Are you kidding me!?" I scream, pushing myself indignantly to my feet. "You're berating me over twenty minutes at our favorite fucking restaurant where you know everyone from the owner to the runners by name, when you left me alone at some fucking party, where I hardly knew anyone for two hours!? You've got a lot of nerve, Matthew Wells."

"We weren't trying to have an important talk that night. Charlotte, I'm sorry. I've apologized profusely for that."

"I'VE BEEN TRYING TO TALK FOR ALMOST TWO YEARS, MATT!"

"Ms. Pierce," Will interrupts me and I shoot him a glare.

"I'm just expressing my feelings. Isn't that what we're supposed to do here? Get it out in the open?"

"And I am glad we are getting to the root of the problems. I just wanted you to take a deep breath."

Our eyes meet and an unspoken conversation passes between us. Him urging me to calm down, me pleading with him to understand. I've been the meek housewife for far too long, and I can't stand it another second. Inhaling, I sigh and turn back to Matt. "I've been trying for so long. You can't up and decide one morning that you are ready to talk. It doesn't work that way."

"Dr. Montgomery said that's exactly the way it works."

"Oh, now we are listening to Dr. Montgomery? Two days ago, you were convinced that therapy and the expensive-as-fuck doctor weren't working. What did you call him again? A *charlatan?*" I smile at him before I take my seat back on the couch.

"Okay, first of all," he looks at Will, "I didn't say it quite like that. Secondly, you are expensive as fuck and you know it. And thirdly, you know what? Fine, I'll say it. This shit isn't working. You're not even trying," he says looking at me.

"I tried. A lot. For a long time. You just never noticed." I look down at my hands.

"Okay, let's regroup. Ms. Pierce, we've discussed that with you attempting to move forward you can't live in the past. He's apologized for things that have happened. You have to let those things go if you have any shot in making it in the long run." I look at him for a beat, careful not to stay focused on him too long.

*Why is he saying that?*

*What are you saying, Will?* I try to ask him with my eyes.

*Nothing, baby—I'm just trying to do my job. You and I are the long run.* I imagine him saying back.

"Fine," I say.

"Let's take a few steps back. Mr. Wells, what makes you think that Ms. Pierce isn't trying?" Will asks and I resist the urge to glare at Matthew.

He doesn't say anything for a while, and when I look over, he's staring intently at the place where the coffee table *used* to be. "I knew something was off, but I couldn't put my finger on it…what happened to the table?" he says looking for the table that Will and I destroyed an hour ago.

"Redecorating. It was time for something new."

"Oh, it was a nice piece. I know good craftsmanship when I see it."

"Full disclosure," Will says and I run a finger over my mouth wondering where he's going with this, "an angry husband broke it."

"No shit?"

"Yes, he got pretty agitated with his woman. The table didn't stand a chance." I see Matthew tense in my periphery.

"Seriously?" Matt says and I know where his mind is going. *Don't take us there. Don't take us there. Please. Matt.* "Is the wife…safe with him? I mean he broke your table, he's probably got a bit of a violent streak." I look at him and see the hesitation and worry in his eyes and in this moment, I'm pissed at him for alluding that Will is violent—although he doesn't know it was Will, and I'm also in awe of his genuine concern for a woman he doesn't know.

I know firsthand that it's genuine. It reminds me of how he was when we met. Matt has no tolerance for violence after having an alcoholic father who used him and his mother as punching bags growing up. When we met, it was like he *knew*. He could sense the similarities between us and he took action. Matt got me out of that hellhole before we were even romantic. He moved me in with him, set me up with the best trauma therapist in Atlanta and ultimately jump-started my healing process. Within days, he and his uncle—who happened to be the chief of police—had the cops at my house hauling that asshole out in cuffs.

My body immediately tenses and I feel the chill in the air, just like I always do whenever I think about that time in my life. Matt's hand laces with mine and I don't miss the look that crosses Will's face.

"Ms. Pierce, are you alright?" he asks. He sees the walls coming up around me as I shut down. *Fast.*

I shake my head willing the thoughts away. *This is not a conversation I want to have with Will in front of Matt.* "Fine."

"Charlotte," Matt says from next to me and I look at him pleading with him not to say anything.

He moves closer to me and I am aware of the man in front of me who is undoubtedly going crazy. "I'm sorry I said that," he says. I nod before giving a small shrug, mostly for Will's benefit.

"It's fine."

"You don't look fine," Will interrupts and I resist the urge to look him in the eye. If I do, I'll lose it. I keep telling myself that I need to tell Will about my past but I also want to keep that part of myself hidden. I don't want him to see that, because of my past, I am still so dependent on Matt.

"Charlotte," Matt's voice interrupts my thoughts, "maybe it's time we tell Dr. Montgomery about Michael."

# CHAPTER
## *Seven*

"**N**o," I tell him firmly and I don't miss the look that crosses Will's face. *I hope he knows not to push me right now.*

"Ms. Pierce, Mr. Wells, if there's something that you feel I should know, that I don't already know, maybe we should discuss it. It's a safe space here."

"Dr. Montgomery, Charlotte and I haven't been very clear on how we met in the first place."

"Matt," I snap at him, "we don't need to get into this."

Matt draws his attention away from Will and eyes me warily. "You refusing to talk about it isn't helping." Condescension drips from his voice and I resist the urge to scream, already overwhelmed by the tension building in the room.

"Are you kidding me? I spent two years talking about it."

"It's a part of our past, and it's something that maybe he can shed some light on."

"God, this is so like you! You think you know everything. You think you know what's best in every situation. I said I don't want to discuss it, so why are you pushing me?" I can hear my exasperation and I'm sure Matt can as well because he shoots me *the look,* the one he uses when he wants me to calm down.

"Maybe you would feel better if I spoke with Mr. Wells alone?" Will asks me. "And then we could speak privately?" I'm about to jump at the idea of getting to be alone with Will and filling him in on the details myself when Matt answers the question for me.

"Charlotte doesn't normally like going into what happened

unless I'm around to fill in the blanks. She prefers if I'm there with her." This had been true once upon a time. There was a time where I couldn't get through it without Matt holding my hand or stroking my back. I'd needed him to say the words that got stuck in my throat. But now, I would much rather explain what happened to me in the comfort of Will's arms, *where I feel safe.*

"Did something happen to you?" Will looks at me and I look away from his intense gaze, knowing that I can't hold it for too long.

"Both of us," Matt interjects, "at different times in our lives." He looks at me. "Charlotte, you shut down just now. I saw it all over your face." I cross one leg over another before crossing my arms in front of me.

"I had a stepfather. He wasn't particularly nice to me or my mother."

*Succinct and to the point. He can fill in the blanks.* I notice Will tense immediately and I try to read his expression, but he's not letting anything show which is for the best. *See why I didn't want to do this now?*

"Understatement of the century. Why are you downplaying this shit, Charlotte?"

"Because it's irrelevant!" I shriek. *Why is he so determined to make me talk? It's just going to take me back to a place that I spent years trying to escape. I'll cry, Will won't be able to touch me, and that isn't good for either one of us.*

A look of horror crosses his face and I immediately regret the words. "It's extremely relevant, Charlotte," he says angrily and the heat behind his gaze shoots through me.

Guilt floods me as I think about the trauma we've both been through. "I didn't mean it like that. I am fully aware of the gravity of what happened, I just didn't think it was necessary to bring it up now."

"I didn't just randomly bring it up, Charlotte. You were fucking triggered."

"You triggered it!" I exclaim.

"And I apologized for it. I just…" He looks at Will who hasn't taken his eyes off of me yet.

*Look away, Will. Please.*

He must hear my thoughts because he manages to tear his intense gaze away from me to look at my husband.

"I met Charlotte when she was twenty and I was twenty-two. The story is still the same, she was a waitress at a restaurant that I went to one night with some friends. We talked, I asked her out, and she turned me down. But it wasn't as romantic as me wearing her down and her finally accepting which is how we tell the story. I went in the next day to see her, but another waitress informed me that she had called out sick. I didn't think anything of it. I went back the next day, same story. I came back a week later and she had this gigantic bruise on her face. I mean…it was awful. She was wearing long sleeves in July…"

I close my eyes, remembering the pain vividly. The purple bruise underneath my eye, the marks on my arm from his strong hands grabbing me. The smell of cheap vodka from his breath surrounds me.

*"Where have you been?" His words boom through the house as I close the door quietly behind me. He's home and he's already drunk.*

*I take a step back, out of arm's reach just in case he decides to take a swing at me. "I—I had class," I stammer, my voice timid and quiet as I remember what happened the last time I apparently "raised my voice" to him. "And then I had to work."*

*"It's almost six o'clock. You were supposed to be home at five."*

*"I—I stayed late at work. One of the other girls called out sick."*

*"You little liar! Where were you?"*

*"I swear, I was at work!"*

*"What did I say would happen if you lied to me again, Charlotte?"*

*"Michael, please, I—" He raises his arm, and I brace myself for the mind-numbing pain the second he makes contact.*

I blink my eyes several times bringing me back to the present just as the memory of his fist hitting my face flashes through my brain. I raise my eyes from the spot on the floor and find Will. Soft, blue eyes bore into me, and I fear he can see the pain of my past as I'm reliving it moment by moment.

"It was a red flag because I knew the signs," Matt continues. "I tried to talk to her but she was just completely void of emotion. There was no life in her eyes, nothing. I basically begged her that night to come have dinner with me because I was so worried for her to go home. I knew someone was doing this to her, I just wasn't sure who it was. The first time we met she said she didn't have a boyfriend, so I assumed it was a parent."

I remember that day like it was yesterday. Summers in Atlanta are brutal and it was the hottest day in July. I wore a black turtleneck sweater to cover both the bruises on my arms and the ones around my neck after his short attempt at asphyxiation. Everyone in the restaurant stared at the woman with bright red cheeks that was sweating profusely as if they knew. They knew what happened to me every night when I went home. I felt their gazes. Their *pity*. I hated it. I knew I hadn't done anything wrong but I still felt the sting of humiliation. The tears run down my face as I hear Matt recount the gritty details of that night. The night my life changed forever.

"I wrote down my number and told her to call me if she ever needed anything. Sure enough, I heard from her that night." I close my eyes and attempt the breathing exercises that my old therapist advised me to try whenever my brain went back to that night. *But I was failing.* I was too far gone. My eyes open and I'm there. I can see everything vividly. My old home that I shared with my mother and then two different husbands after my father died. Michael, my mother's third husband, moved in shortly after they got married.

*I'm hunched over in the corner, my arms around my knees as I try to escape the pain in my abdomen. It hurts every time I take a breath making me wonder how many of my ribs he's broken this time. My head throbs, and I can taste the blood in my mouth from the gash in my lip. I wipe the blood with the back of my hand and I can already feel it swelling under my touch.*

*The house is eerily quiet and I wonder if my mother has been knocked unconscious because I haven't heard her ear-piercing scream in the last few minutes. I stand slowly and breathe a quiet sigh of relief when I don't see Michael in the room. Hot tears pour from my eyes, sliding down my cheeks and fall from my face. It's so quiet, I can even make out the faint noise of the drops hitting the hardwood. Maybe if I can just make it to the door I can go for help... My memory flashes to the sweet man from the restaurant. Matthew-something? The man with the kind eyes and sweet smile that I feared knew the truth. He knew what was happening to me. But why did he care?*

*I tiptoe across the living room, careful to avoid the spots where I know the floorboards creak. My hand is around the doorknob when the hairs on the back of my neck stand at attention. The tears spring to my eyes as I realize I'm not alone.*

*"Where do you think you're going, little girl?"*

*"Mich—ael..." I stutter. "Please don't hurt me," I beg. I beg for mercy, for relief, for—my life.*

*"Where you gonna go, huh? The cops?"*

*"No—I wasn't," I plead as he spins me around and slams me hard against the door.*

*"Don't fucking lie to me," he slurs. He raises the bottle of the clear poisonous liquid to his lips and takes a long sip. "You're not going anywhere." He points behind him. "Upstairs."*

*"But..."*

*He grabs me by my hair and shoves me toward the stairs. "Move it."*

*I begin to move when he grabs my arm and a pain shoots through it making me feel as if every bone is shattering into a million pieces. The pain is so overwhelming, it makes my stomach turn and the bile rises in my throat. For a moment, my vision blurs, large black spots appear in my periphery as the trauma takes over my brain. I plead with myself not to fall asleep. To stay conscious. Who knows what will happen if I pass out? He grabs my arm again and I scream. The pain shooting through my arm is unbearable, and in this moment, I know that my stepfather has broken my arm. I hear a crash upstairs and I pray that my mother is stronger than I am. It's the only way we will survive this.*

Matt's fingers lace with mine, bringing me back to the here and now and I'm grateful for the interruption of my hellish trip down memory lane—even if the hand belongs to the wrong man.

"She was able to sneak out and she called me. I still remember the pain in her voice. How quiet and scared she sounded. It broke my heart. She sent me her location and I found her down the street from her house leaning against a mailbox because she was too weak to stand."

*I couldn't believe how quickly Matt found me. How willing he was to leave the comfort of his home in the middle of the night to help a woman he'd just met. I swear we were just getting off the phone when a silver Honda appeared in front of me and the kind man from the restaurant scooped me into his arms. I don't think I spoke for the next day and a half.*

"I took her to the hospital immediately. That bastard had broken four of her ribs, her arm in three places, and she had a bruise on her left eye to match the one on the right."

He shakes his head as the tears continue falling down my face. "There was no way I could let her go back there. Two days later, the police arrested him. My uncle was, and still is, the chief of police so we moved quickly. The trial…everything. I'm fairly certain he somehow convinced the judge not to let him out on bail until sentencing. I begged Charlotte to testify and she did, as did her mother."

*It didn't take long for me to fall for my knight in shining armor.*

*For the next few weeks, Matt rarely left my side. It helped on the nights that I woke up screaming in fear. Despite the fact that I hardly knew Matt, he let me stay with him as the memories of what Michael had done came flooding back every time I stepped foot in my house. I knew he was gone, but I couldn't shake the feeling that he was— everywhere. Matt did everything and then some to ensure the safety of my mother and myself. There was nothing I could do to express my gratitude to this man that had ultimately saved my life.*

I can hear Matt speaking, but the words are all muffled. I see his lips moving but it's like I'm underwater. I hear nothing. I take a deep breath and try to bring myself out of the past just in time to hear Matt explain my biggest source of anxiety: *Michael's release from prison.*

"And even with all of the testimonies that stated that her bruises and hospital visits started when she was fifteen, indicating that she was a minor when it all began…even with all of that, that asshole only did twenty-four months. When he got out, I wanted to kill him. He had written her letters from jail telling her to watch her back and Charlotte was a nervous wreck every minute. We immediately filed a restraining order but she was still looking over her shoulder. The nightmares had come back full force. I hated seeing Charlotte go through this, but there was nothing I could do. Nothing made her feel…safe. So, I began to keep very close tabs on him. I followed his every move. He's not allowed within a few states of Charlotte or her mother and, as of yesterday, he's somewhere in Virginia." He sighs and I believe he's finally done shining the light on all of the skeletons in the closet. "I may not be the best husband, but I would die to keep her safe and she knows that."

I blink several times as I try to bring my mind out of the dark. *I don't know if it's his words, hearing the story recounted for the millionth time, or the fact that he's said all of this in front of Will who is undoubtedly hurt that I didn't tell him, but I'm wrecked.* He pulls his hand from my grasp and wraps his arms around me, pressing a kiss to my temple and I feel terrible that Will has to witness this. My eyes flit toward him as he stands and walks toward the door. My heart sinks when I watch him disappear through it, closing it firmly behind him.

*Shit.*

"Charlotte, he's gone. It's just you and me," Matt whispers in my ear before placing another kiss on my forehead. *I know he's trying to comfort me, but I really wish he'd stop kissing me, especially in front of Will.* "That story never gets easier."

"He should come back, I'm fine." I wipe the tears away with the tissues that Matt has placed in my lap.

"You sure? I could feel your agitation the whole time I was talking. You spaced out a few times too. I know you were trying to disassociate. Are you okay, sweetheart?" I blanch slightly, but I don't think he notices. Matt rarely uses terms of endearment unless we are in mixed company and it's for show.

"I haven't had a moment like that in a year or so. I'm fine." I nod, willing to say anything for Matt to call Will back into the room. *But what then? It's not like we can talk in private.* I rub my forehead, wishing that for once my life didn't feel so complicated. Matt rubs my back, not understanding the whole reason why the tension is coming off of me in waves. My thoughts are interrupted by a low buzzing noise. My eyes immediately find his jacket knowing that his phone is hidden in his pocket. "Just answer it."

He shakes his head. "We're in therapy, and after that, I'm not taking a phone call."

"It's fine. Just take it."

He looks at me for a minute before taking out his phone, and his eyes widen when he sees the screen. I already know his next words. "Shit, Charlotte, I do need to take this. I just need five minutes."

I shrug. "It's fine." I give him a small smile. The truth is, it *is* fine. I need to see Will and it is the only thing my mind is focused on at the moment. And if I can't be with Will then I want to be alone.

"I'm sorry." He tells me as he stands in a hurry and presses the screen as he attempts to catch the call before it disconnects. He kisses the top of my head and then disappears through the door.

*I wonder how many times I've said the word "fine" in the past twenty minutes. Who am I trying to convince? Matt and Will? Or myself?*

I watch Matt leave the office, shut the door, and I'm left by myself. I reach for my purse, attempting to grab my Blackberry to call the man I've needed for the past half hour but the door opens stopping me in my tracks. Will stands there and I hold his gaze. I know I only have a few minutes but there is so much I want to say.

"I was going to tell you." I can't escape the tears that well in my eyes. I'm so overwhelmed by the events of the past hour and now the man I hope will hold me and take the pain away is less than ten feet away from me.

*But my husband is still twenty feet away.*

"When?"

"It's not something I tell a lot of people anymore. The people who know…they know because they were there. They were a part of my life when I was twenty. It's just not something I discuss with everyone."

"I'm not just anyone," he argues. "I'm your therapist. How did you and Wells not tell me this months ago?" He crosses his arms and regards me warily as he pushes off the door and makes his way across the room.

"You're my therapist now?" I say looking at him with tears in my eyes.

He clears his throat and I can tell he's fighting with himself about whether or not he should touch me. "In this moment, I am. Wells has a similar story?"

"Yes, his father was a drunk. He died when Matt was in high school. His abuse started much earlier though. When he was five or so. Stopped when he was about fifteen after Matt kicked his ass." I sigh. "I'm sorry you had to find out like this. I didn't know…"

"No, *I* didn't know. Do you think I would have made that comment about the angry husband breaking the table if I did? God, Charley, I triggered you," he says rubbing a hand through his hair.

"No, you didn't. Matthew did. I honestly didn't think about it the same way Matthew did. Because I know how the table broke. I thought…I thought you were calling yourself my husband."

"I was." He sits back in his chair across from me and leans forward. Expecting Matthew back any second, he keeps his distance. "Why didn't you tell me?" His voice is low and pained, as if he's going through the same range of emotions. "Did you think that I wouldn't protect you?" He pauses for a second before he continues. "I guess that's only a job for your husband. Someone I'll never be."

I furrow my brows as I try to keep the tears at bay. "That's… that's not true. Yes, Matt got me through some really dark shit but—"

"I always knew there was something you weren't telling me. I was hoping you would open up to me that first time. I even asked you if there was something you wanted to tell me. Did you think I wouldn't protect you? That I wouldn't do whatever Wells has been doing and then some?" The thought warms me. *He wants to protect me as fiercely as Matthew has.*

"Will—"

I hear the door open and I immediately close my mouth when a contrite-looking Matthew walks in. He kneels in front of me, completely ignoring Will who has leaned back in his chair. "We should go, I'll take you home."

"Why? Besides, my car is here."

"I have to go back to the office. Evidently, I'm flying to

Oklahoma tonight. I have a nine a.m. meeting tomorrow. I'm sorry." He looks down at his watch. "It actually works out better that your car is here, but are you sure you're okay to drive?" I try to ignore the look Will is giving Matthew from behind his back, but in my peripheral vision, I know he's shaking his head at my husband's complete lack of empathy in this moment.

*Not that I'm craving it from him anyway.*

"Yes, I'll be fine." *There's that word again.*

"Might I suggest you at least follow her home?" Will says.

"I'll be okay," I say shooting him a cursory glance. *Let him go, so we can finish talking.* "I don't want to drive right now, anyway. I might go for a walk."

"Okay. You know you're safe here right? He can't hurt you. I won't let him hurt you."

"I know."

"Okay, I'll be home around six before I leave. You'll be there, then?"

I nod my head. "Yes."

"Okay, I'm sorry to do this, Charlotte." He kisses the side of my head, and then he's gone.

Will and I sit in silence for a few moments holding each other's gaze after Matt leaves. Now that he's gone, the words have escaped me. *I don't even know where to begin.*

Will stands up after a few moments before he leaves the office.

*Where is he going? Did he really just leave without saying anything?* My teeth find my bottom lip and my nostrils flare as the tears that have been threatening to fall for the past five minutes begin to brim under my eyelids. Will's office feels as if the temperature has dropped twenty degrees and goose bumps break out over my skin. A shudder runs through me in response, and I wrap my arms around myself in an attempt to warm and comfort myself.

After a few minutes Will comes back, locking the door behind him. "I have no words," he says as he makes his way over to his bar. "Do you want a drink?"

I narrow my eyes curiously. I know that nothing could possibly comfort me like his arms around me. "No. I want you." I hold my arms out, desperate for him to join me on the couch. My body is fiending for his touch, but so is my heart.

He takes a sip and eyes me over his glass. "Yeah, of course you do."

I frown at the sarcasm in his voice. "What does that mean?"

"Why didn't you tell me, Charley?" he asks quietly. "Don't you trust me?"

Immediately, I feel guilty. *Why didn't I tell him?* "Of course, I trust you. I'm sorry, I didn't tell you."

He crosses the room, closing the space between us and takes a seat next to me on the couch. He gently turns my face to look at him and traces my lip with his thumb. "How could anyone hurt you?" He closes his eyes as his hand continues to trace my face, my eyes, my nose, my cheeks. "I would kill anyone that touches you." He says it so quietly that I don't think it was meant for me to hear.

I press my hand gently over his, which is pressed against my cheek. "Will, I should have told you sooner."

His eyes close for a moment and when they open they are much colder, immediately worrying me. "This is just who I am in your life…the guy that makes you come, that makes you feel alive, that makes you happy. You fool around with me, and I make you feel good, and then you go back to your husband who makes you feel safe. You get to take a vacation from your life three times a week. God, I'm like your pool boy." He rolls his eyes at the ridiculous metaphor.

"That's not true," I say immediately. "That's not who you are to me at all."

"Then what am I? I'm clearly not the man you trust to keep

you safe. That you feel so loyal to that you won't leave. I'm not the one who's supposed to protect you."

"I…I didn't know you wanted to be that person. You never gave me any indication that you wanted more. You telling me to leave my husband in the midst of fucking because you're trying to lay your claim over me is not the same thing and you know it." I stand up, needing to put space between myself and Will. I struggle between the feelings of wanting him to hold me and not wanting him to touch me at all due to this recent shift in attitude. *After everything that's happened in this past hour, he's really bringing this up, now?* He doesn't say anything, as the weight of my words hang in the air between us. "And now you're learning that I have baggage. Baggage that I was going to tell you about the second we had longer than three hours at a time together. Two of which you're usually inside of me. I'm sorry I didn't tell you. Trust me, part of the reason I was crying is because you had to see Matt and me, like *that.*"

"Why? Charley, that's normal."

"I didn't want you to see Matt…touching me."

"I hated that," he says simply. "But it's bigger than that. You needed contact and I couldn't be that person. I'm not that person."

"But you *are* that person. I needed *you.*" I'm silent for a second. "I need you now." I sit back down and slide off my shoes. I try to move into his lap when he puts a hand up to stop me. "Charley."

The rejection is stifling and I can't seem to get air into my lungs fast enough. "What?"

"I think we should talk about this without touching each other."

"I don't see what one has to do with the other. Can't you see that I need you right now? Or do you still have it in your head that it's not your job?" I scoff, trying to convey how upset I am but I fear it's coming off as bitchy sarcasm.

He runs his tongue over his front teeth and nods once. "Is that why you can't leave him?" he snaps bitterly. "*Won't* leave him?" He sighs after a few moments of my silence. "Because of what you've been through? I've seen it time and time again people associate—"

"Stop," I interrupt him, "don't do that. I'm not your patient right now. I'm Charley, the woman you fucked on a broken coffee table two hours ago. You can't be my therapist right now," I say softly. "I need you to understand… I met Matthew when I was at my lowest." I swallow as the tears begin to slide down my cheeks. "He saved my life and for a while I felt indebted to him. But I also loved him. Maybe a part of me always will. He made me feel safe and secure. I don't worry about Michael coming after me." I stop, wondering how to put into words the thoughts that are constantly running through my mind.

*I've fallen out of love with my husband but the thought of leaving him terrifies me.*

"But things changed, Will. Matt changed, I changed. But was I going to sacrifice feeling safe from the monsters under my bed? Maybe I wasn't in love with him anymore but…maybe I could live with that. Because what would happen if I left Matt? Would *he* come after me? If he did, he'd kill me this time, Will. He'd finish the job he started that night." I sniffle as I try to keep the tears at bay. "If I was no longer under Matt's protection then what would happen to me? You're right," I whisper. "I was complacent… I *am* complacent." I shrug. "But I was okay with that, if the complacency kept me *alive*. Even when I threatened to leave him last year, I'm not sure I could have really done it. I know you think it's about the money…it's not. But it *is* about the protection that Matt's money has provided me and my mother. Maybe that makes me weak. Or stupid. To stay with someone when you're not in love with them, but it was okay. It was fine. Then I met you, and suddenly it wasn't fine anymore. Everything changed." I take a deep breath, relieved that I've gotten all of that off my chest. I look at Will who's staring at me intently. "Please say something," I say after a few moments of deafening silence.

"I don't think that you're weak or stupid, Charley. I think you're incredibly brave and strong." He pushes my hair back behind my ear and gives me a sad smile that makes my heart stop.

*Is this it? Is he leaving me? It's too much. I knew it was too much. That was one of the reasons I hadn't told him. He claims he wants to be this person and yet he's pushing me away when I need him?*

"Do you think you'll ever feel completely safe if you leave him?" he asks.

I shrug. "I don't know. You seemed pretty sure you could do the same if not better a little while ago."

"That's if you want to leave him...which I'm not sure you do."

"I want to be with you," I blurt out, and while I believe that's true, I don't see how we can make that work. The thought that I'll never get to be with Will is sobering and it makes my blood run cold.

"Are you sure about that?" He raises an eyebrow at me, as if he doesn't believe what I'm saying. My lip trembles as I see the look in his eyes. *Why is he asking me that?*

"Are you not?"

"Charley..." He stands up from the couch and I'm seconds from losing it. "It's not healthy to go from one relationship of dependency to another. You'll go from needing him to needing me, and you have to learn to stand on your own. You have to learn who you are outside of a relationship."

"You...you don't need me, too?" I ask. I sound pitiful as the words leave my lips. "You saying I need to learn to stand on my own two feet is basically insinuating that you think I can't. That you think I'm weak." I slip on my shoes and stand. "Ten minutes ago, you made me feel bad for not telling you, you asked me if I could trust you. And I do! But now that it's all out in the open I'm suddenly this different person and you don't want me leaning on you. This is just all too real for you now, right?"

*How dare he do this? How dare he make me feel guilty for not telling him and then turn all of this around on me? As if this day hasn't been traumatic enough.*

"That's not what—"

I put my hand up, effectively cutting him off. "'I'm not that person.' Those were your goddamn words."

"You're taking what I said out of context, I just mean—"

"You've made it perfectly clear what you mean. Maybe you were right. We should stop this. This is all too much for you now." I pull on my jacket and move to the door. "Somewhere inside of me I expected this reaction, but I held onto hope that you'd surprise me." I shake my head sadly. "I guess I was wrong."

# CHAPTER

*Eight*

The tears are still sliding down my cheeks. They haven't stopped since the moment I left Will's office. As I pull into our garage, the door closes behind me, effectively shutting me off from the outside world, and I take a deep breath. I rest my head on the steering wheel as a pathetic attempt to get myself together enough to go inside and potentially face my husband. I stare up into the rearview mirror as I wipe my eyes, my lip trembling even though it's captured between my teeth.

*I look like shit.*

I'm not sure if Will and I broke up but it certainly felt that way and the thought feels like a punch straight to the gut that has left me breathless. Maybe it was true what they say—the grass isn't always greener on the other side. Sure, I have hot, passionate, soul-shattering sex with Will but was that it? Is that enough to completely turn my life upside down? To leave Matt? Despite the fact that he has his flaws, he doesn't deserve this. He doesn't deserve my betrayal after all of the good he's done.

I make my way through the house, the arduous task of climbing the stairs weighing on me as I don't have an ounce of energy. I walk into our bedroom to see Matt coming out of our walk-in closet, with his phone pressed to his ear.

"There you are, I was just calling you," he says walking toward me as he tosses his phone on the bed. I'm shocked by his comment as I can't remember the last time Matt called me to check on my whereabouts. He frowns when he takes in my appearance.

I know despite my dry eyes, they're still red and glossy with unshed tears. "Hey, what happened? I thought you were okay?" He pulls me to sit next to him on our bed. "I knew I shouldn't have left you like that."

"I'm fine. I just…stayed and talked to Dr. Montgomery for a little while." I shake my head. "I hate talking about it." *For once, I'm telling him the absolute truth.*

"What did he say?"

I sigh. Our conversation has been playing on a loop in my mind ever since I left his office. "Nothing I didn't already know."

He nods. "Maybe I shouldn't go," he says staring at his packed suitcase in the corner.

*I know what this is. I've heard it a hundred times. He says that because he knows I'll never ask him to stay.*

"No, you should… I'll be here when you get back." I give him a faint smile, as I do my best to appear "fine" and just a bit shook up over rehashing the demons of my past—not devastated over the wrench that was thrown into my future. "I'm not going anywhere."

*And the hidden truth to that statement feels like a thousand knives piercing my heart.*

He nods once before he takes my face in his hands. He presses his lips to mine and instead of the soft simple kiss I've grown accustomed to, his tongue probes my lips as he tries to gain access to my mouth. I open, welcoming the distraction and the old familiarity of my husband's kiss, reminding me how vastly different he is from the man I'd spent the last few months kissing. It's not a kiss that makes my body come alive like Will's though, and the reminder doesn't help the ache in my chest.

The kiss goes on for a few moments, and when he pulls away, he has a huge smile on his face. "It's been too long since I've done that." I only nod, not knowing what to say. He brushes a hair from my face, probably reading my silence as feeling dazed from our kiss. "We'll talk when I get back." He doesn't wait for my response before heading out of the bedroom to the front door. I follow behind him slowly and lean against the wall, staring as he collects his wallet, keys, and cell phone. "I hate leaving you like this."

"I'll be fine," I say before I take the few steps toward him and wrap my arms around him. *I'm craving the intimacy I didn't get from Will, and Matt is willing to appease me slightly.*

"I'll see you in a few days, okay?" He presses a kiss to my forehead. "I love you."

"I love you too," I say and my heart constrict as the words come out.

*But I'm in love with someone else.*

Once I know he's gone, I slide down the wall slowly, the events of the day washing over me. As soon as I hit the ground, my tears start to flow. Without the watchful eyes of Will or Matt, I let them fall without fear of questioning. I cry for a good hour letting the pain of losing Will and the old wounds that have resurfaced take over my mind.

—

After deciding that an hour was long enough to be lying on the hardwood floors of my foyer, I get up and make my way back upstairs to change for a run. I always run when I need to clear my head, focusing only on putting one foot in front of the other. I slip on my favorite *Lululemon* spandex and tank before I'm out the door. I make it to the end of my street when I notice the shiny, silver BMW parked in front of my neighbor's house. It isn't uncommon for the people on my street to switch out their cars as often as they change their sheets, but Mitch Thompson is a frenemy of my husband's, which means I would definitely have known if they had gotten a new car. I shake it off, determined to put my husband and my boyfriend and anything related to them out of my mind.

I turn the corner off my street, and as I pass the other houses, I wonder how many of them are like mine, beautiful on the outside, but broken and damaged on the inside. I continue my route throughout the neighborhoods trying my best to keep my mind clear, but Will's words continue to creep into my brain.

*"I'm not your husband."*

*"I'm not who you trust to protect you."*

*"You fool around with me because I make you feel good, and then you go back to your husband who makes you feel safe."*

*Is that what I'm doing? Am I using Will for the passion and attention I didn't get from my husband?* I squeeze my eyes together for a moment, trying to stop the twinge of guilt running through me. *So, now, on top of feeling guilty for cheating on my husband, I'm feeling guilty for being married as well.*

About halfway into my three-mile run, I can't decide if it's sweat or tears on my cheeks. I stop, put my hands on my knees, and breathe deeply, my lungs on fire as I desperately try to suck in every bit of oxygen. I turn around and walk slowly as I attempt to calm my heart that is racing from fatigue but also from the tension coursing through my veins. I start back toward my house and I feel a worried frown turn the corners of my mouth down when I notice the same BMW that was parked on my street earlier.

*It can't be the same one, can it? Why would Mitch be following me? Unless it's not Mitch…*

I try to ignore the feeling that I'm being followed, especially in light of the conversations I'd had today, and continue my run back to my house. The last thing I see before I lock the door behind me is the sports car appearing at the end of my street again, where I first saw it.

*What. The. Fuck.*

It's almost 9 p.m., when I hear the doorbell for my back door. No one ever comes around the back, with the exception of our delivery man when we have larger packages, and it's never this late at night. I'm nervous to answer as the feeling of being watched hasn't totally subsided. I had watched the mysterious car leave about an hour ago but I still can't shake the feeling. My hand lingers on the handle and I can feel the spark through the door. I'm about to take a peek through the peephole when I hear his voice.

"It's me, baby." Those three words send a jolt to both my heart and my sex and I whimper in response.

"Will," I say softly and bite my lip knowing that if I open the door, nothing good will come from it. I desperately want to be in his arms after what happened earlier but I can't. "What are you doing here?"

"We need to talk," he says. "I need *you*. Please open the door, Charley."

The devil and the angel are perched firmly on my shoulders pleading their cases over what I should do. It doesn't take long before I unbolt the door to find Will severely dressed down. Dark jeans, a black t-shirt, a leather jacket, and a hat pulled low over his eyes. I immediately feel my body respond to this much edgier look and have to resist the urge to jump into his arms. He looks like the bad boy your mother warned you about and not the intelligent, well-respected doctor you *wanted* to take home to her.

*No, Charley, he doesn't want this and you shouldn't want this either.*

"What are you doing here?"

"Can I come in?"

"No," I say, blocking his entry.

"Please?" he says lifting his head, his blue eyes clouded with hurt and sadness, effectively ripping my heart wide open.

My eyes trace his face, and despite my anger, my heart constricts.

*My pain is his pain.*

I step to the side allowing him to pass, and his signature scent that has a direct line with my hormones infiltrates my nose as I close the door behind him. I stand against it as he walks through my kitchen and looks around. "Nice place," he comments, and I wonder if there's a hint of sarcasm there. "What I expected."

His eyes find mine, his blue orbs boring into mine before he removes his hat and runs a hand through his hair. "Why are you here?" I ask him.

"Because I've been going crazy ever since you left my office. I hate that we left things like that."

"*We* didn't do anything. *You* made it abundantly clear how you felt."

"No. I didn't." He sighs. "I didn't mean what I said. Baby—"

"Charley," I say correcting him and chastise myself for not using *Charlotte*. I need to stop this familiar intimacy with him.

He sighs as he drops to one of my bar stools that surround the island in the center of the kitchen. "I'm sorry for what I said. I…I couldn't grasp what I was feeling. They say doctors are the worst patients…" He chuckles but I can hear the sadness he's trying to hide in his voice. "I had just watched you break down in front of me and there was nothing I could do. I couldn't touch you, hold you, comfort you. It took everything out of me not to say *fuck it* and pull you into my arms and kiss away your tears even in front of Wells. Do you know how much it destroyed me to hear that you went through that? I hate that someone hurt you. That…that I couldn't protect you from that."

"You didn't even know me," I whisper.

"And then Wells…just left you. How could he leave you like that?" He shakes his head and the tears prickle in my eyes. I swallow them down, trying to tell myself I have cried enough today and I need to be strong in front of Will. If I break, he'll want to comfort me and as confused as I am, I would let him. "I wanted to kick his ass. How could he be so thoughtless?"

"We have already uncovered that Matt can be a little inconsiderate when it comes to my feelings." Even as I say the words, even though I've said them before, they hurt. The fact that I have a husband that doesn't care half of the time, hurts. Despite my situation, and the mistakes I've made, *my husband's actions hurt me every day.*

"Still," he says, "it was like it was nothing, Charley. And then he left the fucking state?"

"He had work." I shrug because, honestly, I don't have anything else to say on the matter.

"I would have dropped everything for you, Charlotte." I divert my eyes from his gaze. He walks toward me and takes my hands in his, squeezing them gently. "I'm sorry for how I handled it."

"You told me—"

"I know what I said," he interrupts. "I was wrong to say that. Forgive me. Please."

"Why?"

He lifts my head to look into his eyes. "Because I love you," he states firmly, like he'd said it a million times before. "I am so in love with you, Charley."

My mouth drops open slightly and he gives me a sad smile as if he's worried this won't change anything. As if I'll tell him that it's too late and it doesn't matter. "Wh—what?"

"I know you're afraid to leave Matt because you think that no one will be there to protect you. And I didn't exactly make it clear that I would." He looks down at where our hands are connected before he brings them to his lips. "I love you, I would protect you from anything…everything. I would never let anyone hurt you."

I'm stunned by his admission. *He…loves me?*

I want to cry tears of both elation and grief. He loves me but… I'm not free to give myself to him completely. He must know my thoughts because he places his hands on my face. "I know you're in a tough position, and I'm not asking you to make any decisions right now. I just want you to know that I'm in. I'm all in, Charley."

My teeth find my bottom lip and I chew on it nervously. "Would you like something to drink?" I ask, hoping that the alcohol will calm some of my jitters.

He smiles before he tucks a hair behind my ear. "Can I have a kiss first?"

I stand on my tiptoes as I offer my lips for a quick peck. When I try to pull away, I feel his hands under my bottom hoisting me into his arms. Once I've settled, one hand moves up behind my head keeping my lips firmly planted on his. His tongue moves with mine and it feels like home, a welcomed contrast to the kiss I shared with Matt earlier today. His kiss is passionate and aggressive and his tongue is unrelenting against mine as they find their usual dance.

*This man knows what I want. What I like. How to make my toes curl with just a kiss.*

He pulls away from me and gives me one final kiss on my nose before setting me on my feet. "I'll take scotch if you have it."

I nod, moving to my built-in bar in the corner of my kitchen. "I'll give you a tour later. I need you to fuck me first." I smile and grab the bottle and two glasses with shaky hands. I feel his presence behind me as we make our way up the stairs. My bedroom door is open and once I'm through the threshold, I stop, causing him to run into the back of me, his lips immediately on my neck as he peppers kisses along the length of it.

*Can I do this?*

*He's already in your house, Charley…drinking your husband's twenty-one-year-old scotch*, my subconscious answers.

I turn in his arms effectively removing his lips from my neck. "Actually, can we go to the guest room?"

He looks at the bed behind me and then down at me before

nodding once. We make it to the guest room and I set the glasses down on the nightstand. "Baby, we don't have to do anything," he says wrapping me in his arms. "I didn't come here for sex. I came here to clear things up…to get you back. To tell you I love you."

"You don't want to make love in a bed for once?" I'm not sure what it is I want. I know I want him, but we are in my house—the one I share with my husband. I feel out of my element and the betrayal I am committing is more real than ever before.

"I do, but not at the cost of your sanity. What's going on up here, huh?" he asks, tapping my temple gently, his fingertip grazing down the side of my face and finding my chin. His finger leaves a trail of fire in its wake causing my skin to sizzle.

I pull away slightly, trying to give myself some space for clarity. "What do you think?" I sit on the bed and open the scotch to pour us both a glass. I hand him one and take a small sip of mine. "Am I a terrible person if we have sex here?"

"You're not a terrible person at all, Charley."

"Tell me you love me again," I say, desperate to hear the words. I'm not ready to say the words aloud despite the fact that I was sure I felt the same, but hearing them fall from his mouth sends my brain into overdrive.

He cups my cheeks and I close my eyes relishing in the sensation of his hands on me. I feel his breath on my face before he presses a gentle kiss to my lips.

"I love you, Charlotte," he whispers against my lips and when I open my eyes he's staring at me, his eyes shining with love and adoration.

"We have to figure out a way to see each other more than just during my sessions," I say and I see the look that crosses his face before he nods once. *Don't push me on leaving Matt right now, Will. Please.* "Are you staying the night?" I ask, as a way to transition out of that conversation.

"Can I?"

"I would like that," I say. "Where's your car?"

"Parked around the corner." He pulls my top over my head and buries his face in my bare chest. "I've been wanting to do this ever since I saw you running earlier. The sweat was glistening on your skin, I just wanted to put my face between your beautiful breasts and lick the sweat off of you."

My eyes widen and I grab his head pulling his lips from my nipple. "Wait, what? You saw me running?"

He gives me a sheepish grin before nodding once. "I had to see you. I had to know you were okay. I was waiting for Matt to leave and then I was coming for you."

Realization dawns on me. "You...you have a silver BMW?"

"Yes."

"You were following me?"

"Yes," he repeats as I feel his hand at my breast, toying with my nipple, rubbing it to a hardened peak.

"It made me nervous... I thought I was going crazy."

"I'm sorry, but I just had to see you."

"Is that the first time you've followed me?"

"No," he says simply, and I know the shock is written all over my face. "Once. One other time, after the first time we had sex."

"Where did you follow me?"

"You had mentioned that you'd been waiting for this book to arrive, and you had gotten the email notification that it was in store. The excitement in your eyes when you explained that you were going the next day to get it was so infectious. You were in and out of the store so quick and then I watched you walk to the garage, get in your car, and sit for the next three hours while you read it. I don't know if you finished. But for a while, I was wondering what you were doing. Only until I saw you lift the book over the steering wheel and then I saw that you were reading. You couldn't even wait till you got home to read it."

"You sat and watched me read for three hours?"

"I would watch you sleep for three hours. You fascinate me, Charley. Everything about you." My heart skips a beat at his words. "I'm so jealous of the luxuries that he takes for granted, because I so desperately want them. I want to be with you every second and I can't. He gets to watch you do everything…" He kneels in front of me and strokes my legs starting at my ankle and traces their length, ending at my knees before moving back down.

"But he doesn't. He doesn't even know when my period is, Will, he doesn't see me at all." I scrunch my nose before I pull his face to mine and give him a kiss. "You see me. You see everything."

"I want to see the mundane things, the day-to-day things. Making coffee in the morning, getting dressed, fuck, I don't know, filing your goddamn nails. I just want it all…" He stands up and pushes me back onto the bed before moving to the space between my legs.

I'm topless, but still wearing my shorts, and I feel him pulling at their drawstring before tugging them down. "I want that too." I pant when I feel the air hit my wet sex.

*Between his declarations of love, and the knowledge that he spent an afternoon watching me read, has my arousal pouring out of me.*

"You're so wet," he says as he runs a finger over me. "I am going to worship you." He pulls off his leather jacket and shirt. I take a moment to eye his naked torso before I see him toss his pants on the floor. He removes his briefs and he's left before me, gloriously naked, stroking that steel rod that is standing proudly between his legs. "I think about you every time I touch my cock. You are the star of every single one of my fantasies. You have been for so long."

"When was the first time?" I ask, my eyes focused on his hands as he moves it from root to tip, the veins becoming more evident with each thrust into his palm.

"You don't want to know."

My teeth find my bottom lip and I nod, my chest rising and falling rapidly as I try to control my racing heart. "Yes, I do."

"About a month after you started coming."

My eyes widen at his response. "A month?"

He nods as he rubs his palm against my sex collecting the juices before rubbing it on his cock as lubrication. "I was jacking off in the shower and I couldn't stay hard. Nothing was working, and then your face popped into my mind and I was hard immediately. I hadn't come that hard masturbating—ever."

His words about touching his cock while he thought about me, months before we crossed that line, has me racing toward my orgasm without him even touching me. I think if he were to even breathe on my clitoris I would shatter. "You—touched yourself, thinking about me?" My voice is breathy, the arousal taking all of the conviction out of it.

"I thought about you *every* time."

"What were we doing?" I ask.

"I had this fantasy of bending you over my desk and licking your pussy from behind. Your cum coating my face and dripping down my chin onto the floor."

"Holy fuck." I can barely catch my breath at this point, my chest moving up and down rapidly as I anticipate the deliciously full feeling. I needed that feeling, *now*. My hands have moved on their own accord to my sex, my fingers rubbing the slick skin as I picture his tongue inside of me, his nose probing the space just below my anus as he eats me from behind. His stubble creating a friction that is somewhere in between pleasure and pain.

"Jesus, baby." His voice is hoarse and I watch as he continues to pull at himself. I don't know how long we stay like this, our eyes locked as we push ourselves closer to the edge. Both of us turned on by the feeling of being watched, and the anticipation of being touched. "Spread your pussy, baby. Let me see what's inside."

I swallow hard, trying my best to get moisture into my very dry mouth. I do as he says, parting my folds, exposing myself to him and the cool air of the room. I clench under his gaze and his normal bright blue eyes are so dilated, they're almost navy. "I need to be inside of you."

"Tell me about some of these other fantasies you've had."

He moves closer to me and rubs his cock against me, my fingers still holding myself apart. "You want to hear about every time I thought about fucking you? Licking you? Sucking you? Is that what you want?" He presses harder against me every time he rubs against my clit and I spasm in response, feeling the familiar tingle blaze through me and then fade instantly almost like a shooting star.

"Yes…" I whimper. "Please."

"In the beginning it was what you'd expect: your mouth around my cock as I exploded down your throat, making those perfect full lips of yours, swollen and wet with my cum. I thought about fucking you from behind, my fingers digging so deep into your hips they'd leave marks you'd have to explain to your husband later. Fucking you against the wall, with those sexy heels you wear digging into my ass. You riding me while you played with your incredible tits, bouncing on my cock, your breasts swaying in that delicious way they do when you *really* ride me. I wanted to fuck your tits, slide my cock through the valley between them and then come all over them. Then, I would watch as you licked my cum from your perfect nipples. I thought about fucking your ass especially after the first time you came to a session before you went to the gym. You were in those leggings that made your ass look almost illegal."

He's still rubbing himself against me, and at this point I know we'll explode the second he slips inside of me, both of us on the edge after his pornographic monologue.

"But as time went on, the fantasies got more real," he continues. "They got more aggressive. It got to the point where every time you left my office I was pulling my dick out and jacking off while your scent lingered in the air. It wasn't just raw fucking, it was passionate. I was making love to you in every single one of my fantasies. Waking up with you and slipping inside of your warm, sleepy body for morning sex just as the sun would rise. Worshipping you against the wall after you'd greeted me after work with nothing but panties and a smile. I pictured shooting my cum deep inside of your womb and making you the mother of my baby."

I gasp, feeling a sudden shift in the intensity of this moment. "You've thought about that?"

"More times than I care to admit."

*He wants a baby with me?* I don't speak the words aloud, fearing his answer. Not because I think he'll tell me no, but because I think he'll suggest we start trying to make that fantasy a reality *now.*

"Please fuck me," I manage to choke out.

He ignores me, pushing my hands away and sliding his hand between my legs. He rubs my clit a few times before I interrupt.

"I don't want your fingers," I demand, having had enough teasing. I want to be fucked *hard.*

"What do you want?" He leans over my body, his lips hovering just above mine. His tongue darts out and licks my bottom lip slowly, sensually, erotically. *Fuck me.*

I wasn't sure if I had said the words out loud, but I feel his fingers leave me, and his thick erection move between the lips of my sex before he thrusts into me aggressively.

I clench around him immediately, my body's natural response of wanting to suck him further inside. "Baby, I'm going to lose it if you keep squeezing me like that."

"I *want* you to lose it," I whisper. "I've fantasized about you losing it." I drag my nails down his back, hard as he begins to thrust deeper inside of me.

"You've had fantasies?" he asks, but it's more of a demand. *Tell me everything. Every thought you've ever had. I want to know it. None of your thoughts are safe from me.* I can almost hear it.

"Yes."

"Tell me." He thrusts and the headboard hits the wall with a thunderous bang. "When did they start?"

"I don't want to tell you."

"Tell me," he says as he lifts both of my legs over his shoulders to get in deeper. *He's looking at me so intensely, I wonder if he can read all of my thoughts, if he can see my entire heart and soul. If he can I'm fucked because he's over every inch of it.* I shake my head and he responds by pinching my clit causing me to cry out in ecstasy. "Tell me and I'll let you come."

"As if that wasn't already happening." I narrow my eyes at him.

"I'll stop and make you suck me off."

"You wouldn't."

"Tell me," he grits out.

I moan, feeling close when I feel him drop my legs and his face comes close to mine. He captures my lips in a scorching kiss before he lets his forehead rest against mine. "Tell me," he whispers again, his breath hitting my lips. "Tell me the first time you wanted me, Charlotte. Tell me I wasn't alone all that time."

"After our first session," I breathe out. I try breaking eye contact with him but he grabs my face keeping our eyes locked.

"The day we met? What…what did you do?"

I feel his thrusts slow and I piston my hips upwards indicating what I want. "I'll tell you after my orgasm."

He begins to pick up the pace again, pushing into me harder and harder, his eyes boring into mine as he chases both of our orgasms. "I love you so much and to know you wanted me…the whole time I was wanting you too. You've always been mine. From the fucking start."

"Yours," I moan out.

"No one else's."

"No," I moan, unable to keep the word from leaving my lips. *I do belong to him. I was his. I am his. This part of me that no one has ever gotten to see. The part of myself that I thought could never be revived. The part of my heart that has been closed off for at least two years, maybe longer.*

"Shit. I'm going to come, Charley. I need you to get there."

"I'm so there," I moan out as I feel the first bolt of lightning in my toes. "Harder," I scream and I don't think I've ever made the noises that are coming out of me right now.

"Charley," he groans. "Fuck!"

He thrusts one more time and then I'm convulsing. I dig my nails into his back as I try to tether myself to something physical because I float away. My mind goes blank, and I don't think anything. All I can do is feel; I feel his eyes on me despite the fact that mine are closed. I feel his dick pulsing inside of me as he roars through his orgasm. Most importantly, I feel his heart beating in perfect rhythm with mine.

*Holy mother of God, what an orgasm.*

"Charlotte." My name falls from his lips like a prayer as he continues to pulse inside of me. He's breathing like he's run a marathon and his head drops to my chest. His tongue swipes across both of my nipples before his face finds my neck. "That was incredible."

"I knew it would be good the second we got into bed."

"Fuck," he says and I giggle as I feel him soften inside of me. "I think I came for a full minute." He pulls out of me before pulling me to his chest. He pulls the blankets up from the bottom of the bed and I snuggle against him. "Tell me what happened…when you went home after our first session. Tell me how you fucked yourself, where and with what. Tell me *everything.*"

"You took my breath away the first moment I laid eyes on you. You were charming, and sweet." I smile as I remember that first session. "You were kind to me. You were so chivalrous, and it was something I hadn't felt in so long. Something as minute as waiting for me to sit down before you took your seat had my panties drenched. Truly, I don't know how you or Matt didn't notice the way I was squirming on that sofa. I got home and went straight to my bedroom. Matt had to go back to the office, so I had the house to myself. As soon as I heard the sound of his car start, I had my vibrator out."

"You have a vibrator?"

"Yes."

"Can I see it?" I nod. "How often do you use it?"

"Not as much since we started. But sometimes on the weekend, since I have to wait two days till the next time I see you instead of one."

"So, you took out your vibrator…" he pushes me to continue.

"I thought about you. With your mouth…everywhere. I had this fantasy of you looking up at me from between my legs with your glasses on." I let out a breath, slightly embarrassed that I'm letting this man into the deep corners of my mind.

"Anything else?"

"I fantasized about you tying me up. Spanking me." I roll my eyes. "I read too much smut. Billionaire meets virgin, he fucks her and doing so completely fucks him. The stories are all the same, but they are unbelievably hot."

"You want me to spank you?"

"I want you to do *everything* to me."

He starts to move and I grip him harder trying to keep him in place. "One second, just let me get something," he says. I'm surprised to see he's reaching for his jacket. I frown, wondering what happened that's pushing him to leave, but my expression immediately changes when I see him pull his glasses out. The air leaves my lungs as I watch him slide them on and crawl back onto the bed. "Spread your legs for me." I do as he says and I'm rewarded with the sexiest smile before I see him lower his face between my legs, his eyes never once leaving mine. "Is this what you want, Charlotte?"

"Yes, please," I say in a voice so breathy I don't even recognize it. He kisses the top of my right thigh followed by my left before moving his lips inward to kiss the skin just a few inches shy of my sex. I clench, my body anticipating and responding to his proximity to my wet flesh. He places a kiss on my inner thigh before nibbling on the skin, creating a temporary indentation of his teeth, just as he always does.

*His need to mark me.*

He finally reaches his destination and takes one slow lick through my pussy from bottom to top, stopping at my clit to flick the bundle with the tip of his tongue. "Oh God!" The scream leaves my body instantly, as my hands fall to his head. I look down and push his hair back from his forehead and stare at him through his sexy frames, his gaze still fixed on me. He swipes his tongue back and forth across my clit, almost as if he's as desperate for a taste of my orgasm as I am to have it.

"I swear nothing in the world feels like this does," I moan as I see my juices glistening on his lips, the evidence of my arousal coating his skin.

"Tell me how good it feels."

"Incredible," I groan sitting up slightly on my elbows to get a better view. He continues to work me over, his tongue sliding in and out of me, forcing the orgasm out of me.

"This is better than the fantasy," I groan as he smiles against me. *Fuck me with the glasses on, fuck me with the glasses on.*

"I can't wait to be inside of you again."

"You read my mind."

"I know. You're looking at me like you want to devour me," he says as he sucks my clit into his mouth and I lose it. My orgasm rips through me, tearing me in half and then into fourths. And yet when I open my eyes, I feel whole again. I fall back against the pillows, struggling to catch my breath when I feel his body on top of mine and he's slipping inside me again.

After our second round of sex, I lie on his chest, listening to every heartbeat, and let it lull me to sleep. *I want this. I want this man in my bed, every night and every morning.* "Charley," he says.

"Hmmm?" I'm unable to form any more coherent thoughts, let alone a word. I feel him move and then he's over me staring down at me.

"Baby, look at me," he says cupping my cheek with one hand and putting a hand under my back pulling me closer to him. "I need to tell you something."

"Mmmm," I repeat letting my eyes flutter open and then shut again. "Tell me something."

He shuts his eyes slowly before opening them. "Leave him, Charley. *Please.* I know it's going to be hard, but just…leave him. Because I'm miserable every second I'm not with you."

# CHAPTER
## Nine

**W**ARM LIPS GHOST OVER MY CHEEK AND DOWN MY SHOULDER, rousing me from sleep. A smile creeps onto my face before I'm even fully awake.

"So beautiful." I hear the words murmured in my ear before his lips start a new trail of kisses successfully turning my sore and thoroughly fucked body to mush.

My eyes flutter open and all I see is his perfect head of hair as his lips move down my arm.

"Hi," I whisper so quietly, I'm not sure if he heard it, but his head jerks.

"You're awake." He moves up my body so that we're face-to-face, and he rubs his nose against mine before pressing a short kiss on my mouth. "Morning, baby." Will's used the term of endearment before, but something about waking up in bed with him makes my heart skip a beat. "How did you sleep?"

"The best I have in a while…" I smile. "I wonder why. How long have you been up?"

"Not long. I was going to wake you, but you looked so peaceful. I didn't have the heart to take that from you."

*Somewhere in there is a metaphor and it shakes me to my very core.*

I swallow hard, trying to ignore the fact that I've literally welcomed the chaos into my house and my bed. "Next time, wake me. I don't want to waste a second with you." I roll him to his back and move on top of him to straddle him. I'm naked as the day I was born, and you'd think he'd never seen me this way by the way he's eyeing me.

"I was going to make you breakfast, but you don't have a lot of food…" His fingers play with my nipple.

"We eat out a lot. I used to cook. You know this. But I got tired of eating every meal by myself." I shrug. "Matt's barely been home all week, and I've been staying out of the house."

He nods knowingly, as if he could have predicted my words. "Well, we could go get something?"

I shake my head. "I know too many people in the community. Well, too many people know me…too many people know my husband." I correct myself and wish I would have just said *Matt* after I catch the fleeting look that crosses Will's face. "Wait a minute, you can cook?" I ask, attempting to change the subject.

"I am a man of many talents, Charley." He raises an eyebrow at me and I giggle at his playfulness.

"Oh, I'm fully aware of your talents, but I didn't know you could cook."

"A man's gotta eat, you know."

"I would cook for you." The words are out of my mouth before I can catch them.

"I would be home for every meal." He gives me a sad smile, and he must sense the feeling of dread that takes over my body as the blaring thought shoots through my brain.

*That fantasy may never be a reality.*

"But," he continues, "I think I spotted some eggs in your fridge. I can do something with that."

"I can put an order in for some groceries and have them delivered." I move off of him to reach for my phone.

"Delivered?"

I cock my head. "Yes, you've never had groceries delivered?" I didn't do it often, but sometimes it really was easier than having to go out.

He chuckles as he gets off the bed, his sweatpants hanging low on his hips exposing the perfect V cut that I loved to run my tongue over. "No. Call me one of the mere common folk that still goes into the grocery store."

I wasn't sure if that was meant to be a dig or more playful sarcasm, but I let it go when I see him pulling a shirt on. "Where are you going?"

"To make you some coffee." He presses a kiss to my lips, like he's leaving the state and not just the bedroom, before releasing me. "Order some bacon and something hearty for later. If we're going to continue what we started last night, we're going to need sustenance." He winks before he disappears out of the bedroom.

⸻

The next two days are nothing short of perfect. It is as if Will and I are on our honeymoon.

*We certainly fucked like it.*

It is nice not having to worry about rushing against the clock and being able to savor every kiss, every touch, every thrust. The few times we do sleep, it isn't for long as one of us would wake up, our sweaty limbs still tangled together from falling asleep in each other's embrace and wake the other, demanding the connection our bodies so desperately crave.

Will cancels his sessions, and luckily only had my session scheduled for Friday, so with Matt being away it was also cancelled. Will and I spend the days defiling almost every inch of my house with the exception of my marital bed. The fact that I'm engaging in my affair, in the house my husband pays for, adds a new layer of guilt to my betrayal.

Every time I pass my bedroom, I could almost hear the whisper ghosting over my ears.

*Cheater.*

*You're a cheater, Charlotte.*

Now, three days after Will showed up at my back door, he's gone, and Matt will be home soon from his business trip. Matt had left a day earlier than planned, and so he's coming home Saturday rather than Sunday, which means I have to wait two excruciatingly long days to see Will again.

I still haven't told Will that I love him too. Although I do love him, where does that leave us? *Am I preparing to leave my husband? Are Will and I going to be together?* I'd told him that I need time to process, and he needed to think about his words as well—but he couldn't think about them while he was inside of me.

*Is this what he really wants? Or is he just caught up in the passionate sex we have? Does he really want to be with me? Or does he just not want me to be with Matt?*

God, I'm a cliché. Could I leave my husband? How would I even do it?

*Sorry, Matt, I met someone else?*

My thoughts are interrupted by a slam of a car door and my heart sinks, knowing that it's back to reality. I'm worried about how Matt is going to respond to seeing me considering how vulnerable I was before he left. The kiss we shared runs through my mind, and all I can do is hope that he won't want to pick up where we left off.

I'm in the den reading a book, when I feel his presence in the room. I look up to meet his gaze, and despite the layers of clothes I had put on just for the occasion, he's staring at me as if I'm completely nude, his eyes raking lasciviously over my body.

"Charlotte." He closes the space between us and pulls me to my feet, wrapping his arms around me and burying his nose in my hair. I can hear the deep breath he takes as he inhales my scent, and despite the two showers I've taken since Will left, I wonder if he can smell him on me.

*I wonder if men, like animals can detect when there has been an invasion of their space.*

"I missed you so much." He pulls away before he tilts my face up and kisses me hard on the mouth. I gasp at the aggression allowing his tongue to attack mine. Within a second, I'm being lifted into his arms.

*Fuck, this is what I was afraid of. Pick a fight, Charley. Pick a fucking fight. QUICK.*

He carries me up the stairs and deposits me on the bed before he's on me instantly.

"I've been thinking about this for the past two days." *Maybe I should just do it now. Why prolong the inevitable? But…is it inevitable? Is being with Will the endgame? Once I do this, there's no going back.*

"Matt," I say, his lips finally leaving mine, allowing me a chance to speak, but the words fail me. His lips are on my neck immediately, so I put my hands against his chest and push gently. "How was your trip?"

*Coward.*

"Long. Exhausting. I couldn't stop thinking about being inside of you. Baby, it's been too long, and kissing you before I left… I remembered how good it was between us." He stands and pulls off his jacket and begins to unbutton his shirt.

*Sure, for you.* "Matt, I did some thinking while you were gone."

"Oh? About what?" He tosses his shirt toward the corner of the room and kneels back on the bed, crawling toward me.

"Us."

"What about it?" he continues, and I back up slowly so as to not be in a position where I'm underneath him.

"I think…I think maybe you were right about therapy. Maybe it's not working," I stammer, hoping it will halt his journey toward me. "Or maybe it's not really the therapy. Maybe it's us. We're not working. We don't work anymore."

He stops and I can't escape the relief that moves through me. "What? Charlotte, why are you saying this?"

"Because I enjoyed you being gone far too much," I say honestly, and wince at the harshness of my words, but I need to get his mind away from trying to be intimate with me. *And if he's mad or hurt maybe he won't want me.*

He looks at me as if I've just slapped him across the face, and I guess in a way, I did. "You were all over my dick two days ago, what the fuck happened?"

"I was vulnerable. We had just rehashed all the skeletons of our pasts and then you up and left me there—"

"You said you were fine," he interrupts, his voice hard and cold and suddenly I don't feel so guilty anymore. *This was the man I was used to.*

"If that helps you sleep at night, Matt, fine. But you knew I wasn't. Things were already precarious between us, and then we talked about Michael. My heart had been split wide open reliving what happened, and you up and left five minutes later as if you didn't know the effect it had on me…*has on me.*"

"Charlotte—"

"But you also know I wasn't going to ask you to stay," I continue. "You made your decision. Not that I think it would have made a difference one way or the other. We keep putting Band-Aids on our problems instead of really trying to solve them."

"I am trying, Charlotte. I've been trying for months. I'll admit I wasn't at first, but ever since we started therapy, I've really made an effort. You've been the one fighting me."

I sigh, wondering how I'm even going to argue that. *He's right, ever since I started my affair with Will, I've been less than enthusiastic about reconciliation.* I don't have a reply, so I fix my gaze on a spot on the wall behind him.

My mind begins to spin. *Say I leave Matthew and things with Will don't work out, then I'm completely alone. Is it worth my safety and security for a wild card romance? What if our whole relationship is fueled by just the thrill of the forbidden? What if it doesn't work when our relationship is more than just stolen moments and kisses? What if the spark between Will and me dies along with my marriage to Matt?*

All of the what-ifs are blaring in my brain and I wish I could quiet the questions for just a minute. "I'm going to take a shower. I'm glad you're home," I say, as I make my way off the bed and begin to walk through our bedroom. I've taken two steps before my back is against the wall and my husband is towering over me.

*I know he'd never lay a finger on me, so I'm not worried about that. No, I'm more worried that he's about to drop to his knees and beg. Frankly, in this moment, I'm not sure which is worse.*

"Talk to me," he implores, his pleading eyes boring into mine. "Tell me why you've put this wall up. Why are you keeping me out? What do I have to do to be close to you?" His hands slide down the wall and onto my shoulders before they creep toward my chest. His hands find my breasts, palming them through my t-shirt before he slides them down my body and around to my back. Within seconds his hands are on my ass, cupping me through my pants.

I reach behind me to grab his hands and remove them when one moves between my legs. "Let me make you feel good, baby." *You can't.* I know what his hand is trying to do and my heart begins to race at the idea of him touching my most intimate places.

"Stop!" I say, pushing hard against his chest, and his hand that was trying to make its way into my pants is removed from my body. "I don't want..." I narrow my eyes and I fear the tears will come at any moment.

*Not because of this argument with my husband, but because I feel sick that my husband's hands were all over my body. When it belongs to Will.*

---

I wake up Monday morning, cranky, my mood matching the dreary, gray day outside when I feel warmth beside me. It must be early if Matt is still asleep, but when I check my phone and see that it's a quarter past eight, I frown. *What is he still doing here? I* tap him a few times with my index finger and he groans.

"What, Charlotte?"

"Do you know how late it is?"

"How late is it?" he asks, as he turns to face me, his eyes still closed.

"Eight thirty."

"Okay?"

"Shouldn't you be at work?"

"I'm working from home," he says turning back over.

*Great. How am I supposed to see Will before our session?*

"Oh." I fling the covers back and make my way into our en-suite bathroom, trying not to stomp toward it like a child who isn't getting her way. In the bathroom, I take my aggression out on my teeth, jabbing the brush in and out of my mouth.

*This is fucking ridiculous.*

I lean over to spit and when I stand I feel his presence behind me, his morning wood pressing into my back. I turn around and look at him and he gives me a shy smile.

"I'm going to shower, join me?"

*Jesus, Matt, you haven't been this pushy about sex in at least a year.*

"I'm going to go for a run."

He nods, accepting the rejection, and dropping his shorts before I leave the room. I catch a glimpse of his dick and I realize it's been so long since I've seen it I had forgotten what it looked like. Once I hear the shower turn on, I close the door behind me and bolt for my purse, grabbing my Blackberry and run down the stairs. I know I don't have much time, but I need to tell Will what's going on, and what *won't* be happening today. I'm pressing the send button before I've even reached the bottom stairs, and I immediately hear his voice on the other end but I want to make sure all bases are covered. "One second," I say before I listen to make sure the shower is still running. Once I hear it, I run into the living room and turn the television on loud. "Will," I whisper.

"Baby, how are you? I missed you yesterday." The longing in his voice crushes me as I think about what I have to tell him.

"I know, I'm sorry. Matt is being so…clingy right now. He's barely left my side." I hear silence, and I pull my phone away from my ear, wondering if the call dropped.

*Nope, he's probably just pissed.*

"I can't wait to be inside of you, baby. I got spoiled having you nonstop for two days. Can you come earlier than noon? I need to kiss every inch of your body. I'm touching my dick right now thinking about you." I can hear the desperation and the excitement in his voice, and I hate that I have to burst his bubble.

I groan. "God, I want that…all of that so bad. But…I can't."

"What? Why?"

"Matt is working from home today." There's silence on the other end and I know he's seething. "Baby…"

"So, what, I can't be alone with you at all today?" he demands, and I start to panic at the thought as well.

"I don't know what else to do. Where would I tell him that I'm going?"

"Go for a run, I'll come to you. Now."

"Now? Will, that's…risky."

"I don't care, Charley. I need to see you."

I sigh. "I'll text you."

"Make it work, Charley."

*So, now on top of a clingy husband that won't stop pawing at me, I have a jealous boyfriend that's getting more possessive by the day. I am so fucked.*

"I have to go," I whisper.

"I love you," he says and I wish he knew how much I want to say it back. I almost give in to the urge when I hear my name.

*Close.* I can tell by the volume, that Matt is one room over and coming in fast. I hang up on Will without a word and my heart sinks that I had to do that.

*Please forgive me, Will.*

I bolt for the couch, sitting on my Blackberry without anywhere else close to stash it.

"Shit, why is the TV so loud, are you going deaf?" His hair is still wet from the shower, his torso covered by his Princeton t-shirt and a pair of sweatpants leading me to believe that he has no intentions of leaving the house before our session later.

"Oh sorry, I didn't realize," I say as I turn the volume of the television down.

"I thought you were going for a run?"

"I wanted to check the weather first, I thought it might rain."

He sits next to me on the couch and begins looking through his phone. My heart races at the thought that Will might try and call me back or text me, given that I hadn't had the chance to turn off the Blackberry. Even though it's on silent, I think Matt would feel the vibration. "Can you make the coffee?" I ask.

"Coffee before your run?" he asks, raising an eyebrow at me.

"For when I get back?"

He narrows his eyes at me, no doubt confused about why I would want him to make coffee for me to drink an hour from now but he obliges and heads toward the kitchen. I quickly reach under me and turn my Blackberry off. Will had probably gotten the hint about why I had abruptly ended the call, as he hasn't tried to make contact. I reach for this month's *Vanity Fair* magazine and hide the phone within its pages before heading up the stairs to change into something to wear for my run, gripping the magazine tightly in my hands. I pull on my spandex with the back zipper pocket and store my Blackberry in there while putting one of my flowy tanks on that comes down over my behind. I pull my hair up into a ponytail and move down the stairs. "I'll be back," I say.

"Have a good run," Matt says, his back to me, not bothering to turn around.

I'm out the door, running down the stairs, sprinting for the end of the street, and turning the corner. I power my phone on the second I can no longer see my house. I call the number and I'm shocked when it goes to voicemail. *What?* I call back and again I get his voicemail.

———

**Me:** I'm so sorry, Matt walked in...

**Will:** I can't talk right now.

**Me:** Are you pissed at me?

**Will:** I certainly don't appreciate being hung up on.

**Me:** I'm sorry, I didn't know what to do...please call me back. I want to see you...I went for a run.

**Will:** I can't now.

**Me:** What? You told me to go now! This is the only chance we will have today.

**Will:** I'll see you in your session.

**Me:** That's not the same! I said I was sorry for hanging up!

**Will:** Goodbye, Charley.

I resist the urge to scream as I feel like I am drowning in feelings of anger, sadness, and overwhelming dread, so I continue to run, hoping that it will calm me down. I've barely hit the half mile mark when I stop, and before I can think I'm dialing one of the few numbers I know by heart.

"Hi," I say taking a deep breath. "I need a favor."

# CHAPTER
## *Ten*

"**Y**OU'VE GOT A BURNER PHONE!? JESUS CHRIST, CHARLEY, you're in so fucking deep." My best friend, Lauren Michaels, shrieks as she makes her way onto route 41. I let out a sigh once we're safely out of my neighborhood. I'd called her, knowing that her office wasn't too far from where I live, and she'd be a plausible alibi for what I needed to do.

*And that was the thing about having a best friend; you rang the alarm, and they were there. They just might be a pain in the ass about it though.*

"It's not a burner phone! I'm not a drug dealer." I pull down the mirror and try to smooth the strands back into my high ponytail. My skin is flushed, the adrenaline from my run still coursing through me in addition to the fact that I had my best friend pick me up on the side of the road to take me to Will's office in the middle of the day.

"No, you're right, Hot Doc is the dealer, and you're the addict that keeps going back. He's your drug and he's bad for you."

"Oh, he's bad for me, now? Two months ago, you were dying to hear every explicit detail," I say looking at my best friend who's weaving through the traffic toward the familiar building on Clinton Street. "And…Hot Doc?"

"Yes, Hot Doc. I googled." She shoots me a cheeky grin, her dimple poking in on her olive cheek. Lauren has the type of exotic beauty that stops people on the street, as they try to put her into a box. You can't. Lauren is mixed with a little bit of everything, making her that rare worldly beauty. I'd hate her if I didn't love her so much.

I groan, shaking my head. I can imagine that Lauren has already stalked him on every form of social media out there. "Did you find his Facebook?"

"He doesn't have one...we're sure he's not a serial killer?" I see a hint of worry in her green eyes, but for the most part I see her usual sassy look.

"He's not a serial killer, Lo," I say using my nickname for her. "He's just—private."

"Mmmhmm," she hums as we pull to a stop at a red light just off the interstate. We're only a few minutes away from Will's building, and I'm hoping to keep the interrogation at bay until then. "Char, are you sure you know what you're doing? When this first started, you said this was just sex. Now he's telling you he loves you and to leave your husband and... I don't know. Aren't you worried he might tell Matt?"

I snap my head to look at her. "What!? Lo...no way."

"I'm just saying. He's volatile...he's like a volcano ready to erupt."

"Stop with the fucking metaphors!" I shriek at her as I rub my head.

"And how are you going to explain being gone on this run all this time."

"That's where you come in."

"Me?! I have to get back to work."

"Ten minutes. Drive me back, I'll say you were on your way over because you needed to talk and you ran into me while I was on my run." She sighs. "Lauren, please. You are basically the boss of your office. They don't care that you're gone."

*Oh, Charley, what a tangled web you're weaving.*

She sighs again. "Fine. Do not have sex with him while you're here, I mean it." She shoots me a scolding look.

"No promises," I say.

"You're going to smell like sex. You think Matt won't notice it?" I don't say anything as we pull up to the building. I unbuckle my seatbelt and bolt for the front door when I hear her voice ringing through the air. "MAKE GOOD CHOICES!" she yells. I flip her off before I disappear from her sight.

Once out of the elevator, I push through the wooden door with the words "Dr. William Montgomery: Marriage Counselor" etched into it. Vanessa looks up when I enter, her eyes looking me up and down, no doubt wondering about my choice of attire and why I am three hours earlier for my "afternoon delight" appointment.

"Dr. Montgomery has—" she starts, but I'm already knocking on his door. *Hard.* "Ms. Pierce, he's in a session." I ignore her words and continue to knock, turning normal raps to rapid pounding when the door opens.

"What in the—" His eyes widen when he sees me, shooting fire at me. "Ms. Pierce, I'm in the middle of a session. Now is *really* not a good time." His eyes are almost black with fury and I can only hope that his forcefulness is meant for those in our presence and not because he's actually angry with me.

The tears flood my eyes as I look toward the people behind Will that are staring at me in confusion. "I…" I look back and forth between Will and Vanessa and back away slowly. "I didn't know…that…" I swallow. "Sorry, Dr. Montgomery," I say before I'm on my way back out the door. Once out of his office, I realize the magnitude of what I've just done, and I feel the tears falling down my cheeks.

*What if that couple says something? I mean I guess there really isn't proof but I certainly didn't act like we have a professional relationship.*

I'm entering the elevator before a hand grips my arm, yanking me back and suddenly I'm being dragged into the women's bathroom.

"What the fuck?!" His voice is harsh, but not much above a whisper.

"I'm sorry, I thought…you don't usually have sessions at this time," I say, the tears rolling down my cheeks. "Please don't yell at me."

He closes his eyes and takes a breath. When he opens them, he looks far less angry. "Vanessa told you I was with someone before you started pounding I'm sure. It was a last-minute decision to see them." He looks at my attire and narrows his eyes at me curiously. "Did you run here?" He looks at his watch. "There's no way, I just talked to you."

"I…got a ride."

"From who?" I swallow guiltily and realization dawns on him. "Who knows about us, Charlotte?"

"Lauren," I say, and he sighs.

"I didn't realize you had told anyone."

"She's my best friend."

He shakes his head, and I know he's irritated, but I think deep down he understands. "What are you even doing here?"

"I thought you wanted to see me… I wanted to see you. I felt bad that I hung up on you and I knew you were mad."

He crosses his arms and gives me a stern look. "So, you felt the need to come here and interrupt my session?"

"I said I was sorry and that I didn't know." I shrug sadly. "I just thought…" I bite down on my bottom lip and feel his presence surrounding me.

"You thought what?" He lifts my chin so I'll meet his gaze. "That you could show up here unannounced, half dressed, and I would drop everything and fuck you?"

My lip trembles at the harshness of his words. "I just—"

"Because you're right." His lips seal over mine and within

seconds I feel him fumbling with his pants. "We have to be quick. I left them yelling at each other."

I start to pull my spandex down when he shakes his head. "No."

"No?"

"I want your lips wrapped around my cock," he says rubbing my bottom lip with his thumb and I smile before dropping to my knees in front of him. His impressive erection juts out the second I lower his briefs and I run my tongue up the underside of his shaft before taking him into my mouth and hollowing out my cheeks. "Fuck…" I pull him out of my mouth, a trail of spit connecting my lips to his cock. I swirl my tongue around the tip before glancing upwards at the man who I somehow can bring to his knees, even when he's pissed. He's looking down at me, his eyes hooded with raw lust when I feel my butt start to vibrate indicating my *burner* phone is ringing.

"Shit," I mumble around his cock.

"Don't you dare," he groans, holding onto my ponytail to keep me on his dick.

"It's Lauren…"

"I don't care if it's Jesus. Suck."

"Well, get there fucking faster," I whimper around his dick as I start to suck harder and faster, needing to get him to the finish quicker when I feel him start to spasm.

"That's right, baby. Take it, fucking take it all." I feel my eyes start to water as he pushes to the back of my throat and empties himself. I swallow every drop, as always. He finishes and zips himself back into his pants before I'm even off my knees. He lifts me off of the ground to my feet.

"So, this was all about you? You're not even going to attempt to fuck me?" I ask narrowing my eyes.

"I thought you had to go," he says rubbing a hand through his hair, the smugness evident in his voice.

"You're a fucking asshole," I growl at him before I look in the mirror and rub my hands under my eyes to wipe the stray tears away. "I came here to try and apologize and talk and spend time—"

"Spend time? Charley, don't you dare even go there. Like this," he points between us, "is enough."

"I know it sucks but—"

"But nothing. Make a fucking decision, Charley."

"Is that what this is about? You said you wouldn't push me."

"Is that what this is about? Did you really ask me that? That's what ALL of this is about! Sneaking around and lying and you showing up to my office in your workout gear because you had to sneak out of your house under the illusion of going on a run! Your best friend calling you while your mouth is on my cock summoning you back. Me only being able to see you when your husband is ignoring you. I'm not trying to push you, but I told you I love you. How long do you expect me to wait?" He looks at me.

"Please don't do this now… I don't know when I can see you again."

He shakes his head at me. "That's exactly what I'm talking about," he says before he heads for the door. "I'll see you at three."

He leaves the bathroom, and it's suddenly much chillier than when we entered. I can't focus on anything except getting out of this building, as I make my way out of the elevator and toward the familiar car.

"God, I was about to come in after you," Lauren says as soon as I close the door behind me.

"It's been like fourteen minutes," I say, looking at my phone.

"I take it things didn't go well."

I give her a deadpanned look. "Brilliant deduction."

"'Kay. can we check the attitude before I leave you on the side of the road?" She puts the car in gear to drive me back home.

"Good one."

"What happened?"

"I sucked his dick. He's still pissed."

"Clearly you didn't do it right," she jokes and I shoot her a glare.

"I'm serious. I'm in so deep, Lauren. I don't even know how I got here." Hot tears stream down my face.

"Just…stop, Charley. You have to stop."

"But…I can't," I whisper.

"Yes, you can. You have to. Forget about Matt and the fact that you're married and cheating on him. Think about you. Look at what it's doing to you!"

"Please don't tell me to give him up," I cry, the tears beginning to flow more rapidly at the devastating thought.

She sighs and looks at me as we sit at a stoplight. "I would never tell you what to do. And I know you haven't been happy with Matt but…you know I've always been straight with you." I nod, knowing I'm not going to like what I'm about to hear, but knowing that I need to hear it. "This is going to blow up in your face. Both of you. Will is going to lose his practice, you're going to lose Matt and who knows what else."

"Am I going to lose Will too?" I ask, needing the reassurance that this man will be with me even in the end.

"God, Charley, is that all you care about? All of this is going up in flames, and it's like you will gladly burn if it means he's right there with you?"

"Isn't that what being in love is about?" I ask quietly as she turns onto my familiar quiet street.

"You're in love with him?" she asks me, her eyes confused and curious but not at all judgmental.

I nod once. "I haven't told him that yet."

She sighs. "Well, then you know what you have to do."

"I know. I've known for a while. I just… I don't know how to do it."

"This is going to sound terrible but maybe…maybe Will can be there when you do it. You know as your unbiased counselor," Lauren says, raising an eyebrow at me.

"I just want to be sure first, you know? I'm turning my life upside down for a guy that I've been sleeping with for four months and have known for seven. What if I end things with Matt and… things with Will don't work out?"

"And that's a reason to stay with Matt? Because you're what— afraid to be alone?"

"It's so much deeper than that and you know it," I snap at her.

"I know. There are things that go bump in the night and they terrify you, but you're not really living right now, Charley. I know you're scared of the unknown and being left unprotected, but is that what all of this is about? Or are you using that as an excuse to hide the fact that you have a fear of being alone. And you'd rather have someone to come home to at the end of the day—even if you can barely stand them half the time—than no one at all. As much as you want to throw caution to the wind and be with Will, you're used to stability and doing that would invite chaos into your life."

*I want so badly to call her a bitch. The worst friend ever. Storm out of her car, slam the door, and tell her to fuck off. But she's right. And I hate it when she's right.*

"Even a broken clock is right twice a day," I grumble as she pulls next to my car.

She gives me a weak smile. "I have to get back to work, but you know I'm here."

I'm about to answer when I see my husband standing in front of her car with his arms crossed. I immediately tense as I slip my phone back into my back pocket and zip it shut as he comes over and stands next to Lauren's window. She rolls it down and looks up at him.

"What's up, Wells?"

"Ladies." He nods. "I was wondering where you ran off to. You didn't even take your phone," he says looking at me.

"Totally my bad. I was on my way over to talk. Emergency. This fuckboy won't call me back." Lauren shrugs and I resist the urge to smile at how quick she covered for me. "I ran into her on her run so I kidnapped her."

"I see, well I'm sure he's just a bit overwhelmed at the Lauren Michaels whirlwind." He raises an eyebrow at my best friend and I smile thinking about their usual banter.

"What can I say, not everyone can handle me." She looks at me and we share a look that only we understand. "Call me later?"

"Yes, of course," I say, hugging her a second longer than usual in an attempt to express my gratitude.

I get out of the car, and walk quickly into the house, before moving up the stairs.

"Next time, just take your phone," Matt says, following close behind. "I'm surprised you didn't. You always listen to music."

"It's…it's a new thing. Running in silence," I lie.

I think even he hears the lie in my voice because he eyes me warily. "Well, I've got some work to do before our session. I'll be in my study if you need me."

"Okay," I say, thankful that he didn't try and kiss me with the flavor of Will's cum still in my mouth.

# CHAPTER
## Eleven

I RUN MY HAND THROUGH MY HAIR, MY KNEE BOUNCING aggressively as Matt and I sit in the waiting area. His hand wraps around my knee giving it a gentle squeeze. "Stop fidgeting. What's with you today?"

I stare at his hand, noting how foreign his touch feels. "Sorry," I say.

"Mr. Wells, Ms. Pierce," I hear and look up to find Will in his doorway, his eyes darting back and forth between us and settling on Matt's hand on my knee. I stand and follow behind my husband as we make our way into the room.

"Well, I haven't seen you two in a while. How are you? Mr. Wells, I trust your trip went well."

"Yes, great. I don't think I really needed to be there, but it is what it is," he says.

"So, what's—" Will starts when Matt interrupts.

"I have something. I've been waiting to talk about this, and Charlotte is going to be pissed but frankly I want some goddamn answers."

My eyebrows furrow. I have no idea what he's going to talk about but I brace myself for the worst.

"Charlotte blatantly refuses to touch me. If I even go near her, she shuts down."

*Yep, as bad as I thought it was going to be. Well, at least Will can be assured that I'm not sleeping with him.* I'm silent, completely at a loss for what to say.

My eyes find his.

*Will, I'll let you field this one.*

He clears his throat clearly uncomfortable by this, and I can see he's not reading my thoughts as well as I'd hoped. "Ms. Pierce?"

"Yep?"

"Do you have anything to say to that?"

"No, I don't think so."

"Is there a reason you don't feel the pull to be intimate with your husband?"

"Ummm, migraines?"

"Don't be a smart-ass," Matt says.

"That's all I got." I shrug.

*The only way to get out of this is to berate him into a fight or just act so indifferent that he loses it. Do not engage him on this, Charley. Do not engage.*

"We are in marriage counseling for Pete's sake, Charlotte. If we are trying to fix our marriage, we need to be intimate."

"Says who? You know tons of people believe sex is only needed for procreation." I shrug. "And last I checked, we weren't doing that." Will rubs his hand over his bottom lip, and although he's hiding it well, I can see the amusement in his eyes.

"Don't you have anything to say?" Matt asks, looking at Will.

"I think you two should talk this one out."

"Is that what this is about? That I'm not ready for kids? So, if I was willing to start trying, I could at least see you fucking naked?"

"First of all, that's a low blow to try and manipulate me into bed by offering me something I want more than anything. Secondly, we are not going to have a baby to try and fix our marriage. That is the worst idea."

"I would have to agree with that," Will interjects just a little too quickly.

*Relax, Montgomery. That's not happening. The only kids I'm interested in having now would be calling you Daddy,* I try to tell him with my eyes.

"So, that's it? We're just never having sex? You certainly had me fooled after Wednesday." He looks at Will and I immediately stiffen. *Fuck.* "She was all over me when I was leaving—"

"All over you? Please! I hugged you goodbye and we kissed. Give me a break."

"We haven't kissed like that in months."

"Well, I'm sorry. I was upset after Wednesday's session," I say, glaring at Will, daring him to get upset after the way he treated me after that. "I just wanted…to be held."

"And then two days later I come back and you've reverted to being the ice queen. I just want to know what changed. It just keeps leading me back to square one, thinking that there's someone else."

I bite my bottom lip. I don't know what else to do and I need to focus on something. "I don't know what else to tell you."

"How about the truth for once?"

I look at the man in front of me and then the man at my side. "I'm sorry that I'm not particularly up for sex. You ruined a lot of my self-esteem, you've shattered my confidence after months of pushing me to the side. You made me think that I wasn't good enough, that you were bored, that the idea of sleeping with me repulsed you. That it was some arduous task to make love to me. I'm sorry that I'm not eager to jump back into bed with you now that you've got months of cum backed up and you need a release. I don't work that way. And for the record, all those months that you were pushing me away, am I supposed to just believe you didn't look elsewhere for sex? Please."

"I didn't."

"Like you'd tell me. Matt, I saw you like seven hours a week, don't insult my intelligence."

"Don't turn this shit around on me, Charlotte. This is the first time I'm hearing of this hypothesis and now that I've accused you of it, now all of a sudden you think I've been unfaithful too?"

"Just because I never said anything doesn't mean I never thought it."

"How would that make you feel…finding out that Matthew had been unfaithful?" Will asks me and I resist the urge to tell him to back off with this line of questioning.

"Why are we even talking about this? I've never been unfaithful!" he screeches. "Give me a fucking polygraph."

"Look, I never had any proof, it was just a theory because I never saw you. Just like you have a theory now."

"Whatever."

*Okay, Charley, this might backfire but…do it.* "Seriously, Matt, when I'm not with you at some god-awful work function, I'm shopping or at spin class, maybe yoga, with Lauren, or here at therapy. So, unless I'm sleeping with Dr. Montgomery, I don't think there are any other options."

*I don't even chance a look at him, because I know I'll lose it.*

"Don't be so inappropriate, Charlotte," Matt scoffs and I still haven't looked at Will after my comment.

"Don't Charlotte me. I am so sick of hearing you question whether or not I've been unfaithful. If you truly think I am, then leave me! For the love of God, if I'm so horrible, why are you still here?" *Ask yourself that same question, Charley.*

He narrows his eyes at me. "When did you get to be like this?"

"I don't know, probably somewhere around our third year of marriage," I snap.

"You can be such a bitch when you want to be," Matt snaps back and I see the fire in Will's eyes briefly before he reins in his temper.

"You know I don't put up with that in here," Will interjects. "Apologize."

"For what?"

"You know what." He glares at Matt and I wonder if Will is

this strict with all of his couples, or if he just hates the thought of anyone talking to *me* like that.

"She's acting like it and you know it," Matt argues.

"Not the point. Use different words."

"Fine. Sorry," he says, and I shrug, unmoved by his half-assed apology.

We're silent for a second when Will finally says something. "I can't believe after seven months you still haven't gotten to the root of your problems."

"Isn't that what we're paying you four hundred dollars an hour for?" Matt asks.

"I've tried to spoon-feed it to you, but I can't do the work for you. I can't have the epiphanies for you. Mr. Wells…Matt, tell me why you want to be with Charlotte."

I narrow my eyes, not liking where this is going. "Because I love her and we took vows. And we've been through a lot together. No one knows her like I do and vice versa."

"Does she make you happy?" Will asks, as he taps his pen against the pad.

"Most of the time."

"Are you telling the truth?"

He hesitates slightly. "Yes."

"Does *she* make you happy? Or are the good memories of the beginning of your relationship…what make you happy? Because those memories won't keep you warm at night."

"She makes me happy. She's supportive and kind and caring… she's been there with me through so much. She was with me when I had nothing. When *we* had nothing."

"That's called loyalty, not love, which has already been made abundantly clear that you two have for each other."

*Not so much on my end anymore.*

"It can be both," Matt says.

"Yes, but they're not synonymous."

He looks over at me. "What do you have to say about all of this? You're awfully quiet."

"I think…I think I'm scared of what not having you in my life means. It's been eight years and…not having you in my life seems strange. I basically became the person I am today in part based on our relationship. For all intents and purposes, we grew up together. We became adults together. But, Matt, we haven't been happy in…what? Two years? I will take responsibility for the last several months but there was so much that happened that led me here. I got fed up, I am fed up. I'm exhausted from feeling like I'm in this marriage by myself. But at the same time…" I feel the tears building. "…at the same time, I'm terrified of leaving this marriage and…not having someone to look out for me. You've fought so many demons for me that I don't…I don't know that anyone else will understand what it is I need. I have baggage and not everyone can handle that." I don't look up for fear of seeing the look in Will's eyes.

*Pity? Anger? Sadness?*

"I understand that," Matt whispers. "But does that mean… that's the only reason you want to stay married?"

*This is it…my out. Take it, Charley.* "I just don't think…my feelings for you are enough to stay married."

I see the tears in his eyes before he clears his throat. "Do you want out?"

I bite my lip and realize this isn't a conversation I can have with Will in the room. "Can we talk about this at home?" I see Will's flash of confusion though he quickly recovers.

"Why wouldn't we talk about this here with Dr. Montgomery?" Matt asks, and I sigh at his logic. *Of course, that makes sense if I'm not thinking about leaving you for him.*

"I just…" I sigh, unable to find the words as the sound of Matt's phone ringing breaks the silence.

I look at his chest pocket, toward the source of the ringing.

The small object that has caused such a rift in our marriage. The item that controls his every move. "Just answer it," I say, shaking my head. "You know you need to."

He pulls his phone out, looking at me and then the phone and then me again. "Five minutes," he says getting up.

*I have to admit, it never gets easier realizing that I will always come second. It's a bitter pill, even if I'm sleeping with someone else. This is such a precarious time in our marriage, you'd think for once he would choose me. The fact that he still doesn't think of turning his phone off while we're in therapy speaks volumes.*

Then he's out of the room, and the door closes behind him.

"Baby," I hear his soft voice in the quiet room and I look up at him, the tears threatening to spill from my eyes, "please don't cry. I can't touch you right now."

"What...what was that earlier?"

"I was angry... I had told you I loved you and then you just hung up on me. I know it was poor timing, but it hurt. And then you showed up here, which...I loved. But then, I didn't have enough time with you. And then Lauren called and..." He takes off his glasses and rubs his hand over his face before putting them back on. "I made a mistake treating you like that. I'm sorry." I nod and he looks at me harder. "Are you going to tell him you want out?"

I look up and shake my head. "You've got to stop pressuring me. I'm ending my marriage, it's not that simple. I've known him almost a decade. I owe him the conversation even if he hasn't been the best husband. A conversation I can't have in front of you."

"Are you? Ending your marriage?"

I look down at my engagement and wedding rings and begin to fiddle with them. "Yes."

"That's all I needed to know." He shoots me a soft smile. "This is the first time you've said that."

"I want to be with you," I whisper.

"I want to be with you too."

# CHAPTER
## Twelve

THE REST OF THE SESSION CRAWLS BY AT A SNAIL'S PACE, MATT pressuring me to open up, and Will doing his best to keep Matt in check and the spotlight off me. All I wanted to do upon leaving is go home and climb into bed alone so I can have phone sex with Will. I need to get off and I need some connection with him to get me there, but it seems the gods are not in my favor as Matt trails into the house behind me.

"We need to be out of the house by six," Matt says as we make our way through the foyer of our home. These are the first words he's spoken since we left Dr. Montgomery's office and I don't miss the edge in his voice.

My eyes widen as I realize I have somewhere to be tonight, which will throw a wrench in my plan for phone sex. "What?"

"We have plans with Bree and Nathan? Remember? We are trying that new Mediterranean restaurant?"

My stomach growls immediately. *Goddammit I've been dying to eat there.* "Right. Sorry it just slipped my mind. I'll be ready." *Maybe this is just what I need. A night out. I can talk to Bree about mindless shit while my husband talks to Nathan and it'll be fine.*

As I put on my favorite piece of jewelry, my Cartier watch—a wedding gift from Matthew—I finger it gently, recalling that day. I was so blissfully happy I don't think I stopped smiling the entire day. I was marrying the love of my life and I was ecstatic. I close my eyes and I feel like I'm transported back to a simpler time.

*Maybe God will grant me a do-over. I can go back and not marry Matthew and then I don't have to hurt him.*

I know I've become quite selfish but I wasn't always like this, and sadly, I don't even know the person looking back at me when I look in the mirror—when I can even look myself in the eye. I pull my hair, tightening the messy, high ponytail, the tips ghosting over my shoulders. I walk out of the bathroom to see Matt sliding on his jacket. He frowns slightly as he takes in my appearance. "That's what you're wearing?"

I look down and then back up. "Yes? I… Is there a problem?"

"We aren't going out to a bar, Charlotte."

"It's a jumpsuit."

"Where's the rest of it?"

I look down at the endless black material around my body. "It's a cropped pant!"

"There's no straps!" I look down to my chest, that's completely covered by the fabric going straight across hiding any potential cleavage. *It's a strapless jumpsuit. Give me a break, Matt.*

"So?"

He shakes his head before walking by me without another glance. "Whatever."

I look at my closet, wondering if I should change, but roll my eyes instead. *Fuck that.* I send Will a text, telling him I'll be out for a while and that I will text him when I can, before heading downstairs.

"Okay, I'm ready."

He looks at me again. "Wait, so you're not going to change?"

"No, Matt, I look fine. What is your problem?" *Better than fine actually.*

"Just wish you were looking a bit more conservative. What if we run into people from work?"

"I would never wear this if we were meeting people from your job, but we're having dinner with Bree and Nathan. I toe the line when it's necessary but give me a break," I say, crossing my arms.

"Let's just go," he says walking out of the house in front of me and toward the car. I sigh as I lock the door behind us and pray to the gods for an endless supply of wine.

———

"You look gorgeous!" Bree Cunningham says as we approach the table. She hugs me for a second too long and I almost break down feeling someone squeeze me that hard *and tell me that I look nice.* "I've missed you. Let's do something soon, okay?"

I nod. "You look great too, Bree." Nathan pulls me into a hug before kissing my cheek.

"Hey, Char." *I always wonder what Matt divulges to Nathan. If he paints me in this horrible light. If I am the bitchy, nagging wife that doesn't suck his dick anymore. But if he does I would never know it, because Nathan is always such a gentleman.*

We sit around the half-circle booth, Bree and I in the middle, while Matt and Nathan sit on the sides. I'm grateful for the wine that's already on the table so I reach for it, but Matt's hand stops me. When I look up, he's shooting me a look I've been on the receiving end of many times; that look of irritation that tells me I need to *knock it off.*

"I'm with Charley, let's crack it open. It's been a hell of a day," Nathan says as he rubs his head and points at the bottle. "The chef is sending over everything, so we don't need to order. Apparently, this wine is the best on the menu."

I glare at Matt before passing the bottle over. "So, how's it going?" Nathan asks, observing the tension between Matthew and me and obviously trying to defuse it. *Bless his heart.*

"Good," Matt says immediately, "I finally closed that deal at work."

My lips form a straight line that he jumps at any opportunity to talk about work even though the conversation was directed at both of us.

"And how are you?" Bree asks me as the guys continue to talk.

I'm grateful for the wine that's been placed in front of me and I take a long sip. "I'm okay, Bree. Thank you for asking." I look at my lap willing this night to be over so I can talk to a man who cares about what I have to say or a woman that I don't have to lie to.

*People that love me for me and not the front I put up. As sweet as Bree is, I can't be honest with her, which makes talking to her just as tedious at times.*

An hour and three bottles of wine later, Matt switches to Manhattans and I realize he's barreling toward intoxication. I'm feeling buzzed myself, and I wish I would have suggested to Matt that we Uber to the restaurant, as I know we'll end up leaving our car here later. I've started to loosen up slightly and I've even laughed a few times. I see Matt putting a freshly filled glass to his lips and I pull it away from his mouth before he takes a sip. "Maybe you should slow down?" I ask quietly.

"Oh, come on, we're amongst our friends."

"Yeah, come on, C. Let him cut loose like we used to before Matt went and got that big fancy job and couldn't hang anymore," Nathan says.

*Ah, so it's not just me that got pushed to the wayside, then?*

I shake my head as I see Matt shoot Nathan his middle finger. "Oh shit!" he chuckles and I look at him, surprised by his out-burst. "It's our marriage counselor," he chuckles.

Adrenaline courses through me at his words, and my body hums in anticipation. *Calm the fuck down, Charley, he can't fuck you here.* "Oh, and he's got a woman with him! Good for him. I was wondering his situation." He shrugs while I begin to burn with rage.

*That can't be right. That cannot be fucking right.*

"Should we go say hi?" I ask. *Yeah, I'm playing with fire but I want to know what the fuck this is about.* I'm trying to control my thoughts that have me barreling toward rabid fury, but he's sitting at a table with two women and another man. *A double date? What the fuck?*

"Interrupt his date?"

"It may not be a date," I counter, annoyed that Matt has picked up the same vibes.

"Two girls and two guys? Looks like a date to me, but sure, come on, let's go chat," he says, sliding out of the booth and not bothering to wait for me before he heads toward the table.

*Shit, he is drunk. I'm not far behind him. Before he reaches the table, Will's eyes find mine and widen. I see him prepare himself for the explosion heading his way.*

"The good doctor!" Matt says and Will stands. "You're out amongst us commoners," he jokes. "We just wanted to come over and say hello."

"I'm glad you did," Will says. "It's good to see you." He rakes my body in appreciation. *In front of my husband?* Matt doesn't seem to notice though, as he finishes the rest of his drink. "Oh hey," he whistles at a waiter that passes by. "Can I have another one of these?" He sets the glass on his empty tray.

"Matt, that's not—"

"Yes, sir," I hear the waiter say and I am thoroughly embarrassed. *I hate when he gets like this. Only when he's drunk does he become this entitled asshole. I hate it.* I glare at him before realizing that we are still in mixed company and I turn back to Will.

"Who are your friends?" I ask, looking at the table.

I can see the look he's trying to give me. The soft, kind look as if he's begging me to give him a chance to explain. "This is my brother, Andrew, his girlfriend, Olivia, and her friend Renee. Everyone, this is Matthew Wells and Charlotte Pierce." *I love the way he introduces us. You would never know we are married, which I think is his point.* I resist the urge to chuckle.

"So, it's a date." Matt smirks at me and under normal circumstances I would be thoroughly embarrassed. Instead the embarrassment is replaced with anger and hurt. "Told ya," he says to me and all I want to do is mark my territory all over Will so this bitch knows who he belongs to. *My name is all over his dick, honey, so don't even try it.*

Will chuckles. "No, it's not a date," he says immediately, I'm sure for my benefit, and I see Renee's face fall and his brother shoot him a glare. *So, it is a date? But my guess is it is one being forced by his brother. But still, what the fuck? Was he just not going to tell me?* "How many of those have you had, Matthew, you feeling okay?" He looks at me. "I hope neither of you are driving."

"Oh, take off the counselor hat for a second. Come have a drink with us. Bring your friends."

"There's not really a ton of room…" I don't want to bring that kind of negative energy to a table with myself and my drunk husband. *Tension is already at an all-time high.*

Will looks toward our table to see Bree and Nathan behaving borderline obscene. Nathan's hand curls around Bree's shoulder and dancing around the top of her shirt before diving inside. I roll my eyes but at the same time I'm jealous of how easy their marriage looks. I mean even if they're pretending, which I don't think they are, at least they *look* happy. The waiter brings Matt's drink and Will stops him. "Can you bring us a round of shots? What do you guys say? Tequila?"

My eyes widen and I look at the people behind him staring at me. "What! We've had enough. That's very nice of you, but—"

"Oh, come on, one shot for Will's friends!" his brother chirps as he waves the waiter over.

"We aren't his friends." Matt perks up as he takes a healthy sip of his drink. "We pay him to make sure we don't kill each other."

"Oh, you're one of his couples?" Andrew nods at us. "Well,

nice to meet you both. Didn't know you were married the way he introduced you," he finishes and I see Will shoot him a look.

"Yeah, she didn't change her last name. Can you believe that?" Matt snorts.

"I never understood why women don't change their name when they get married. Why didn't you?" Renee asks. *I'm sorry but was anyone talking to you?*

"Renee," Andrew's girlfriend scolds her, "that's not your business."

"I ask her that all the time. I don't think she even knows," Matt says. I can't control the look of disgust on my face for airing our laundry like this in mixed company.

Trying my best to keep the anger out of my voice, I say, "We should go back to the table."

"What about our shots?" Matt asks. *Don't you think you've had enough?*

"Stay and take them if you want," I snap. "I'm going back to the table."

"Don't be such a brat. Dr. Montgomery ordered them for us."

"I don't want them," I say before storming off. I walk past the table and toward the bathroom slamming my clutch down before sitting on the couch. It doesn't take long before I hear the door open and close. I don't anticipate that it's Will, but I am a bit surprised to see Bree come into view.

She sits next to me on the couch, and before she says anything she wraps her arms around me. "I'm sorry, Charley."

"For what?"

"Not being a better friend to you."

"You're a great friend, Bree. Why do you say that?"

"Because you're so sad every time I see you. You should see the hurt written all over your face every second and it's gotten worse over the past few months. Charley, why don't you leave him?"

I shrug. "It's not that simple," I say. "Or maybe it is…" I feel the tears streaming down my face and I know exactly why. *I'm slightly intoxicated and seeing the man I love out on a date with another woman regardless of his level of interest is a punch in the gut. I know he probably has similar feelings with me being married but this is the first time I've experienced it. And it sucks.*

"Oh, honey, I'm so sorry." She squeezes my hands before giving me another tight hug. "You know I'm always here for you. I'm always here to talk."

"Thanks, Bree. I know." I give her a small smile as I wipe the unshed tears forming in my eyes.

We head back to our table, and I see Matt has returned. I let my eyes glance at Will's table and his eyes find mine immediately. I hope in that moment he can see what I'm feeling. We haven't had a moment alone since the few minutes during our session and we haven't had contact since the blow job I gave him that left me feeling empty and hurt.

*He didn't even kiss me goodbye. And now he's on a date.*

I want nothing more than to leave, when I feel eyes on me. A lot of eyes. I look up and see Will's gaze fixed on me and out of the corner of my eye, I see Matt's on me as well.

I turn toward my husband. "What?"

"You look hot in that. That's why I wanted you to change. Too fucking hot," he says, and I roll my eyes at his drunkenness.

"Thank you." I take another sip.

"Can I touch you when we get home?" he asks so quietly I almost miss it.

"Matt…" I don't want to rehash this in public.

"Charlotte…? What is it? What can I do to make it better?" *Where was this man a year ago?*

"Can we not do this here? Right now?" I ask, even though I know Bree and Nathan are in their own world.

"I just think we should try."

"You're drunk."

"You know that's when I'm the most fun." He wiggles his eyebrows at me and I can't help the chuckle that moves out of me.

*He won't even remember this conversation later and the chances he'll even be able to get it up are slim.* My eyes find the table again and they widen when I see that Will is absent. *Where did he go?* I see Renee so I know that he's nowhere with her. *Thank God.*

"I have to pee again," I say motioning for him to move. "You know once you break the seal." He lets me out of the seat and I start walking toward the bathroom when I feel hands wrapping around my wrist and I'm being hauled into a room marked, Employees Only.

I look around and see it's a small office, and before I can think I'm pushed against the door of the office and lips are everywhere. My cheeks, my lips, my neck, my chest. "I'm sorry, I'm so sorry. Please don't hate me," I hear in my ear as I feel his erection pressing against me.

I push on his chest hard and he stumbles back. "What the hell is that? Who is that? Touching you and…" I cross my arms. "Is that what you want?"

"No! Of course not, baby. I want only you."

"Then what are you doing on a date with some girl who is clearly dying to suck your dick?" I grit out.

"You know exactly what this is, Charley. My brother and his girlfriend and his girlfriend's friend that they were trying to set me up with. I didn't even know until we were on our way here that this was the plan!"

"Were you even going to tell me?"

"Of course, I was. The next time we were together."

"It's easy to say that now," I say.

"I've never lied to you, Charley. Speaking of, were you going to tell me about your little make-out session last Wednesday with Wells?"

"You're kidding me, right?" He shoots me a look, and I snap.

"After you basically told me you couldn't be what I needed? I was vulnerable, and he was there. *You weren't.* He initiated it, and I didn't stop it. And for the record it was hardly making out."

His features soften dramatically as he's reminded of the details of my past and I think he opts to cut me some slack over my moment of weakness with Matt. "Keep his tongue out of your mouth, Charlotte, I mean it."

"Sounds like you don't trust me now."

"Like you trust me? You can't if you think Renee means anything to me."

"I trust you, it doesn't mean I'm happy watching you with someone else."

"And you think it's easy for me?"

"Stop throwing that in my face, Will. We're talking about you out on a date with another woman the day I told you I was going to leave my husband!"

"It's not a fucking date! Why are you doing this? Why are you picking a fight with me when I should be inside of you?"

I ignore his accusatory line of questioning. "And buying us shots? What the fuck is that? Did you think we were just gonna eat, drink, and be merry!?"

"I was playing along. Wells is hammered."

"You think?"

"I need to make sure you get home safe," he says, moving toward me.

"No." I put up a hand to stop him from coming forward. "Don't touch me."

"Wh-what?"

"You walked out of that bathroom today when I needed you, after treating me like your own personal cum dumpster, so now it's your turn to know how it feels." I turn on my heel and walk out the door and back to my table.

# CHAPTER
## *Thirteen*

T HE RIDE HOME IS SILENT; ONLY THE SOUNDS OF THE windshield wipers fill the Uber as we pass through the streets of Atlanta, well past midnight. The skies have finally opened up, letting the torrential rain fall from the sky in buckets. It's the storm they've been calling for all week and I'm caught in it.

*Much like the other storm I'm currently caught in.*

My husband was nearly incoherent when we left the restaurant, leaving me to question if I'm the reason he drank half his weight in whiskey.

*Or is there something else bothering him? I'm not stupid, I haven't touched him in months… Is it possible that he's fucking around as well, despite his protests that he's been totally faithful?*

We make it home and Matt stumbles out of the car and up the stairs toward our door, not bothered that the water is beating down on his shoulders and back, soaking him. I follow close behind, holding the umbrella over my head that I'd brought just in case. I'm surprised he's able to get the keys in the door but he does and he's inside without a care if I've made it in behind him. I'm almost inside when something catches my attention out of the corner of my eye. A silver BMW, parked at the end of my street.

—

The good thing about a drunk Matt is that once he crosses the threshold of full blown intoxication, it's only a matter of time before he's completely passed out, and we're getting close. I grab him a bottle of water from the refrigerator and head upstairs to find my husband flinging his shoes across the room.

"You—" he slurs before he points at me, winking once, "—are so fucking hot."

I clear my throat. "And you…are so fucking drunk." I smile before setting the water on the nightstand and heading to the bathroom for a bottle of Advil. I come back in the room to find his pants also discarded. He's leaning against our headboard drinking water with his eyes closed. I set the Advil on the nightstand and he reaches for my hand, lacing his fingers with mine, and I look at where our hands are joined.

"Sit, Charlotte." I worry what he could possibly say, and as much as I want to bolt for the man in the Beamer outside, my blood alcohol content and my curiosity get the best of me. I oblige his simple request.

"What?" I ask softly as I pull my hand out of his grasp.

"I thought about it…" he starts, "cheating on you." He sucks down another gulp. "When things changed between us…but I never did." I nod, not liking where this conversation is going. "But you…pretty and perky Charlotte Pierce," he runs a hand down my face and I shiver, "I don't buy that you haven't had anyone between your legs these past few months. And I just want you to be straight with me." He hiccups. "Just tell me…is it Nathan?" My eyes widen in horror at the thought of sleeping with my husband's best friend. "I mean tit for tat, right? I did sleep with Bree, and I don't think Nathan has ever gotten over it."

"You…you slept with Bree?" My eyes are wide, and I know the shock is written all over my face.

"Years ago. Before they got married." He shrugs, and his eyes are getting heavy, as it's taking longer and longer for him to open them between blinks. "They were just dating at the time."

"But…that's your best friend? You…how could you betray him like that?" *Whoa, Charley, reel it in. Don't be a complete hypocrite.*

His hand finds my shoulder, still exposed from the strapless jumpsuit I'm wearing. He draws circles with his thumb before he leans forward and kisses the skin. "Matt," I say, backing away slowly. He reaches for my ponytail and his face inches toward mine. I back up not wanting to feel his lips on mine and heeding Will's instructions—well, demand to keep Matt's mouth off of mine. In an instant, his body is covering mine, and I'm ready to snap at his invasion of my space when I hear his light snoring. I look down to find his head leaning against my chest, sleeping soundly. I try to move him slowly, when I feel wet lips being dragged along my cleavage.

I move out of his grasp and lay him down, pulling the bottle of water from his hands and put it on the nightstand. Once Matt falls into a drunken sleep, I know he's out for the night so I don't have to worry about him waking up and realizing I'm not here. I pull off my jumpsuit and replace it with a pair of shorts and a sweatshirt.

*I just want to get the hell out of here and into Will's arms. Despite the fact that I'm mad at him, I don't know when I'll be alone with him again, and I want to feel his arms around me. It's the only thing that will calm the uneasiness coursing through me.*

I grab my keys and both cell phones, sliding them into my pocket before I move down the stairs. I look out the window to find the Beamer still parked at the corner, and immediately my heart starts to race. It has stopped raining, although it's misting slightly, so I pull my hood up over my head and walk down the street as I attempt to move out of sight range of my house. I also don't want to be seen by any nosey neighbors getting into a random car. I'm a few streets over when the car pulls up next to me and I slide in quickly, closing the door behind me, and pulling my hood down.

I look over at the man I so desperately want to touch when he leans across the console and slides his hand behind my neck to pull me closer to him. I was expecting an aggressive, possessive kiss but instead I'm greeted with a soft, warm, gentle kiss that sends a spark through every extremity. His tongue finds mine immediately and we start the dance we both know by heart. His hands find my cheeks as he strokes them with his thumbs. I pull back slowly when I feel his nose rub against mine and then graze my lips before he pulls back slightly still keeping his hands on my cheeks. "Hi, baby," he says softly.

"Hi," I say, the air leaving my lungs. "Why—how are you here?"

"I left when you did."

"What did you tell your brother?"

"I wasn't going to stay, not knowing how you were getting home, or if you would safely. Once I saw you leaving, I told my brother that my woman wasn't pleased that I was out on a date when I should be buried inside of her." He rubs his forehead. "I'm sure I'll get a load of follow-up questions about that tomorrow."

I nod once before I stare out into the starry night. The rain has subsided completely, making it easy to point out every twinkle in the sky. If my life wasn't so fucked up in this moment, I would think it was magical. "Will…"

"Please don't leave me over what happened earlier. I was such an asshole to you and you didn't deserve it." I can see the worry etched over his face. I reach out to stroke his jaw, letting my fingertips brush his stubble. His eyes close and he leans closer, into my hand.

"No, I did deserve it," I say, the tears brimming in my eyes as I drop my hand from his face. "I've jerked you around and I've made you wait for months and months. I've made you this dirty little secret and it's not fair to you and I'm sorry," I sob. I wasn't expecting this breakdown and I certainly wasn't expecting it right now, but it's here and I have to deal with it. He reaches for me, pulling me into his lap to straddle him. Normally I would find this position sexual and I'd be dying to have him inside of me, but right now I just need to be held, and for the first time in months I'm not thinking with the space between my legs.

He pulls my hands from my face and kisses them gently before he looks up at me. Our faces are so close, we're almost touching. "I'm not giving you up," he whispers. "I'll wait as long as I have to."

"But you said—"

"Fuck what I said, Charley. I know I can't push you. And I know that I have. I've taken my frustrations out on you, and I'm sorry," he whispers. "Please forgive me."

"I should be asking *you* to forgive me."

"For what, baby? We're in this together. I knew what I was getting myself into when we started."

"For letting this go on for so long…" I sniffle. "For falling in love with you. For letting you fall in love with me. It would be so much easier to walk away from you if I didn't…" I look away from his gaze having realized what I said.

"Say the words, Charlotte," he says so quietly that I almost miss them.

"I…I love you," I say, the tears pouring from my eyes and landing on my sweatshirt. "I love you so much that…that I have no idea how I could possibly give you up. And I don't know what's going to happen, but I know in my heart that I want to be with you. You're it for me, Will. I just…I have to figure out where to go from here." I finally look up into his eyes and I'm met with the most beautiful shade of blue. I've never seen Will cry before and maybe he won't actually shed a tear but his eyes are glassy and I see them brimming under his lids. "I'm scared," I whisper, my fears roaring loudly in my head.

"Charlotte," he whispers back, and then his lips find mine. His kisses are gentle, soft, and loving. "I love *you* so much. I would do anything in the world for you—so either of us walking away from this…it would kill me," he says against my mouth, before he pulls away to pepper kisses down my face and neck. They're so light and sensual that I almost combust from the sweetness of it. "Don't be scared, Charley. I'll keep you safe. *Every* part of you. Especially your heart."

I roll my neck to the side giving him more access as I sink further down on him allowing for direct contact between our pelvises. He groans when he feels the warmth of what's under my shorts straddling him. Only his slacks and my thin shorts keeping us from the touching of our most favorite parts. "I need to be inside of you. I need to feel you. Every inch of you," he says as he presses a kiss over my sweatshirt directly over my heart.

I look around and he moves his seat back into the reclining position and although it's not the most comfortable I couldn't care less. I'm with the man I love, and right now, in this moment, we are all that matters. I move back into my seat so that I can pull my shoes, shorts, and underwear off opting to leave my sweatshirt on in case someone happens to pass by.

*Right, like it'll matter if you're riding a man's lap who is not your husband.*

I ignore my subconscious, knowing that I need Will's touch so bad, in this moment, I probably wouldn't care if Matt himself walked by.

I climb back into his lap and his hands wrap around my waist instantly pulling me to his chest as I slide down on him. I sigh feeling content as I haven't had him inside of me since he left my house on Friday almost three days ago.

*I hate this.*

I don't move, and neither does he, we just stay like this relishing in the feeling of this intimate position. I nuzzle my face in his neck before my mouth finds his and we begin to kiss, slowly mirroring our moves below the waist as I start to move up and down on him. I break the kiss, wanting the eye contact more, and I stare at the most beautiful man that has trusted me with his heart. I'm overcome with emotion as I feel my orgasm building and see the emotion in him as well. "Will," I say, my eyes never leaving his. I'm too afraid to even blink for fear I'll miss what I think his eyes are telling me.

*I love you.*

*I'll never leave you.*

*It will be okay.*

*I'm here.*

"I know, baby. I'm right there with you."

"It's so much," I say wanting to be even closer to him. "I can't breathe." But the thought doesn't scare me. It revives me. And I haven't felt this alive ever. "I'm going to come," I say quietly, "but… you knew that."

He smiles that smile I fell in love with all those months ago, that dimple poking out is just enough to make my heart melt. "Eyes on me, baby. Don't close your eyes when you come, I want to see you come apart."

"Yes," I moan. "You're close too, I can feel it. I can feel every inch of you when we're together. What you're feeling, what you're thinking… I know the depths of your mind and your heart. And you know mine."

"Two halves of the same whole."

"Fuck," I whimper. "Where were you eight years ago?"

"You don't want to know how many times I've asked myself that."

"Tell me you love me," I gasp, on the precipice of a soul-shattering orgasm. *I'm so close I can taste it.*

"I love you so much." I cry out hearing his words, the first wave of the orgasm taking over and my hand goes to the ceiling of the car for leverage. His mouth is on my neck as I move up and down on him faster as the rest of my orgasm rips through me. He fills me deeply each time I make my way down to the base of his cock, our pelvic muscles pressed together completely.

Sweat rolls down my back as he rips my sweatshirt over my

head, leaving me completely naked in his arms. His tongue traces my nipple, collecting the beads of sweat that have formed and sucking them down like it's the sweetest drink before he tugs the sensitive pebble between his teeth.

"I want you to come inside of me. I want your cum inside me for the rest of the night. I want to go to bed with it there," I say and it's as if my words are his undoing, he comes, growling my name in my ear as he stills, filling my body with everything he has to offer. His orgasm finally wanes after what feels like a blissful eternity, and I can still feel him pulsing inside of me. I clench once letting him know he needs to stay put, and he chuckles.

"I wasn't going anywhere. I want to stay inside of you for as long as possible."

"Forever?" I ask.

"Forever." He rubs his nose across mine and we sit in the afterglow of our lovemaking. Only after a few minutes does he break the silence. "I love coming inside of you, baby, even though it's risky as hell. You're still on the pill, right?"

I nod, knowing a baby would be the worst thing for us right now, especially if we want to escape this with minimal destruction. "Yes, I am."

"Okay, just stay on it a little longer, alright?"

I cock my head to the side as I try to move the damp hair off of my neck. "Then what?"

"What do you mean?"

"I mean…when we get together…"

He smiles a shy smile. "I thought you knew how I felt?"

My eyes furrow wondering if we've had this conversation and I somehow missed it. "I don't—I don't remember talking about it?"

"I'm all in on kids, Charlotte. I want you pregnant the second the ink on your divorce papers dries."

I swallow. "You don't even want to marry me first?" I ask, cocking my head to the side.

"I want it all. Marriage and a baby—babies. I want a life with you, Charley," he shakes his head, "so much that…"

I eye him. "So much that…?" He looks out the window, avoiding my gaze completely. I pull his chin to look at me, staring into his worried eyes. "So much that…" I repeat, urging him to complete the sentence.

"I bought a house." He rubs the back of his neck, something I've noticed he only does when he's nervous.

"You bought a house?" I ask, the shock evident in my voice.

"Yes…for you to live in…with me. For us to live in together… and raise our family." He looks as if he's nervous to tell me but I'm so overcome with gratitude and love for this man I can't imagine why he would be apprehensive.

"You bought us a house?" I ask, the tears brimming in my eyes. He nods still unsure of my response to this life-changing news. "Oh my God, Will!" I wrap my arms around him and squeeze before I place a kiss on his lips. "Do you have pictures? Can I see it? Can we go see it soon? Please?"

"I do have pictures, yes," he says.

"When were you going to tell me? When did you buy it?"

"I saw the house about a month ago, and I thought of you instantly. I mean…I could see you there with me. But at the time you hadn't said you were definitely leaving him. I thought you might eventually, but I didn't know that it definitely meant you'd even want to be with me. The realtor is a friend of my brother's— really an old girlfriend, and she said she'd keep an eye on it until I was sure. I guess she saw my hesitation to give her a definitive no. And then we had those two days at your place, and I knew. I knew that you were feeling what I was feeling. That you loved me and wanted this as badly as I did… I do."

He rubs his hands down my shoulders and squeezes. "I called her and asked for a week. She obliged. And then today…you said you were leaving him…"

I gasp. "Did you do it…today?"

His nerves are back as he reluctantly nods before lowering his head. "I signed the papers today, after you left my office."

I place my hand under his chin and bring his gaze back to mine. "You bought us a house today?"

"And then went on a fucking date," he says as he rubs his forehead. "Stupid."

I shrug. "I was on one too. I'm sorry I got so mad at you for that."

"Yeah, but at least I know you're going to go out with him from time to time. I'm sure it surprised you to see me with another woman."

I bite my lip to prevent the tears from forming. "It certainly was unexpected."

"Look at me," he says, grabbing my face. "There is no one else. Just you. Just like I trust you aren't doing anything with Wells you have to trust that I'm not doing anything with *anyone*."

"I do trust you. Like I said, it just hurt to see you with someone else. Just like I know it hurts you to see me with Matt. I'd never felt it before and I guess I got a glimpse of how you feel. It sucks and I'm sorry I put you through that."

He chuckles before pulling me to his chest and breathing in my scent. "Yes, it's difficult, but I'm sorry you had to see that."

I nod, rubbing my face against his chest that is still covered by his white dress shirt. I unbutton his shirt and press my face to the warmth, needing to feel the skin-to-skin contact and not caring that it's coated with a layer of sweat. "You bought us a house." I look up at him as the tears start to flow. "Do you have any idea how unbelievable that is. How unbelievable *you* are? I'm in awe of you."

*And it's the truth. I know Will loves me and knows how I feel about him, but he still took a huge risk. He gambled on me and bought a house. A house for us to raise our kids.*

"Honestly, I thought you'd be pissed I jumped the gun like this. And without talking to you…"

I perk my head up off of his chest. "Oh my God, no. Not at all. I can't believe you did this for me. For *us*. This is amazing."

We stay like this, talking, kissing, and just sitting in silence, letting our fingertips do the talking for us as they explore every inch of each other's skin. The morning is quickly approaching and I know our time is up. I feel the tears forming in my eyes the second the realization registers on both of our faces. *It's late, and we can't stay out here all night.*

"I'll see you Friday, baby. We'll go see the house?" he says in an effort to cheer me up, but I hear the sadness in his voice that, again, I have to leave him.

"Our house?" I whisper, feeling a tremor move through me as the words leave my lips.

"Yes," he smiles, "and we'll christen it while we're there. It's not going unnoticed that I haven't tasted your pussy today."

I bite down on my bottom lip out of sheer arousal and frustration as I had *definitely noticed*. "So, Friday?"

"Yes, ma'am, be prepared to have my mouth reacquainted with *every* inch of you," he says in a voice so low and seductive that I almost convulse. I know I have to get out of this car *now* before it results in round two.

I reach for the door handle before I turn to look at him. "What I said, Will? I meant it. Please don't forget that. Even if I can't take your call or see you when you need me right now, please don't forget that I'm yours. So completely and irrevocably yours. Maybe not on paper, but mind body and soul…" I say sadly, knowing that my life inside this car is vastly different than my life outside of it, and as soon as I climb out of this silver BMW, my reality will change once again. The reality that I'm not with Will.

*I really feel for Cinderella in this moment. Who says you have to go back to reality at midnight?*

I climb out of his car and start the quick trek back to my house. I see him watching me out of the corner of my eye as he inches along the street a few yards behind me. I shoot him a quick wave before I'm in the house. When I'm safely inside, I pull out my phone and send him a text.

Me: Drive safely. Thank you for coming to see me.
Will: Sleep tight, call me when you can. I love you.
Me: I love you too. I can't wait until I can go to sleep in your arms every night.
Will: Ditto, baby. My bed is waiting for you.

# CHAPTER
## *Fourteen*

I'M LYING IN BED STILL REELING FROM MY NIGHT WITH WILL— the orgasm, the "I love yous," and the house he bought us overwhelm my thoughts, making it impossible to shut my eyes. I stare at the ceiling, unable to turn off my brain as my thoughts begin to drift.

*How did I get here?*

*I know I'm in this situation because of the decisions I've made, but the act of cheating on Matt was not what broke my marriage. It might just be the straw that broke the camel's back.*

I close my eyes praying for sleep to claim me when I'm reminded of all of the things that had a hand in the demise of my marriage. The late nights, early mornings, cold looks and kisses, forgetting my birthday—*ah, my birthday last year.* I squeeze my eyes shut as I try to stop the tears from falling.

———

*September 23, 2016*

*I wake with a start on my twenty-eighth birthday with a huge smile on my face. I was never someone that hated birthdays. Maybe I'm not old enough to view them as something sad or morbid—I guess that comes with age. I like the attention, the cake, the people reaching out that you haven't talked to in a few months calling to wish you well on your day. I loved all of it. I turn my head to the side and frown when I don't see my husband—or anything for that matter.*

*When we lived together, before we got married, I was roused from sleep on September twenty-third by his mouth on me, his lips bringing me to an orgasm before my eyes were even fully open. The first year of our marriage, it was the same, and the smell of bacon tickling my nostrils. After year three, when things started to go downhill, Matt wasn't in bed with me, but he left flowers and a note. Last year, it was just a note and the instructions that I was to have a spa day with Lauren. But this year, I frown when I don't see anything.*

*No flowers, no note, no husband.*

*I sit up in bed, stretching my limbs to the ceiling. When I walk downstairs, I wonder if my husband is trying something new this year. I search the house top to bottom and don't see any sign of him or anything celebratory. The dishes from the meal I had alone last night still lie in the sink along with the wine glass I'd filled to the brim at least three times as I brought in my birthday alone. My eyes dart to the foyer and I see that his briefcase and keys aren't there, leading me to believe that he's already left for work. I pull out my phone and press his contact, my hands shaking as I anticipate the disappointment.*

*"Matthew Wells."*

*Jesus, Matt, did you even bother to look at the person calling? "Hi," I say softly, "it's me."*

*"Hey, I'm walking into a meeting, can I call you later?"*

*"Oh…I…I mean…" Did he…did he forget? I wonder. No, that's impossible. This has to be setting me up for something huge. A surprise maybe. "Yeah, totally fine," I say, my optimism taking over.*

*"Great, later," he says without so much as a term of endearment. I hear the line go dead and I set the phone down.*

*I spend the day with Lauren, who'd had the foresight to take off work, and we have mimosas at our favorite spot. The bartender even looked the other way and honored the bottomless mimosa deal only reserved for weekends even though it was Wednesday. I wasn't drunk, but buzzed enough to feel the tension building over my husband's indifference to my day of birth. Lauren hadn't been* the biggest fan of Matthew, so I didn't want to spoil the day or our buzzes talking about it.

After all, there was still tonight.

I got home around five, and after a day of mimosas and pedicures—two of my favorite things—I showered before putting on a black dress that I'd bought especially for the day. I assumed we'd go to dinner, and I wanted to look and feel as beautiful as September twenty-third always made me feel. I curled my hair in loose waves and did a smoky eye. The works. I poured myself a glass of wine, swinging my feet as I sat perched on the barstool, the lasting effects of brunch starting to melt away. I hear his keys in the door and smile brightly as he walks through the door.

"Hi!" I call as he walks in still staring down at his phone.

"Hey," he says, not even bothering to look up. I clear my throat and when he finally does look up at me, I see a small smile cross his face, as if he wasn't expecting me to be dressed this way. "You look really pretty."

I blush slightly, sad that something so minor causes my heart to skip a beat. It's as if any attention or affection from my husband makes me unreasonably happy as it's so rare that he gives me either. "Thank you, it's new." I smile. "I bought it for today."

"Today?" he asks. "You going out with Lauren?" He grabs a wine glass from our cabinet and pulls out the Merlot I opened last night. He looks at it before pushing it aside and opening up a new bottle. Something so simple and idiotic, but it makes my heart constrict. He even hates my wine choices.

"Ummm. We…we aren't going anywhere?"

"No? I'm exhausted, and I still have a ton of work to do."

"But…"

He's already out of the room before I have a chance to say anything and I feel the nausea bubbling inside. I've felt the distance for months now, coming up on a year. I attributed it to work, and stress

but…*forgetting my birthday? I follow him to his office and stand in
the doorway with my arms crossed.*

*"Matt," I say, and he looks up from his computer shocked to see
me in his space.*

*"Yeah?"*

*"What's today?" I ask, praying that he'll break out in a smile or
laugh. A simple "gotcha" would turn my whole day around.*

*What I don't anticipate is his response.*

*"Wednesday?" he asks as he cocks his head to the side.*

*"No…the…the date," I whisper.*

*"The twenty-third?" he says, and the wind is knocked out of me
by the fact that it still hasn't clicked.*

*"You…you forgot," I say, the combination of the mimosas and
wine causing the tears to flow out of me like a fountain. My lip trembles and I bolt from his office. I hear him calling after me but I fling
myself on the bed and cry. Not just because he forgot my birthday;
I'm not a child. No, it's so much bigger. I cry because, in that moment, I know it's over. I cry and cry until I feel the bed dip behind
me and I'm pulled into his arms. I want to fight him so bad and if I
were stronger I would, but I'm weak and exhausted and I just want
him to love me again.*

*Why is that so hard? Why am I so unlovable?*

*I close my eyes, the tears leaking out of me when I hear a series
of "I'm sorrys," "I'll fix this," "Anything you want," "Jewelry."*

*I cry well into September twenty-fourth, and then I'm done.
The walls move up over my face, my eyes, and most devastatingly
my heart.*

*I ask for a divorce the following day.*

⎯⎯

I look at Matt, the hurt and anger at how inconsiderate he was almost a full year ago still coursing through me. I turn on my side;
I can't stand to look at him for another second, but my heart still

races out of anger. I turn onto my back and shut my eyes, my last-ditch effort to calm down. When it doesn't work, I fling the covers off of me and make my way out the bedroom, hoping some chamomile tea will calm my nerves. I start our electric kettle and prepare a cup before I sit on the floor, leaning up against the island in the center of our state-of-the-art kitchen. I pull out my Blackberry and put the phone to my ear as I hear it ring.

"Why are you still awake?" I hear him say sleepily and I wince, remembering how late it is.

"Sorry I woke you; I couldn't sleep. I miss you."

There's silence on the other end as well as some shuffling, and then his voice is louder, making me believe he's fully awake. "I miss you too, Charley. I wish you were here."

I feel the tears lodged in my throat, and I'm seconds away from answering his question about why I'm awake in the first place, when my libido has a different idea. "What would you do if I was?"

I hear a sharp intake of breath and then his voice is low, sinful almost. "Charlotte." The single word rings through the phone and has a direct line to my sex. "Where are you?"

"Kitchen."

"Are you sure you won't be…heard?"

"I'm sure. Tell me." My hand dances at the hem of my t-shirt, my fingertip rubbing the skin just above the waistband of my shorts. "Make me forget, Will," I whisper. "Please."

He's silent for a moment. "I should come back."

"No. I'm fine, I just… I started thinking about my birthday last year."

I don't hear anything for a moment. I even pull my phone away from my ear wondering if I had dropped the call. "You have this blue dress," he starts, and my eyes widen. I wasn't expecting him to start talking about my wardrobe. "You wore it a few weeks ago, on the first warm day of the season. It clung to you in a way that made me hard for your entire session. It showed a hint of cleavage and I couldn't stop fantasizing about licking the tiny bit of skin exposed between your breasts. It was a bit short, and I'd hoped you'd worn it for my benefit, especially every time you crossed and uncrossed your legs. My heart stopped every time you did because my eyes automatically went to the space between your legs, hoping for a glimpse of your panties. Wells was next to you… I swear he had to have known."

I gasp at his confession about my *Alice and Olivia* dress. I hadn't missed the way his eyes raked over me in appreciation when I walked into his office, my silky-smooth legs out on display for the first time since the prior year.

"I wanted to rip that dress off of you the second I laid eyes on you," he continues. "Lay you on my desk and lick your pussy until you screamed my name." My hand moves between my legs, rubbing myself through my shorts feeling myself build even underneath two layers of fabric. "I would take my cock and rub it against your slick clitoris. I wouldn't slip it inside of you. *Not yet.* I would rub my cock against you. Torturing you, slowly. I would tap my cock against your sweet spot, over and over."

*Fuck, I wish I had my vibrator.*

"Touch your pussy for me, Charley." I do as he says, sliding my fingers underneath my panties to the slick folds that have been wet ever since Will answered the phone. "Are you?"

"Yes," I breathe out, hoping I don't sound like a cheesy porn star.

"Good. I'm touching my cock."

"I wish it was inside of me." I squeeze my eyes shut as I continue to rub harder.

"So do I, baby. Tonight, in the car wasn't enough. I need you so badly I can't think. If I were there, I'd have you on your back, your legs over my shoulder as I fucked you mercilessly. I would fuck you so hard, you'd wince every time you moved tomorrow.

Every time you cross your legs, you'd feel the emptiness of not having my cock there. You'll ache for me, Charlotte."

"I already do."

"Do you? Does your pussy hurt when I haven't paid it attention in a while? When I haven't kissed it or fucked it? Does it cry for me?"

"Yes!" My fingers slide inside of me just as Will would do if he were here.

"When you rub your pussy, do you picture me?"

"Yes, every time!"

"What are you picturing now?"

"Tell me what I should be picturing."

"My fingers." And I close my eyes trying to pretend my thin dainty fingers are his thick ones, burrowing deep inside of me up to the knuckle. "I love feeling your juices coating them, the smooth skin of your lips that tremble just before I touch you. That quiver while I'm inside of you, around my fingers. I love touching your clit with my thumb as I finger you, rubbing circles into the engorged flesh as I hook my finger around your g-spot. And then you moan." His breathing speeds up and I wonder if he's getting close. "Fuck, baby, your moans are like music to my dick."

Right on cue, one escapes my lips as I feel myself nearing my climax. "Will, I'm so close."

"I'd pull my fingers from your pretty pussy and lick the juices from them, the smell filling my nostrils of my favorite scent…you know that's why I always smell your panties, right? Why I run my nose along the wet fabric just after I take them off?"

"I—I had an idea," I stammer, my orgasm only a few strokes away.

"Let me hear you come, baby. I know you're close."

The strokes along my clit become more vigorous as I approach the edge, knowing that I'm so close to sweet release. "Will!" I cry out, my hand gripping the phone with one hand so tightly, as I fear I may drop it on my hardwood floor.

"There it is," he says, his voice gravelly as if he's just had an orgasm of his own. "Hearing you come is just as hot as watching you."

"I wish you were here to watch me. Did you come?" I ask him.

"The second I heard you gasp out my name, sweetheart."

I'm not sure if it's his words or the after effects of my orgasm or a combination of the two, but I feel drained. My body is suddenly exhausted and wanting nothing more than to be in his arms.

"I want to spend my birthday this year with you."

"I would love that."

"Is it possible? Can we make that happen?"

"I'll make it happen, if that's what you want. Anything you want."

"Anything?" A smile finds my face as I picture all of the possibilities.

"Anything," he repeats.

I sigh, thinking about the one thing I want most. The thing that can lead to me getting everything else I want in life. "I want a divorce, Will."

He lets out a breath. "Do you want me to come get you?"

*I know he would. If I asked him to, he would walk right into this house, pull me up off this kitchen floor and carry me to his car without thinking twice.* "No. But I think…I think I'm going to talk to Matt tomorrow."

"Tomorrow? Baby, don't you want me to be there?" he asks, knowing that tomorrow isn't one of our scheduled sessions.

"I don't know… Maybe? But what are you going to do? Urge us to work it out? Tell me not to make any hasty decisions? You try to remain impartial during our sessions. It's not going to work if you're being all reasonable, trying to appear as if you're an unbiased third party."

"I just don't know how he's going to take it…what if he…"

I can imagine where his mind is going. "He won't hurt me."

"Everyone has a breaking point, Charley. Matt isn't violent because he has to actively work at not being so because of how he was raised. Violence *is* a learned behavior that is embedded deep in Matt's psyche. He has to constantly battle his demons, telling himself that he doesn't want to become his father. It may not be a natural reaction. And if he's upset, his natural reaction without thinking might be to cause harm to you."

His words make sense and if it were anyone else I would agree, *but this was Matt. My Matt. Well not mine anymore. But I know him.* "I'm not worried, but if you want to be parked down the street just in case you can be."

"I want to be," he says instantly.

"Okay."

"So, tomorrow?"

"Yes.

"Tomorrow, I ask for a divorce."

# CHAPTER
## *Fifteen*

**Me: We really need to talk, tonight. Do you think you can come home early?**

I stare down at the text I sent Matt well over three hours ago that is still unanswered. I roll my eyes, frustrated with the usual bullshit, and press the phone to my ear. An exasperated sigh leaves my lips as I hear the beginning of his voicemail. I don't even bother leaving one, knowing that he either won't listen to it or he'll delete it as soon as he sees the red number flash on his screen.

**Me: This is important, Matt.**

The day passes at a glacial pace, my nerves on edge as I picture how this conversation with Matt is going to go.

*How should I start it?*

*"You know we haven't been happy in quite some time…"*

*"Despite everything that's happened between us, I want you to be happy…"*

*"I want to be happy and I'm not…"*

*"I met someone…"*

I look at my phone for the millionth time today, my pulse racing every time I reach for it, expecting a text message from my husband.

*Still nothing.*

I begin to pace the length of my bedroom, my heart in my throat as I picture his response to asking him for a divorce… *again.* He broke down in our living room, his knees finding the space on the floor just between my feet as he promised that things would get better. That he loved me more than anything, and he wanted a chance to fix it. When I was hesitant to respond, he went for a different tactic: *fear.*

"*What about Michael? What are you going to do if Michael comes after you again? You need me, Charlotte. You need me just as much as I need you.*"

"I don't *need* you, Matt," I speak into the air, my voice cold and angry. I jump nearly three feet when I hear my phone beep with the notification of a message.

*Except it's not the phone that Matt would be texting me on.*

My heart races even faster, when I realize it's not my husband, but the love of my life.

**Will: Hi, beautiful. How is your day?**

**Me: As good as a day where I can't see you could be, I guess.**

**Will: Tomorrow.**

**Me: What time should I meet you? And send me the address!**

**Will: Anxious, are we?**

**Me: You have no idea.**

**Will: Have you talked to him?**

We've done our best to keep names out of our texts, not that I thought Matt would ever find my phone—or be able to unlock the impossible passcode I had on it—for that matter.

*Being able to hack someone's password required them to know deep intimate details about the other person and Matt didn't know much about me anymore.*

But, on the other hand, you could never be too safe when it came to technology, so we tried to keep specifics out of our messaging as best as we could.

**Me: Nope. I've called, texted, he won't respond or take my calls.**

**Will: Unbelievable. He must suspect what's coming.**

**Me: How?**

**Will: He can't possibly think you two are happy. That YOU are happy.**

**Me: Doesn't mean he suspects that I want a divorce. He's just inconsiderate and oblivious.**

**Will: Clearly.**

**Me: Can we talk about something else?**

**Will: Fine.**

I can tell he's irritated that I still haven't had this conversation with Matt, indicating another day is going by that I'm not free from the shackles of my loveless marriage.

**Will: What color are your underwear?**

**Me: Now we're talking.**

I spent the next hour, talking to Will, with my clothes off and on…and then off again. By the time we stop, I'm sated, yet physically and emotionally wrecked.

*I wanted to be with Will. Now.*

I stay up until my eyes can't physically stay open for another second, and drift off to sleep on my couch in the den. I'd hoped he would have woken me up when he came home, but when I wake up the next morning, around five thirty, it's to the sound of the front door closing, and I have an inkling that maybe Will was right.

*He's avoiding me.*

I frown, annoyed that he's so opposed to talking to me that he would let me sleep on our couch all night. I don't know why the thought makes me so emotional, but it does and before I can stop them, the tears are moving uncontrollably down my face.

*Why does he hate me so much?*

⸺

It's 10 a.m., and I'm driving to the house across town that Will had bought. I'm so happy to get out of the hustle and bustle of the city, and looking forward to an area of peace and quiet that could only be found in suburbia. I put my phone down as it tells me "I've arrived" and I stare up at the house in front of me. A vast contrast to the mansion I share with Matt, this house is much smaller but has the warm, inviting feel I've always longed for. It's a gorgeous, gray house with white and blue accents, in a neighborhood just outside of Atlanta. I get out of the car and put my hand over my eyes to shield them from the sun and to take in the beauty of what's before me. My eyes take it in from top to bottom and by the time I get to the white picket fence, I can't help the smile that crosses my face.

"Do you like it?"

I turn to him, my brain telling my body that I can't mount him in the front yard. "I love it! It's beautiful and…there's a white picket fence!"

"Did you think I'd buy you a house without one?"

I'd always wanted a house with a white picket fence because to me it represented that perfect family. Call it watching too much *Father Knows Best* and all of those older sitcoms that portrayed a family that lived in a perfect house, on the perfect street with white picket fences surrounding their perimeter. Matt didn't seem all too concerned with that, and while our mansion is gorgeous, it's also ostentatious and doesn't exactly have the *home* feel that Dorothy wished for.

*This* feels like home…or maybe *Will* is my home.

He leads me inside, pushing me against the wall the second we are safely behind closed doors. "Hi, beautiful." He cups my cheeks gently, stroking his thumbs over the space beneath my eyes. "How are you?" he asks, his eyes scanning my face, knowing I can't lie as easily to his face as I can over the phone about being *fine*.

"I'm okay, I just… I think you're right about Matt suspecting what I want to talk about. I fell asleep on the couch waiting for him to come home and he didn't even wake me when he got in last night."

"He left you there?"

I nod. "It's stupid. I hate that it bothers me so much. And our couch is comfortable." I shrug.

He steps away from me, rubbing his jaw. "He's such a fucking asshole."

"Will…" I say, reaching for his hand in an effort to calm him down.

"Don't, Charlotte. You know he is."

"Yes, but I also know it's not helping for you to get all worked up over it. You're the level-headed one. I'm the emotional one, remember?" I joke and he shakes his head, his eyes finding mine.

"This isn't funny. Nothing about this is funny," he whispers as his fingers find my hair, gently tucking a strand behind my ear. "I'm ready for this—all of this. Aren't you?" He waves his hand around the foyer and I'll admit I'm dying to see the rest of the house, but clearly, we need to get a few things straight first.

"Yes, Will. I do, more than anything, but I'm ending a marriage. One I was in for five years, with a man I've known for almost a decade. Counselor hat on, please, boyfriend hat off. I know you can't possibly be telling me that this isn't a big deal. This isn't something I can blurt out on my way out the door."

"It just seems like you're dragging your feet a little."

"Me?" I push him gently on the chest so that I can put some space between us. I cross my arms defensively. "Matt's never home."

"That's nothing new, Charlotte."

"What do you want me to do? Hide his keys? Force him to sit down and pay attention to me? If I knew how to do that, we wouldn't need you." I roll my eyes and, in an instant, he wraps his hand around my wrist and pulls me into his arms.

"Don't be a smart-ass," he scolds, pressing a finger to my lips when I try to protest. "This is going to be difficult. Perhaps the most difficult thing you've ever done, but if this is what you want. What you truly want…not just what you think *I* want, then you need to do this. In the end, only you have to deal with the choices that you make."

"This is what I want, Will. I wanted this before I even met you, and I let him talk me out of it. I let him talk me into marriage counseling. I thought it would work." I pull out of his arms again. "I don't regret what's happened between us, but I would be lying if I didn't say that this definitely did *not* work."

"Or did it?" Will asks. "You found yourself, slowly but surely. You were a completely different person when you started; now you are the strong, confident, passionate, sexual woman that had been lying dormant for years."

"Yes, because of *you*." I smile, thinking about how much of my confidence that Will had instilled in me.

As if reading my mind, he says, "No, baby. *You* did that."

—

After we've done a complete tour of the house, I want nothing more than to christen the grounds with the man that had done all of this for me—*for us*. With each room, I saw my life slowly transforming before my eyes. I saw my very pregnant self walking through the halls, hand in hand with the man I loved, the cool metal of his ring, pressed against my palm.

I saw the nursery painted blue—and pink, both of us hovered over a tiny bassinet after we welcomed our tiny human into the world. I saw the faint pencil marks on the wall indicating their growth. I saw baby number two, *and three, and four.*

*Shit, Will and I are busy.*

I pictured where the Christmas tree would go—there's a perfect spot next to the fireplace—where we can cuddle in front of the roaring flames as Christmas Eve turned into the next day.

There's a balcony on the second floor, just off the master suite where we can watch the sun set during those warmer summer nights.

Then there was the kitchen, a place where I had spent so much time alone. Cooking dinners for one, and then eating them by myself, the sound of my fork hitting the plate the only sound in the room.

I saw his arms wrapped around me as I cooked us breakfast in the morning. His mouth on my neck as I prepared dinner for us and our offspring, rubbing my belly that was full of new life.

*Barefoot and pregnant in Will Montgomery's kitchen.*

After all of that, I couldn't contain the river that was flowing between my thighs, my arousal dripping into my panties with every step. I excuse myself to the bathroom and strip myself of everything except for my underwear I know he'll rip from me within seconds. Walking into the kitchen I find him leaning against the breakfast bar, talking on his phone, when our eyes meet. He gazes upon me salaciously, his tongue darting out to run over his lips causing me to shudder. He almost drops his phone into the sink before I hear, "Vanessa, I have to go."

His words are jarring. *Do guys really end work phone calls the second their naked woman walks in the room? I'm pretty sure Matt wouldn't even notice me if I walked into a room on fire.* I don't think Will even waits for Vanessa's response before he's moving toward me. "Charlotte," he says, his voice hoarse with want and need.

"I…I thought we could christen our new home."

"Yes," he says and I immediately wrap myself around his body, still fully clothed in his black suit; a vast difference to me, who is completely nude aside from the scrap of fabric between my legs that's getting wetter by the second. I close my eyes, relishing in the feeling of his thumbs rubbing my nipples to hardened peaks. He drops his hands, as his mouth engulfs one of them, his tongue rubbing against it before he suckles it. He grazes his teeth over my nipple, before letting it go with a pop. His mouth finds the other. "You have beautiful breasts, Charlotte," he murmurs with his mouth attached as if he's trying to fit the entirety in his mouth.

"Turn around." I do as he says, putting my hands above my head and resting my forearms on the wall. He presses against me, trailing his hands down my naked body and I wish he'd lose the clothes for us to have skin-to-skin contact. I smile when his hand moves to the inside of my panties, his fingers parting the lips of my sex. I groan, letting my head fall back as he begins to massage my clit with his index finger. Walking around this house was nothing short of a powerful aphrodisiac, so I know it won't take much for me to come all over his hands. He must know this too, because after a few swipes over my clit, he removes his hand much to my disappointment. He takes a step back and gets on his knees, pulling my panties down, slowly. They're barely around my thighs when his mouth kisses and bites the flesh of my ass.

"Mine," I hear him growl as I feel him begin to nibble on the skin. I'm not surprised when he full-on sinks his teeth into me as he's been known to do, and I yelp. His tongue soothes where I know there are indents of his perfect teeth, branding me. "Will," I whimper, the need for him too great to be quiet.

"Bend over, baby, halfway." I know what he wants so I oblige, bending my body at a ninety-degree angle so he can access every part of me. It takes no time for him to settle between my legs, his mouth working me over from behind. When he spreads my cheeks and drags his tongue upwards, the goose bumps pop up instantly, as if I'd stuck my finger in a light socket. I let out a sigh as his tongue probes the place that only he's been, claiming me in the dirtiest way. *And yet I don't feel dirty. I feel desired, wanted, loved.*

He stands up and within seconds his slacks hit the floor, the belt clanging against the hardwood and his cock is at my entrance, dragging his tip through my sex, tortuously slow. "This is going to be hard...and rough," he says hoarsely.

I nod my head having lost all ability to speak only moments ago. He pushes through me inch by inch, allowing me to feel the thickness of his member before he slams the rest of the way into me causing my hands to slide against the wall and me to lurch forward. Before my face can make contact with the wall, his arms wrap around me, his much larger frame engulfing my petite one.

"Hold on, baby," he chuckles and I giggle. I rest my head against my forearms and brace myself for him again when he pushes inside of me. I whimper with his body pressed completely against mine. "I'm going to move now."

And he does. *Fast and hard.*

I reach between my legs and graze the place where we're connected feeling him as he moves in and out of me, before I continue on my journey. I reach my destination and I cup his balls gently before I massage them harder.

"FUCK," he roars and his hands tighten on my hips, moving himself more aggressively in and out of me. My hand is still between us, his balls in my palm, our arousals dripping out of us and down his shaft and onto my hand. I clench at the raw sexiness of it and a beat later I feel his balls tighten, the first telltale sign he's about to unleash his seed inside of me. "Touch your clit for me, baby." I press my hand, that is coated with a mixture of our cum, against me and just the mere thought of rubbing his cum into my pussy has my orgasm brewing.

"Will, I'm going to come," I breathe, and it's like the words are his undoing because he shoots his load into me chanting my name like a prayer. His hand moves mine out of the way as he begins to rub me, hard, and within a second, I'm convulsing in his arms. At some point he must have pulled out of me, because when the aftershocks have passed, I'm in his arms, my back resting against his chest with his hand cupping the space between my legs almost protectively.

"I love you." He nuzzles my cheek before pressing a gentle kiss to the space behind my ear. "I just want you to be happy." He strokes my arms gently and I let my eyes flutter closed as I lean against his chest, letting him hold me upright.

"You make me happy," I tell him. "I love you too, and I know what I have to do…today."

—

We still have a bit of time to kill before we have to be back, so we spend it sitting on a blanket on the floor of our new house.

*The start to our new life.*

He had thought ahead, thinking that I might be hungry or that we would have worked up a sexually charged appetite, so he stocked the refrigerator with a few things.

We feed each other the spread of fruit and an array of cheese and crackers when a memory flashes through my head. "Oh my God!" I shriek. "I can't believe I forgot to tell you. Matt slept with Bree!"

"WHAT?" he yells, and I realize what he must be thinking.

"No, no, no, before me," I say and I see him simmer down and nod. "Evidently before Bree and Nathan got married but *while* they were dating! I don't know all of the specifics, but it's so crazy; Matt and Nathan are like brothers. They've known each other since they were kids! I don't even understand how he could do that to him. I know, I don't exactly have a lot of room to talk, but I was stunned when he told me," I ramble as I nibble on a cracker. "Nathan never did anything to deserve that. Not that I'm saying that Matt deserves to be cheated on, but he's certainly not innocent in all of this. So, what I'm trying to figure out is what did Nathan do to Matt?"

"Interesting," he says stroking his jaw. Will is well aware of who Bree and Nathan Cunningham are to us, so I'm sure he's just as shocked to hear the news. "How did you find this out?"

"Matt told me that night we saw you at dinner. He was drunk and it all spilled out. He asked if I was cheating on him with Nathan."

*I still have a hundred questions regarding Matt's affair with*

*his best friend's girl. When exactly did he? I know that it was be-*
*fore me, but how long before? How did Nathan find out? Does he*
*definitely know?*

Will's eyebrows shoot up. "Tit for tat style, huh?"

"Evidently." I shrug. "I'm surprised Bree never told me."

"Maybe she didn't want things to be awkward or uncomfortable?"

"So, all three of them are sharing this secret and no one told me?"

"Nathan knows?"

"The way he told me, it sounded like it? But I didn't ask him straight out."

"And Nathan is okay with it?"

"He married her, so I guess so?"

"Hmmm. I would like to take a look inside *that* marriage."

"Enlighten me." I giggle. "Tell me how you'd counsel a cou-ple where you're not head over heels in love with the woman." I smirk and he raises an eyebrow at me.

"Head over heels, huh?" He takes a sip of water and I have to will myself to look away so that I don't get turned on watch-ing the water slide down his throat. *He makes everything look so goddamn erotic.* I shoot him a look telling him to get on with it. "Well, first, I would need to know if Nathan knows. Did Bree tell him? Did Matt tell him? Did he find out somehow on his own? I mean all of the biggest problems arise when someone is dishonest."

His words are sobering. "Like me."

"Charlotte…"

"No, I'm not asking for you to placate me, or tell me that it's different. I know what I'm doing. I'm a…*cheater.*" My eyes squeeze shut as the word leaves my lips like a dirty little secret.

"I wasn't going to placate you…or tell you that you're differ-ent. I was just going to tell you that I'm being dishonest as well. That you aren't in this alone. *We* are in this together, baby." He grabs my hand and brings it to his lips, dragging them over each finger. "You and me," he whispers quietly before his lips are on mine, his tongue begging for access to my mouth and finding my tongue instantly.

We kiss like this until I pull away, knowing that we're running low on time. "We should go."

After getting dressed, and tidying up, we walk toward my car and he helps me inside. I start the engine and roll the window down to lean out of it.

"I'll see you soon," he says running a hand through my hair. "I love you."

"I love you too, and I love our house."

"I can't wait to fill it with babies." He smiles and I can feel my cheeks turning pink.

He chuckles before his lips find mine, coaxing my tongue out of my mouth and into his for the final time today. "Drive safely," he says, rubbing his nose against mine. I nod and as he leaves my window, I watch him walk behind my car and get into the familiar BMW parked behind me.

# CHAPTER Sixteen

MY LEG IS BOUNCING NERVOUSLY AS WE SIT IN WILL'S OFFICE, waiting on Matt, who of course is late. "I'm so over this. I wouldn't be surprised if he just didn't show up at all." I rub my forehead, feeling a slight headache forming behind my eyes.

"Sweetheart, breathe. You know he comes whenever he pleases." I notice him fiddling with his pen, something I've noticed he does when he has the urge to touch me but can't.

"That's my fucking point!" I say getting up to pace Will's office. "Why…why after all this time does he still not give a fuck? You would think at this point since he's 'trying to work on his marriage,'" I say using air quotes, "that he would at the very least be on time for our counseling sessions." I move toward him to try and sit in his lap when he shakes his head at me. "What, Vanessa isn't going to announce him? He's just going to waltz right in?" I say, cocking my head to the side and putting my hands on my hips.

"Don't get smart with me, Charlotte," he says with a firm tone but I can see the humor all over his face.

After twenty minutes of Will and me eye fucking each other, Matt finally arrives. He walks in and I can't even help the icy stare I give him. *Breathe, Charley.* "I'm sorry I'm late, I—"

"Don't bother apologizing. You're late every week. It's always the same. Traffic blah blah blah," I say waving my hand in the air. "The apology only means something the first ten or so times."

"Okay, what is your problem, Charlotte? I literally *just* walked in the door, how are you already pissed at me?"

*You're my problem,* I think to myself but take a deep breath before I speak that into existence.

"How about we take a breath?" Will says. "You two are coming out the gate running today."

"Dr. Montgomery," I say, giving him my warning tone and I think he's taken aback.

"By all means, Ms. Pierce," he says waving toward us both.

I'm quiet for several moments, wondering how I should start this, my mind drifting back to all of the sentence starters I had worked out. Clearly my brain and mouth aren't working together at the moment, because I blurt the words out without any thought. *Rip the Band-Aid off, Charley.* "I want a divorce," I say bluntly.

"What?" Matt says, his eyes wide. "Because I was late? Charlotte, don't be dramatic, I—"

*Did he just—?* I watch as Will closes his eyes slowly, knowing that I'm absolutely about to explode, and when he opens them, I see the look he's giving Matt.

*Do you know **anything** about women?*

"DRAMATIC?" I screech. "Did you just call me dramatic?" I say. "You're kidding, right? You're not kidding?" I look at Will. "He's not kidding? After a year and a half of treating me like an afterthought, an annoyance, an obligation? You're calling *me* dramatic? After you made me feel like I wasn't good enough for you? Not perfect enough for you?" Tears form in my eyes. "You pushed me aside, you ignored me, you lost all interest in me. I'd be sitting at dinner with you, and you'd look through me. You didn't care what I ever had to say. And you kept me locked up in our house and only let me out when you needed me for show. You didn't want me to work, but you gave me no reason to stay home. You wouldn't give me a baby when you knew I wanted one. What was the point of spending all that time and money and resources to put me back together after what happened with Michael if you were just going to break me all over again?!" I yell, my hands shaking violently. "I'm not happy and I'm not living like this anymore. I don't deserve this." I shake my head as I wipe the tears from my face. "It's over."

"Charlotte, you don't mean that. You know how I feel about you."

"No. No, Matthew, I don't. And frankly…I don't care anymore. You've changed. I've changed. We've changed. You're not a bad person, Matt. You're just not the right person for *me*. And clearly I'm not the right person for you either."

"Charlotte…" he says moving closer to me and I move back, letting myself sink into the couch.

"Don't," I say, putting a hand out. "You can't suck me back again. I should have done this a year ago, when I wanted to, instead of letting you waste forty thousand dollars on therapy." *Part of me wonders if I ever would have met Will though. I know he wonders the same when I see a look of sadness cross his face.*

"Not that you haven't been lovely, Dr. Montgomery," I add, shooting him a knowing smile even through my tears.

"You can't leave me, baby. I love you. I love you more than anything, you know that. It's why I'm here… I'm fighting for you, for us."

"Are you? Have you really tried? Is that why you've been avoiding me the last few days? Why you won't talk to me? I asked you yesterday to come home earlier. I called you, I texted you, but you wouldn't even grant me the courtesy of taking my calls. *I'm your fucking wife, Matt.*" The words come out harsher than I intend, and I resist the urge to look at Will, praying he doesn't react too noticeably over my comment.

"Yesterday was crazy, Charlotte. I had such a busy day, I barely had a chance to do anything."

"A simple 'Okay' or 'I'll try' would have sufficed. It would have taken less than ten seconds. You blatantly ignoring me is just the giant *'fuck you'* that you love to stick to me."

"That's not true, Charlotte."

"Isn't it? You won't even call me Charley. *Every* person that I have some sort of intimate relationship calls me Charley. My grandmother was the first to call me that, and you *know* what she meant to me. I love the name, and yet you only call me Charlotte—"

"Oh, give me a break," he interrupts.

"Let her finish." I hear Will's even voice washing over me and I'm instantly calmer.

"It matters. It's something so minute, but it means something. It just further explains how little you take my wants or needs or feelings into consideration."

"Because I don't call you Charley?"

"It's all a part of the bigger picture. You don't want to be married—at least, not to me."

"How can you say that? After everything we've been through together? Eight years, Charlotte. Oh, I'm sorry—*Charley.*" He rolls his eyes, and I shake my head.

"You still don't get it. We've grown apart, Matt. We want different things."

"Is this about me not being ready to have kids?"

"It's part of it." I nod.

"Fine, Charlotte. If it means so much to you, we can try."

From the corner of my eye, I see Will tense and I do my best to calm him with my eyes, but I don't think it's working as he shifts in his seat. "No, Matt. It's too late for that. And I know that's not what you really want. I'm not going to force a child on you."

"If it's that or a divorce, I'll take the former. I'm sure the idea will grow on me."

"Do you hear yourself? Matt, it's okay to not want kids. But in the same breath, it's okay for me to *want* them and to not want to be with someone who *doesn't.*" I shake my head. "Don't get me wrong, if we were happy and in love and our marriage was strong, maybe I could accept the fact that we'd never have kids because *you* would be enough. Because being without you would hurt more than being without a potential baby I had never met. But we aren't happy at all!"

"Says who?"

"ME! I'm not happy! Can't you see that? I'm drowning in this marriage and you don't care! And if you would be honest with yourself for two fucking seconds, you would see that you're drowning too, you've just thrown yourself into work to avoid the issue."

"That's not true, I do love you."

"You love the person I was. The people we *were*. We are different people now, Matt. I might be asking for a divorce now, but let's face it, Matt, you left me two years ago."

"That's not true—"

"I've been in this marriage by myself for so long," I say, the tears back with a vengeance as they move down my face, "that at this point if you tried... I mean really tried... I don't think I could even let you back in. I can't get past all of the things that have happened. I was in love with you, Matt. Madly. But I'm a different girl than I was when we met. I was in love with you back then. But to be honest, I don't know who that girl is anymore and you don't know the guy you were either. Maybe that's on me too. Maybe I should have fought harder for you, or for us..." I wipe my nose with the tissues that Will keeps on the table for moments like these. "I don't know what else I could have done but...it's too late now."

"It's not too late." I hear his voice breaking and I look to see the tears threatening to spill out of his eyes. "Charlotte, please don't do this to me, I'm sorry."

"I know..." I say with a sniffle. "I am too. But...we just can't do this anymore. We are too young to be living like this. *So unhappy*. I'm not just talking about me, Matt, you're not happy either."

He shakes his head. "Don't project that shit on me. I refuse to believe it's over."

"Okay," I say sullenly, unsure of what to say if he's going to flat-out refuse a divorce.

He's silent for a moment, and I think he realizes that I'm not giving in. I see the moment the look in his eyes changes from hurt to anger. "I'm not signing shit."

"Okay," I repeat.

"How can you be so fucking cold?" he spits out. "You act like we haven't been together for eight fucking years, Charlotte, and you come in here and end it like it's nothing."

I shake my head. "Like it's nothing? You think this is nothing? Like this was easy for me? Like anything about the last two years has been *easy*? Tell me you aren't this delusional, that you didn't see this coming? We've been in therapy for months, and it's not working! We just don't work anymore!"

"You're just upset. We can work through this."

"Fine, Matt. Maybe we *can* work through it, but the fact of the matter is I don't *want* to. Not anymore."

He looks as if I've slapped him and he shakes his head at me. "What are you going to do without me?"

"I'll figure it out," I say softly.

"What are you going to do, go out and get a job? All that fancy shit I buy you costs money, sweetheart."

"Don't fucking patronize me, Matt. I never asked you to buy me anything. I was there, Matt, before your bank account had all those zeros? I was there, and I loved you more then. I never wanted you for the shit you bought me, and you know that. So don't act like I'm some pretentious, spoiled housewife that can't leave her husband because she doesn't want to give back her credit cards, because frankly I don't give a fuck," I growl at him, angry that he would even insinuate that I was with him for the money.

*The security maybe but no, not the shit he bought me. I'm actually surprised he hasn't thrown that in my face. The fact that he won't be able to protect me from Michael if we aren't married. Maybe that's too low, even though right now he's angrier than I've ever seen.*

"It still doesn't explain what you think you're going to do about money."

"I'll figure it out, Matt. I'm a smart girl."

"Are you? You're sure not acting like it." I don't say anything back and he continues. "I had no idea you were capable of being this cold-hearted."

"I'm sorry that you feel that way," I say, unable to come up with any other words.

"Fuck you and your apologies, Charlotte. Don't think that I don't know what all of this is about. I still think that you're fucking someone else. So, what? He's promised to give you the world now if you leave me? You're going to be with this other guy? I know you, you'd never not look before you leap. So, tell me, Charlotte, do you have someone in line to take my place? You wonder why I haven't touched you? Because I don't know how many men you've whored yourself out to and I don't fucking trust you."

"OKAY, ENOUGH!" I hear Will's voice roar through the room, and my eyes widen as I anticipate that he's about to rip Matt a new one for talking to me like that.

*Baby, don't do anything reckless!*

"I've sat back and watched you attack her for the past ten minutes. Enough. If you don't have anything to say that doesn't involve you defaming your wife's character I suggest you keep quiet." *I'm shocked that that's all he says to Matt. I was half expecting him to rip his head off the second he called me a whore.*

"Doc, relax. I'm sorry that I'm not more pleasant to the woman who's leaving me after eight years." He turns to me. "You really want to do this?"

I nod. "Yes," I say, fresh tears rolling down my face.

He shakes his head, and he doesn't say anything for what feels like an eternity. "I want your shit out of my house," he says and I turn to look at him. "Tonight. What you don't take with you, I'm tossing," he says. "And for the record, it's not lost on me that you haven't denied anything I said about you leaving me for someone else. If you think you're getting a dime out of me after you fucking played me, you're out of your fucking mind." He gets up and walks out the door, slamming it behind him.

I expect to feel his hands around me immediately, but instead I hear his door open and shut again. I look up to see that I am completely alone in the room and I wonder if that is foreshadowing of what's to come.

*No, Will wants you. You're not alone.* I sigh. *Part of me believes that maybe I do need to know what it's like to be alone. Frankly, the thought scares the shit out of me.*

My thoughts are interrupted by Will coming back through the door and locking it behind him. It only takes him a few steps before he's on the couch next to me and I'm in his arms. "Where did you go?" I ask, as my face finds solace in the crook of his neck.

"To talk to Wells," he says, and I can hear the agitation in his voice. "Dick," he mumbles into my hair.

I gasp. "What did you say?" I sit up to look at him.

"Just that he was out of line talking to you like that and throwing out or damaging your things won't look good in the divorce. Also, that you'd be well within your rights to press charges for damaging your property."

"Is that all?"

"That's all I said, but I also wanted to make sure he wasn't coming back." He places a kiss on my forehead.

"I need to figure out how to get all my stuff," I say sadly. "I'll call Lauren and my mom. I wonder if he'll do anything to my stuff between now and when I get there."

"I don't like the idea of you going there alone. Maybe Lauren can go with you." He squeezes me tighter. "I hate that I can't go with you."

"No. We need to lie low for a while."

"I know, but this means you have no reason to be coming back here right now," he says and I can hear the implication in his voice. *That means we shouldn't see each other.*

"How will we see each other?" I ask, the anxiety over not seeing Will for an extended period of time blooming in my chest.

"I'll figure out something. but I wouldn't be surprised if he got someone to follow you now," he tells me, and a tremor skates through me.

"Will, he's not so mad that he would let *him* come back, right?" I feel like someone has a vise grip around my throat, the oxygen not flowing quite as well as it was a few moments ago, thinking about Michael finding me, finding my mother, and finishing what he started all those years ago.

"No," he says, putting my face in his hands and swiping his lips over mine. "At least, he better not. I'll kill them both," he says so low that it sends a chill through me. I rest my head on his shoulder letting my lips rest against the skin on his neck. He wraps his arms around me as I fall into a troubled sleep.

# CHAPTER
## Seventeen

WAKE UP, DISORIENTED, CONFUSED, AND GROGGY, MY BODY feeling like it's aged five years. Despite the discomfort, the scent surrounding me is calming. I press my nose against his chest, inhaling him and I'm instantly revived. My eyes flutter open and I look up into piercing blue eyes and a smile.

"Hi, beautiful."

I blink my eyes a few times. "How long have I been asleep?"

"About forty minutes. Lauren called twice... I hope you don't mind, I answered the second time."

"Does she know?"

He nods. "Yes, I assume Matt called her."

I roll my eyes. "I'm not sure why. Does he think he can turn her against me?"

"I couldn't tell you your husband's motives for a lot of things, Charley. Nevertheless, Lauren is coming here."

"What?" My eyes widen in shock. My best friend is finally going to meet the man that I haven't been able to stop talking about for months.

"I don't want you driving and I can't drive you."

"But—"

"No buts, Charlotte. Now do you want to rest until she gets here?"

"Sure," I whisper. I lay my head back down on his shoulder when my phone rings again. I look at the screen and groan when

I see the word "Mom." "Did he call my mother, too?" I place the phone to my ear.

"Hi, Mom." I don't even try to hide the exasperation in my voice.

"Charlotte Elizabeth, what is going on?!" I roll my eyes at her use of my first and middle name. She's using that shrill tone of voice she uses when she's excited and I have to pull the phone away from my ear slightly.

"I suppose you've talked to Matt?"

"He just called me…in borderline hysterics."

"I don't know why he called you." *Was he just trying to turn everyone against me? Good luck trying that with my mother.*

"He says you asked for a divorce?"

"I did."

"Why?"

"What do you mean, why? You know how difficult things have been. Mother…I can't do this right now," I sigh, resigning myself to the fact that my mother is going to try and convince me that this isn't a good idea.

*But does she really not understand where I'm coming from? Has she not been paying attention to anything that's been going on the past year?*

"Matt has been so good to you, Charley…you can't jump ship just because it's hard."

"If that were the case I would have left him a long time ago. I tried."

"He thinks there is someone else."

I'm silent. *I've never flat-out lied to my mother. Sure, I've lied by omission a ton over the past several months, but she's never asked me point blank if I was cheating.*

I swallow hard, my mouth suddenly dry as I prepare to tell my mother the truth. "I know."

"He also says you don't deny it. You have in the past. But you didn't today."

"What do you want me to say, Mother?"

*I am getting more frustrated with this conversation with each passing second. It doesn't even sound like she's on my side.*

"How about that he's mistaken?"

I put my hands over my eyes feeling like I could scream, when Will's hands begin to rub my back. I'm still in his lap and he's listening to every bit of this conversation. He gives me a small nod that I take to mean, *it's time we start coming clean.* "He's not."

I hear a sigh on the other end. "Oh, Charley."

"I know, but…I'm happy. He makes me so happy."

She sighs. "How long?"

"Going on five months."

"Jesus, Charley, five months!" she shrieks.

"I know. I just… I couldn't help it. I—I'm in love."

"With this other man?" she gasps, and I think she's shocked that I've used the L word.

"Yes. Mom, he cares about me…so much. He actually cares about what I have to say. My thoughts and dreams… I've been in a marriage for so long with a man that knows nothing about me. He pays me zero attention, Mother. Not that this is necessarily anything to be proud of, but I've been having an affair for months and he's only just now suspecting it. He doesn't notice anything about me."

"And that's a reason to cheat? Because he doesn't pay you any attention?" she accuses.

"I'm not making excuses for my behavior. I know it's wrong, but I fell in love," I say keeping my eyes on Will. "I love him more than anything." His hand moves from my back to stroke my cheek and the simple gesture sets my skin ablaze.

*I need him. Now.*

"Does he love you?"

"Yes," I say. "He bought us a house." I smile as I look at him.

*If I can't be honest with my mother, I can't be honest with anyone. I trust her like I trust Lauren, and although she's upset with me right now, she would never betray me to Matt. She would take my secrets to the grave.*

"There's so much you don't know. I know that you're disappointed, and one day soon I'll tell you everything, but I just need time to…decompress."

"Okay. Where are you?"

"I'm…not at home."

"Are you with him?"

"Not now, Mom."

"What's his name?"

"I can't tell you that yet."

"Oh God, is it someone we know? Someone Matt knows? Please tell me it's not one of his friends."

"No, it's not," I say, answering only her last question, "but actually, do you think you can meet me at my house soon?"

"Of course, but why?" *And I can already hear her shuffling around in the background getting herself together.*

"He told me I had to have all of my stuff out by tonight or he would throw it away. I don't know, maybe he'll toss it in a dumpster and set everything on fire." I chuckle at my dark humor as I rub my forehead. "I just want to make sure I at least get all of my important things."

"He said WHAT?" I pull my ear away from the phone as I hear her shriek. "He can't do that! He better not touch any of your things, and I can't believe he's just kicking you out of the house like that. Charley, how can he? Isn't your name on the deed?"

"Well, yes, but…"

"Then technically he can't," she says and Will gives me a look that says, "she's right."

"I don't want to be there, he doesn't want me there. It's fine."

"Where are you going to stay? Do you need to come here?"

"With Lauren." *Hopefully that's okay with her.*

"Are you sure you aren't staying with your boyfriend, Charley? You know you need to lie low right now if you don't want things to completely blow up in your face. At least until you're legally separated."

"I know, and yes, I am staying with Lauren." Will stiffens underneath me, probably realizing that means we wouldn't be seeing much of each other. *If at all.*

"Okay, when should I meet you?"

"Like an hour?"

"Okay, Patrick is coming too," she says, referring to my current stepfather, "just in case that husband of yours gets out of line."

I chuckle thinking about my stepfather that wouldn't hurt a fly. After Michael, my mother was wary about remarrying again, but Patrick Daniels was a breath of fresh air and my mother was smitten with his kind heart instantly. A man that would surely be the opposite of her previous husband. "Sure, Mom."

"Charley."

"Yes?"

"I'm beyond disappointed right now, but you know I'm always on your side, right?"

"Yes…" I say hesitantly, the tears forming immediately at the words "I'm disappointed." I hated disappointing my mother or *anyone* for that matter.

"Okay, I love you."

"I love you too." I hang up the phone and let out a breath when I feel his hands on my face.

"Well, that could have gone worse."

"My mom would never take anyone's side over mine. She may be disappointed but…she just wants me to be happy."

"Sounds like a good mom." He smiles, but I can see something behind his eyes that I can't quite detect. I didn't know much about Will's family—*you don't know much about Will in general, Charlotte.* I shake my head, trying to clear the thought that I'm jumping feetfirst into the unknown with a man I don't know other than in the biblical sense.

"She's the best. She will love you," I say, giving him a smile. "Eventually," I add as an afterthought.

———

"So, you're the man that has me battling midday Atlanta traffic so my best friend can give you a blow job. Pleased to meet you." Lauren struts into his office as if she owns it, before sticking her hand out for Will to shake.

I shoot a look at her. "Lauren!" I hiss.

"Oh, are we being coy now? What's the protocol for this because I don't know."

"It's nice to meet you too. I've heard a lot about you. Charley has only good things to say," he says and I can see her resolve weakening already. Despite Will's formalities, I can see a bit of amusement in his eyes. *Lauren made people comfortable even in the most uncomfortable situations. It was one of her most lovable qualities.*

"Flattery will get you nowhere," she says with an eye roll, though a smile plays at her lips. "Okay, so you ready?"

"Yes, but we have to go to my house."

"Whatever for?" Lauren asks with an eye roll. "I'm really not in the mood to mediate you and Matt. Isn't that your job?" Lauren points at Will before she chuckles. "Can I just say you're a really shitty counselor," she snorts.

"Lauren! Can you not?" I narrow my eyes at her. Normally I loved her sarcasm and quick wit, but right now I really wasn't in the mood. "I need to grab a few of my things before Matt purges everything I own."

"He's not going to do that, Charley."

"I don't know what he's going to do, but either way I literally have the clothes on my back and my purse. I just want some of my things. My mom and stepfather are meeting us there."

Lauren looks at Will and I shake my head. "He's not coming," I say, already knowing Lauren's thoughts.

"As much as I want to be there…" He looks at me as if he's rethinking his choices.

"No, baby, I'll be fine."

He puts his arms around me and pulls me into his arms before his hands move up to frame my face. "Do not get too close to him."

I nod. "I'll have people with me, he won't…he's not going to hurt me."

"You have one hour."

"What?" I ask confused at his time constraints.

"Until I'm coming in after you."

"No, Will. You can't."

"Technically I can, if I feel you're in danger. Do not test me, Charlotte, I mean it."

"Will, I will have three people with me."

"None of whom can protect you like I can."

My heart skips a beat at his words and the fact that he wants to love and protect me so fiercely. "One hour." I nod. He rubs my cheek and gives me a small smile.

"Call me if you need me, you know where I'll be."

"Parked at the end of my street?"

"Absolutely."

———

I sigh as we pull into the garage. We left my car at Will's office so I didn't have to drive and to prevent Matt from doing anything to my car. *Although he paid for it, it is mine. It was a gift and I'll be damned if I'll allow him to wreck it in a blind rage.*

"You ready for this?" Lauren asks, and I nod. "You and Will…

you guys together… I'm not sure what I was expecting, but that was intense."

"Is that a good thing?"

"I don't know yet." Her eyebrows furrow. "He looks at you like you're his reason for breathing. Like you're the center of his world. The way you look at each other…" she shakes her head, "I've never seen you like that with anyone."

"I've never felt this way about anyone." My eyes drift to my house, the one that I share with my husband, the man that I should be feeling *that way* about.

"You know I've got your back in there, right?"

I nod, before we make our way to the door. The first thing I hear when I cross the threshold is my mother *screaming. Shit! My mom beat us here.* "How dare you kick her out? What kind of man does that!?" she yells, and I groan.

"Mom!" I make my way into the living room to see my mother standing with her hands on her hips, a scowl crossing her features.

"I see you told your mother," he snarls at me.

"Excuse me? You called her. I was perfectly fine leaving her out of it for now," I bite back.

"Why do you even give a shit that I told you to leave? Don't you have a boyfriend to stay with?" he asks as he nurses a drink in his hands. *I wonder how many of those he's had. He can be an angry drunk every once in a while.*

"Is that all you're going to keep throwing in my face? Your hypothesis that there's someone else? Be a fucking man and own up to the problems in this marriage that *you* caused," I snap before I move up the stairs to our bedroom.

Forty-five minutes later, I've packed up two suitcases of clothes and shoes, a few pieces of jewelry, my favorite books, and my laptop. I'm moving toward the bedroom door when I pull one of my favorite items from my dresser. A music box that was my grandmother's. It looks like a snow globe but inside is a woman and a man that spin around when you wind it up. When I was younger, my grandmother would tell me it was my parents and I relished in the fantasy as my birth father died when I was a baby. I would stare at it for hours, pretending that it was my parents before me. When she died, I slept with it for a week. I press it to my chest before setting it in my open *Louis Vuitton* tote. I take one look around the room that has been my home for the last five years before making my way downstairs with Lauren, my mother, and Patrick behind me.

Matt is sitting in the same chair, one leg crossed over the other looking at me with disdain. "Did you get all the shit I gave you that you want to take?"

I don't dignify his question with a response. "I'm leaving. Whatever you don't toss, I'll come get later, I guess," I say sadly, "and I'll file in the morning."

"Who the fuck says you get to file?"

"Okay…?" I wince. "You can if you want." *At this point, I want out of this house before Will makes good on his word. We're dancing really fucking close to an hour.*

He snorts. "Of course, you don't care."

"Matt, you're drunk," my mother says. "Maybe we should call your mother…or Nathan."

"No," he hiccups, "just get her the fuck out of my sight. I don't know how she gets to just walk into my life and take everything from me and just walk out when she's done. Fuck you, you ungrateful bitch," he snarls at me.

"Now just wait a minute—" my mother interjects, not liking anyone taking that tone with me.

I interrupt her, knowing that there is really no reasoning with this highly intoxicated man. "Matt…it's not like that at all. You know it's not." My bottom lip trembles, hearing him spew those hateful words.

"I don't know shit. I don't even know who you are anymore.

The woman I fell in love with wouldn't do something like this," he says getting up and moving toward me. I back up wondering if he is going to get violent when Patrick pulls me out of the way. "You think I'm going to hurt you?" He chuckles. "You really don't know me, do you?" I sigh with relief, *I knew he wouldn't.* "After all this time you think I would lay a finger on you? Despite the fact that you ripped my heart out?"

"Ripped your heart out? Matt you barely tolerated me half the time!"

"I loved you," he says, his voice so low, "and you broke my fucking heart," he adds bitterly. "So, now I'm going to break yours." My eyes widen as he reaches for my tote that I left sitting on the table. I know what he's going to do and I move around Patrick to try and stop him but it's too late. Lauren and my mother scream for him to stop, knowing what that music box means to me, when it leaves his hands. As if in slow motion, I watch as it shatters against the wall. It splinters into a hundred pieces, much like my heart and the pain rips through me dropping me to my knees instantly, the ability to keep myself upright gone.

*How, how, how! Of all the things! How could he do that to me!?*

I'm vaguely aware of my mother screaming in the background before Lauren has me off the floor, moving me toward the back door, shielding me from the broken glass all over the floor. I don't know if I have any of my things when she puts me in the car. Everything around me is white noise, all of the blood rushing to my ears and drowning out the sounds of the world around me. My lip trembles as I think about the two people, outside of the globe, no longer holding hands as they spin in a circle.

"I'm going to go get your stuff, stay here," Lauren says, putting my purse in my hands. She fishes through my bag in search of my Blackberry and pulls it out. "We're leaving in five minutes, follow the white Lexus," I hear her say before she hands it back to me, and heads back into the house.

"Charlotte?" he rasps through the phone, his voice laced with concern. "Baby, are you there?"

"I—I'm here." I manage to get the words out.

"What happened? Why are you crying?"

"I'm o-o-okay," I stammer.

"Don't lie to me, Charlotte. What's going on?" The panic is evident in his voice.

I hear the door open and shut behind me and I imagine it's my things. "I'll call you right back." I don't wait for a response, before I hit the end call button as my door opens and my mother's arms engulf me. Her familiar scent is the only source of comfort I'm desperately clinging to.

"Oh, honey," I hear. "Patrick will make you a new music box, okay?" she says in my ear. "What an asshole." I look up at her and shake my head.

"I'm the asshole. I did this to him," I sob.

"No. No, honey, you didn't." My mother tucks a hair behind my ear and kisses my head. "Here," she says opening her hand and revealing the two tiny figures that were inside my music box. "They can put these in a new one."

"It's not the same," I whisper.

"I know. Your grandmother had that when I was a little girl," she says sadly, "but no one loved it as much as you did."

I swallow. "I want to be with Will now," I say not caring that I've said his name.

"Is that his name?"

I nod. "Yes, he's around the corner. He wanted to be here but… it would make things complicated."

"Matt knows him, doesn't he?"

"Yes," I say simply.

"Honey…who is it?"

"I can't tell you," I whisper.

"Yes, you can," she says back.

"He can get into trouble, and I've already wreaked enough havoc on his life…on everyone's lives," I say as I see Lauren moving back toward the car. She climbs in and my mother looks at Lauren wondering if I will say it in front of her. I nod, indicating that she already knows.

"Charley, if you can't tell me, who can you tell?" she asks, linking her pinky with mine like we did millions of times when I was growing up.

"It's our marriage counselor."

# CHAPTER
## Eighteen

**I**'M NUMB.

I feel nothing as we back out of my driveway, Lauren's back seat full of my belongings. My mother is in a state of shock by my reveal but she knows this isn't the time or place. I am still too emotionally wrecked by what happened to discuss it. With a promise that, "We will discuss this later, young lady," she had left. I open my hand, and the small metal people have left indents in my palm from squeezing them.

*How could he be that cruel? Of all the things he could break? He broke the thing that meant the most to me?*

"He's such an asshole, I can't believe he did that! I have a good mind to go back in there and rip his balls off!" Lauren screeches as she grips the steering wheel tightly.

I shake my head, although I know she's not looking at me. "I brought this on myself," I say softly, the tears falling down my cheeks. I don't think I could stop them if I tried. The feeling is so fresh and raw.

"That was so cruel and heartless. He knew your grandmother gave it to you and how much it meant to you."

"I left him, Lauren. People do awful things when they're hurt, and he thinks I left him for another man. Which I *did*."

*I'm not making excuses for him, what he did was the most heartless thing anyone has ever done to me. But isn't what I'm doing to him just as bad? No, Charley, you aren't doing anything to him. You both did this. You both wrecked this marriage. But on the other hand, you're the one saying "it's over," and you did betray him.*

I want to scream just to quiet the thoughts in my head.

"Did you though?" she asks.

I look at her, my eyes narrowing in question. "Did I what?"

"Leave him for another man."

"Uh…where exactly have you been?"

"I just mean if you were happy, if Matt treated you right, didn't ignore you for months and take you for granted, perhaps the affair with Will would never have happened. And it's not like you went looking for trouble. It just happened. You fell in love, no one can fault you for that."

"I'm fairly certain Matt's lawyer can fault me for it."

"Oh, fuck him," she says.

I'm silent again, the events of the day playing through my mind on repeat.

*New house. Sex with Will. Leaving Matt. Music box breaking. He thinks I'm a whore. I'm a whore.*

*I'm a whore.*

*I'm a whore.*

The thoughts are blaring in my head as the car slows to a stop. I look around to figure out why we've stopped when my passenger door opens and I'm being pulled into strong arms, and against a broad chest. My body calms immediately, feeling safe for the first time since I left his office. His arms wrapped around me is the only time I ever feel truly safe anymore. Physically, mentally, emotionally.

"What happened? If he touched a hair on her head, I'm going back there," he barks as I unbuckle my seatbelt and wrap myself around him. I know he's talking to Lauren but I pull back slightly and look at him, sure my eyes are glazed and red. His hand stops rubbing circles into my back before kissing me lightly. "What happened, baby?" he asks in a much different voice than he used with Lauren. I open my shaky hand slowly, and I'm almost afraid I'll drop them when he sees what I'm holding. His face falls, realization dawning on him. "Is this from—" he starts, having heard the story about the music box, and I nod.

"He's so mad at me," I whisper sadly.

"Asshole." His demeanor softens as his hands find my face and starts to pull me from the car.

"Wait—" Lauren says, and Will puts a hand up.

"I've got it. I'll bring her to your place later."

"Are you sure that's a good idea?"

"I need to be alone with her," he says and my eyes flash to his. I expect to see lust and desire but those feelings must be lying dormant within him because all I see is love and devotion in his eyes.

She looks out into the woods in front of us and then at me in frustration. "Do you want to do this? Charley, he can come to my apartment. I just don't think it's a good idea for you to go traipsing off with your boyfriend, five minutes after you leave your husband."

The tears stream down my face hearing my life spelled out so simply. *Go traipsing off with your boyfriend five minutes after you leave your husband.* I know she meant it more literally and not so metaphorically but is that what I'm doing? The house and marriage and kids talk? Should I take the time to let the dust from my marriage settle before I go jumping into this new life with Will?

I glance up at him and shake my head. *Maybe I am, but that's what I want.* For the past two years I've done everything that I thought would make someone else happy. *Well, look how that turned out. It's time to do what I want for a change.*

"Lauren, we won't be too late," I say simply before he pulls me from the car, shielding me from the world behind us.

Sliding me into his BMW, I watch as he talks to Lauren briefly before I see her pull off into the night. He gets in the car and I scramble across the console into his lap. "I love you," I say into his neck desperate to hear him say it back. Matt's words are still blaring in my head, and I'm hoping Will's words will eradicate them.

He pulls me out of his neck, the tears swimming in his eyes, and I'm shocked to see one travel down his face. "I'm so sorry," he says sadly.

"Why?" I whisper. *He's the last person that should be sorry.*

"Pushing you to do this, I—"

"No," I say putting a finger to his lips. "You didn't push me to do anything. This needed to happen whether you were in my life or not. I wasn't happy."

"You thought you were until I came along," he says sadly.

"Did I?" I cup his face. "Baby, look at me," I order and his eyes meet mine. "Do you love me?"

"More than anything," he says, urging me with his eyes to believe that despite what he's saying, he's not going anywhere. "It's just…the way he talked to you…what you will have to deal with in divorce proceedings…" He squeezes me tighter in his lap. "I hate that you'll have to go through that, and I can't even be with you." He strokes my closed fist which holds the people from my music box and I open it. "I'll fix it."

I shake my head. "You can't. He smashed it." The vision of it shattering against the wall into pieces plays over and over in my head.

"It was broken when you got home?" he asks, and I shake my head.

"He threw it at the wall when I was leaving." The tears form all over again.

His eyes widen as his thumbs find my cheeks wiping away my tears. "In front of you?"

"Yes."

He swallows hard and looks out the window as he tries to rein in his temper. I'm curious what's going through his head right now when I hear him say, "Stay with me tonight."

"What? I can't—"

"Yes, you can." He runs his index finger over my cheek gently.

"I don't think it's a good idea—" I start when he interrupts me.

"I don't think it's a good idea for us to be apart."

"I think that's the *smart* idea." I raise an eyebrow, questioning him.

He sighs. "Fine, then I'm coming with you to Lauren's."

I nod before changing the subject. "I told my mother it was you." I lay my head on his shoulder allowing him to resume stroking my back.

"Oh really? What did she have to say about that?"

I'm about to answer him when Will's cell phone rings through the Bluetooth in his car. I turn my head out of habit to see who's calling when I see my husband's name flash across the screen.

"Answer it," I urge, gesturing toward his phone.

"Charley…" he starts, and I shake my head.

"It'll be okay, please?"

He clears his throat before pressing the button to connect the call. "Dr. Montgomery."

The line is silent but only for a moment before his voice roars over the line. "She left me. She really left me."

"Did you think that you could have convinced her otherwise?" he asks, his voice even, clinical. *Dr. Montgomery is here now.*

"I don't know." I hear him hiccup. *I wonder how much of that whiskey he's put away since I left.* "I fucking hate her." The words wash over me when Will lifts my chin to meet his gaze. *I love you,* he mouths. He smiles and swipes his lips across mine quietly not caring that we are on speakerphone with my husband. "You there, Doc?"

"Yes," he says, still looking at me. "I can understand your anger, but what is it that you're looking for at this point? An apology?"

"I don't want anything from her, just *her.*"

"As that's so evident by your behavior."

"What the hell does that mean?" His voice is laced with anger and accusation.

"It means you took your wife for granted, Mr. Wells. She was screaming for your attention and you wouldn't give it to her. She felt unappreciated and unloved…so she left, but not before giving you chance after chance."

"So much for you being impartial. Why do you always take her side?"

He rubs his nose against mine and smiles again at me.

*Always,* he mouths.

"Mr. Wells, this isn't about sides. This is about you and Charlotte. Frankly, my opinion doesn't mean all that much. Your wife decided to end your marriage, so she did. There's nothing I could have done to change her mind." I shake my head back and forth at him.

"I have one of the best lawyers in Atlanta if she thinks for one second she's getting anything she has another thing coming."

I can feel him tense underneath me, and I sigh. "So, you're just going to leave her with nothing?" I wave my arms in front of his face, signaling that I don't want anything from him but he waves me off. "You'll be required to pay alimony if a prenuptial agreement was not in place."

"All that shit goes out the window if I can prove she cheated on me."

"Why are you so convinced that there's someone else?" My eyes widen at his words. *You're playing with fire, Will.*

"It's just a feeling, you know? She hasn't let me touch her in months. She barely looks at me."

"Those are all assumptions and hunches…do you have any proof? Phone records, pictures, letters, text messages?" *I guess this is smart in a way; we can know what I'm getting myself into by knowing ahead of time what he knows.*

"No, I just…it's just a feeling…you think you wouldn't know if the woman you were with for ten years was sleeping with someone else? She's just different."

"But so are you," Will interjects. "You've both admitted to being different people than when you first met. You met before you were finished growing…and sometimes in the process of growing, couples grow apart. It's not anyone's fault, it's just you were only meant to be together in one particular part of your lives. The Charlotte and Matt as adolescents were perfectly compatible…but not the fully grown adult versions of Charlotte and Matt."

"Can't you help me get her back?" His voice shakes and my lip start to tremble fearing Will's next words as he tries to remain unbiased.

His hand strokes my cheek before he shakes his head. "No," he says tersely. "No, Matthew, I can't. I can't convince her to give you another chance."

"Yes, you can. She listens to you. She trusts you."

*More than you could even imagine.*

"Mr. Wells, I have to go. If you'd like to set up a private session, please contact Vanessa. But I'm not going to go in circles with you right now when it's clear that you've had too much to drink. We will talk when your mind is clear." He doesn't even wait for the reply before he presses the end button on his car. He checks his phone to make sure that the call has really ended before he cups my face. "Are you okay?"

"I want to come with you…to your house. I want to be alone."

———

"I always tried to picture where you lived," I tell him as we pull into the garage of his townhouse on the outskirts of the busy city of Atlanta. His house isn't small, but it isn't ostentatious or what I would imagine for a bachelor pad. It sits on the end of a row of four houses, a one-car garage nestled underneath the three levels. The red brick is accented by white shutters, and a long staircase leads from the parking pad to the front door.

The garage door slides down behind us, shrouding us in darkness and I look around the small space, a vast difference from the four-car garage I'm used to.

"I know it's probably not what you're used to but…it's just me here." He seems to read my thoughts, and I grab his arm as he makes a move to get out of the car.

His eyes meet mine and I grab his face, pressing my lips to his. When I pull away, I see the hint of disappointment in his eyes. "Now it's you and me," I say, trying to convey as best as I can that he is all I need. "And a house full of babies," I add, my teeth finding my bottom lip at the mental images of tiny versions of Will and me running around.

A smile tugs at the corner of his mouth. "Should we go upstairs and start practicing?"

I almost melt into a puddle of need in his car upon hearing his words. "Yes, please."

He places a kiss on my lips before he's out of the car and opening my door so I can step out. I'm suddenly aware of a sharp pain in my hand, reminding me that the tiny people from my music box are still nestled tightly in my palm. I slide them into my purse and the movement catches Will's attention.

"I can't believe he did that." He sighs as he sets my small overnight bag down.

"You can't? You heard him, he fucking hates me." I repeat Matt's words as I move closer to him and into his arms. Wrapping his arms around me, he kisses the top of my head, then tilts my chin up to kiss my lips gently.

When he pulls away, he takes me on a short tour of the main floor. The house is beautifully decorated, leading me to believe that he probably had someone do it for him. The space warm and inviting, but still masculine. "Your place is beautiful, Will. Did you hire someone to do this?" I ask him, my hand running along the black granite countertops in his kitchen.

"I did. As much as I wanted a place full of IKEA furniture, my mother would have had a fit. She took care of it. Within two weeks of moving in, she had her decorator in here making all kinds of decisions. I eventually had to rein her in."

I nod, feeling a twinge of jealousy as I think about a woman decorating Will's place. *It's her job, Charlotte.*

"You can decorate the next one for us," he tells me, his hands finding my face, again as if he's read my thoughts.

I slide off my heels, my feet aching with the pressure. *As a matter of fact, my entire body aches.* The adrenaline from the day is wearing off, and I'm suddenly exhausted.

"Are you hungry?" He opens the refrigerator and I note how organized it is. I'm acutely aware that I haven't eaten much today, but to be honest, food is the furthest thing from my mind right now. I shake my head. "Baby, you have to eat something. We haven't eaten since that fruit and cheese at the house earlier."

Hearing him reference our house makes me feel warm

all over and I shoot him a smile as I walk toward him. "What house?" I ask him, my eyes dancing playfully.

He seems to understand what I want to hear, as he sets down the bottle of wine he had been in the process of opening. "Our house," he whispers.

I lunge into his arms, my legs immediately wrapping around his waist. "Say it again."

"*Our* house," he groans as my lips find his neck.

"Take me to your bedroom." My words come out breathy, my sex taking control of my voice as I rub my core against his torso. I pull away and his lips find mine as if they are drawn to each other like magnets. One hand threads through my hair and one holds my bottom, cupping it possessively as we begin to move. "I love you," I whisper against his lips. My breaths are labored as the tears become lodged in my throat and I'm unable to keep the emotion out of my voice as the events of the day come crashing down on me.

He sets me on my feet and I take a second to admire my surroundings. I've fantasized about being in this room a million times, but nothing could have prepared me for how I would feel actually being here. This whole room smells like him and my body immediately reacts—but not in the way I expected. My heart beats wildly in my chest, my nerves suddenly going haywire as I think about what I've done. *What I'm doing.*

*I'm in the bedroom of my lover, the man I left my husband for...*

*I left Matt.*

*I'm getting a divorce.*

"Are you okay?" he asks so quietly I almost miss it. I wonder if what has happened is setting in for him as well. I nod, the connection between my brain and mouth not working. He runs his hand down my back and finds the zipper of my pencil skirt. I'm still wearing my clothes from the session and I'm desperate to get them off of me. *Desperate to get this day off me.* The skirt pools at my feet and I'm brought back to the first time he pulled a pencil skirt off of me four months ago. His hands find the buttons on my blouse and he peels it off of me slowly. His lips brush over my right shoulder before he trails kisses across my chest to my left shoulder.

"Will," I moan, my nerves and anxiety slowly melting away under his skilled lips. I let my head fall back letting the feeling of his mouth on me take over my mind.

*There is so much shit I have to deal with, but not right now. Not in this moment. Right now, my only concern is this man with his lips and hands on me making me feel things I've only ever felt with him.*

*Love.*

*Passion.*

*Desire.*

*An overwhelming need to be possessed by another so fully.*

"You are so beautiful, and you are *mine*," he groans against my neck and only then do I realize my bra and panties have been ripped from me. I look down to see that I'm completely naked, and the tent forming in his pants in response. He brushes his thumbs over my nipples, making them pebble instantly. "Get on the bed," he says and I follow his instructions.

I lie on my back and my eyes follow him around the room as he peels off his clothing like a well-choreographed dance. He pulls off his tie, sliding it through the collar of his shirt, his eyes never leaving mine as he unbuttons his shirt. My heart races seeing his naked torso as if I'm seeing it for the first time. At the sight of his abs I lick my lips, longing to feel the hard ridges against my tongue. He unbuckles his pants letting them fall to the floor, his strong thighs on display dying for me to sink my teeth into them as I make my way toward the hard muscle standing proudly between his legs.

"See something you like, Charlotte?" His arms flex, the veins protruding in that sexy way as he slides his gray briefs down his legs, revealing his cock, hard and pointed directly at me.

"You are unreal, you know that?" I smile as he makes his way toward me, kneeling on the bed and crawling up the space of his California king bed until he's between my legs. He lowers his mouth, hovering over my mound that is quivering in anticipation of his touch.

"Is that so?" He presses a kiss to the skin and I hiss, dying for the stimulation. "So wet," he says, and I wonder if he's talking more to himself because his eyes haven't left my sex as if he's memorizing it. A moment later, he is working me over, kissing me as if it were my mouth. His tongue rubbing my clit the same way his tongue massages mine and I whimper as my hands find his hair. He pushes two fingers inside of me, hooking them around *that spot*, rubbing his fingers against it, all while his mouth never leaves my clit.

I whimper, my release imminent, as I shut my eyes feeling the first wave of my climax. "Will!"

His licks become more rapid, as he slides his fingers out of me, his nose continuing to stimulate my clit as he fucks me with his tongue. The bite of his stubble heightens my arousal, and I'm finding it difficult, not to clamp down on his face, keeping him in place and the consistent delicious prickle on my thighs. "I love the taste of your pussy." He pulls away, my orgasm dangling in front of me like a proverbial carrot.

I look down and I almost come at just the sight of him. The bottom half of his face is slick with my juices while his blue eyes are dark with pure, unadulterated lust. "I get to do this whenever I want now," he continues. "I can mark you and not have to worry about anyone seeing it but me."

"I'm yours," I moan out. "Mark me. I belong to you... I've

always belonged to you," I say, my eyes finding his between my legs. His hands move under my bottom and cup me, lifting me up to meet his mouth.

"Fuck," he groans as his eyes flutter closed. I expect to feel his tongue again but I don't. I hear him inhale and my mouth drops open as I realize it's his nose nestled between my legs, breathing in my scent. "I want to bottle your fucking scent," he says, letting my bottom drop to the bed. He trails kisses up my body and lies on top of me, his dick working on its own accord to find its way home inside of me. "I want to smell you all the time. Your pussy, your perfume, the way your hair smells…the way your skin smells… I need all of it. On me. All the time," he says into my ear as he begins to rock back and forth inside of me.

His hands find mine and he brings them up over my head, lacing our fingers. His face finds the crook of my neck as I wrap my legs around him. "Charlotte. Fucking. Pierce," he says, each word tied to a thrust. "You. Are. Mine."

"Yes," I moan. "Every part of me is yours." He continues to thrust. "Even my name," I whisper. He stops instantly, pulling his face out of my neck, looking down at me, and questioning what he knows I'm trying to say.

"What—but you've never…" I think he's struggling with the words not wanting to talk about my marriage while he's balls deep inside of me so I cut him off.

"No one has ever…" The intensity of his gaze is penetrating. I try to look away but I can't. "It's different with you," I say finally.

"You…want to take my name?" he asks and I see the surprise in his eyes. I hear it in his voice.

I bite my bottom lip and nod. "Yes, please," I whisper.

"Charley," he murmurs, both of us building toward our

release. "You don't know what that means to me. To know you want to be mine…in every possible way."

"Please!" I exclaim, both in response to his comment and the orgasm that is so close I can taste it. I squeeze my eyes shut feeling the telltale signals.

"That's it, baby. Come for me," he groans in my ear and I shatter, the fireworks shooting behind my eyes and exploding throughout my body. Goose bumps break out on my skin, the hairs standing on end as he pushes through his orgasm as well, my name on his lips, like a prayer. I'm still in a fog from my orgasm but I could have sworn I heard him say *Charlotte Montgomery*. He pulls out of me after a few moments and pulls me to his chest. I draw circles on his skin before dragging my lips across the same place that's covered in sweat.

"Did you call me Charlotte Montgomery?" I ask looking up at him with a smile. He tightens his hold on me and winks and I know I have my answer.

*Charlotte Montgomery*

My name has never sounded better.

# CHAPTER
## Nineteen

'M NOT SURE HOW LONG WE SLEEP, BUT THE SOFT BUZZING OF my phone rouses me. My eyes flutter open to find Will and I are both on our sides, clinging tightly to each other, his arms cradling my head to his chest protectively. I don't want to leave this peaceful, safe embrace but I need to see who is looking for me.

*Probably everyone I've ever met.*

I roll him to his back gently and try to pull away but his grip tightens around me. *Note to self—sneaking out of a bed with Will is no easy feat.*

"Baby, I have to get up."

"Mmm-mmm, you're too warm," he says sleepily and clutches me tighter rolling me to my back, immersing his face in my chest before sucking a nipple into his mouth. His arms wrap around me as he uses my other breast as a pillow. He lets me go with a pop and drags his face up to mine to kiss me deeply. "Hi, beautiful."

"Hi." I grin at the man in my arms, still in a sleepy haze, not wanting to let me go for anything. *Somewhere in there is a metaphor for our relationship.* "I have to answer the phone," I say kissing his nose. He finally relents and lets me go with a final squeeze of my ass. I giggle and find my phone in my purse. It's a little past nine at night, meaning it's been three hours since I officially walked out of my house setting the wheels in motion to end my marriage.

*The first step toward a new life, a new love, and a new Charley.*

I see that it was Lauren that had called and I press the button to return her call. Before I can even say hello, she's barks out, "So, are you just not coming here?" I can hear the irritation in her voice.

"Yes…I mean, eventually," I say looking at the naked man in bed staring at me like he wants to devour me again.

"Eventually? Charley…you've got to be smarter about this. Neither of you have filed, hell you're not even legally separated. If this gets back to Matt, his lawyers could argue that you had a fight and that's all this was. A Rachel and Ross 'we were on a break' of sorts."

I smile at her FRIENDS reference as I move back to the bed and climb in next to him, back into his arms. "Definitely not just a break."

"Yes, I'm aware, I have a car full of your possessions that would agree."

I wince. *Shit, I've dragged Lauren into this and just ran away with Will. Not that I could have stopped her. Lauren would walk through hell with me. I know her irritation is stemming from more than just the space I'm taking up in her car.* "Shit, I—"

"You should come here, Charley," she says, and I see the look of defeat Will is giving me. He can obviously hear her.

"Tomorrow. I just—" I look at Will, the love for me written all over his concerned face. "Tomorrow, Lo."

"And what do I do if Matt shows up here?"

"Why would he?"

"Hell if I know, but your husband is a wildcard right now. He's a man that's been hurt and he wants his woman back."

"I'm not his woman, Lauren. Not anymore."

"Fine. He wants his wife back. That you still *are*." Her voice is authoritative, almost motherly. I half expect her to call me *young lady*.

"Tell him I'm at my mother's…or a hotel. I don't know, Lauren." *I hate that I've put her in this position.* "I'm sorry for getting you involved."

She's silent for a moment. "I've been involved since college, Pierce." I smile hearing her words, and I don't even notice the tear trickling down my face until I feel his mouth on my cheek kissing the wetness from it. "Just be careful, and make sure you know what you're doing."

"I'll come tomorrow, okay?"

"I'll have wine poured."

"Thanks, Lo…for everything."

"No thanks necessary. You know I've got your back."

"I know." I smile into the phone before I hang up.

"I wish you could stay here with me." He pouts and it's literally the most adorable thing I've ever seen. I have a flash of a smaller human that looks exactly like him giving me a similar pout and my heart melts.

I cup his face and brush my lips across his. "I don't want to be away from you either, but I want to be smart about this."

"Maybe you can stay at the new house."

"Oh, because that's not obvious." I roll my eyes and I'm met with a pinch on my side.

"Don't roll your eyes at me," he growls before he pins me down and presses his lips to mine.

———

Later that night, I'm in Will's kitchen in nothing more than his t-shirt and my panties. Will had ripped my pants off the second I tried to put them on. I'm standing on my tippy toes as I reach for a bowl, having a taste for pancakes even though it is almost ten at night. He reaches over me and pulls the bowl down, giving me a boyish grin. Pretending to hand it to me, he snatches it away raises it high above his head out of my reach. I jump to reach and grab it but it's absolutely no use. I glare at him jokingly and cross my arms before he boxes me against the counter pressing his lips to mine. Setting the bowl on the counter, he reaches for me, snaking his hand under my shirt when I hear someone approaching.

"Oh shit, my bad, bro, sorry!" I look at the source of the voice and my mouth drops open when I realize who is in front of me.

*From the restaurant earlier this week—Andrew, his brother.* SHIT!

I wonder if Will has told him about me, but by the look on Will's face, I take it he has not.

"Don't you fucking knock?" he yells, pulling my less-than-clothed body behind him. I wonder if it's just because I'm barely clothed or because he doesn't want Andrew to put two and two together.

"Sorry, but we had plans to watch the game? I've been calling you for hours...no wonder you haven't answered," he jokes.

"Oh right...sorry. As you can see, tonight isn't good..." Will points to the door.

"So, you're not going to introduce me to..." He signals toward me even though I'm successfully hidden behind Will. Andrew attempts to come closer when Will takes a step back, backing me against the counter to shield me from his brother.

"Back off, Drew," Will growls.

No one says anything for a few seconds when I hear, "You've gotta be shitting me, bro. The woman from the restaurant? Your patient?" Andrew accuses. Will's shoulders sag with defeat having been caught when he turns to face me.

"Baby, go back to my room."

"Baby?!" his brother exclaims as he finally has a good look at me. "Aren't you married?"

"Andrew," Will barks at him before he turns back to me. "I'll be there in a few minutes, okay? Let me just get rid of my brother... that doesn't know how to knock." He glares at him. I nod and he places a gentle kiss on my lips. I leave the kitchen and thank God that there's a wall separating the kitchen from the living room because I'm absolutely about to eavesdrop.

"What the fuck, man? She's married, isn't she? The woman who's married to the guy that got so hammered the other night? The one that didn't take his last name when they got married? I never forget a hot woman, Will. Don't you dare lie to me and tell me it isn't the same one from the restaurant."

"Watch it," Will warns him.

"Is that why you put such an emphasis on calling Renee *Olivia's* friend? Because you didn't want to piss your married girlfriend off?"

"Keep your fucking voice down," Will snaps.

"She's your woman? The one you had to get 'home' to? Are you insane? She's married, Will."

"Her name is Charlotte, and…she's getting a divorce." Even though I can't see him, I can hear the agitation in his voice.

"Oh, for the love of God, Will. Are you kidding me with this? You're a therapist and you can't see through that bullshit? People do this shit all the time! Promise the world and that they'll leave their spouses for their mistresses or…what are you anyway? Are you her mistress?"

"Fuck you, Andrew. I was there when she asked for the divorce."

There's silence and I wonder if they've started whispering. I crane my neck to try and hear better. "How long has this been going on?"

"Five months."

"You've been fucking this married woman for five months. Are you out of your mind? A woman that pays you to counsel her and her *husband?* You're supposed to *fix* the problems in her marriage, not create them! Do you care about your license? Your practice? Your life? You're throwing all of that away for a piece of ass?"

I hear a chair skidding across the floor and then a bang against the wall. "Next time that will be your face, if you EVER say something like that again," Will growls. There's silence and then I hear him again. "I'm in love with her, Drew."

"Are you shitting me right now?"

"I didn't mean to…I swear. I tried…for months to stay away from her. I counseled her and her husband for months before I did anything…before I touched her. I couldn't take it another second. I had to have her."

"She wasn't yours to have!" Drew exclaims.

"She loves me too."

*More silence.*

"You are so fucked, you know that?"

My heart sinks. *Are we? Are Will and I just being naive that we think that we can get out of this with minimal damage?*

"It'll be fine once she's divorced."

"Tell me you aren't that naive! You can't be. You do this for a fucking living. I know I don't have to tell you that divorces take time, sometimes they want you to be separated first…does her husband know? Have any ideas?"

"No…her husband wouldn't notice her if she was on fire."

"So, she went looking for a man that would give her attention?"

*No! Of course not. Is that what people think? That Matt was ignoring me so I went looking to start an affair?*

"It's not like that."

"Then what's it like?"

"You don't understand." His voice is almost pleading. I don't know much about Will and his relationship with his brother, so I'm wondering if Andrew's reaction is judgmental.

"Clearly. Make me understand."

"I don't know what you want me to say. We fell in love."

"But she's your patient. She and her husband are your patients. You say she's getting a divorce, but is it official? Has she even filed before you have her here half naked in your house cooking dinner? Has she even fully moved out of her house before she came here and set up shop? Do you know how bad this could be for you? For your reputation? For your life? Does she know? You say she loves you but does she care that you've risked it all for her?" The questions are shooting out of him in rapid succession. I can barely keep up.

The tears are rolling down my cheeks fast, and before I know it my feet are moving forward and I'm back in Will's kitchen. "Of course, I know!"

Will's and his brother's heads both snap toward me and I see the hurt look in Will's eyes that are a direct reflection of my own. "Baby." He moves toward me and I stop him.

"I know that he's risked everything to be with me. I know that me being here is risky but…we just couldn't help it. I couldn't help it. I love him, more than…anything in the world. And I'm here because it hurts too much to be apart. We've had to be apart for months, and I don't want to do it anymore. He showed me what it feels like to be in love. Totally and completely in love," I say softly as I wipe the tears from my eyes. "I know how this looks but…I tried to get a divorce last year. I won't bore you with the details, but it just wasn't working. My husband begged. Got down on his knees and begged me for another chance and he came up with this idea to go to counseling. I was skeptical at first, but I agreed. And then I met Will." I look at him and give him a small smile. "I didn't mean to fall in love with you…" The tears start to fall again. "I'm sorry! I never meant to screw up your life." I back away slowly out of the kitchen, the sobs wracking my body. I don't make it three steps before I'm cradled in his arms, inconsolably crying into his chest.

I hear the faint sounds of his voice soothing me but my sobs are so loud it's all I can hear in my ears. He pulls my face out of his chest and cups my cheeks, wiping my eyes with his thumb. "Hey, why all the tears?" he asks, rubbing his nose against mine. "You know I don't feel that way."

"Hearing…all of that… I hate that I've done this to you."

"He doesn't understand, but he will soon, okay? He didn't know that we are in love, Charley." He rubs my back and hugs me tightly. "Come on, stop crying. You didn't do anything to me. We are in this together."

———

I don't remember falling asleep but the next thing I know my eyes pop open. His brother left moments after his intrusion, and Will brought me back to bed, holding me in his arms until we fell asleep. It's dark, only the light from the adjacent bathroom creeping out into the room. Will is no longer in bed next to me, and I'm immediately on the move to his bathroom. I see him in the shower, his balled-up fist against the tile next to his forehead that is resting against it. I pull off his shirt and my panties and climb into the shower with him. I move forward and touch his shoulder, pressing a kiss to his shoulder blade. "Why didn't you wake me?"

"I thought you needed to sleep…and I needed to think."

He still hasn't faced me so I pull on his bicep in an attempt to get him to look at me. "Think about what?" I ask, immediately fearing that his brother's words are resonating with him.

"Not what you're thinking, baby," he says, turning around. He must have heard the insecurities threaded through my words. "No matter what happens…" he starts, "being with you…us being together is the most important thing to me, Charley." He rubs his wet nose against my dry one. *I'm sensing a "but," and I don't like it.* "That being said…maybe we need to do a better job of lying low, at least until your divorce is finalized."

"How?" I ask, although I know what he's going to say.

"You can't stay here." I look down and nod once. "You know I want you here all the time. But if we want to get out of this with minimal damage, we need to create some space. If Matt finds out then we deal with it, but right now he doesn't know about me which means we—you have the power here. If he somehow gets proof…things become difficult."

I nod. "So, I can't see you at all?" I ask, my heart constricting at the thought of being away from Will for so long. "Can't we continue having sessions?"

"I might be able to throw in some 'post-marital' sessions. And I can meet with Matt as well… I can't imagine not seeing you for a month, but—"

"A MONTH?!" I exclaim.

"That's how long it takes for an 'uncontested' divorce to be final in the state of Georgia starting with the day you file and the papers are served."

"I'm filing tomorrow," I say rubbing my forehead. *I need these wheels to go into motion ASAP.* "Fuck, I need a lawyer, and you heard Matt. He's got a great lawyer. I—"

"I'll ask my father." *I remember him telling me that his father is a lawyer, but is that a good idea? Involving his family?*

"Is that a good idea?" I ask, voicing my concerns. "Not only would that raise some red flags to Matt but…won't your father have a lot of questions? Certainly not how I would like to start them off meeting me," I say.

"Oh, because your mother has the best impression of me?" he asks. raising an eyebrow at me.

"Touché." I roll my eyes, thinking about the inevitable line of questioning that will happen when he meets my mother, starting with, *What the hell were you thinking!?*

"I'm not going to ask my father to represent you; just if anyone in the firm can take your case. But he is my lawyer, so in case I need him, it wouldn't hurt to keep him in the loop."

"I'll protect you from Matt as best I can. If it comes down to it, I wouldn't want you to lose everything over me."

"I'd give it all up for you," he whispers against my mouth.

"You'd eventually resent me."

"No, I wouldn't…never, but we aren't even near this bridge, baby. All we have to do is make it one month, as long as Matt doesn't contest it."

"One month," I repeat, "and then we can start the rest of our lives together."

———

I don't know how long I've been awake staring at the ceiling, but it was dark when my eyes first opened, tears leaking from the corners and streaking down my face as I think about how Will and I have to be apart.

*He did say we could maybe work around it, but we certainly won't be seeing each other three times a week like I'm used to…and even that isn't nearly enough time in the first place.*

As the night has turned into early morning, the anxiety creeps in. Will reaches for me when the early morning turns to 8 a.m., his hands parting my legs and he slips inside, holding me…loving me…worshipping me. We make love for the better part of an hour, savoring every part of each other before we enter into a period of absence. The tears stream down my face, delaying my orgasm. "It'll be okay, I promise," he whispers. "We'll still talk. You have your Blackberry."

"Promise me once it's official we'll be together."

*What if he meets someone else? Or…decides it's too much? No… Charley, you've got to relax. He bought you a house and he wants a family with you. Babies—with you.*

The thought calms me as he traces kisses along my face and whispers, "Always…forever…the second it's official…"

I wrap my arms around him as the final moments of our love-making come to a close. I feel his climax rip through him and I'm a beat behind. I've never cried during an orgasm…*well, a few times with Will but that was because I was so overcome with pleasure.* But I've never come with tears in my eyes out of sadness. I can't seem to stop them as I say goodbye to the man I love more than anything.

*Even if this is just "see you later," I hate it.*

We get dressed in silence and soon my phone is ringing, letting me know that Lauren is here to pick me up. His hands wrap around me as I end the call.

"I love you."

"I love you too." I sniffle.

"A month is nothing," he says and I raise an eyebrow at him. "In comparison to the lifetime we'll have together?"

My heart melts hearing his words and I reach up to pull him into a hug. "Call me later?"

"Of course, and who knows…we can probably still see each other…just file and give it a week or two to settle."

I smile. "Okay."

"I have something for you," he whispers, and I eye him curiously. He reaches into his pocket and pulls out a small but very recognizable red box; the gold *Cartier* script causes my heart to skip a beat. My eyes widen and he smiles. "Not an engagement ring…yet." I open the box and see the familiar ring and I look up at him, overcome with shock. Matt had hated this collection, stating it wasn't classic like the *Love* Collection, of which I have a dozen pieces. I remember the first time I bought a "Nail" ring for myself since my husband refused. I had been so excited but when I got home, he told me it was tacky and too edgy for me, and to take it back. The tears run down my face that he's bought me the same exact ring I returned two years ago.

"I don't think it's tacky… I think it's you." He smiles.

"Will you put it on?"

My left hand still wears the two rings of another man, so he slides them onto my right ring finger before placing a kiss on it. "I promise we'll be together."

"Okay," I say, giving him one final hug and pressing my lips to his. "See you later."

I force myself to keep walking and not look back. I have to push myself to put one foot in front of the other, out of his house, and toward Lauren's car. Before I know it, we are out of his neighborhood and moving away from Will and my heart that I've left with him.

# CHAPTER
## *Twenty*

"**H**AVE YOU LEFT THIS BEDROOM ALL DAY?" LAUREN ASKS AS she stands in the doorway of the guest room in her apartment. I sit up and run a hand over my eyes trying to pull myself out of the final moments of my second nap of the day. "Are you just planning to sleep the next month?"

"It's been one day, give me a break," I whine as I fall back into the pillows. *Although the idea of sleeping through the next thirty days doesn't sound like a bad idea. I wouldn't mind fast-forwarding through this time without Will. Besides, I am mentally exhausted.*

It had been one day since I left Will's apartment and I'm already miserable. True to his word, Will had already found a lawyer that worked at his father's firm to represent me. I'll be meeting with him tomorrow to draw up papers and then they will be served to Matthew.

"A month is not that long, Charley." I glare at Lauren and she shoots her hands up in defense. "I just mean it might give you some clarity. The space might do you good! Give you some time in between Matt and Will. It's not healthy to jump from one relationship to another so quickly. You're coming off of an eight-year relationship and a five-year marriage, let yourself decompress. He will be there after you've gotten yourself together."

"Since when did you become so wise?" I grumble.

"I just don't want you jumping feetfirst into this relationship with Will and…have it blow up in your face."

"It won't! I love him, Lauren. You know I do."

"You loved Matt too at one point."

"That's not fair." I shake my head at her and pulling my covers over my face as I try to block out the world—and Lauren's logic.

"I don't know what about this situation makes you believe that life is fair," she says sitting down next to me and yanking the covers from over my head. "Come on, let's go get margaritas."

"What about my attire leads you to believe that I *want* to leave this apartment?" I say, throwing her sarcasm back at her.

"Your love for tequila? Come on, Charley…you haven't left this bed in almost thirty hours except maybe to…shower? Tell me you've showered."

"Fuck off, I've showered." I frown before turning my back to her to face the wall. I feel the covers pulled from me again and sent off the bed, and I sit up shooting her a glare. "I don't want to."

"I don't give a shit. You're staying at my house you have to do what I say."

I roll my eyes and hop out of bed. "What are we in, grade school?" I say before heading into the bathroom to try and fix the rat's nest that is my hair.

———

I can't escape the giggles that come out of me as Lauren and I take on our second pitcher of margaritas. *Okay, maybe I did need this. Time with my best friend and tequila and tacos. Three of my favorite things.* "So, who's bigger?" Lauren asks and I almost spit out the drink in my mouth.

"Lauren!" I say, my cheeks getting hot, and I don't know if it's from the alcohol or my best friend's line of questioning.

"What? If you can't tell me, who can you tell?" She leans forward urging me to answer her.

I look around, to make sure no one is listening. "Will…by a long shot."

"It's been so long since I've gotten any. I think I've forgotten what it feels like," Lauren complains as her head finds the table.

"Well, I'm about to be in the celibacy boat right along with you."

"Hot Doc is going to find a way to see you over the next month, don't be so dramatic!" I giggle at her nickname for him.

"That's the opposite of trying to lie low, Lauren. And didn't you say that I should let things settle before I go jumping into another relationship... I love Will more than anything, and I want to be with him," I say, swirling the straw in the pale-colored drink in front of me. "But I would be lying if I didn't say I might need some time to breathe. I don't want to go from being reliant on one man to reliant on another." I'm silent as I look out at the traffic passing by. "I hate the idea of being alone." I wince, hearing myself say the words out loud for the first time. "And I hate that I feel that way. Yes, it stems from Michael and...all of the issues with my mother and her multiple husbands but I'm twenty-eight."

*Fuck, I'll be twenty-nine next week. Happy fucking birthday to me.*

"I'm an adult, I should be able to...stand on my own two feet." I feel myself on the edge of a breakthrough...or a breakdown.

"Tequila: the best truth serum," Lauren says, raising her hand up toward the waiter who I assume is behind me. "We're going to need another one of these," she says, pointing at our pitcher that is nearly empty. "Charley, everyone needs to feel safe and loved and protected. There is nothing wrong with needing someone. Hell, we all need someone to lean on sometimes."

"Please don't quote old-school songs to me right now."

Lauren's mouth drops open and she smiles. "That's a great song."

"If you start singing, I will get up."

"Lean on meeee," she starts and my eyes widen as I look around at the people around us.

"I'm serious, Lo."

She continues and I put a hand over my eyes trying not to make eye contact with anyone who might be watching. Her voice gets louder with every line. "Lauren…God, what did I start?" I say, rolling my eyes.

She looks around, her voice getting quieter. "Okay, I'm done. Thank you, you've been a beautiful audience."

I sigh and shake my head. "I can't take you anywhere."

"I'm serious though, Charley. No one is faulting you for needing someone to be there for you. I just don't want you to get hurt by moving too quickly."

"I feel like it's inevitable though, right? I cheated on my husband. Why do I get to walk away from this scot-free?"

"Because although you did something bad, you're not a bad person."

*Is it bad that I need to hear that? As annoying as she can be, Lauren always knows what to say.*

"And Matt isn't totally innocent in all of this anyway," she continues. "I mean come on, how many times did he make you feel unimportant…unloved…"

"Is that a reason to cheat though?" I ask, suddenly doubting all of my decisions of the last four months. "Maybe I should have just left Matt the second the feeling to fuck Will was getting too great."

"Look, you and I both know this is bigger than the fucking. If you just fucked Will once or twice, you could probably tell Matt, he'd be mad and maybe not trust you for a while, but he would get over it. You guys could move forward. You didn't end your marriage because you cheated on your husband and you just couldn't live with the guilt. You ended it because you fell in love and you can't live without another man that's not your husband." She shrugs. "It sucks, but it's the reality of the situation. This is so much bigger and deeper than the physical act of penetration."

I sigh letting her words sink in as she gets up to use the ladies' room. I pull out my Blackberry and my mood is instantly lifted when I see a text from Will.

**Will: I wish I was coming home to you tonight.**

I press the green button on my phone to place a call, needing to hear his voice more than our flirty text banter.

"Beautiful." He answers the phone after the first ring.

"Hi," I say soft and breathy and I hear him groan over the phone.

"Should I have my dick out for this conversation?" he asks, and I smile. The idea of phone sex flashing through my mind.

"Where are you?" I ask, trying to calm my libido that has been sparked both by the alcohol and the mental image of Will naked.

"In my office…I have a session in a few minutes. Where are you?"

"Getting margaritas with Lauren," I hiccup.

"I see, and how many of those have you had?" he asks, but I can hear the humor in his voice.

"A lot."

"How are you getting back to Lauren's?"

"An Uber… I don't think either of us are in any place to drive," I giggle.

"If she's anything like you, then no, neither of you should be driving." I giggle again. "I mean it, Charlotte."

"I know. I won't, I promise."

"Good. Now go have fun with Lauren and call me later, okay?"

I nod, my drunk mind not recognizing that he can't actually see me. "Yes, okay!" I say.

He chuckles. "I love you."

"I love you too."

"Who do you love?" Lauren asks, coming around the table and sitting across from me.

I hang up the phone and give her a look. "Who do you think?"

An hour and another pitcher later, Lauren and I have gotten

the bill. I have to fight her to let me pay. Since I'm staying at her apartment it is the least I could do. The waiter comes back to the table and I take the bill from him, expecting to see the familiar receipt under my card when I just see my card and I look up at him confused.

"Ma'am, I'm sorry, but your card has been declined."

"What?" My vision is a little blurry, but I know I could find my American Express Platinum Card in my sleep. I put the card close to my face and sure enough it's the one I was trying to use.

"There must be some mistake, this card has no limit." I smile. "Can you try again?"

"Yes, ma'am," he says before walking away.

"So weird." I shrug as I take the last sip of my drink.

A few minutes later, he comes back. "Still didn't go through, ma'am. Do you have another card?"

"That's impossible. I use this card all the time. Okay, sorry. Not your problem. Let me grab you another one." I hand him my Chase card and surely enough he's back within moments telling me the same. "Are you sure your machine is working? I've never had any issues with these cards before."

The waiter, who probably isn't older than twenty looks at me, the annoyance evident. "I…don't know. Maybe? I can try another machine?"

I sigh. "No, it's okay. Umm, here," I say, pulling out my bank card.

"That's so weird? Why would none of your cards be working?" Lauren asks, and I shake my head, confused when he comes back with the same growing scowl to tell me this card has been declined too. At this point I'm furious.

*What the fuck?*

"Just let me pay, and then we can figure out what's going on?"

I nod as Lauren pays the check and my heart sinks when he

comes back with the receipts for her to sign. "Why would—" I start when I have a sobering thought.

*Matthew has access to all of my cards.*

"He wouldn't," I say and Lauren's eyes widen, as she understands where my mind is going.

I pick up my phone and dial the number on the back of my card. "Thank you for calling American Express, can you please tell me who I have the pleasure of speaking with?"

"Charlotte Pierce."

"Hello, Ms. Pierce, what can I help you with?"

"I—ummm, I'm trying to use my card and it won't go through," I chuckle. "Very embarrassing…can you tell me what's going on?"

"Of course, Ms. Pierce. I do apologize for the inconvenience, can you please provide me with the last four digits of your social security number?

"Three zero one four."

"And the last four digits of the card you are calling about? I do see a few different cards here."

"Four zero zero five."

"Okay, yes, I see here that the account holder has cancelled this card. I see a notation that you have misplaced your card and we are actually in the process of sending you another."

"That's…not possible. I'm looking at my card right now."

"We received a call earlier today from the cardholder and we were told to cancel this one."

"That's impossible. I'm the cardholder."

"Well…can I place you on hold, for a moment?" she asks.

"Don't bother," I say. "Just tell me, this cardholder, was it Matthew Wells?"

"I'm not at liberty to say who called, ma'am."

"Unbelievable," I chuckle. "Thank you for all of your help." I hang up the phone and look at Lauren. "That asshole cancelled all of my credit cards."

"Do you have any cards in your name?" she asks.

"Yes, one I think…" I rub my forehead. "Unless I cancelled it. What the fuck?" I growl. "So, what, he's just going to take everything?" I ask. "I mean…I guess I can't expect him to be supporting me. I just thought he'd at least tell me first. Am I not allowed that courtesy?" The tears well up in my eyes as I think about the fact that I don't have a dime to my name. I haven't had a job the entire time we've been married, and what little bit of savings I had going into this marriage I put in our joint account. Then the light bulb goes off in my head. *Joint checking account. Well, if that's how you want to play things, Matt.*

———

I crawl my way into bed after we get back to Lauren's with the multiple margaritas and shots I consumed roiling in my belly and pull out my Blackberry. "I was wondering when I would hear from you," he says sleepily, and only then do I notice that it's well past 1 a.m.

"Shit, I'm sorry it's so late." I lie on my back, my eyes fluttering closed as the alcohol prohibits me from keeping them open.

"Don't be. I always want to hear from you, *any*time. Did you have fun with Lauren?"

"Yes…I wish you could have been there."

"Me too, baby."

*I debate telling him about my plan for tomorrow but decide against it, knowing that he would probably offer to give me anything I need.* "So, will you be at your father's office tomorrow?"

"When you meet with your lawyer? It's probably not the best idea."

"Does your father know?"

"He knows that you are a…close friend of mine. I think he's probably connected the dots. I just wanted you to file before I tell him everything."

"Everything meaning?"

"The house, you, me…*everything*."

"Your family isn't going to like me very much are they? If your brother was any inclination," I murmur.

"They'll love you once they meet you and get to know you."

"Mmmhmm," I say, feeling myself on the precipice of sleep.

I hear him tell me he loves me, and it's the last thing I remember before sleep finds me.

⸻

Sitting across from my divorce lawyer—John Cromack Esq., of Meier, Carr, and Cohen—I sign my name on the dotted line. *I had no idea that filing for divorce would be that simple.*

"This is only the first step, Ms. Pierce. Once your husband is served these papers, is when the hard part comes like the negotiations, the back and forth…deciding what it is you both think you should be walking away from this marriage with. Ms. Pierce, Georgia is a 'no-fault' state so we don't necessarily need to prove that there was any fault. We are just citing irreconcilable differences. The partners want this to be at the top of my priority list, so it is. You must have some friends in high places."

*Or boyfriend's father in high places. I pray to God that I don't come face-to-face with said boyfriend's father while I'm here.*

"Now, there was no prenuptial agreement, and because you haven't worked for the entirety of your marriage you could be entitled to some hefty alimony payments, as well as half of the assets acquired during your marriage," he tells me and I shake my head.

"I don't want half of everything. I told you what I wanted."

"Yes, your…" he looks down at his notes, "Audi Q3, and certain gifts that Mr. Wells has given you over the course of your marriage. Gifts are a given, Ms. Pierce." He removes his glasses and tosses them across the table. "Frankly, you will probably be leaving this marriage a very wealthy woman, or at the very least, extremely comfortable. Are you familiar with the phrase 'just and equitable division of property, assets, and debts'?"

"I can guess what that means."

"No judge will grant your husband everything, after you haven't worked, thereby leaving you destitute. To be honest, you may be granted your home, even though he purchased it and makes the monthly mortgage payments. Any property that you bought with money that has been earned during the marriage is community property. Each party's income during the marriage is community property. Fortunately for you, Ms. Pierce, you had no income. So, you have nothing to lose from this divorce, only to gain. Anything that was bought during your marriage, belongs to you both. It does not matter what paycheck was used—and in this case all major purchases were done by your husband, correct?"

"Yes."

He nods. "But these are all things that will be discussed once he is served the papers. In the meantime, since you don't have access to your credit cards, do you have any idea what you are going to do for money? Do you have access to your joint checking account?" *It's like this man can read my mind.*

"Yes."

"I see. And are you going to do something about that?" he slides his glasses back on and looks at me from over the top of them. I bite my bottom lip, looking to the side, out the window, as my mind drifts to Will.

*Is he in a session? Is he thinking about me?*

I talked to him this morning, after I woke up with my phone next to my ear alerting me that I probably fell asleep with him on the phone. But we didn't talk for long, as I was rushing out the door to meet my lawyer.

"Yes."

"I would say that's wise. How much are you considering taking?"

"I don't know, what do you think? You're my lawyer."

"Well, based on his records," he says, looking down at my husband's bank statements, credit card statements, investments, stocks, and bonds. "I would say fifty thousand is a nice round number."

I let out a breath and raise my eyes to the heavens. "That's a lot. I was thinking more like ten?"

"Ms. Pierce. You probably only have one shot at this. Once he realizes that you've taken money, he will probably at least attempt to move it or perhaps freeze the account so that neither of you have access until the divorce is finalized. Do you know if he is the primary account holder? Or did you open it together when you got married?"

"We opened it together."

"Perfect." He slides the papers across the table that my husband will be served within the hour. The words *Summons* and *Petition of Divorce* stand out at me as if they're written in bright red, bold print and not basic black print. "This is your copy. His copy is on his way to him as we speak."

"You are serving him at work?"

"Yes, Ms. Pierce, we are very discreet though, and we are aware that he has his own office."

I nod, hoping that he's alone and thereby not embarrassed in front of his very conservative partners. "I have another question," I say taking a deep breath.

"Yes, Ms. Pierce?"

"Well, anything we talk about here is confidential correct?"

"Yes, ma'am. Nothing you say here can be spoken outside of these four walls. Attorney-client privilege."

"Okay," I breathe out as I prepare myself to open up another can of worms. "Matthew believes that I'm having an affair."

"He believes…? Or he knows for a fact?"

"He believes. He doesn't know anything."

"So, there is something to know then…"

"Yes."

"I see," he says grabbing a pen from his jacket pocket and jotting down some notes on his memo pad. "Once? Twice?" I bite my bottom lip and he raises an eyebrow. "More than twice?" I nod. "Okay, better question, how long has this affair been going on?"

"Five months," I whisper.

"Are you still engaging in this affair?"

"We decided to stop…until after my divorce is final."

"That's not exactly what I asked. Maybe you two aren't seeing each other but are you still communicating with him?"

"Yes," I tell him honestly. "Matt doesn't know, and I plan to keep it that way. But…say he finds out…what does that mean?"

"Well, Ms. Pierce, due to the 'no-fault' divorce clause, the court does not consider which spouse 'caused' said divorce and given that you are filing and not him it has nothing to do with how property is divided. The court may consider your conduct if you're demanding certain assets but it won't affect much else. Are you sure that he doesn't know?"

"No…he has no idea."

"You've been having an affair under your husband's nose for four months and he didn't notice? Damn, no wonder you're getting divorced," he says, leaning back in the chair.

I laugh nervously at his humor, before my lips form a straight line and my eyebrows rise to my hairline. "You don't know the half of it."

―――

It's been an hour since I left my lawyer's office, and I've been sitting in the parking garage ever since, worried that I don't have the ability to operate a vehicle yet, as I hold my copy of the summons with shaky hands.

*I'm ending my marriage. I'm getting divorced. I'm supposed to be going to the bank and withdrawing a lump sum of money from our joint account. As angry as he makes me, I can't bring myself to do it. Regardless of the fact that he's attempted to leave me with nothing, taking money from him just feels…wrong. No, Charley. This is money that you deserve. Stop being such a wuss. Take what's yours!* I try to quiet the voices in my head as I hear my phone whirl to life.

"Hi, Matt," I say quietly. I pull my Blackberry out, remembering my lawyers warning that I should be recording all conversations with Matt going forward. I press record as I hear his words move through my Bluetooth.

"Are you out of your fucking mind?" he growls so low and menacing my blood runs cold.

"What—what are you talking about?"

"Don't play fucking stupid, Charlotte. You had papers delivered to my office? DO you have ANY idea how that makes me look? Everyone has been staring at me for the past hour! They know that I was served, you heartless bitch!"

His harsh words sting. "I…I didn't know they were going to serve you at work."

"Why the hell did you file at all?" he snaps.

"I told you I was going to," I snap back. "What, did you think I was kidding? Or did you think that you could bully me into coming back by cancelling my credit cards and attempting to leave me with nothing?"

"Didn't think it was fair that you got to throw your little temper tantrum on my dime," he snarls.

"It's not a temper tantrum, Matt. If so, it's an expensive one as the lawyer is billing me four hundred and fifty dollars an hour." Not one hundred percent true. I think the case is being handled pro-bono thanks to Will, but I'm sure they see me as a cash cow based on my circumstances.

"I am going to fight you, Charley. On everything. Every single fucking thing. If you think that I am just going to roll over and accept these bullshit terms just because I didn't fuck you every night you have another thing coming. You aren't entitled to half of everything just because I didn't have the foresight to make you sign a prenuptial agreement. If I knew you were such a vindictive, spiteful whore, trust me, I would have. I will never forgive you for this, Charley. Just remember, karma is a fucking bitch," he says before I hear a click.

I'm shaking as I turn the recorder off on my Blackberry. Tears well in my eyes, and as much as I want to break down, I can't.

*There is something I need to do first.*

# CHAPTER
## *Twenty-One*

WITH A CERTIFIED CHECK FOR FIFTY THOUSAND DOLLARS IN my purse from our joint checking account, I make my way to a different bank and deposit it. I'm sitting in the parking lot, the thoughts of what I just did running through my head. Before I took Matt's phone call, I did feel bad about it, but after hearing his words—his hatred toward me, and remembering the fact that he attempted to manipulate me into staying by cancelling my cards, I didn't think twice about taking what was rightfully mine.

*Go ahead, Matt, be pissed. Make my fucking day. Not a court in America will make me give it back. But what am I even going to do with that much money? Maybe I should donate it? Or maybe take a trip. A divorce-moon. Go see the pyramids in Egypt, go swim in the Mediterranean Sea…* My thoughts are interrupted by my phone ringing.

"Hello?"

"Ms. Pierce?" I hear and recognize my lawyer's voice.

"Yes, Mr. Cromack?"

"I assume you've been to the bank?"

"Yes, sir," I whisper.

"Splendid. I've just heard from your husband's attorney. I will be in touch with you about a meeting by the end of the week."

*That soon?* "The end of the week?" I whisper.

"Yes, ma'am. Is that a problem? The sooner we start, the sooner we can end it. Frankly, Ms. Pierce, they want to play hardball, but this is going to be a pretty open-and-shut case."

"Do you think we can get this resolved sooner than a month?"

"I do think the negotiations and the agreement will be done within that time period, but you still need to wait the full month for the divorce to be final. I doubt we will need to go to trial."

I sigh. "Fine."

"This boyfriend of yours waiting for you?"

"You could say that," I say.

"Lie low, Ms. Pierce. You've got the upper hand, don't let your hormones ruin that."

"I know."

"Good. I want no surprises, understood?"

"Yes."

"So, there's nothing I need to know before I meet with his attorney?"

"No."

"You're sure?" I furrow my brow as I wrack my brain for anything that Matthew and his lawyer may be able to use against me. "Ms. Pierce?" he pushes and I assume he's taking my silence as guilt or withholding information.

"Yes, I'm sure!"

"Alright, I'll be in touch."

———

"God, you are so beautiful," are the first words out of Will's mouth when our Skype connects. I smile and reach my hand to the screen as if it'll be the warm skin of his face and not the cold hard screen of my computer.

"Hi…" I shoot him the smile that's only reserved for him and I'm granted a smile to match.

"So, you filed."

"I did." I nod.

"How do you feel?" He cocks his head to the side sexily.

"Free."

"I'm really proud of you. I know it's not easy. Especially being together for so long."

"In the end, it really wasn't that hard. Even if you weren't in my life…" I recall my conversations with Matt earlier today and I know without a shadow of a doubt that any man that thought it was okay to talk to me like that, regardless of the situation, is not the man for me.

*My mother would have a fit. Not that my mother has provided me with the best examples of how a man should treat a woman, but I know one man that wouldn't dare ever talk to me like that. And I'm looking at him.*

"A lot happened today…"

"Oh?"

"I don't want you to panic."

He leans closer to the screen, one eyebrow raised. "That's not the way to start things off."

"Okay, so I told my lawyer about you."

"About me specifically?"

"No, just that I had an affair… I'm *having* an affair."

"And what did he say?"

"Not much…just to lie low."

"Okay, why would I panic about that?"

"I'm working up to that."

"Mmmhmm," he says staring at me skeptically.

"Matt cancelled my credit cards."

"He did WHAT?" His eyes widen.

"Are you that surprised? I mean of course I was caught off guard in the moment when I was trying to pay for dinner last night, but I'm really not all that shocked."

"So, he didn't even tell you?"

"No."

He runs his hand through his hair, visibly agitated. "Do you have any card that is in your name?"

I shake my head. "No," I whisper. "I thought I still had one, but I cancelled it a while back."

"So, he has access to all of your cards."

"I guess that's what happens when you don't work," I say sadly. "Note to self, don't do that again," I muse aloud.

"*I* would never do that to you," he says, and I realize how that must sound to the man that wants to marry me and share a life with me.

"I'm sorry, I didn't mean it like that, I just…"

"I get it. I'm going to have to pay for some of his mistakes." He shrugs sadly.

"NO!" I shriek. "No, I'm just…"

He interrupts me. "Going to be more guarded."

"I would say, more careful."

"You don't need to be careful with me, but I'll prove that to you. I just hope you give me a chance to."

"Of course, I will."

"You say that now, but it's easy to think that I'll do to you what he's done."

I bite my lip, not knowing what to say. *Does he think he's capable of doing that?*

"I think…I just want to know that I can stand on my own two feet. And that has nothing to do with you. I would think as a counselor you can understand that."

"I do, and I admire it. I'm proud of you, Charley. Your strength is remarkable."

"You're shrinking me," I groan before giving him a smile.

"What else? Wait, first, what are you doing about money? Are you okay? Do you need money?" *I knew that was coming, and as much as I don't want to lean on him financially, it warms me that he wants to take care of me.*

*God, Charley, you've really got a type, don't you?*

"No." I smile. "I don't, but thank you… I withdrew money from our joint account."

"A lot?"

"More than I initially wanted, but he called me before I did it and pissed me off."

"How much?"

"Fifty thousand…it's what my lawyer suggested."

"It's what I would have suggested as well. Baby, why didn't you call me?"

I shrug. "I don't know. I'm already your problem in so many ways," I chuckle. "I didn't want to add financial burden to the list."

His brows furrow in anger and he leans forward. "Don't you ever let me hear you say something like that, again. You're not a problem at all. I love you and I want to protect you and take care of you. Let me."

"Okay." I nod, a feeling of warmth washing over me as I hear his words. "So anyway, he called," I say softly, "after he got the papers."

"How did that go? I hope you recorded it."

"I did…it…went how you'd expect." I reach over to grab my Blackberry. "I sent the file to myself and forwarded it to my lawyer. Do you want to hear it?"

He nods and I play the recording. I watch as the man I love grows more and more agitated hearing Matt speak to me in such a hateful tone. He shakes his head before running a hand over his mouth. "Fucking dick."

"So…" I take a breath. "Yeah. My lawyer is meeting with his lawyer tomorrow and we're all meeting on Friday."

"All of you? Like you and Matt in the same room?"

"Yes."

He nods. "Are you going to be okay?"

"Yes, I'll be fine."

"Matt is trying to set up a session with me," he says.

"Oh?" I ask, raising an eyebrow. "Is that ethical?"

"You're questioning my ethics *now*? Jesus Christ, Charley. Really?" He rolls his eyes. "As I mentioned there is post-marital counseling."

"And you think you're the right person for the job?" I narrow my eyes at him.

"I am if I want a session with his wife as well," he says before running his tongue over his bottom lip causing me to shudder with lust.

"Weren't we supposed to be lying low?"

"This is true, but I am a professional, Ms. Pierce, and if Mr. Wells would like to meet with me, it's only fair that I meet with his soon-to-be ex-wife as well."

"Mmmhmm." I giggle. "Don't agree to it yet."

"Why?"

"Because I'm not sure I trust you not to act like a possessive caveman over a woman he's still legally married to and that would be a huge tip-off," I say matter-of-factly.

"Fine. For now, I'll keep him at bay." I go to pull my shirt off, wanting to get to the fun part of our Skype sessions when he stops me. "Wait."

"What?"

"I've been looking into your stepfather's whereabouts."

I stiffen, my body going rigid and tense with the news. "Oh? Have you found anything?"

"Not yet. Where is the last place Matt's guy reported?"

"Earlier this month Matt told me he was still on the east coast somewhere. He was in Virginia at one point."

He nods. "I can't hire a full-time PI, but I can protect you just as well without one, Charlotte. I will keep you safe."

I nod. "Thank you." I smile knowing that Will really plans to protect me just as fiercely as Matt. *Probably more.* "I really appreciate that," I say, moved to tears as I think about my lover already possessing the traits I need in a husband.

He nods before pressing his fingertips to the screen. "Please don't cry."

"I just wish you were here," I sniffle, wiping under my eyes.

"Me too, baby." He shoots me his panty-dropping grin. "So, you want to show me what's under your shirt now?"

———

The following day I wait to hear from my lawyer about how the preliminary meeting with Matthew's lawyer went, and when my phone rings I lunge for it. Fearing the worst, I shakily put the speaker to my ear.

"Hello?"

"This is going to be easier than I thought," he says and I breathe a sigh of relief.

"That's great!"

"They don't have a leg to stand on."

"Wonderful, the sooner the better."

"Only thing, you didn't tell me you saw a marriage counselor?"

"Oh…I didn't realize that was necessary. It's not like he helped," I chuckle. *Well not in the way he should have.*

"Seven months is quite some time. We'll need his testimony."

"For what?"

"It's not always necessary, but our firm likes to have their testimony on file if it's applicable. We'll summon him sometime next week."

I rub my hand over my jaw. "Okay…do Matt and I need to be there?" I have a fleeting thought that maybe I should divulge to my lawyer that he's the man I'm having an affair with but decide against it. I mean he's a marriage counselor, and Cromack is a divorce lawyer. *Conflict of interest much?* Surely, they could cross paths again. So, I'll just keep this little bit of information to myself.

"No, no, we'll meet with him separately. We would need his

impartial evaluation without you two staring at him awkwardly."
*Awkward indeed.*

"Great. So, I'll see you tomorrow?"

"Yes, eleven thirty."

"Sounds great."

—

"Why the *fuck* would I give her my house?"

"Because it legally belongs to both of you. You purchased the house together," Cromack retorts.

"Correction, I purchased it and she lived there," Matt says. We've been going back and forth for the past hour and a half, and just as Matt said, he's fought us on every little thing down to our frequent flyer miles.

*God, this man is petty.*

"Well, maybe don't live in Georgia. Because in this state, if you purchase something while you're married and there is no pre-nuptial agreement in place it is community property and will be divided as such upon divorce," Cromack says.

"This is horseshit," Matt growls.

"It's the law," Cromack states calmly. "Mr. Wells, frankly you're wasting all of our time with your antics. This is all fairly standard." He turns to Matt's lawyer. "Honestly, Stein, I thought you prepped your client better than this."

"Your client is wanting to take half of everything which everyone in this room knows she didn't rightfully earn. I think my client is well within his rights to be angry."

"And that's our problem...how? Oh wait, it's not! Jesus, Stein, maybe we need to go over how the law works again, to refresh your memory?" He leans back in his chair like the smug bastard he is. *Smug or not, he's one hell of a lawyer.* "We have been more than fair, your house in the Hamptons, which was a gift to my client. The timeshare in Cape Cod, and Hilton Head…frankly he's getting off easy."

"Except the house that's worth the most!" Stein roars.

"I don't even want the house," I perk up. "We can sell it for all I care." *There's another house across town where I would rather be anyway.*

"Of course, you don't care," Matt spits.

"I think what Ms. Pierce is saying," Cromack says looking at me with a look to pipe down, "is that she isn't going to take your house if you have such strong ties to staying there. But maybe it would be a good idea to sell. The market is doing better, and it's in a prime location. It could be sold by the spring. You could probably make double what you paid, due to the renovations and updates that Ms. Pierce did."

"With my money," Matt adds.

"Semantics, Mr. Wells, if that is your only argument here, then we have nothing more to talk about. As far as the state of Georgia is concerned, every dime that you earned during your marriage is just as much hers as it is yours. Now if I were you, I would not continue down this path of insinuating that you won't be coming up off of some significant money. Though my client doesn't want it, she IS entitled to it whether you like it or not. So, your best course of action, is to get on board. The longer we drag this out, the more you'll be paying."

"This is bullshit," Matt says leaning back in his chair and shooting me an angry look.

"Matt," I plead, "please, I don't want all of this. I just…I just want a divorce. You can have everything."

"Except the fifty grand you took?"

"A drop in the bucket and you know it," I say, wondering when on earth Matthew became so stingy. *Frankly, before this started, he spent money like it was nothing.* "The only reason you're so up in arms about fifty thousand is because you know that's all I need to start over and get my life together. I'm not a frivolous spender, and I never needed all of that shit. Sure, I grew accustomed to the lifestyle when you started shoving it down my throat, and while I appreciate everything, you and I both know I didn't need that. You cut me off because you thought I would panic not having anything and come running back to you. I'm stronger than that, and you know it. Honestly, if you get out of this marriage fifty thousand less, I say you're getting off easy, but you're making this so difficult. Why? You don't love me. You don't want to be married to me."

"Says who?!"

"Your actions. Your words. In the past week, I've been vindictive, spiteful, a whore, a bitch…and that's just what you've said to my face. Who knows what you've said behind my back, and you want me to just say, 'okay, never mind, let's stay together'? Please!" I shake my head. "You dragging this on is just ridiculous. Fighting me over our gym membership? When I'm the only one that uses it because you work out in your office gym? Fighting me over the artwork in our bedroom in the house in the Hamptons?"

"You know that piece is worth at least two hundred thousand dollars now," he argues.

"I'M AWARE! I stalked it for months. I did the research, I bought it!" I put my hand up. "And I swear to God, if you say with your money, I'll scream. Matthew, I'm trying to be civil and patient and understanding because I know you're hurt, but you are testing my limits and testing how far my patience and understanding will go. If you want a fight, and a messy sticky divorce, we can do that. I promise it won't work out well for you," I finish, crossing my arms.

"I'm not giving you anything without a fight." He stands and buttons his suit jacket. He looks at his lawyer. "You know what I want. Don't settle until we are all on that page. I don't want to see her again until then."

I nod my head. "Mature, Matt."

"Mr. Wells," his lawyer says trying to stop him, "you have to be here for negotiations."

"Well, we're finished for the day. I need to get back to work."

"Of course, you do," I murmur under my breath.

"What was that?"

"You can't even block out enough time to take me to dinner on my birthday, why should I be surprised? You couldn't care less when it comes to me."

"I'm sorry, should I have cleared my schedule to come here to argue with you? Charlotte, I'm sorry I have shit to do, but hey, why are you complaining? As long as I keep making money, it's more for you in the end, right?" he snarls before he's out the door slamming it behind him.

His lawyer grabs his papers and heads for the door as well.

"Stein, don't waste our time again. Get your client in line, and tell him to watch his mouth around mine," Cromack barks before Matt's lawyer is gone as well.

Cromack spins toward me and smiles. "This is going to be like taking candy from a baby."

"I don't want any of Matt's candy, Mr. Cromack."

"I know, Charley. You're a good kid…you don't strike me as the gold digger type. Your husband's kind of a dick, huh?"

"He wasn't always like this. He changed…hell, I changed too," I say, rubbing my head.

"Look, I know you don't want to take money you don't think you've earned but think of it this way. All the time you've spent unhappy in this marriage? Think of it as a job. All the cooking and cleaning…consider it back pay. The children he didn't want to give you? That comes at a price when you get divorced. So, stop thinking of it as taking something from Matt that you don't deserve, and start thinking about what you've *earned* through-out this marriage. You and Matt both have stated on record that it was Matt that pushed you to quit your job when you entered this marriage. Ms. Pierce, that alone is cause for the salary you would have earned times the years you were married. You were an events coordinator for a large hotel chain? That job starts roughly at about sixty thousand dollars, and that's if you weren't promoted, and received no bonuses or raises. Multiply that by five years and that's three hundred thousand dollars. So, even if he were just to pay you that, after he forced you not to work…that's still more than what you're originally asking for."

*I guess that does make sense. Damn, three hundred thousand? Wow.*

My thoughts are interrupted when I hear Mr. Cromack's phone ring. I tune out his talking, still stuck in my head, when I hear his voice next to me. "Did you hear me?"

"Oh sorry, what?"

"Another senior lawyer wants to meet with you."

"Oh?"

"Yes, apparently your case is the buzz amongst the partners, that and when husbands storm out during negotiations, it draws attention. He's one of the nicer ones; probably just wants to make sure you're okay," he chuckles and I smile. *Cromack's a shark, but he's also one giant teddy bear.* "I'm going to go to my office. You come see me before you leave."

"Okay."

He exits the conference room and I hear him greet whoever is taking his place. I stand up when the man, who I assume to be the senior lawyer, moves through the room and toward the table.

"Charlotte Pierce," I say, holding my hand out.

"I know who you are." He smiles before taking my hand. "J.R. Montgomery." My heart sinks. *Shit.* "You are certainly prettier than your pictures."

*I'm having a hard time reading him and it's stressing me the fuck out.* "Mr. Montgomery…"

"Call me J.R."

"J.R...." I'm not sure what he knows about me or my involvement with his son, so I'm at a loss for words not wanting to share more than he knows.

"You are certainly the talk of the office. Cromack has had wonderful things to say about you. Says your husband is an asshole. And here I thought my son was biased because he's been sleeping with you for the past five months."

*Fuck!*

My cheeks turn bright red hearing his words and I reach for the glass of water that is in front of me as my mouth has gone dry. "I know how this looks but…I love your son very much."

"Hmm." He draws a finger over his lips. "The first time I meet my son's girlfriend is during her divorce proceeding. You're not starting off very well, young lady."

I swallow and look down at the ground, the tears welling in my eyes. "I know," I say.

"Do you think I should trust you?"

"Yes."

"And why is that?"

*God, he's lawyering me!* "Because your son does."

"My son is blinded by…well…" he waves his hand over me, "you're a very attractive young woman, Ms. Pierce. Who wouldn't be?"

"I—"

"I am giving you one chance, Ms. Pierce," he interrupts. "If you screw my son over, I will ruin you. You won't be able to talk your way out of it like you are with your moronic husband that didn't make you sign a prenuptial agreement."

I nod, knowing that I've made my bed and now I have to lie in it. "I understand." *I mean if I were J.R. or Will's mother I would be skeptical too. They're just looking out for their son. Gotta have thicker skin, Charley.*

"Good. That being said, there is someone here to see you."

"Me?" I ask, my eyes widening, praying that it's not another surprise like Will's mother, for instance.

"Consider your lawyer's office, a...free space," he says. "Attorney-client privilege, remember?"

My eyes dart to the door as I see Will walk through it and my eyes widen. Tears fill them as the feeling of not seeing him for the past four days comes crashing down on me. *Damn, Charley, four days? You have got to get it together.*

"Dammit, J.R., what did you do to my girl?" He shoots his father a glare as I stand up and let Will pull me into his arms. *He calls his father J.R. as well? Not Dad?*

"We just had a little talk, right, Ms. Pierce?"

I nod. "Yes, sir."

"Good, now don't be in here all day, and open a window when you leave," he says, turning on his heel and closing the door behind him.

# CHAPTER
## *Twenty-Two*

THE SOUND OF THE DOOR SLAMMING SHUT ECHOES OFF THE conference room walls. "You're here," I gasp, taking a small step forward. Four days, and it has felt like four months. My body responds as it always does when he's near. Fire and heat and want. "I can't believe you're here."

"Of course, I'm here. I will always show up for you, Charley, *always*." He closes the space between us, lifting me onto the long cedar wood table with ease.

———

I'm lying flat on my back as the warmest sensation takes over my body. I feel like I'm floating in and out of consciousness, pleasured into oblivion. The love of my life's head hasn't left the space between my legs in what feels like close to an hour, his mouth giving me multiple orgasms. I let my eyes flutter closed, letting the feeling of Will's mouth on me lull me to the edge of sleep. His movements speed up, and I feel his tongue moving rapidly over my clit, as two fingers slide inside of me. I faintly hear him ask—demand—me to come but he sounds so far away. My body tenses as I feel my orgasm hit me hard and I bite down on my bottom lip as a moan escapes me. I open my eyes again and Will is staring up at me from his chair positioned between my legs, my arousal spread all over the bottom half of his face. I sit up from lying flat on the cool, wooden conference table and I move into his lap to straddle him.

He rubs his hand over his jaw effectively removing my orgasm from his face but the aroma of my wet sex still lingers in the air. "I've missed your pretty pussy," he whispers sinfully into my ear.

"Mmm," I moan as my lips find the area behind his ear that I know drives him wild. "It's missed your mouth." I graze his ear with my teeth and I feel his cock pulse underneath my naked mound. He had long since removed his pants, knowing that it would be a dead giveaway if the evidence of my arousal were all over the crotch of his slacks.

He pulls me back, his face serious despite our state. "What did my father say to you?"

I shake my head not wanting to get into this now. "Nothing I didn't expect."

"That's not what I asked."

"Will, it's okay…I can handle it."

"I didn't ask what you can handle. I asked you what he said. Don't make me ask you again, Charlotte." Despite his gruff tone, I can't help but be turned on by his demands. *Maybe because he's so fiercely protective of me—from everyone?*

"Just that he was going to be watching me, that's all… I mean, Will, this is the first time he's met me. I wasn't really expecting a 'welcome to the family.'" I see his nostrils flare and I rub my knuckles down his cheek causing his shoulders to sag, alerting me that the tension is slowly leaving his body. "I'll gain their trust. Them being skeptical of me just means they love you and want to protect you."

"If they try to come between us, I swear," he mumbles before he looks away from me. I shake my head and pull his face back to mine and plant a kiss on his lips, tasting myself.

"They won't," I whisper as I find his cock between us and slip him out of his underwear. I slide down onto him inch by delicious inch until he's fully sheathed in me. "It's just you and me."

He nods as I start to move up and down on him, his hands grasping my hips and finding a rhythm. "I can't wait to have this every day."

"Anytime you want it, baby, it's yours," he groans in response as he leans his head back and looks up at the ceiling. His eyes flutter closed and I know his body is taking him to new heights as my inner walls begin to massage his cock. My hands grip his shoulders as I slide up and down on him, my legs already falling asleep and I know the second we are together in the open, I'll never take for granted being able to fuck my man in a bed.

*I've fucked him on more tables, in more chairs, and standing up more times—and I'm ready for the days of lazily making love on our couch, our bed, and the lounger on our porch. I'm craving the days of just…being still. Not hurried kisses and touches and fucks but caresses and lovemaking that lasts well until dawn. I'm ready for a love past the forbidden romance.*

"I love you so much," he tells me, his eyes staring straight into me as if he can see my soul. I wonder if he's feeling the same things I'm feeling because he stops thrusting and crushes me to his chest. "I can't take it another second."

"Take what?"

"Being away from you. It's making me fucking insane." He runs his fingers through my hair, gently massaging my scalp before his fingertips dance down my spine, and I shudder at the gentleness of it all. "I'm starting to feel out of control, and Matt is becoming too much of a liability where you're concerned."

I sit back in my chair and look at him confused, completely aware that he's still throbbing inside of me. "What do you mean?"

"He's cruel to you and hurtful. I don't like how he speaks to you," he says as he leans back in his chair. "I know he's pissed but you were together so long, for him to say these things to you is ridiculous. I know that you think he would never lay a hand on you, but I'm just not so sure."

I feel my heart skip a beat at his words. *I still don't think he ever would but I hate that Will is so uncomfortable.*

"Promise me you won't be alone with him," he whispers low. "Promise me you'll keep yourself safe until I can do it properly."

I nod, not knowing what else to say. "I promise." I rub my nose against his to get his attention back on me as he's been looking down for the majority of this heavy conversation. He looks at me, the worry and apprehension written all over his beautiful face. "I wish you wouldn't worry so much. It's going to cause wrinkles in that pretty little forehead of yours," I say, drawing my index finger over his frown lines.

"Don't make light of this," he says softly and I nod.

"I'll be safe," I say, "and soon enough you can do it for me."

He clears his throat and I wonder if the fact that he's inside of me coupled with the intensity of the moment has him out of his element. "Thank you, for trusting me."

"Of course, I do," I say pressing my hands to his chest. "You're the only person I completely trust, Will. Wholeheartedly." I smile, hoping he will feel better about all of this, when he returns my grin, warming me all over.

I know that I've only known him for such a short time, but there's something inside of me that tells me that I can trust him. That he loves me unconditionally, and he's in this with me. The way he looks at me…*hell, the way he's looking at me now tells me that this is all real for him.* Maybe it's a leap of faith, throwing away years of marriage for what started out as a fling, but I've never been surer that there is someone waiting at the bottom to catch me.

———

"I mean do you blame them?" Lauren asks as she plops down on her plush, white sofa next to me. She hands me a glass of wine filled practically to the brim. I had left my lawyer's office completely sated, but with Will's father's words still ringing in my head. "I mean come on, Charley, Will's father—a lawyer none-theless—is meeting you for the first time as you take your husband to the cleaners after cheating with his son? You kind of look like a man-eater and their son is just too blinded by your pussy to see it." Lauren's words wash over me. *Amazing. At twenty-eight years of age, I've had sex with two men, and I'm a man-eater.*

My cheeks heat up as I take a sip of my wine. "I don't blame them, Lauren. I just…I want them to like me."

"And maybe that will take some time." She shrugs. "I wouldn't worry too much yet. You're still married, so it's not like you'll be going to their house for Sunday brunch anytime soon." She rolls her eyes and I scoff at her.

"Are they ever going to like me?" I sigh. "Or am I forever going to be the slut that cheated on her husband?"

She's silent. "Maybe when you start popping out their grand-children they'll get on board. Children may not fix everything, but *grandchildren* certainly do."

"Great," I sigh.

"Aren't you and Hot Doc talking about children? I thought he was trying to knock you up, like yesterday." She purses her lips in a questioning way and I have to resist the urge to smack the smug look off her face.

I ignore her comment. "First, his brother and now his fa-ther," I say putting a hand over my eyes before running it through my hair. "I can only imagine what Mrs. Montgomery is going to think of me."

"That you're a whore who's not good enough for her precious baby boy," she says and I look over to see her picking at her nail beds.

"Rude!"

"Okay, maybe not, but…prepare for the worst. Not everyone

is going to be like Mama Wells who would let Satan himself in from the cold if he needed a place to stay."

*It was true, Matthew's mother was a saint. Fuck. I should really call her. I'm sure she's plenty mad at me right now.*

"All I'm saying is they may not love you right away and that's okay. You have to accept that. And yes, you can cry and bitch and complain to me and I'll bash them for not seeing what a wonderful person you are but the reality of it is, they don't see what a wonderful person you are…right now. They see a woman that stepped out on her marriage, got herself in way too deep, all while risking their son's livelihood." She shrugs. "I want them to like you…to love you, and accept you, but right now…you can't be mad if they don't." I nod, letting Lauren's words soak in and I love her right now for her blatant honesty, although it's a bitter pill. "Look, just get divorced, okay? One thing at a time."

———

I slide my Chanel sunglasses over my eyes as I walk out of my spin studio, the sweat glistening on my skin. It's been a few days since my sexy tryst at my lawyer's office with Will, and I'm starting to feel the itch to see him again.

*Settle down, Charley. No.*

I take a long swig of my Smart Water and make my way to the garage toward my car when my Blackberry vibrates in my purse.

My day is instantly better at the idea of speaking to him. Coupled with the endorphins from my exercise, I'm on cloud nine. "Hi!"

"Hi, baby."

"What are you doing?"

"Sitting in my car watching my insanely gorgeous girlfriend walk down the street."

I stop in my tracks and I look around as the women filter

out of the studio toward their slew of Range Rovers, Audis, and Beamers. "You have another girlfriend?" I joke.

"No," he growls at me. "Just one that's currently making me desperate for a taste of the sweat dripping off her."

I put my hand on my hip as I scan the street again. "Where are you?"

"One street over."

"Are you following me?"

"No, I wanted to see you. We need to talk, Charlotte."

"Talk?" I'm immediately on high alert. Years of experience *and pop culture* remind me that "we need to talk" is never a good thing. *The fact that he called me Charlotte isn't helping either.*

"Come," he tells me, and as if I have no control over my own legs, I obey knowing that this is the furthest from lying low.

*Getting into Will's car in broad daylight in front of your spin studio where you spend three days a week. Smart, Charley.*

I've barely settled into the car when I feel hands tugging me into a familiar lap and squeezing me tight. "Baby," he breathes into my ear. I'm mildly aware that I'm sweaty and smelling of the floral aerosol deodorant I sprayed before I left the studio and I try to move out of his arms.

"Will, I…" I strain as he literally crushes me against him. "I'm sweaty and disgusting and…I should move." I note that he's dressed for work, and the last thing I want to do is ruin his clothes with my sweaty attire.

"No," he growls in my ear. I can't see his face, but his voice leads me to believe that he's extremely anxious. "Never move," he says softer and loosens his grip around me. I slide back to look at him and he traces a hand over my face, giving me a sad smile. He looks out the window and my heart sinks knowing that he's about to drop a serious bomb on me.

*I can feel the tension radiating off him in waves and I'm not sure I want to even know why.*

"I just want to keep you safe," he whispers.

"From what? Or...who? Is this still about Matt?" I ask.

"Everything. I...I don't know anyone well enough in your life to trust anyone."

"What—what does that mean?" *He doesn't trust Lauren? My mother? What does he know that I don't?*

He opens his mouth and it's as if the words fail him because he closes it immediately. He shakes his head, before the heel of his hand finds his eye. "I hate that I have to tell you this. I hate that there is so much that I can't shield you from," he murmurs and my brows thread together, wondering what he could possibly tell me that is causing this much inner turmoil. "But first and foremost, this is good news," he says and I feel slight relief rush through me. "Above all else, I'm pleased with what I have to tell you."

"Then what—" He stops me by putting a finger to my lips.

"Because you're going to flip."

"I won't flip." I shake my head. "Just tell me." He sighs and my body shakes with worry. *It's good but it's bad? What in the world, Will? Spit it out!*

"So, I have some news about your ex-stepfather." *My blood runs cold at the mere mention of him. What does that mean? He's involved? Nothing about him could be good news.* The goose bumps rise on my skin despite Will's arms that are still wrapped around me. "I followed the very vague trail that you gave me about what Matt has told you."

"Uh huh," I say, needing him to get from point A to point B a little bit faster, because right now I can barely hear him over the loud pounding in my ears. I swallow and my mouth has already gone dry. The knot in my stomach is twisting over and over again.

"I found something. At first, I couldn't believe it," he says, "but it checks out. Charley, Matt has been lying to you for about a year and a half now."

*About Michael's whereabouts? Is he closer than he told me?* "Lying to me? About what?"

"Your stepfather is dead, Charley. He died from an overdose. Apparently, he got into heroin at some point…or maybe he always was, I don't know if you ever saw that," he rambles, "but he's dead."

"Wait, what?! How long ago? Are you sure?" I blurt out.

"Yes, he died about a year and a half ago. I can show you the autopsy reports, police reports, everything." He pulls a folder from a briefcase sitting next to us.

I'm numb. Completely numb. My mind has gone blank and I don't think I can even formulate a sentence at the moment. A smile cracks across my lips and before I know it I'm laughing. *Hard.* Harder than I've laughed in months, because really, what about my life isn't funny?

*Michael is dead. He's been dead. And yet, earlier this month Matt told me that his PI pinned him on the east coast. Roanoke, Virginia, to be exact. And he's been dead for a year and a half? When I tried to leave him ten months ago, at one point he even said "don't be stupid, Charlotte, what about Michael? I need you safe." THE WHOLE FUCKING TIME!?*

My mind is screaming at me, and the laughter stops when I feel hands on my cheeks and lips. "What the fuck?" I whisper.

"I know," he says quietly. He shakes his head. "He let you go on being scared for longer than a year."

"I should have done my own research…I just never…I never thought to look," I say, still trying to root through the millions of thoughts running through my brain.

"You trusted him and he betrayed that trust." He shakes his head and tucks an errant strand that has escaped my ponytail behind my ear. "What reason would you have to check his sources?"

"I should go," I whisper.

"What? Baby, I think you're in a little bit of shock."

"No. I see things perfectly clear."

"No, you're in shock," he repeats. "You were just laughing, hysterically—which is normal," he explains. "Laughter is often a natural reaction to trauma, but it also means—"

"Don't shrink me right now," I say looking to the right and out of the window. I see a woman walking down the street with a man. They stop, they kiss, they take a selfie, and I find myself jealous of this woman I've never met.

*Why isn't my life that easy? Why can't I walk down the street hand in hand with the man I love, kiss him, document our love on social media, and boast to the world how happy and in love I am? Why must I have a husband and a boyfriend and a mountain of lies and deceit?*

I turn back to him and press my head into his neck wanting nothing more than to climb inside of him for protection from all of the bullshit that is surrounding me like a tornado. "Run away with me."

"What?"

"We can go to Europe, and get married, and be together. And not deal with all of this." I shake my head. "We can be together all the time. Screw the next month."

"Charley…" He cocks his head to the side and stares at me with, what? *Pity? Sorrow? Remorse? I can't tell.*

"Don't look at me like that…isn't that what you want? To be with me?"

"More than anything, but we can't run away from this."

"Why not?"

"Because we can't, baby. You know that."

"Nope. I have fifty grand and…I can sell all my stuff. We can go live a happy, Parisian life." I smile. "I'm not going to be able to get a job here anyway." I shrug sadly.

"I'll help you," he says, rubbing a hand down my face and I scoff.

"More help from the man that loves me. I don't want another Matt, Will." I raise my hand up to stop him from panicking at the comparison. "I just mean I don't want a man that wants to spoon-feed me…my *life*." I feel my lip tremble. "It's fine if you don't want to go," I say softly.

"I would go anywhere with you," he whispers as he raises my chin. "And after a good night's sleep, and a cry, and some tequila…" he smiles, "if you still feel this way in the morning, we can talk about it. But the natural reaction for you right now is to run, and that's normal, but you can't, baby. You have face this. I will *help* you."

"How could he just…let me be afraid? Was it all just to keep me under his thumb? Keep me reliant on him? Let me think that if I didn't have him looking out for me that Michael would come after me?" I sniffle and wipe my nose gently. Will pulls a handkerchief from his pocket and wipes under my eyes and then my nose. "How could he do this to me?" I ask, the tears starting to fall, as the initial reaction has turned to a more genuine one. "I'm not a hypocrite, okay? I know that what I've done is wrong… but…this is so different!" He wraps his arms around me and pulls me back to his chest.

"I know, baby. I know." He strokes my back, his lips finding my forehead.

*I'm not sure what it is, maybe just a series of I love yous, and I'm sorrys, but I can't quiet the rage in my head. I know that there are five stages of grief, but I find myself wondering what the five stages of learning that your husband has been harboring a secret for a year are? Shock, laughter, sadness, anger…what's after that?*

I pull out of Will's hold and run a hand under my eye, wiping the tears away for the hundredth time. "I should go."

"Go? Baby, you're not in any position to drive. Let me take you home," he says as he continues to stroke circles into my back.

"No." I shake my head. "I'll be fine."

"Charley," he says, and I look into his sad blue eyes, "I don't want you alone with Matt. At all."

I nod. *I no longer even know the man I was married to for so long. I don't trust Matt. I don't know the person he is.* "Are you looking into Matt as well?"

"You bet your ass I am."

"Have you found anything?"

"No." He shakes his head. "I don't think he's cheating on you, Charley. I don't think he's ever cheated on you." His words are sobering, the line between lover and marriage counselor blurrier than ever before as the man I love sits here assuring me that my husband isn't cheating on me.

"I wouldn't care if he had."

"I know, but…I just thought you should know. Part of me always wondered," he says. "With the trips and working all the time…he really is married to the job. *You* were the mistress," he says with a hint of humor, and I can't help but chuckle sadly at his joke.

"I'm going to go." I pull myself out of his grasp.

"Wait…" He holds my hand, squeezes it, and I look at him, praying that I can keep the tears at bay just until I get out of the car.

"I'm going to follow you back to Lauren's."

"Fine," I say before his lips find mine in a heated kiss. It's not aggressive or possessive; it's loving and passionate and takes my breath away. With every stroke of his tongue against mine I feel myself getting more and more worked up as I think about Matt. I pull away knowing that I'm not in the right headspace to continue this kiss. "I'll call you later."

He nods and presses a kiss to my forehead. "I love you."

"I love you too," I murmur.

I don't remember my walk from his car to mine, but some-how, I make it. I don't know what to even think as I start my car and rest my forehead on the steering wheel. I sit in my car and stare into space, my mind racing a mile a minute as I re-call every time over the past year that Matt handed me a bullshit story about Michael. By the time I get to his most recent lie, I'm enraged. I pull out of the space with a new mission in mind. My thoughts go back to the five stages I was thinking about earlier. *Shock, laughter, sadness, anger…what's after that?*

**Rage**.

# CHAPTER
## Twenty-Three

S INCE I EXITED THE FREEWAY AND BEGAN TO MOVE THROUGH the familiar streets that do not lead back to Lauren's house, my phone has been ringing nonstop. Will had started calling me the second he realized what my intentions were, and I've sent him to voicemail every time.

*No. This has nothing to do with you, Will. I know you're worried he's going to do something to me, but honestly the way I'm feeling right now, I wish he fucking would. I dare him.*

I park my car in my usual spot and sprint for the elevator, before I see the car that has been following me for the past twenty minutes pull into a spot. I hear my name shouted from behind me, and then I'm in the elevator. He calls me again and this time I answer.

"Stop. I need to do this."

"Charlotte, bring your ass back down here right now," he demands.

"No," I say.

"I will come up there and get you."

"No, you won't."

"Charley, think about what you're doing."

"I am. Fuck the money, fuck the houses, fuck it all, Will. This is so much bigger than that now. He can have every dime, but he's going to answer my fucking questions and he's going to do it today," I growl as I end the call and slip the phone back into my purse.

*I am well aware that I am spiraling. That I'm out of control, that I'm probably a liability. My lawyer is going to have a fit. But I don't care. This isn't reason, it's instinct. I never really understood the term crimes of passion, but right now, I think I've completely grasped the concept. All reasoning has gone out the window and I'm acting on basic urges and instincts.*

*Those instincts are telling me to rip Matthew's balls from his body.*

I storm through the halls of my soon-to-be ex-husband's office without a care in the world for the scene I'm about to cause.

*Hell, I might be a widow before I'm a divorcee.*

"Is he in there?" I bark at his assistant, a sweet middle-aged woman, who's probably sent me more flowers over the course of the last two years than my own husband. *Sorry, Sarah, you've been caught in the crossfire.* She nods, her eyes wide. I assume she's taken aback, both by Matt's estranged wife storming through the office, and her sweaty workout attire. I open the door and slam it behind me so hard that his Princeton master's degree shakes on the wall. His head shoots up, his eyes wide at the intrusion.

"Charlotte? What the hell? You can't just—"

"Shut up," I growl, my voice menacingly low. "Don't you say a motherfucking word. Or I will scream this entire building down."

He leans back in his chair and eyes me, knowing that I'm just reckless enough to do it. I'm sure he's worried about me causing a scene in front of his entire office. I take a few breaths, attempting to calm my nerves, when I look down at my hands and see them shaking violently. *I need to punch something. A wall, a punching bag, Matt's face.* I walk toward his desk and grab what I know to be a picture of the two of us. I don't even think before I'm sending it barreling toward the wall. The glass shatters and I know, in this moment, this is truly the end. I'll be shocked if I don't end up telling him everything just to stick the knife in deeper.

He still doesn't say anything.

My whole body is shaking now and I don't even know how

to start this so I just cut to the chase. "I know Michael is dead," I blurt out and I see his face go through a hundred different expressions in the course of thirty seconds. "You selfish, manipulative, arrogant, pathetic excuse for a man," I say shaking my head. "How could you do that to me?" The tears form in my eyes and roll down my face. "A year and a half?" I shake my head as my lips form a straight line.

I slam my hands on his desk and lean forward. "A YEAR AND A HALF?" I back up and begin to pace the length of his office. "'If we split up, who's going to watch out for Michael?' You said that, when I first wanted to leave. You said those words, and it shook me to my core. You knew he was dead. You played into my fear to keep me in this marriage! You fucking asshole!"

"Wait a minute, Charlotte. I didn't—"

"Don't lie to me, don't you fucking dare sit here and lie to me." I take a step closer. "YOU OWE ME THAT MUCH. You wasted a fucking year of my life. YOU OWE ME THE TRUTH. You let me think he was out there, waiting for me. That I needed you or he would come for me." The tears are falling down my face and a part of me is so angry for letting him see me cry. *I wanted to be strong and confident but it's still so raw. The pain is deep.*

"How—who even told you that? Where are you getting this information?"

"I hired a private investigator of my own," I say. "I didn't think you'd continue looking into Michael so I wanted to have it in place for when we broke up." I shrug. "Were you ever going to tell me?"

"Who is this guy?" he asks, and I'm getting angry all over again by the fact that he's avoiding the issue and not answering my questions.

"Answer my questions," I grit out.

"How do you know he's not ripping you off? I've worked with my guy for years…you know that."

"Oh, and you're telling me that he keeps reporting that he's alive? That you've been paying upwards of ten thousand dollars a month and he's just been feeding you lies on his whereabouts?"

"Charlotte," he says standing, but I put a hand up. "I would not come within kicking range of me because your ability to have kids will be put into jeopardy." I cock my head not passing up the opportunity to throw in his face one of the many reasons we are divorcing. "Guess it doesn't matter though, it's not like you want them anyway." He stops, heeding my warning. "You lied to me. You lied to me about something BIG. This isn't…there's nothing you could have done to me that was bigger than this. You tainted the one thing that made you a hero in my eyes. The one thing that made me feel that deep down you were a good guy. Despite how you've treated me, I thought on some level you cared about my well-being."

"I do—"

"Bullshit," I interrupt him. "My overall well-being. That includes my mental health, and you know that deep within me I still feared Michael coming after me and ending my life. And you let me go on thinking that was a fucking possibility. So, what? I would lean on you? Need you? Stay with you? Are you that pathetic? That desperate for the love of a woman that you'll take someone who stays with you for that reason only? I should have left you. Months ago. Probably a year. But I was scared. And you exploited that." I see the moment that the sadness in his eyes turns to anger and I clench my fists wondering if he'll actually try and put his hands on me.

*Try me.*

He doesn't move toward me and I shake my head. "You honestly have nothing to say for yourself?" He's quiet and looks out the window, his hands buried deep in his pockets. I shake my head. "Yeah, I wouldn't be able to look at me either," I say before I turn on my heel and walk out the door, the tears flowing down my cheeks faster with each step.

I hear the ding of the elevator and I'm walking to my car when I see Will still parked a few spaces down. I get into the car and start the engine. I half expect him to appear at my car to rip me a new one, but I'm sure he suspects there are cameras covering every inch of this fancy garage.

I drive for about ten minutes when I pull into an empty park parking lot. I've barely turned off the ignition when my door opens and Will is pulling my seatbelt off of me and yanking me from the driver's seat, hard.

"Get the fuck in the car, Charlotte." I do as he says wondering why he didn't just join me in mine.

"I know you're mad—" I start.

"Mad? No, Charlotte, I'm furious. What the fuck did you do?"

"You have to understand how I feel, Will. You're a shrink."

He sighs, pinching the bridge of his nose. "What did you tell him?"

"Nothing about you. This isn't about you or us right now, believe it or not."

He snorts. "We'll come back to that smart-ass comment in a second. You just ran to his office and showed him your entire hand, you could have used this to your advantage."

"See, you're not getting it. I don't care about blindsiding him or using anything to my fucking advantage. This is my *life,* Will. These are my feelings. And I'm not interested in discussing this with my lawyer or Matt's lawyer. I wanted answers from Matt. I wanted to yell and scream and…I wanted him to see and feel my raw anger. I didn't want to wait and calm down, so what, he would get levelheaded Charley? Fuck that! He deserves my anger and my pain. My devastation over being deceived by the man I trusted the most!"

"I get that, Charley—"

"And I can still use this to my advantage, Will. I'm going to tell my lawyer."

He looks out the window. "Where did you say you heard the information from?"

"I said I hired a private investigator of my own since I was worried that he wouldn't keep looking into my supposed living stepfather. Why are you asking me all of this? I confronted him, he had nothing to say. It gave me my answer. Why does it matter how I found out?"

"Because it matters, Charlotte! You are getting divorced. Everything. Fucking. Matters." He rubs his forehead and looks at me finally. "Did you hit him?"

"No."

"Did he touch you?"

"No"

"How did it end?"

"I walked out when he had nothing to say. He barely said anything the entire time I was in there. He just kept asking how I knew, asked if the guy was lying…" I look at him. "You're sure about all of this?"

"Yes," he says and grabs the folder that he pulled out earlier but never opened. "Here," he says softly, his anger subsiding now that he knows things didn't go as bad as he was thinking. "You promise me he didn't touch you?" he asks as I begin to thumb through the overwhelming amount of evidence that Michael Taylor no longer walked the earth. I nod and he leans back in his seat. "You're going to kill me, Charley."

"Sorry," I say, although we both know that I'm not.

"We've talked about that." I smile faintly at his inability to stop being a counselor for two seconds. "You're going to need to tell your lawyer."

"I know."

"Today."

"Fine, Will." I try to keep the irritation out of my voice.

"That was risky," he says after a few moments. I don't reply because I don't know how to. "Do you feel better?"

"I'm glad to have the truth out in the open. I'm glad that he knows that I know the truth."

He nods again and the awkward silence becomes deafening. It feels like there's a mountain of unsaid words between us and neither of us are making the first attempt to climb. "It's not about you or us, believe it or not?" he says, repeating my words back to me. "What the hell was that about?"

"I just meant I hadn't told him about you. At this point he'll probably drop the cheating hypothesis as he doesn't even have a leg to stand on. He's a lying, manipulative bastard. Glass fucking houses," I grit out. "I dare him to keep accusing me without proof."

*I'm exhausted. The adrenaline from the last hour and a half is wearing off by the second and I wonder after rage if there's a sixth step: exhaustion or maybe defeat. I'm exhausted, I'm drained, I feel like I've run a marathon, and I just want to crawl into bed and sleep for a week.* He nods and I know that he has something to say. "What?"

"It's just the way you said it that's all."

"The way I said what?" I say, not able to curb the irritation in my voice.

"Don't pick a fight with me, Charlotte."

"I'm not."

"You are, and I'm not giving in to this bullshit. Everything about this situation affects us, every decision you make affects me too, whether you want to admit it or not, because you have this fear of repeating the cycle of being the wife of someone who doesn't give a shit. But we *are* in this together, Charley. *I* give a fucking shit."

I bite my bottom lip as tears pool in my eyes and I almost want to get out of the car and leave. But the fear of not knowing when I'll see him again stops me. *Sure, I'm pissed right now, but in two hours I'll want him to hold me and tell him I love him and I may not have that luxury. So fast-forward two hours.* I move toward him and despite his *fuck off* demeanor his rigid posture softens dramatically when I climb into his lap. "I'm sorry," I whisper. *And I actually am this time.* "I shouldn't have said that."

"You're right, you shouldn't have."

My hands find his face and I slide them across his cheeks and into his hair, pulling his head down toward my lips. He plants a kiss on them and when I try to slide my tongue through his he stops. "Charley."

"What?"

"You should get home."

"Why?" I ask as I begin to kiss his neck, my tongue rubbing the skin just over his pulse point.

"Because we are in a park in the middle of Atlanta."

"So?"

"And it's two in the afternoon."

I shrug and he shakes his head. "This is not lying low." *I guess, but I'm feeling vulnerable right now and I need you.*

"We can talk on the phone, but I think we've played with fire enough times today."

I pull out of his arms and I can still feel the wall between us as I move toward my door. "I'll be at Lauren's." I place one final kiss on his lips. His coldness feels a bit like rejection and I want out of this car that is making me feel as if the walls are closing in by the second.

# CHAPTER
## *Twenty-Four*

IT'S BEEN A WEEK, OR AS I LIKE TO REFER TO IT, TWENTY-ONE days left, when I'm sitting in my lawyer's office waiting for him to wrap up a final meeting so we can talk about a few things. I had told Cromack about Matthew's yearlong lie and he was almost drooling over the information.

"Hell, that man is literally trying to throw money at you," he'd said, and I could see the dollar signs flash in his eyes. Although he is handling the case pro-bono, the amount of the settlement does count toward his end-of-year bonus, so I've read from some research. And when the numbers start getting up around where my settlement will be, the bonuses look a lot like yearlong salaries. I'm a little early so I pull out my Blackberry to find messages from Will. Things have gotten back to normal between us, after that day when I learned about Matt. The next day we both apologized for our tempers, our words, and our actions, and chalked it up to dealing with this shitty situation the best way we can.

One thing did come out of that though. We are on the same team, the same side no matter what; turning against each other isn't an option. He showed up at Lauren's house that night with flowers and pizza, and we watched a movie with Lauren, then retired to my room and made love for hours. I couldn't even stop the tears from falling when he woke me around 4 a.m. to slip out of my bed. *You're so close, Charley. There's a light at the end of the tunnel.* I haven't seen him since then and we are both climbing the walls.

**Will: Skype sex later?**

**Me: Absolutely.**

**Will: Great. Bring your vibrator. The pink one.**

I smile thinking about the video I sent him this morning of me masturbating with it. Not only did I masturbate, I did it to completion, giving Will a very up close and personal look of my orgasm as his name left my lips. Needless to say, it resulted in immediate phone sex, and intermittent "sexts" throughout the day.

I go to send him another text when Cromack walks through the door. "Charlotte Pierce."

"John Cromack," I giggle and his face, usually cheerful, is stoic.

I'm not stupid; Cromack is usually so happy to see me because this case is pretty much a cakewalk and it's making him look damn good to the partners. When he sees me, our chats usually consist of what I've done that day, questions about what to do about his rebellious teenage daughter, or if I've seen my secret boyfriend. But right now, he does not look pleased.

"Everything okay?" I ask.

He eyes me, running his finger over his bottom lip. "I think I underestimated you."

"What?"

"You've played all of this perfectly. If you'd be willing to take the LSATs and go through three years of law school, I'd say you'd make one hell of a lawyer."

"I don't understand." *I take that to mean I'm a good liar? Good at manipulation? Going straight to hell?*

"I asked you from the beginning if there was anything about this case that would surprise me. I said no surprises, Ms. Pierce."

"I—I don't know what I'm hiding from you," I whisper softly and in this moment I don't.

"Tell me about your marriage counselor," he says, crossing his arms in front of him and I know without a shadow of a doubt he knows.

"Your face tells me *all* I need to know, Ms. Pierce. So, what are

we going to do about our communication problem? Because…
when I told you I would be meeting with your marriage counselor, it didn't behoove you to tell me that he's the man you've been
sleeping with for five months? You didn't think that was important to mention?! Before I went into a meeting with him and your
husband's goddamn attorney!" he shrieks, and I wince.

"I—" I sigh. "I'm sorry. I just… Will said he could keep it together and that you wouldn't be able to tell." Tears well in my eyes,
knowing that this is all about to blow up.

"Oh, you couldn't. Stein is none the wiser. Your boyfriend
played it well. Wasn't too biased. Made pretty general, blanket
statements. Even said some things about you…not sure if it was
just to even the playing field or due to doctor-patient confidentiality. Regardless, I only know because I started thinking about
the coincidences."

"Coincidences?"

"Like, your marriage counselor being the son of one of the
partners here. But then I thought well, you know, maybe he just
felt bad and offered to help her out by putting her in touch with
someone here. Not a conflict of interest; it's his job to help out either party of the marriage and if your husband already had the
attorney you would certainly need help finding a good one. But
then…why would I be doing this pro-bono? Of course," he crosses
his arms, "this case is no longer pro-bono due to this recent chain
of events. But then I remember Montgomery—his father—wanting
to speak with you, and hearing rumblings that day that his son was
in the building. He's around from time to time for divorce cases,
so it's not unheard of for him to be in the building. But then seeing him during our interview, it just all clicked. It was just a hunch
and I was only about eighty percent sure, but you confirmed it."

"I'm sorry I didn't tell you," I whisper.

"Mmmhmm," he says and I wonder if he hates me now. I look

up to see him stroking his beard and looking at me from over his glasses. "You're a ballsy lady, Ms. Pierce."

I clear my throat. "What happens now?"

He shrugs. "Nothing. We go about business as usual. We continue the proceedings as we have been."

"What did Will say?"

"A lot of psycho-babble generic bullshit to be honest. There's only so much he can say without violating your doctor-patient confidentiality and also without implicating himself on top of that."

I thumb the hem of my dress and look up at him. "Your attorney-client privilege only applies to me though, right?"

"Mmmhmm," he says, steepling his fingers under his chin.

"Well are you—I mean…" I stumble over my words. "Are you going to tell anyone?" My hands begin to shake as I think about this entire thing blowing up in our faces when we are this close.

"Ms. Pierce, Dr. Montgomery did not *tell* me anything. If he would have said, 'I have been sleeping with this woman for months,' then Stein would have left me in his dust as he raced to the ethics board. But he didn't. I had a hunch and you confirmed it. *You*, Ms. Pierce. And as you said, *you* and I have attorney-client privilege."

I nod getting his point.

My secret is safe.

Will's secret is safe.

*We* are safe.

At least for now. *Thank God for loopholes.*

"Thank you."

"Do not thank me, Ms. Pierce. It's my job. And thanks to your marriage counselor not being able to control his erections around his patient's wife, you're about to make me a very rich man. Well, more so than I already am," he chuckles.

*Great, so he's probably gone to Will's father shouting accusations. Hell, J.R. probably confirmed it long before I did. Ergo, a hefty chunk of change that the firm probably did not want to part with.* "Lawyer hat off, still attorney-client privilege," he says, "but I know you don't have any decent father figures so I have to ask… you sure you know what you're doing?"

I let his question sink in, wondering what in the world I should say. I go with the truth. "No, I don't."

"I admire your honesty, Charley." He pauses, and I smile thinking about how this is the first time he's called me Charley. "Do you love him?"

"More than life itself."

"He feels the same about you?"

"Yes."

"Let me ask you something," he starts. "What are you going to do when this is all over, you're divorced, you're free, you've got more money than sense," he says waving his hand around, "et cetera, et cetera, et cetera…"

"Be with him? Get a job? Try to regain some normalcy."

"Mmmhmm, and are you planning to stay in Atlanta?" he asks and I wonder where this line of questioning is going.

"Yes."

"And you think that Mr. Wells isn't going to put two and two together if he sees you two together? You two just realized your feelings right when you signed? Nothing at all before?"

"Well at that point it shouldn't matter. We'll be divorced, names signed, the end. Right?"

"Wow. You are ruthless."

"Will is the endgame." I shake my head. "I've come too far to just…give him up, and that isn't an option. So, if I have to deal with an ex-husband that lives here that I have to see from time to time, then so be it. We aren't going to rub it in his face; for the first few months we will be lying low, but at some point, it should be expected that I move on."

"Charley, you need to be careful. Scorned ex-husbands don't always go away so quietly. Should I even bother negotiating alimony payments? They're going to be null and void the second you walk down that aisle. I assume you'll be getting married rather soon?"

"Not right away."

"You know that the payments stop the day you remarry."

I nod. "That's fine. I don't need him to pay me anything. The settlement should be more than enough." At this point, I should be coming out of this marriage with a little over half a million after taxes in terms of all our liquid assets. Matt had finally been convinced to sell, so our house will be going on the market at the end of the month.

"Just…be careful," he says. After a few moments he speaks again. "Was it Montgomery who figured out about your stepfather?"

"Yes."

He seems impressed. "Good man."

"He's the best," I whisper.

"But a shitty marriage counselor."

# CHAPTER
## Twenty-Five

I'M PULLED FROM MY SLUMBER BY KNOCKING ON LAUREN'S apartment door. Pushing the blankets back, I rush to answer it, not wanting to miss whoever it is. I peek through the tiny window eyeing a delivery man on the other side. I open the door and he smiles at me, holding a vase of white roses in each hand. "Good morning, Ms. Pierce, special delivery for you."

*Twenty-four long-stemmed roses, and I know exactly who they're from.*

Remembering social etiquette, I head back to my bedroom to grab my wallet. "Oh, hold on let me get—" I start when he raises his hand to stop me.

"No, ma'am, it's already been taken care of. Happy birthday," he says, and before I can protest again, he disappears out the front door. A card is nestled inside one of the bouquets and I reach for it.

*Happy Birthday to the love of my life.*
*Looking forward to seeing you later to celebrate*
*the first of many birthdays together.*
*I'm so glad that you were born.*
*I love you,*
*WM*

It's not lost on me that I've only been twenty-nine for about eight hours, seven and a half of which I was sleeping, and Will has already wished me happy birthday twice. It is so different from last year when the man that supposedly loved me never mentioned it at all. I run to my room, excitedly, and pull out my Blackberry to call him immediately. I'm met with his voicemail, and realize he's probably in a session. I decide to text him and mid-sentence my phone whirls to life.

"Hi!" I chirp cheerfully, my lips widening into a smile so wide that my cheeks hurt.

"There's my birthday girl. How are you?"

"I'm good, wonderful. Thank you for my flowers, they are so beautiful."

"You're welcome, I know that white roses don't symbolize love quite like red ones do, but I know they're your favorite."

*He's right; white roses are my favorite flower, and despite Matt knowing this he—well, his assistant—always defaulted to red or yellow roses.*

"I'm glad that you like them…and as much as I hate to cut this short, I have to get back to my session."

"Wait, you called me in the middle of a session?"

"I told them it was an emergency, it's okay."

The tears flood my eyes as his simple words, that hold so much meaning, wash over me. "But—it wasn't an emergency."

"Baby, anything with you is top priority. If you call me, it's important. I will always make time to talk to you. You've been on my no-wait list for months."

"No-wait list?" I ask.

"Yes, if you call the office, Vanessa knows to put you through no questions asked."

*My mind drifts back to the early days when I didn't have my secret Blackberry, and I would call his office to not have his personal cell on my phone records. I always wondered how I got through so fast, knowing that Will is a very sought-after counselor and often has back-to-back sessions. I didn't understand how I could get him so easily on the phone. Now I do.* I lick my lips as his words not only move me, but turn me on.

*Over and over again, his words and actions prove to me that he is nothing like my soon-to-be ex-husband. He's kind and considerate and courteous. He's the man I should have been with from the beginning.*

—

I'm driving to my lawyer's office for my meeting with Matthew and our lawyers when my phone rings.

"Hi again," I purr.

"I'm sorry I couldn't talk earlier," he tells me and hearing those unfamiliar words render me speechless.

*"I'm sorry I couldn't talk earlier." Not "I can't talk right now. I'll call you later," and then doesn't. Or acting as if I'm a bother when I do call. Who is this amazing human? Am I that jaded that I truly believe that Will would change from the caring man that he's been all along?* "Charley?" I hear him say and I wonder how many times he's said my name while I was stuck in my head.

"I'm here," I say, my bottom lip trapped between my teeth as I think about all the things I want to do to the man on the other end. "When can I see you?" Last night, after a heavily sexual Skype date, he promised that we would see each other today, no matter what. It may have been the orgasms talking, but I was holding him to that.

*I just pray that Matt doesn't have anyone following me.*

"Anxious, are we?" he says in a low voice that causes goose bumps to pop up all over my skin.

"Yes," I breathe out.

"Me too," he growls. "Will you meet me at our house?"

I smile hearing him refer to our house so casually as if he's been doing it for years. "I would meet you anywhere. What time?"

"Maybe around seven?"

"Yes, of course."

"Park in the garage. I'll leave it open for you."

"Okay. Are we staying the night there?"

"I thought we could," he says, and my body comes alive thinking about our first night in our new house. "I know it's risky but… there's only so long I can go without seeing you. The need to see you sometimes is so great, I can't breathe," he says as if he can hear my thoughts about Matt finding out about us.

His words send a jolt of electricity through me, touching me every way it can. *My head, my heart, my soul, my sex. I didn't know it was possible to be so unbelievably moved and turned on at the same time.* "I feel the same," I say, unsure of how I manage to get the words out.

"Bottom line, Charley, you're worth the risk. You always have been." I can't believe the words coming out of his mouth. *I didn't know a man could love a woman like this. Love **me** like this.*

———

"Charlotte," I hear from behind me before I enter our usual room for an hour of cold looks and harsh words as we attempt to divvy up five years of marriage. I turn around and Matt walks toward me, his hands tucked in his pockets as if he's not looking to start an argument, rather as if he comes in peace.

*I don't.* Just seeing him reminds me of the last time we were in the same room. Suddenly, I feel angry all over again. *Just keep it together, Charley.*

"Matt." I nod and turn to walk through the door when he grabs my elbow gently and squeezes. My eyes dart to his hand on my elbow and then back to his face. Through narrowed slits, I glare at him. "Yes?" I hiss venomously.

He lets me go as if he's been burned. "I just wanted…" He shrugs and I actually see the hurt in his eyes. "Happy birthday."

*He actually remembered this year. Wow.* I nod. "Thank you, Matt."

He nods. "Are you doing anything today?"

*Yes, letting my boyfriend fuck me within an inch of my life.* "Nothing in particular. I think Lauren wanted to do something," I lie smoothly.

He nods again. "Well, I was thinking…" he says quietly as if he's scared to say the words. "We could have dinner and talk?"

My eyes widen. *What could he possibly have to say? I entertain this whole "let me try and be nice to Charley because I fucked up and forgot her birthday last year AND she just found out what a liar I am" charade, but my patience only goes so far.* "Talk about what? The year of lies you've been sitting on?"

*Glass houses, Charley. Put down the stone.*

"I know you hate me, Charlotte…but I can explain."

"No, you fucking can't," I bite out and walk through the door, not caring what he has to say.

The hour of negotiations is pretty tame today. I let Cromack do most of the talking as I stare down at the ring Will gave me under the table and fantasize about being underneath him tonight. I happen to tune in just as Cromack and Stein begin to discuss the artwork on the main floor of our house. Matt can have them. I never even liked all of those tacky pieces he chose. There was a gallery in New York I was in love with that had an entire theme that I wanted, but Matt felt it was too feminine and therefore nixed all of my ideas.

*How did I not see it from the beginning?* His disdain for me and all of my choices, my ideas, my dreams. Hell, after he made me quit my job, I'd expressed an interest in publishing because it was something that I could do from home, but he'd talked me out of it before I could even blink. *"Publishing houses are a dying career,*" he had told me. "*Everything is done virtually, anyway. Amazon, e-books; they're the way of the future. No one buys hardcover books anymore.*"

I certainly do, and I happen to know a certain doctor that fucked me against a massive bookshelf filled with hardcover books.

My mind drifts to Will, and the excitement over seeing him tonight, sends a spark to my sex. It's been a week to the day since I've seen him and all I want is to curl up in his arms and make love through the night. Tears spring to my eyes as I feel the situation beginning to take a serious toll on me.

"Ms. Pierce?"

I clear my throat, attempting to hide the tears that have formed. "Yes?"

"Is that okay with you?"

"Is what okay with me?" My cheeks heat up, realizing everyone in the room knows I'm not paying attention.

"Cromack, your client is not taking today seriously, and I don't have time for it. She's disconnected from this entire process. I can't—" Matt's lawyer starts when a familiar sound fills the room.

*Matt's cell phone.*

"Didn't I advise that you need to at least have the decency to silence your mobile device, Mr. Wells?" Cromack asks as he fiddles with his pen. "It's disruptive and frankly disrespectful."

"Relax, Cromack. My client is a very busy man," Stein argues back all the while I watch Matt looking at his phone.

"I do have to take this." He looks around the room, his eyes stopping on mine almost apologetically, and I can't stop my eyes from rolling to the back of my head as he leaves the room.

"I couldn't imagine why you two have marital problems," Cromack muses aloud.

Stein looks down at his memo pad before putting his face in his hands, assumedly just as irritated with Matt. A few minutes later, Matt returns, taking his seat across from the table, and his eyes find mine. An outsider looking in would say that his demeanor hasn't changed from earlier, but I can read his body language, I know his expressions. *He's pissed.*

*But…why?*

I fight the urge to ask if everything is okay, but then I remember that I'm still angry with him. Do I really care if one of his deals fell through? Or if one of his subordinates fucked up a contract?

*No. I don't.*

I turn my gaze back to Cromack. "Shall we continue?" I ask.

"I know we haven't discussed this in detail, but I would just like to make it clear that I refuse—absolutely *refuse* to pay alimony. I'm not supporting you, Charlotte." His green eyes are so cold, almost venomous as they bore into mine.

"I never asked you to."

"No, you're just taking half of everything I've earned." He holds his hand up, effectively silencing my lawyer. "I know. I KNOW, Georgia is a no-fault state, but it's fucked up that you get half of everything I worked hard for. Fine, I have to, whatever." He waves his hand. "But I'll be damned if you get another penny out of me when the ink on our divorce papers dries." He shakes his head, his tongue running over his front two teeth, another telltale sign that he's severely agitated.

"Matt, I don't know where this hostility is coming from all of a sudden, but don't take your work shit out on me."

He chuckles, his hands finding his eyes. "You're so good at playing the victim, aren't you?" His eyes narrow, the smile leaving his face to the point that he's almost void of emotion.

*I don't know this look. I've never seen this look.*

I look away, not wanting to hold his penetrating gaze for another second. "Let's proceed," Stein says.

"It seems both parties are clearly not in a good space at the moment. Might I suggest a short recess or perhaps reconvening on Monday?" Cromack interjects.

"Monday," Matt says. His voice is even, yet still cold. "I honestly can't look at you another second." His voice is laced with anger and resentment before he's up and out of the door.

———

I'm walking through the garage of my lawyer's office, my nerves still unsettled over the switch in Matt's demeanor. My phone rings and I dig through my purse to find it. When I see the name flash across the screen, I flinch. "Fuck!"

*Mama Wells. Okay, Charley. You knew you were going to have to deal with this eventually. Now or never.*

I climb into my car, knowing that this conversation may hinder my ability to keep myself upright.

"Mama Wells," I say using my nickname for her.

"I didn't even think you'd answer," she says and I don't detect any anger in her voice, only sadness. "Hello, darling."

"How…how are you?" I rest my back against the seat and let my shoulders sag.

"I've been better…seems I'm losing a daughter."

I squeeze my eyes shut as I feel the prickling in my scalp begin. *Don't cry, Charley. Don't cry.* "I should have called you," I say honestly. "I'm sorry that I didn't. It just…it got to be too much, Marian. You have to know I tried. So hard."

I hear her sniffle and ice rattling against a glass and I wonder if she's poured herself a stiff drink to help get her through this conversation with her estranged daughter-in-law. "Don't give up on him, Charley. Don't give up on my baby. He's just—lost."

"I didn't give up on him, he gave up on me. A long time ago. Or did he just tell you I left him out of nowhere?" I ask harsher than I intend.

"I'm no stranger to a man that works too much and doesn't always put his wife first. Matthew's father was like that. I put up with it…on top of the abuse. I guess that makes you stronger than me, huh?" *After all of this time, I can still hear the pain in Marian's voice when she discusses Matt's father, but she's also developed a defense mechanism for it. Dark humor.*

"No," I whisper. *I'm the furthest thing from strong. Some would probably say that I'm weak. I was weak to the urges and gave in to the temptation of sleeping with a man that wasn't my husband.* "I'm not stronger than you in the slightest. You're the strongest person I know, Marian."

*And it's the truth. Knowing what she had been through…what she sacrificed, she was admirable and brave. I look up to her more than she knows.*

"I couldn't protect Matt then, and I can't protect him now." *Protect him from me, I assume? From the pain I'm inflicting? Matt's father physically abused both Matt and Marian for years before, finally, one day when Matt was fifteen, he fought back.*

*And won.*

*After that Marian thought everything would get better. Matt begged her to leave, but she never did. Granted, Matt's father never hit either one of them again, but the decade of damage had already been done. Matt hated his father and their relationship was broken beyond repair. A year after that, Matt's father died from cirrhosis of the liver after he'd spent years soaking it in whiskey.*

*Matt didn't attend the funeral.*

She hiccups and only now do I realize how much she's put away. "There's no hope for you two?" she whispers and I feel a tear slide down my cheek as I realize this breakup with my husband's mother will be harder on me than the one with my actual husband.

"No, Marian. There isn't. We both need to move on. We're different people now."

"You won't come see me anymore, will you?" She sniffles and I feel my heart break hearing her words.

"Of course, I will," I say, the words flying out of my mouth before I even have a chance to think about how my new husband will feel about the relationship I intend to keep with my ex-husband's mother.

"Do you have plans today? I know it's a special day for you. Happy birthday by the way," she says and I know it's taking everything out of her to try and be happy for me. I don't have a chance to answer when she says, "I have something for you. Would you like to have dinner tonight?"

I feel all of the air leave my lungs. "Marian…I have plans tonight, but we can get together soon, okay?"

"Next week sometime?" she asks sadly but with a hint of hope in her voice.

"Okay," I say, again without thinking but I smile when I hear her gasp.

"Really? Oh, Charley, that would be lovely. I can't wait to see you, sweetheart. It's been so long."

"I know, a few weeks?" I know that isn't that long in the grand scheme of things but it is for me and Matthew's mother, as we usually had a weekly standing lunch date.

"Too long, I'll see you then, Charley."

"Right," I whisper back as I wonder how the hell I was going to face her.

# CHAPTER
## Twenty-Six

T HE RIDE IS SILENT ALL THE WAY TO THE NEW HOUSE. I DON'T even turn the radio on, needing the silence as I try to wrap my brain around the last few hours. Between Matt and his mother, I'm drained. I'm skeptical about telling Will about Matt's attitude, knowing that he doesn't think very highly of him at the moment. I can just hear him now: *This is precisely why I didn't want you around him, Wells is so unstable!*

I pull into the garage and I see Will standing in the entrance to the garage sporting a sexy smile. Grabbing my overnight bag out of the passenger seat, I sprint to the man I haven't seen in person in seven long days. "Will," I say dropping my bag to the floor and flinging myself into his arms. It isn't long before my legs are wrapped around his waist and his lips find mine. Kissing me, possessing me, his tongue rediscovering every inch of my mouth with wild abandon. I don't know how long we're kissing against the wall of the cold garage, but after some time, he pulls away and sets me on my feet. I smile when I see my berry lip stain has smeared all over his mouth. My eyes glance down to his crotch, my lip sinking into my bottom lip, thinking about the same color all over his cock.

"Are you looking at my dick, Charlotte?" His voice low with traces of humor.

"Yes. It's mine, isn't it?" I take a step forward, pressing my freshly manicured index finger into his chest. "It's mine to do with what I want?"

"Fuck," he says barely audibly and I drop to my knees, hitting the cold cement in front of him. Ignoring the discomfort to my knees, I take his dick from out of his slacks and rub it along my lips, smearing my lipstick along his shaft.

*Marking him, branding him. I want his dick to be stained this shade of fuchsia for as long as possible, reminding him where I've been and who this dick belongs to.*

He groans clearly sensing the possessive feeling that has come over me. "Charlotte," he says hoarsely, "put me in your mouth, baby."

"Say please," I say batting my lashes sweetly at him. I run my tongue from root to tip, still not wrapping my lips around him fully. He jolts forward attempting to get his member inside of my warm mouth but I move back. "Beg for it."

"I think you're forgetting how this works, Charlotte," he growls. Yanking on my hair, he tilts my head up to stare into his hungry gaze. I know he would never hurt me, and I trust him to know what's going too far, but right now I'm loving his dominant side. His other hand grabs his dick and guides it to my mouth running it along my lips. "Stick your tongue out," he commands and I oblige. He rubs his dick against my tongue, his velvety member penetrating my mouth. "Wrap your lips around me, and it's *not* a question. Do it now."

"I want you to fuck my mouth." The words fly out of me faster than I can catch them, and I feel the blush paint my cheeks.

"Char-lotte." His breathing is labored, his chest heaving up and down with what I assume to be excitement.

"I want your cock so far down my throat I can feel it in my pussy." I bite my bottom lip for emphasis.

"Jesus, woman. You're going to kill me." He takes a step closer, rubbing my lips with his cock. "Tap my leg if I need to stop." He grits his teeth.

I shake my head in response. "I don't want you to stop."

Tilting my head back, I open my mouth and his cock slides through my lips and down my throat. I swallow once, my teeth lightly grazing his shaft in the process and the roar that leaves him is almost animalistic.

"FUCK, Charley!" He looks down at me, and our eyes lock. I suddenly feel so exposed despite the fact that I'm not the one half naked. I shut my eyes, needing some sort of barrier between Will and me as the intensity of the moment overwhelms me.

"Open them. Let me see those eyes." My eyes pop open obediently. "You are so fucking beautiful and your mouth…holy fuck." My eyes begin to water, and his thumb gently wipes away the tears as he thrusts into my wanting mouth. I let him continue to control the speed, my mouth responding to his invasion. "You're going to make me come, baby." He thrusts again and again, his hands on each side of my head as he grits out his orgasm. My hands reach for his ass, sinking my nails into his skin to steady me. He jolts in response, the mild pain sending him over the edge.

"Christ, Charlotte," he groans as he spills down my throat. I pull back, and suck him hard through his orgasm, his body shaking with the force of his climax. When I know he's fully come down from the high, I slide my lips off him. Will lifts me into his strong arms and attacks my lips instantly.

"I've missed you so fucking much," he tells me between kisses. Each kiss is frantic but leaves me dizzy after each one. "Come, let's get out of the garage."

He pulls me through the living room, the sexual thoughts of what happened the last time we were here playing through my mind on a loop and heating my skin. We enter the den and there's a blanket laid out in front of the fireplace with a bucket of champagne, chocolate-covered strawberries, a few other foods, and two small boxes. My feet are glued to the spot, surveying the romantic scene in front of me. "Come," he says taking my hand in his.

I move to sit between his legs on the blanket as he hands me a glass of champagne. I lean back against his chest and clink my glass with his. "Cheers to you, Charlotte Pierce," he whispers in my ear. Turning my head, I capture his lips knowing that I need the taste of him far more than the bubbly beverage in my hand.

"This is all amazing," I murmur, looking at the variety of other foods on the blanket. I turn around to face him just as he plucks a strawberry and moves it toward my mouth. I wrap my lips around the fruit not once breaking eye contact with him and moan in appreciation. The fruit is still in my mouth when his mouth crashes onto mine. "It tastes even better when it's been in your mouth first." I bite my bottom lip as I feel a slight wave of naïveté at this man's overwhelming kinky streak. We play with our food for another twenty minutes or so, sharing kisses in between when he stops. "I have something for you."

"Will…you didn't have to get me anything, you already bought me beautiful flowers," I whisper. "And besides, all I really want is you." *And it's true. I had years of getting tangible items as gifts that collected dust in a room somewhere, and while I treasure the ring Will bought me, I don't want him to feel that he needs to get into that habit.*

He cocks his head to the side as if he doesn't understand that he's my greatest gift and holds a small box out for me. It's bigger than any jewelry box I've ever seen so I wonder what it could be. It's so beautifully wrapped, I don't want to rip the paper. "This is beautiful, Will." I finger the gold bow that's wrapped around it. "Who wrapped this for you?" I giggle and he gives me a sheepish grin.

"I do have an advanced degree, Charlotte. I've seen it done enough times that I know how to fold some corners and cut and tape," he jokes.

*He wrapped this? He actually took the time to wrap a gift for me. The thought doesn't just count. The thought is everything. I was always more than aware that Matt had his assistant wrap all my gifts. Half the time he didn't even know what the gift was in the first place.*

"Will." I rub his jaw, letting my thumb skim his bottom lip. "I am...moved, beyond words. Thank you."

He smiles a boyish smile and I swear I see his cheeks turn a little pink. I start to open it and when I peel the paper off I see it's a plain brown box. I look at him curiously and when I open it I almost drop the item out of my hands. The tears fly out of my eyes in an instant when I pull the familiar snow globe out of the box, my hands shaking more violently with each passing moment. "You...you...how?" I ask quietly, as I see the familiar people that I believed were still tucked in my purse.

"I took them from your purse when you stayed with me. I actually thought you'd notice."

I shake my head, trying to force the words to come out of my mouth but it's no use. I spin the dial twice and I hear the same music that used to play, as the two spin around the globe. I cradle it to my chest as I move into his lap, wrapping my arms and legs around him and squeeze him tight. "Thank you, thank you, thank you," I say through my tears. "You have no idea what this means to me."

*And I don't think he does.*

I set the globe down, so as not to break it again, and my hands find my eyes as I begin to sob. *I don't think I've ever had this kind of reaction to a gift.* I feel Will's hands stroke my back and his lips dancing across my bare shoulder peppering gentle kisses as my sobs turn to hiccups then sniffles. I don't know how long I've been crying when I feel his hand lift my chin. "Don't look at me, I'm a mess," I half cry, half giggle, as I wipe the tears from my eyes.

"You're beautiful," he says, "and I told you I would fix it," he whispers.

*I wonder if he even hears the irony in his statement.*
*I told you I would fix it.*

*The snow globe, me…everything. Maybe he's not such a bad counselor after all. I smile at my attempt to be funny when he smiles back not understanding my inside joke.*

"What?" he asks, his head cocked to the side.

I shake my head. "It's just…you've fixed a lot more than just my snow globe," I whisper.

He nods and I wipe my eyes for the final time, hoping I've cried enough for one day. I don't even want to know what my face looks like. Mascara runs from my tears, and lipstick is smeared from the aggressive kissing, but he's looking at me as if he's never seen anything so beautiful in his life.

"I want…I need you, *everywhere,*" I breathe out, knowing that Will's possession of me is something that grounds me faster and more fully than anything.

*I want him to understand how much I'm totally and completely his. Every part of me.*

He groans his appreciation as his hands fist my flowy dress, bunching it up around my waist and then pulls it over my head, leaving me topless in his arms. "Let me see, baby. I haven't touched your pussy in so long." His lips find my breast, sucking the skin into his mouth as his fingers find their way into my panties. He strokes my sex, that is already saturated from the mere thought of him touching me. "Lie back," he says and I lie on the blanket, after Will slides the food out of the way. I'm barely on my back when he yanks my underwear off me and the cool air hits my sex. "You waxed recently." He eyes me hungrily.

My teeth find my bottom lip as I nod. "Two days ago," I whisper. I feel him stroke my mound, and he nods in appreciation, his tongue darting out between his lips as he licks them lasciviously. He flips me effortlessly and pulls me to my hands and knees, spreading me, exposing me to him completely. I hear him pulling ice from the bucket and I shiver in anticipation.

I yelp when his hot tongue and an ice cube come against my

clit. "Oh my God," I moan, as I feel the sensation of warm and cold against me. My sex pulsates under his skilled mouth. "Will..." I groan. I hear him slurping against me, as the ice melts and I feel it dripping down my thighs. When the ice has melted completely, I feel his tongue between my cheeks that he has spread completely, and rims me as if I was his last meal. The taboo feelings of having him somewhere so intimate flood me, and I feel the arousal mixed with the moisture from the ice trickle down my thighs.

"You are mine, Charlotte. Every inch of you." I hear the sound of his belt buckle and within seconds I feel his cock at my entrance. He slides in torturously slow allowing me to feel every ridge of his cock as he pushes himself to the hilt.

"Fuck, I'm close," I moan feeling his balls slapping against my clit with every thrust.

"Get there faster, goddammit," he grits out and I move faster knowing he's waiting for me. *That I'm fucking a man that actually cares if I get off. That I'm making love to a man that loves the feeling of my cum running down his cock as much as he loves to watch it drip out of me.* "I see your toes curling," he groans and he's right, they're curled so tight, they might remain permanently that way. *Not that I'd care.* "You're right there, Charley. Give it to me, baby, come for me."

"FUCK!" I groan as my orgasm flies through me, my hands bunching the blanket below us as I feel him pick up the pace and then still inside of me and his cock releases his orgasm. Each following short pump rubs against my inner walls. He fits so snug inside of me, I feel each pulse. He wastes no time letting me come down when I feel him remove himself from me. I'm still on my knees, my body bent over, so I look between my legs and see his cock glistening with our arousals, his cum still dripping from the tip, his dick still hard. I hear the squirt of the lubricant and I see him fisting his dick between my legs. "You ready?"

"Yes, please." I feel him rub it against my puckered opening before he pushes in slightly. I clench at first, my body not used to the intrusion.

"Relax, Charley. Remember? Deep breaths, baby."

I nod remembering how good it felt once he was inside but how excruciating the first few thrusts can be. His hand finds my clit, his fingers ghosting over the bundle of nerves. "Will," I moan. I want to tell him how good it feels but I don't think the double stimulation will allow it.

I'm so focused on his fingers on my clit that I forget that he's inching his way into my asshole, bit by bit. He's been pushing in gently when his hips rest against my ass cheeks and his lips on my shoulder. "I'm in, baby," he whispers. "Can I move?"

"Yes!" I cry out, a tremor moving through me as the delicious release begins to build in my core.

He starts to move in and out slowly, and soon I'm meeting him thrust for thrust as he moves faster. "Tell me the only person who's been here. Tell me, baby."

"Only you, Will," I whine, when his hand leaves from between my legs to grip one cheek hard, his thrusts getting more aggressive as he chases his climax.

"Fuck, say it again, Charley. Say it."

"Only you," I whimper knowing he needs to hear it. "I'm yours. I've only been yours."

"Charley." He grunts out his release as he shoots his seed deep inside of me. A few moments later his lips drag down my back. "Fuck," he whispers. "You are the most incredible woman I've ever met."

―――

After our dirty romp in front of the fire, we go straight to the tub, where he washes me from head to toe, not forgetting any inch of my body. He makes me come twice with his fingers and his lips as he cleans me. Now we're in a bed that he had ordered for our guest room, reminiscent of the first time we were in a bed. We lie on our guest room bed, the only piece of furniture in the room, having just made love again, my head resting on his chest, and I decide to bring up what I've been putting off.

"Will?"

"Mmmhmm?" he says rubbing his lips over my fingertips and my heart flutters at the simple gesture.

"So, you may not know this…but, I'm relatively close with my mother-in-law."

"Is that so?" he asks. "I think you've mentioned that you care very deeply for her."

I nod against his chest. "Yes, we've spent a lot of time together over the past eight years."

"I see. And how does she feel about you and her son getting a divorce?"

"She's not…taking it well. I hadn't talked to her. I should have called her. But…I guess I just figured she hated me. I should have known that was not the case at all. Marian doesn't have a hateful bone in her body."

"But she's Matthew's mother."

"What do you mean?"

"It means by every rule that ever existed in life, she's going to take his side."

"She asked if we could work it out." I feel him tense beneath me and I rub his chest. "I told her no, Will." I feel him relax and I look up at him. "You couldn't have thought differently."

He shakes his head before he presses a kiss to my forehead. "No, but what is the point of telling me this."

"Well, she asked if I would have lunch with her next week."

"And you said?" His voice is already laced with irritation, so I know he won't like my response.

"I told her yes."

I swear I could hear a pin drop as the silence envelops us and

Will moves from under me to on top of me and looks down at me. "My counselor hat is coming on."

"Why?" I groan.

"Because you pissed me off, and I don't want to be mad at you on your birthday."

"Why are you pissed off?"

"Don't push me, Charlotte."

"I'm not, but it's not like I'm having lunch with Matt. It's his mother who is the sweetest woman I've ever met."

"Mother of your soon-to-be ex-husband," he says simply.

"So?"

"So, what reason could she possibly have to want to go to lunch with the woman that broke her son's heart?"

"Marian understands."

"Charley, I don't think it's a good idea."

"Well…I wasn't asking your permission. She's been like a second mother to me, and I completely understand that she won't be a part of my life going forward, so I certainly owe her a proper goodbye."

He eyes me warily before shaking his head. "I don't like this, Charlotte."

I reach up and rub my nose against his. "Do you want my ass again?" I ask playing into his caveman urges.

"No, Charlotte. I don't," he growls as he pulls out of my arms and gets out of bed.

"Where are you going?" I ask, feeling a chill in the room that wasn't there a minute ago.

He stands in the doorway. "I can't think when you're rubbing up against me like that."

I smile and I move to get off the bed toward him, but he puts a hand up. "Stay on the bed."

I bow my head submissively. "Yes, sir," I say before shooting him a wink.

"Don't try and fuck your way out of this, Charlotte."

"What do you think is going to happen? She'll convince me to take him back? To get back together? Do you think I'm that easily swayed? Will, I'm fairly certain you're the only person that could convince me to take him back," I say honestly.

*It's an irony not lost on me.*

Before I realize what's happening, he's on the bed, I'm on my back, and I feel his dick sliding inside of me, feeling harder than it looked twenty seconds ago. "Those words turned me on far more than they should."

"I trust that you know what's best for me, Will. I've trusted you since the second we started this," I whisper. "But there is nothing to worry about with Marian." I feel him moving gently in and out of me. "I love you. Only *you*."

"Only me," he whispers, and I nod.

"Kiss me."

We kiss, our limbs intertwined well past midnight, and around three in the morning, I feel the last of my energy pulled from me as I fall asleep safely in the comfort of Will Montgomery's arms.

# CHAPTER
## Twenty-Seven

"**Y**OU LOOK HOT, PIERCE," LAUREN TELLS ME AS WE PREPARE for a night out. My best friend believed that there was only one true way to celebrate your day of birth: tequila shots. So, here I was, in a black bondage skirt that looked as if it were painted onto me and a white top that showed a bit more cleavage than I normally do. I'm wearing my favorite Christian Louboutin heels and the black leather jacket that I scored at a *Barneys* sample sale. I've pulled my hair into a ponytail on the top of my head, knowing that the club Lauren chose will be hotter than actual hell and I want my hair off my neck.

I'd sent Will a picture, and he'd called me immediately after swearing that I was trying to kill him. He also expressed that he wasn't pleased that I was going to be out *in that* without him around to keep men away from me. Something told me I might be seeing him tonight despite the fact that being out in public together was risky.

"What did Hot Doc say?" Lauren asks as she applies a thick coat of red lipstick. "I'm surprised he didn't show up and rip my door off its hinges to get to you."

I chuckle at her exaggeration. "He was…pleased." I purse my lips. I can almost feel his words moving through me.

*Every man in that club is going to be staring at you. Wanting you. It pisses me off because you are mine, Charlotte. But you look sexy as fuck, baby.*

"And not so pleased," I add.

She shakes her head. "So, will he be showing up then?" she asks, a twinkle in her eye.

"Don't encourage his recklessness, Lo. He shouldn't show up, but I wouldn't put it past him."

"I've only had two interactions with him and just from those brief encounters I can tell that he is one of those overprotective, *don't even look at my woman*, type of men."

"He does have a bit of a caveman streak, but I think my response to it fuels it." The goose bumps pop up all over my skin as I think about how possessive he can be *and how much I love it.*

———

Friday nights in an Atlanta club are notoriously crowded. Like "line down the block and around the corner" crowded. Not to mention, the covers to get in are usually outrageous, especially if you have a penis. This is why it helps to know people, and luckily for us, Lauren knows the right kind of people, which is how we're ushered to the front of the line of *Bar Twelve* and are currently following the manager down the long hallway toward the main area of the club. The sound of the bass resounds off the walls.

"When are you going to let me put a ring on it, Lauren?" The manager is a tall blond guy who is built like a linebacker. A linebacker in an Armani suit and loafers that I know ran him at least a few thousand.

I giggle. "I'm ready when you are, babe," she flirts back.

He puts a hand over his heart. "Jet is ready to take us to Vegas."

"Private jet, huh? You're really pulling out all the stops tonight, *but* I think your girlfriend would probably have a problem with our little trip."

"Girlfriend! What girlfriend?" His eyes widen as if he has no idea what she's talking about.

"Oh, Josh, you wound me. I could teach a class on social media stalking, ya know?"

He runs a hand down his jaw, stroking his beard. "I'm breaking up with her," he admits, realizing that he'd been caught. I roll my eyes. *Tale as old as time.* Not that I had to worry about Lauren getting caught up in that. She spoke fluent fuckboy and handled situations like this brilliantly—with sass and class.

"In the meantime, though, can I borrow your jet?"

---

Going out with Lauren is something out of your typical debaucherous movie. The night consists of shots, cheering every time a song comes on, and more than likely watching as she ends up making out with someone before the night's over. She is a bona fide party girl, and while I retired from the game long ago, I still let my hair down every once in a while. I'm watching her politely decline a drink when I notice something in my periphery.

I look up to see a man that can be no older than twenty-one giving me a boyish grin. "You come here often?"

"I think that line is older than you are." I force a smile and shake my head.

"It got you to smile though. I'm Chris."

"Nice to meet you, but I'm married."

*Well, that tasted weird coming out. I guess technically I am married still but…not for much longer.*

"No ring though?" He points at my naked ring finger and I immediately rub it as I always do when I notice the empty space. The ring had rarely left my hand in the last five years, and now it's gone; a permanent reminder of how my life is changing. "I—" I start, not knowing what to say without being either caught in a lie or giving him the opening by telling him I'm getting divorced.

*Or you can say you have a boyfriend.*

"It's being sized," I tell him, not wanting to tell this ex-frat guy my business.

"Really?" He raises an eyebrow indicating that he doesn't believe me.

"You don't want to just save face and buy the lie? Obviously, she's not interested and she's trying to preserve your feelings. Let her." I hear Lauren's voice right next to me as she slides an arm over my shoulder. "But for the record, she *is* married." She gives him a smug grin and he turns away in a huff.

"*It's being sized*? What kind of lie is that?" Lauren snorts.

"It slipped out that I was married, and then what was I supposed to say? Oh, I'm actually getting divorced, but I have a boyfriend, no, thanks?"

"Sounds perfect. Makes you sound real complicated, and God knows men run from that." She takes a dramatic sip of her vodka soda before scanning the crowd.

I take a peek at my phone, surprised that I haven't heard from Will when I hear my name being shouted from next to me. I turn to see who it is and I inwardly groan, wishing that Lauren hadn't chosen this moment to get us more drinks, and that I could use her as a buffer.

*Fuck. Does this mean Matt is here somewhere?* I wonder as I see his best friend, Nathan, walking toward me.

"Birthday raging?"

I smile at Nathan's consideration. *Even he remembers my birthday. Also, had Matt not told him what was going on?* "You could say that."

"Or celebrating something else…" He raises an eyebrow at me. *So, that's a yes.*

"Nate, can we not do this now?" I'm not in the mood to talk about this at all, let alone in the middle of a crowded club while I've had one too many gin and tonics.

"That man is crazy about you."

I snort. "First of all, you don't even believe that anymore, and that's not the point. I asked if we could not discuss this now. Can you just respect that?"

He huffs and shakes his head. "You here by yourself?"

"No, I'm here with Lo."

He nods in understanding when I catch the eyes of some-one moving toward us, *quickly.* My eyes widen as I see the storm headed my way. Hurricane Will is moving toward us, and it is going to be disastrous. Before I have a chance to signal to him to stop I hear his words flying out of his mouth.

"Back the fuck off," he growls.

Nathan's eyebrows almost shoot off his face and he looks around to ensure that Will is talking to him. "Excuse me?"

I take a moment to take him in, having not seen him for a few days. *God, he looks good.* He's wearing a white button-down shirt, rolled up to his forearms, and black pants as if he just came from work, but without his jacket and tie.

"You heard me, back off." I take a break from ogling the man that I love, so I can try and do damage control.

"Will." His eyes find mine and I'm doing my best to start an unspoken conversation with him but he must be too riled up.

"Baby," he breathes out and before I can reply, his hands are on my face, his lips descending on mine. "I couldn't stay away." He smiles just before his lips touch mine.

*Fuck, this is bad. Very bad. Well, you're already fucked, you might as well let him kiss you.*

"Baby?" I hear behind me as Nathan pulls me out of his grasp. "Charlotte, what the fuck is going on?"

"What part of this aren't you getting? She doesn't want you, asshole. So, move on." *Don't do it, Will.* "She's spoken for."

I don't even know what to say at this point.

*Do I say that Will is lying?*

*No. Not that.*

"Will, stop," I tell him, pulling on his arm gently. *God, where the fuck is Lo? She would know what to do. Because I am certainly not helping.* I set my drink on the table behind me, knowing that the alcohol is prohibiting me from thinking rationally.

"Oh, I'm aware that she's spoken for. She's married to my best friend," he says looking at Will before shooting me a furious glare. "So again, I ask what the fuck is going on?"

*Shit.* The intensity of the situation coupled with the alcohol has my eyes welling up with tears.

I don't have a chance to answer before Lauren returns. "Sorry it took me so long, the line was longer than—" she starts when her eyes widen to the size of saucers at the sight of Will. They go even wider when she sees Nathan. She focuses on me and I think she's confused as to who knows what. But I know that she can sense my worry.

*HELP!*

"What's going on here?" Lauren asks.

"That's what I fucking want to know. Charlotte. Answers," Nathan growls at me.

I sigh. "Will…this is Nathan Cunningham." A moment of re-alization crosses Will's face followed by a look of remorse.

"And who the hell is this?" Nathan asks. Will is silent as he assumes I should probably do the talking. "Not so tough now, are you?" he sneers at Will.

"Nathan, stop." The last thing I need is for this to turn into a pissing contest.

"Don't tell me to fucking stop, when you've got some man with his hands on you while you're still fucking married." He shakes his head and a look of judgment crosses his face. "So, Matt was right, you've been cheating on him this whole fucking time? And you have the nerve to do what you're doing to him?" he yells.

"Don't talk to her like that," Will barks at him. *Not helping, Will.*

He puts his hand up. "I know you are not talking right now. Who the fuck are you? I've known her almost a decade. I was her husband's best man in their wedding, so you can shut the fuck up." He turns back to me. "Call this joker off, we need to talk, Charley."

I can feel the tension radiating off of Will in waves and, right now, as I watch my life go up in flames, all I care about in this moment is knowing that no matter the outcome, Will and I would be together. "Nathan, I'll be right back. I'll…explain when I get back." I grab Will's hand and move through the crowd. I vaguely hear a *what the fuck?* But I ignore it, moving out of the main bar and into a more secluded hallway.

"Fuck. Baby, I'm sorry. Guys were coming up to you left and right and—"

I stop him, pressing my hand to his chest and planting my lips to his. Our tongues tangle for a moment, and I moan, my body reacting to the taste of whiskey and mint. "I've missed you," I whisper.

"You have no idea." He lets his forehead rest against mine. "It's been a long fucking week." He rubs his nose against mine. "I was becoming unhinged."

"I see that. Nathan, of all people?!"

"I didn't fucking know, Charley! That night at the restaurant…I didn't get a good look at him. I'm sorry." He rubs my arms in an attempt to calm me, but it's not working. I'm worked up and wound so tight, I might snap any second.

*I am going to feel like shit the second I open my eyes tomorrow.* The emotional hangover coupled with a physical one. *Just kill me now.*

"That's Matt's best friend that just watched you all but pee on me in there, Will! And now I have to tell him. He's going to tell Matt." I put a hand over my eyes, feeling a headache beginning to form behind them.

"Tell me fucking what, Charley?" I hear Nathan say to the left of us and I sigh. There's no denying what's happening between Will and me right now as I'm pressed against him, his arms wrapped around me.

I take a step back, untangling myself from Will. "Nathan…" I take a deep breath, "this is…"

"Your boyfriend? Yeah, that much is obvious. What I want to know is how long?"

*At least he doesn't seem to know exactly who Will is.*

"A few weeks?" I tell him weakly and even I don't buy the lie. *Come on, Charley, sell it better than that.*

"And you're already that familiar with him? Fuck off, Charley. I'm not stupid."

"You have one more time, talking to her like that," Will growls at him, taking a step toward him.

"Stop, it's okay," I tell him. "Nathan, we didn't…" I sigh. "What do you want me to tell you?"

"Let's go with the truth."

"Oh, like you all told me the truth about Matt and Bree?"

He freezes. "You know about that?"

"Matt got drunk and told me…that night the four of us went out last month. Right before I filed." I wince, recalling that Will was there that night, and drawing Nathan's attention back to that night may jar a subconscious memory of seeing him.

"Then you know he didn't cheat on you. Matt and Bree betrayed *me*, not you, Charley. And one has nothing to do with the other. If you cheated on Matt—"

"I didn't," I tell him, preparing myself for this blatant lie. "We realized that we had feelings for each other before I filed but… we haven't…"

"You haven't slept with him? Yeah, okay, Charley. He looked like he was about ready to murder me when he saw me touch you." He snorts and I wince at his reference to Will's possessive behavior. "How long, Charley. Be straight with me."

"To be honest, it's none of your business," Will interjects. I close my eyes, the effects of the alcohol catching up with me.

"Nathan, can we not do this now?"

He shakes his head, ignoring my pleas, and Will's comment. "So, he was right. You were cheating on him."

"No," I start, wondering how I could spin this but I come up empty. "Nate, it's so much more complicated than you can imagine. But this really isn't the time or place."

"Christ, Charley," he says running a hand through his hair. "I don't even know who you are right now. This isn't you. You don't hurt people…I thought you and I were alike in that regard. Loyal, good people. You think you know a person." He shakes his head.

"I am a good person. The world isn't so black and white. There is so much gray everywhere."

"You're really defending your actions, right now? You cheated on my best friend, Charlotte."

"I didn't say that!" Nate has no proof, and I certainly wasn't about to just openly admit anything. "And don't you dare try and act like you have any fucking idea what goes on in my marriage, Nate. You have zero clue." My fists clench as I feel the anger coursing through me. *What had Matt been telling him?*

I can tell Will wants to add in his two cents, but I think it would be a huge tip-off, if he started rattling off some counselor-type wisdom. *No talking, Will.* He must read my look, because he doesn't say anything.

"And while we are on the subject, he asked if I was cheating on him with you."

"Son of a—" he yells. "I told him multiple times that I wouldn't go there." He shakes his head. "He keeps thinking I'm going to retaliate because of Bree." He shakes his head and rubs his jaw. "Them doing that to me…a part of me has never gotten over it. But I would *never* do that to Matt."

"You're a good person, Nate. Better than me or Matt or Bree. We've all done bad things and we've hurt people. I can't speak for them. Only myself. But…things change, Nate. And for me, they happened in a way that I didn't realize until it was too late. Until I was already in it. My heart decided my fate long before my brain even realized what was happening."

He looks around the hallway, and for the first time I spot Lauren at the end of the hallway, staring down at her phone to ensure she was close in case I needed backup. I smile inwardly, at her protectiveness. "Look, Charley, you need to tell him, *whatever* it is that's going on here. Tell him, or I will."

# CHAPTER
## Twenty-Eight

TRIED TO HEED NATE'S WARNING BUT, PER USUAL, IT WAS impossible to get in touch with Matt; I'd called him, texted him, left word with his assistant four times and he'd yet to contact me. He'd even been absent for a meeting with our lawyers. My infidelity was something I wanted to discuss in person, and he was making it absolutely impossible. *Unless he was avoiding me.* I wasn't sure if Nate had already told him his hypothesis and I was getting more anxious by the day.

*Maybe I should just show up at the house?*

I'd considered that, but Will had killed that idea before it had fully formulated.

*"You cannot be alone with him for this conversation, Charlotte. Absolutely not."*

*"Oh, you want to be there?"* I'd snorted. *"That's a great idea."* I *wasn't planning to tell Matt who the man was, praying that Nathan was just drunk enough to not remember Will's name or anything that would allow Matt to put it together.*

*"I don't give a fuck. Do not go to your house."*

So, now I'm pacing the length of Will's office, under the ruse of a post-marital counseling session, trying my best to keep calm as we plan the next course of action. "He must know."

He taps the space next to him. "Baby, come sit down. You're so anxious."

"You think?" I stamp my foot. "Matt is avoiding me, and his best friend knows that there's another man, regardless of the specifics… It's been a week, he must have told him by now." The morning after, Nathan had called me and informed me that he would give me time to tell Matt the truth. That the last thing he wanted to be was the bearer of *that* news. That he deserved to hear it from me, and that *I* owed him that much. But I wasn't sure how long this courtesy would last.

"He said he would give you time to tell him, Charley." I continue to pace when I feel his hands gripping my waist and dragging me toward the couch and into his lap. "Breathe, baby."

I take an exaggerated breath and he nuzzles his face behind my ear, rubbing his lips against the spot that he knows makes me weak in the knees. "Will…" A whimper escapes my lips.

"I need you, baby. I have to fuck you," he groans into my ear. "You knew you were going to tease me with this short-ass dress of yours. So now I need a taste of what's underneath and you need to release some tension."

I grind my ass into his growing erection and before I can think he's ripped my dress from me and flipped me onto my back, his head ascending up my legs within seconds. He pushes my panties to the side, and presses his lips to the slick flesh, running his tongue over my clit before sucking it into his mouth. He swipes his tongue back and forth several times before I grab his face, pulling him up my body. "Fuck me," I moan, needing the kind of fullness that only his cock can give me.

His dick is out within seconds, and I look down, the very second it touches my sex and I squeeze my eyes shut, as I attempt to memorize the visual. He's not even inside of me and I feel myself on the edge, waiting for the orgasm to rip through me. He taps his dick against my clit a few times and I feel my toes curl in response to the pleasure shooting through my brain. "I can't wait for this to be over."

"We're so close, baby," he says as he begins to thrust inside of me over and over again. I feel myself building, the sounds of our lovemaking bouncing off the walls of the room. I haven't been this wet in some time and the sounds it causes my body to make when he thrusts makes this feel even sexier. "I can't wait until you're finally mine."

"I am yours," I moan. "I always have been." And it's as if those words are his undoing as he pushes into me a final time and I feel him shudder on top of me.

"FUCK," he roars before his lips attack mine in a searing kiss and my own orgasm follows right after. I squeeze my eyes shut as I feel the lightning bolt shoot through my body. I squeeze him to me, dragging my nails down his back as the pleasure I'm feeling becomes too much.

"Oh my God," I breathe out as I try to calm my racing heart. "That was…"

"Everything," he says in my ear as he captures it between his teeth. "I'm going to fuck you every day for the rest our lives, Charlotte Pierce."

I let out a moan. "Is that a promise?"

"Fuck yes. Should I write that in my vows? I solemnly swear to love, honor, cherish, and fuck you into oblivion for the rest of our lives."

"Yes, exactly like that." I smile.

"I do promise that, you know." I look at him, my eyes narrowing in confusion as to what exactly he meant.

*Promise to fuck me? Thank God.*

"To love, honor, and cherish you. To never take you for granted. To be the husband you deserve. To protect you. To show you how beautiful and sexy and enticing you are every single fucking day," he says before he drags his teeth across my pulse point. "To keep you safe. To never lie to you. To always put you first because you're the most important person in my world, Charley. You always will be. I love you so much…I always have." He presses a gentle kiss to my lips.

I can't stop the tears that have escaped my eyes as I hear this beautiful profession of love for me. "Will…" I'm so moved by his words that I'm at a loss for my own.

*How do you even reply to that?*

"I—" I start when Vanessa's voice comes through the room successfully cutting me off. I can see the annoyance in Will's eyes immediately and I hope he doesn't rip her head off too badly.

"Dr. Montgomery? Hi…ummm…" I hear the uncertainty in her voice and I wonder what has her so nervous. "I apologize for the interruption but…Mr. Wells is on his way upstairs. *Now.*"

# CHAPTER
## Twenty-Nine

V ANESSA'S WORDS SEND ME INTO PANIC MODE, MY WIDE eyes a direct reflection of the terror coursing through my veins. He's still inside of me so he pulls out immediately and I wince from the loss of contact as well as the emptiness that floods me.

"Holy shit," I exclaim as I pull my dress over my naked torso. "What do I do...what...did you know he was coming? Should I hide?" I scurry to the bathroom, pulling my hair up into a ponytail and securing it at the back of my head as I move. I keep a bag of toiletries hidden deep in the back of his cabinet, and I quickly search for the hairspray to lay down my just-fucked hair.

"No, I didn't know and no, you shouldn't hide. Get dressed. You're technically scheduled for a session, so we just have to play this as if everything is normal. If you hide and he figures out somehow that we had a session and that you were here, *that's* worse." Will has just finished putting on his jacket, and he runs a hand through his hair. I'm sure he's just as anxious as I am, but he remains calm. *My guess, as an attempt to keep me calm.*

"Are you nuts?" I begin to take an actual bath in my perfume spraying it all over myself, to mask the scent. "It smells like sex in here." Despite the fact that we started lighting candles to mask the smell, the scent of sex still lingers in the air. Usually we had about ten minutes to air out the room, but the two to three minutes that we have until Matt is here is not enough time. "Your face probably smells like...*me.*" Will moves quickly into the bathroom to swish some mouthwash and splash some water on his face, trying to remove the smell of my orgasm.

I'm in the process of opening a window and spraying some air freshener when I hear him. "I can be in here with Vanessa."

"What?" I ask, and I'm sure my face is a mix of confusion and a twinge of hurt as I sense where he's going. Him and Vanessa would be in here...having relations.

"I'll bring Vanessa in here, if it smells like sex well..." He runs a hand through his hair and slides his glasses on.

"And I'm here...what? Watching?" I ask, my eyebrows rising to my hairline, as I pull on my jacket.

"No, you'll be outside in the waiting room. You're early," he says and I'm trying to run through every scenario in my mind as quickly as possible.

*That could work.*

"Fine," I grab my bag as I move toward the door. I unlock the door, my hand on the knob when I freeze, hearing Matt's voice just on the other side of the door. I turn to look at Will, my eyes wide with horror as I dash to the couch.

*It's showtime.*

I sit in my usual spot, crossing my right leg over my left and smoothing my dress down. I reach for my light pink lipstick and swipe it across my lips, my hands shaking as I slide it back into my purse. I place my hands in my lap and look at the man that I love more than anything. I give him a small smile as I brace for impact. He rakes his eyes over my body once, but I don't think it's sexual, rather protective.

*Relax,* he mouths, *I love you.*

I mouth the same, when I hear the door fly open. We both

turn our gazes to the source of the noise as if we're surprised at the sudden intrusion, to find Matt staring at us angrily.

"Mr. Wells—" Will starts. I assume he is preparing to chastise him for his interruption when he closes the door behind him.

*Well, shit.*

"Oh, so you didn't even attempt to hide?" he sneers at me.

"What?"

He strides across the room, sitting down next to me on the couch and I shift uncomfortably in response. "Oh, come now, Charley. Let's not play games here."

"Mr. Wells, Ms. Pierce and I are in the middle of a session, this intrusion—" Will starts when Matt interrupts.

"Oh, it's Ms. Pierce now? That's what you call her?" He crosses his legs and narrows his eyes at him, and I know in this moment he knows.

*He's fucking with us, and he's going to enjoy it.*

"Not…Charlotte? Or *Charley*…" He leans forward, his hand under his chin. "Not…baby?" "Tell me, what do you call my wife when you're balls deep inside of her?" He raises an eyebrow.

Hearing the words fall from Matt's lips makes me feel like someone has knocked the wind out of me.

*How does he know?*

*Did Nathan tell him?*

*Nathan didn't even know anything for sure!*

*Fuck! I knew I should have just showed up at his office or at home. Now everything is a mess!*

"Matt, what are you—" I start, but he interrupts me again.

"Don't you dare fucking lie to me. Don't act like you have no idea what I'm talking about. Stop playing me for a fool! I'm so sick of the fucking lies, Charlotte. What I want to know is how long?"

I look at Will, unsure of what to say when he snaps. "Don't fucking look at him, look at me, Charlotte. *I'm* your fucking husband!"

"I—I—" I stammer, my brain-to-mouth function not working.

"HOW FUCKING LONG?!" he bellows and I flinch at his volume.

"That's enough." Will moves to his feet in defense, as if he's preparing himself for attack.

Matt turns to look at Will and smirks. "The Doc speaks." A sinister smile crosses his face before he stands and strolls across the room toward the bar and pours himself a large glass of scotch. "Tell me, Montgomery. When did you *start* fucking my wife?" At this point, he's moved back toward me, standing within arm's reach of me, looking down at me.

He strokes a hand over my head, running a finger down my cheek, and I immediately shrink away from his touch. "She's soft, isn't she? Her skin feels like silk," he says. "Does her pussy still taste like—" I'm about to speak up, not wanting to tolerate his crass language, when Will has pushed him away from the couch, taking a protective stance in front of me.

"Stop," he growls, his fists clenched at his sides.

I am praying to every higher being I can think of that this doesn't come to that.

"Stop what? We're all friends," Matt chuckles. "Hell, we're like those special brothers now, right? Fucking the same woman and all."

*I don't understand his angle and I have so many questions. Why isn't he yelling? Screaming? We are a week away from my divorce being final and now things just got a whole lot more complicated.*

*And that's if Matt doesn't go to Will's ethics board.*

*Fuck.*

"How?" Will says, the one word that was as good as a confession. His eyes dart to mine, apologetically.

He looks back and forth between us and he chuckles as he sees the look Will and I share.

He crosses his arms in front of his chest. "I had you followed." He points at me. "I knew something wasn't adding up, but I just wasn't sure *who*." He shakes his head. "But then things started coming together. Finding out your father is a lawyer for the firm representing my wife got me thinking. While he informed me there wasn't anything wrong with it, Stein thought it was odd as well. He said your body language was very…familiar. So, we started talking…and Stein, he suggested that maybe you two were closer than you let on." He shrugs. "But I wanted proof. I *needed* to know, once and for all. And sure enough, my PI confirmed it, followed you to a house across town. That day we were in the meeting with our lawyers. *That's who called.*"

*Fuck. That was a week ago. He's known since then?*

"What I don't know is how long, but you're going to fucking tell me. How long you've been playing me for a fool. Was this all along? Before we even started counseling? Was this a plan to fuck me over and take my money? After everything we've been through, Charlotte?"

At this point, the tears are flowing down my face and I sniffle. He drops to his knee in front of me and puts his hand on my knee. "Oh, honey, why…why are you crying? Because I see you for what you really are? Because you have to drop the good girl act? You can no longer play the victim in our divorce?"

I try to push his hand off my knee but he grips it harder. "Does he fuck you good, Charlotte? Is that why? You went crying to our therapist because you're a horny bitch?" He stands up just in time for Will's hands to find his chest, pushing him away from me.

"Fucking stop, right now," Will snarls.

"And you—ballsy as hell. Fucking a married woman you counsel? Risking your practice? Your license? Your life? Was the pussy worth it? I know she's hot, but damn, really, Doc?" he snorts, and I can tell Will is resisting the urge to put his fist through his face as he knows that would just make everything worse. But it doesn't stop him from grabbing Matt by his suit jacket and dragging him to the wall, slamming him against it.

"You are going to STOP fucking talking about her like that," Will barks. "Unless you don't want to leave this room with all of your bones intact," he adds.

"And now he threatens," Matt chuckles. "You're making my case so easy." I see Will loosen his grip on him and his hands drop to his sides.

*Oh my God, is he going to sue Will? Could he? Fuck, fuck, fuck!*

"Matt, stop it!" I move toward them. "I…" I let out a breath as I'm at a loss for words. "I—I'm sorry. This is all my fault."

"You're sorry? Are you fucking kidding me? That's all you have to say for yourself?" Matt shakes his head. "Nathan was right."

"Nathan?" *So, Nathan did tell him about the other night? I really thought he would have at least given me a chance.* My breath comes rapidly and I wonder if I'm on the verge of a panic attack.

"You really thought he wasn't going to tell me? You thought you could—what, convince him I didn't deserve to know as some sort of sick payback? Did you play up the fact that I slept with Bree?"

"He said he was going to give me a chance to tell you!" I cry, my hands beginning to shake violently.

"I can't believe you even *thought* that he wouldn't tell me he saw you all over some other man. Nate's loyalty lies with me, not you, Charlotte." He shakes his head. "God, you had me fooled. You had everyone fooled. You're a terrible person, Charlotte Pierce." He looks down on me. I wasn't prepared for his words, *and I'll admit they sting.* "How long?" he snaps, his eyes as dark as night. "The fucking truth."

I bite my lip, nervously feeling as if I've been backed into a corner. *Will, what do I do?* I look at him for help, but I can't read his face. His cold eyes are trained on my husband and not looking at me. "A few months."

"What the fuck is a few?" he asks, not accepting my vague timeline.

"Two months, Matt."

"Bullshit," he snaps.

"It's not."

"You're so full of shit, you know that? You act like I haven't known you ten goddamn years. I know when you're lying, Charlotte."

I swallow hard before I relent. "Five," I whisper, my hands finding my eyes as the shame of lying to him for so long hits me like a ton of bricks.

*I should have dealt with this months ago. Why did I do this to myself? To Will? Even to Matt? He's right, I am a terrible person.*

He shakes his head. "You've been fucking my wife for five months?" Matt says, looking at Will. "This whole fucking time." He shakes his head.

"Matt…I never meant for you to find out this way," I tell him.

"You never meant for me to find out at all. You thought you could just take my money and ride off into the sunset with your boyfriend," he says.

"Matt, I didn't even want anything from the divorce. I tried. You know I tried. I don't want anything from you. I told you to keep the house, keep everything. I wanted my car, my fucking

Cartier watch, and some jewelry that had some sentimental value or ones that I bought my damn self. Don't make it seem like I wanted half of everything."

"Georgia and its goddamn divorce laws," he growls. "Even with this, I can't do anything to you," he says before turning his sinister gaze to Will. "You on the other hand," he narrows his eyes at Will, "I can bury you with this."

Fresh tears form in my eyes and my scalp prickles hearing him threaten Will's job. "No!" I shriek. Will is still somewhat in front of me, so I push him to the side so that I can be face-to-face with Matt. "Your issue is with me, not with him."

"It's with both of you."

"Don't take it out on Will," I whisper. "I'll rip up the settlement."

He doesn't respond to my comment, he just walks toward the window. He stares out of it for a moment. "How many times did you fuck in this office, and I came in right after? The unknowing idiot husband?" He shakes his head. "No, I want something so much more than money. You betrayed me. Both of you did." He turns around and looks at us. "Tell me, Charlotte, you think the doc loves you? Is going to be with you forever? How many wives do you think he's fucking? You can't be that naive that you think you're the only one—do you think you're special?"

"She is the only one," Will jumps in. "I *am* in love with her." His tone is firm, full of conviction.

*At this point, we might as well be transparent.*

"He took advantage of you as your counselor, Charlotte."

I glance over at Will and I can see in his eyes what he's thinking. *Not true. Don't believe it, baby.*

*I don't,* I try to tell him as best as I can with my eyes.

I shake my head. "Matt, it wasn't like that!"

*We just...fell in love.*

He snorts before turning his focus to Will. "And let me guess, she loves you? Until she does the same thing to you that she's done to me? Until she gets bored with you and finds another plaything? What makes *you* so sure that you're the only one she's in a relationship with now? You two have weaved this web of lies and deceit, how can you even trust each other?"

"Because we love each other, Matt," I answer. "I know you're hurt, and I'm sorry." I wipe my eyes as the tears blur my vision. "I fell in love, but our marriage was broken beyond repair before Will came into our lives. We were just putting Band-Aids on the problems, but they were only temporary solutions, and if you were honest with yourself you would admit that. You aren't brokenhearted over this," I continue. "You're embarrassed and your ego is bruised but you haven't loved me for a long time. This isn't about me sleeping with someone else."

He shakes his head. "You don't know shit about what I feel, Charlotte. What I've learned through this whole process, is you only care about yourself. When you needed someone to get you away from your stepfather, I was there. When you needed a place to stay, I was that person. When you needed someone to pick up the pieces of your life and go with you to therapy and hold your hand, I was that person. And then you changed. Once you were strong enough to stand on your own, something you were never able to do before, you realized you didn't need me anymore. It's always been about you, Charlotte. You're the most selfish person I've ever met in my entire life and I wish I had never met you." His words are like knives slicing through my heart.

*He's hurt, Charlotte.*

*You hurt him.*

"How can you even say that to her. You know she doesn't have a selfish bone in her body. She stood by you longer than she should have. You treated her like shit, Matt, and you know it. You lied to her about her fucking stepfather. You ignored her, neglected her…the list is endless. She was strong enough to walk away because she *had* to be. You have nothing to do with her strength," Will interjects.

Matt is silent as if he's letting Will's words sink in before he looks at me. "Charlotte, you can keep the money. All of it. At this point, even if I can prove an affair took place it wouldn't matter much. So, you keep the money, because when I'm finished with both of you, it'll be all you have left." He starts moving toward the door before turning back to look at Will. "It's funny, all this time you were sleeping with her, did you really think that if this blew up in your face she would be around after you were disbarred? Lost your practice, your license? Everything? Did you really think that a woman that you were fucking in *marriage counseling* was a loyal and faithful, *be there with you till the end* type of girl? You see what she does after she gets what she wants, don't you? She leaves," he says, "and she'll leave you too." With those final words my husband slams the door behind him leaving me and the man I'd left him for.

**Will and Charlotte's Story Continues Summer 2018**

## *Will*
*Seven Months Earlier*

"**D**r. Montgomery, your twelve o'clock, Mr. Wells and Ms. Pierce, are here." The voice of my assistant, Vanessa, floats through my office just as I finish reading through their file.

"Thank you, Vanessa," I say. "I'll be right out." I run a hand through my hair and pull my glasses from my face.

*The first session with a couple is crucial. Everyone is usually on their best behavior but I catch little things. I learn their body language with each other even though they are trying to act as if things aren't as bad as they appear to be. The eye rolls that they think I don't see, the shoulders that tense up when their partner talks, the obvious disdain that they try to hide.*

I open the door and almost take a step back in awe when the most beautiful woman I've ever seen is sitting there in my waiting room. I resist the urge to stare at her as the air slowly leaves my lungs, and fail.

Her legs are crossed, her hands folded in her lap, and her back so straight it's like a string is attached to the top of her head, keeping her perfectly erect. Her shiny, chestnut hair is cascading down her back and over her shoulders in waves that I swear belong in a shampoo commercial. Her lips are full and plump, and currently formed into a pout, though I notice her mouth ticking slightly upwards as I move closer to them. I scan her face, and when our eyes lock I feel the electricity move through me. She blinks her eyes a few times, attempting to break the trance between us, but

I don't remove my eyes from hers. Her brown irises are bright, hidden behind long, well curled eyelashes, and I'm convinced she has the most beautiful eyes I've ever seen.

*What the hell is this woman doing in marriage counseling? Any man married to her should be on his knees worshipping the ground she walks on. Okay, Will, you know the beautiful ones are the MOST crazy. Just wait till she reveals it.*

"Mr. Wells, Ms. Pierce," I say, realizing that I haven't said anything this entire time I've been ogling another man's wife. Although, I don't believe that he's noticed as I see now that he's engrossed in his phone.

"Dr. Montgomery." Mr. Wells nods and shakes my hand, firmly of course, doing his best to assert his dominance. He walks through my door ahead of his wife without another word and I want to scoff at his lack of manners. *Chivalry is dead and gone in this marriage, huh?*

"It's a pleasure to meet you," Ms. Pierce starts and her voice is so soft and sweet, it's as if she sprouts wings and a halo instantly, because she sounds like an angel. "Thank you for meeting with us." She walks by me, her scent flooding my nostrils and sending a spark to my groin.

*Holy fuck, what is that? She smells divine. Christ, Montgomery. Get it together.*

I close the door behind me and sit in my chair in front of them as I take in the two painfully uncomfortable individuals sitting on opposite ends of my couch.

Mr. Wells looks almost hostile, his arms crossed, leaning back, one leg over another as his index finger traces his lips, cockily. He's looked at his watch at least twice since he's sat down and it's obvious he'll be one of those husbands that don't take this process seriously. Ms. Pierce on the other hand, looks nervous. She's fidgeting with her rings and her teeth keep finding her bottom lip. I try not to focus on it because it's distracting as hell.

I look back and forth between them before I begin. "So, why don't you tell me a little about yourselves? Ms. Pierce?"

"Well, Matt and I have been together eight years, we got married about five years ago," she says giving a small smile. "And things have just been…difficult as of late," she says, and I give her a small smile.

"Ms. Pierce, I admire your diplomacy, but you're in marriage counseling, now isn't the time to be diplomatic. I have read all of that in your file, and we will come back to that. Right now, I want to know about *you*."

"Oh, right, okay, sorry," she says nervously and my eyes narrow. *Why is she apologizing?*

"You've done nothing wrong, Ms. Pierce. No apologies necessary. Continue."

"Right. So, I graduated from UGA with a degree in marketing. When I graduated, I was offered a position as an events coordinator for The *Wyndham Hotel Group*. I worked there for a little while, until I got married. Then, I quit." She blanches, and although I can't hear it in her voice, I can see it on her face. *That was not completely her decision and I can sense a bit of resentment regarding it.* "And now I…" she starts before she looks down at her hands and I know this is the moment. *The moment every couple has at some point after they cross the threshold of this room. Sometimes it's an hour in, or a day in, or a week in, but with Ms. Pierce it's ten minutes in. She's about to lose it. And then we go to work.* "Now I don't do anything," she says and looks up at me, the tears amplifying the color of her eyes. "I'm a prisoner of my own life."

I hear a snort from the other side of the couch. "Here we go." It's the first time he's spoken since his terse greeting.

"Heaven forbid I'm honest about my feelings in therapy," Ms. Pierce snaps immediately.

"A prisoner of your own life? Really? God, you can be so dramatic." He rubs a hand over his eyes, clearly exasperated.

"Okay, in here it's better if we refrain from personal attacks or direct insults. I know it's a bit of a cliché, but we need to start sentences with 'I feel.' Mr. Wells, you can say 'I feel that I don't understand what you're saying.' This is a safe space for both of you and I don't want either of you to feel stifled, *but* you *do* need to respect each other."

The rest of the first session went similarly to how it started and it quickly became clear to me that Mr. Wells treated his wife like she was a burden. He didn't pay her much attention, he knew nothing of her current dreams, her drive, her passion, her love of literature. He used her as a pawn in his life because she fit into his *American Dream.*

*But did he love her?*

The jury was still out on that, and I had yet to pass judgment.

—

We were about a month into our sessions when Ms. Pierce started to open up more. She had quickly become one of my favorite patients and I started to look forward to seeing her every Monday, Wednesday, and Friday. She was witty and smart, and had a smile that stopped my heart the few times she flashed it at me. She was kind and courteous and I watched as Mr. Wells unabashedly walked all over her during their sessions.

"Mr. Wells, tell me how you feel about children?" I ask one Wednesday afternoon and he immediately shakes his head.

"She knows I'm not ready for that."

"Does she know why? She's made it clear about her feelings on the matter, and yet I don't think I know why you are so against it."

"I'm only thirty, I'm doing well in my company, we're still young. She's twenty-eight. It's not like her biological clock is ticking. She has plenty of time," he says as if he's rattled off these bullshit reasons a time or two before.

"While that may be true, she believes that she is ready and

it might be something worth discussing. This is a marriage, Mr. Wells, it's about compromise."

"You can't compromise about a kid. If I'm not ready, how is that fair to them?"

"What about it makes you feel that you aren't ready? Do you think you wouldn't make a good father?" He shrugs but doesn't offer up any explanation and I wonder if there is more to that story. I know that his father died when he was in high school but he hasn't discussed it much.

*There is something these two aren't telling me. I can sense it.*

"So, what do you think it will take for you to be ready?"

"I don't know," he says, brushing me off as he looks out my window. "Time?" He shrugs.

"How much time?" I hear her voice ring through the room, not accusing or harsh or angry, rather meek and timid. "I want a baby," she says softly.

"Well, that's not happening right now. Deal with it." He's still looking out the window and not making any effort to look at his wife.

*But I do.*

I see her lip tremble and the tears flood her eyes. She clears her throat, swallowing them down, and while I've never been one for having contact with my patients, I want to wrap her in my arms and let her know that everything will be okay. That I'm here for her. That I care. The sound of her husband's cell phone rings through the air, and I try to control my look of disapproval as he tells her that he *has to take it*. She doesn't even respond before he's moving toward the door.

Her eyes follow him out of the room and linger at the door long after he's gone. I'm not looking at her straight on, but her body language shows that she's hurt, but also that she's not totally surprised at his lack of empathy.

"Ms. Pierce?" My voice is soft and her eyes flit to mine. "Are you ready to be a mother…*right now?*"

I know she can hear the true meaning of my question, because she nibbles on her bottom lip nervously. "I *am* ready to be a mother. Father aside…I didn't exactly grow up with the best father figures." She swallows, and for a moment I see the darkness cloud her beautiful features. Then she shakes her head as if trying to rid the thoughts from her brain.

*What was that about? Did someone hurt her?*

"If my mother could do it, so can I."

"That sounds like you're prepared to do it alone."

"It's not ideal but…why should I keep denying myself what I want?"

I don't say anything in response, because frankly, I'm at a loss for words. I'm not in a position to advise her on her options if Matthew isn't a part of the plan, and I'm not about to go putting thoughts in her head.

I'm ripped from my own thoughts when she speaks again.

"You ever look at your life and wonder how the hell you got here? One minute you're twenty-one and completely in love and the next minute you're twenty-eight and you're wondering—where did the years go? Where did my life go? When did my relationship change? When did…when did Matt's feelings change? When did *my* feelings change?" She shakes her head and I see the tears building in her eyes. "I can't live the next sixty-plus years of my life like this, Dr. Montgomery. Hell, I won't make it another sixty years in this relationship." She looks around and takes a deep breath. "I'm…miserable," she says, and I wonder if it's the first time she's said the words aloud.

Her words wash over me, seeping into my soul. The room is quiet, her soft gaze holding mine before she shrugs. "Ms. Pierce—" I start, wondering which words of wisdom to offer her.

"I should go," she interrupts me as she stands. "I don't know how long his call will take, but our hour is almost up." She looks down at her watch and smiles. "I'm sorry to waste your time like this, Dr. Montgomery."

"It's not a waste of time," I say giving her a genuine smile. *Truth is, I enjoy Ms. Pierce's company, probably far more than I should.* "We are going to unpack what you said on Friday, alright?"

"Forget I said anything."

"No. That's not how therapy works," I tell her. "You need to continue to be honest about your feelings."

She nods. "Okay."

"Ms. Pierce," I call out to her as her hand finds the door.

"Yes?" She stops to look at me as I make my way over to her.

*I don't know what to say to her. She looks so completely broken. So fragile. Her husband is slowly breaking her and I'm doing a shitty job of stopping it.* "Keep your head up, okay?"

She seems surprised by my words but she gives me one of her heart-stopping smiles and nods as if I've given her the most profound advice. "Thanks, Dr. Montgomery."

⸺

"I'm not happy, Matt. I haven't been for a year!" Charlotte rarely raises her voice, but when she does it is usually because of Matt's evident indifference.

*He can be such a dick.*

"And you think I am? You think I like this?"

"You're not doing anything to try and change it!" Charlotte shrieks as she begins to pace around my office.

"What do you want from me?!" he yells back.

"To care! To talk to me. To want to spend time with me! Hell, something! I'm in this marriage too, Matt."

"I'm aware of that, Charlotte."

"You don't even look at me anymore."

"I don't have time for this," he says, getting up from the couch.

Charlotte pushes against his chest. "NO! You don't get to walk away from me! You don't get to push this aside and brush the problems under the rug *again*! We have to deal with this. Why won't you talk to me? Why do you hate me so much?"

"I don't hate you, Charlotte. Don't be ridiculous," he says as he runs a hand through his hair.

"Then what is it?!"

"I DON'T KNOW!" he roars and I'm seconds from telling him to rein in his temper when he cools off. "I'm sorry for yelling, I'm just…tired. Tired of dealing with this. This is exhausting. I am tired of feeling like I'm failing as a husband, failing at this marriage. And I just—I don't know that I can do this shit anymore," he says, and just as quick as the words are out of his mouth, he's gone.

Charlotte is frozen in place, staring at the door that her husband just walked out of and then she's on her knees, sobbing violently into her hands. I've been around crying women before, *often*, but seeing her cry like this, does something to me that I've never experienced and before I can think I'm kneeling next to her, rubbing her back.

"Hey, it's okay," I say soothingly and it only makes her cry harder. "Hey…" I pull her face from her hands and looking into her glassy eyes. "Let's get off the floor, okay?" I say softly. She nods and lets me lead her to the couch. I hand her the box of tissues that sits on my coffee table and I sit in front of her on the table.

"Thank you," she whispers. "I'm sorry I lost it like that."

*She's got to stop apologizing. I have to break her of that.* "Nothing to be sorry for." I am toeing the line right now but my hand finds her face and I wipe the tears that have streamed down her cheeks. Her mascara has run, leaving black smudges underneath her eyes that are red and a bit swollen.

*But she's still the most beautiful woman I've ever laid eyes on.*

"I think my time is up," she sniffles as she grabs her purse and stands.

"Ms. Pierce," I stop her and she turns to look at me, "you will be happy again." I smile at her. "We'll get you there."

*Two weeks later, I had sex with Charlotte Pierce.*


*Present Time*

It's been an hour and we haven't said anything. Charley has barely looked at me. She's been staring at a spot on the floor since Matt left, the slam of the door effectively kick-starting her shock. I held her, kissed her gently, stroked her hair, nothing. I've gotten no reaction out of her in over sixty minutes and it's starting to worry me. The only words I've uttered were to Vanessa when I thanked her for the Chinese food that was now sitting between us on my coffee table. I finally muster up the courage to say something.

"Baby, you need to eat something," I say, looking at her untouched food.

"I'm not hungry." She takes another sip of the dark liquid that's swirling around the tumbler I gave her.

I push her hair behind her shoulders and stare at her. She's staring straight ahead and hasn't so much as glanced at me. "Just a few bites?"

She shakes her head slowly and although I'm not looking at her straight on I can see the vacant look in her eyes. *She's in shock and almost catatonic.*

"Charley," I say grabbing her face, and finally, her eyes find mine. The warm chocolate eyes I'm used to seeing are replaced by foggy, lifeless ones. The tears have made her perfect lashes damp and smudged. "It's going to be okay."

She blinks slowly a few times before turning her head again. "I'm sorry that this happened."

"Don't apologize. We knew this risk. I knew it. It's going to be fine. We're going to be together. I know all of that shit he said isn't true, about you leaving me." *The thought sends a chill through me, and although I don't believe it, it did stop my heart hearing Matt speak my greatest fear.* "I know you're in this with me."

"You shouldn't want me in this with you. You shouldn't want me at all." Again, she doesn't look at me.

*Okay, Charley clearly needs a counselor more than her boyfriend right now.*

"Charlotte," I say, commanding her attention and she turns her head slowly, "you're in a bit of shock. Which is normal, but you have to snap out of this. *Now.*"

"I should go," she whispers, the tears building again in her lids.

"No," I say instantly, "you aren't going anywhere."

*At this point she doesn't need to be anywhere but with me. There's no sense in going to Lauren's now. There's no one left to hide from. Everything has been brought into the light.*

"I'm sure you need to call your lawyer and do damage control. I don't know…whatever you can do to minimize the damage to your reputation. It probably won't help to do that while I'm here," she says softly.

*Gone is the fiery, confident Charley, and replacing her is a scared, devastated girl who believes that she's not good for me.*

"I need you here. You are my main focus right now. Everything else can wait."

"Why?" she asks as the tears begin to fall down her cheeks. "This is going to ruin your life. I ruined someone's life," she says sadly, "and it's the person I love most in the world." Her lip trembles and it takes everything out of me not to lean forward and take the lip in between my teeth and nibble on it gently.

*Even when she's vulnerable, I want her. Need her.*

"Say it again," I say moving closer to her.

"What?" she asks, looking up again.

"That you love me."

She wipes her tears and I move her hands away gently so that I can do it for her. "I do love you, which is why I hate myself so much right now."

"No hating yourself," I growl. "You're still talking to a counselor right now. None of that in here," I say, smiling at her, trying my best to lift her mood just a bit. "We both did this. We both got ourselves into this mess and we are going to get out—together. But I need my strong Charley. I'm nothing without her and I can't do this by myself," I say giving her another small smile.

She gives me a half nod before she's in my arms holding me as tight as I'm holding her. "I'm in this with you," she says so quietly. "I would never leave you. I don't want you to lose anything…but if you do, I'll still be here."

I can't stop the smile that moves across my face. "That's nice to hear."

"You didn't actually believe what he said."

"No." I shake my head. "Doesn't mean I liked hearing it."

"He knew what to say to get in your head. He's good at that. And I'm the only manipulative one," she says, rolling her eyes, and I'm happy to see glimpses of my girl coming back to life.

We sit in silence for a few moments before she buries her face in my chest. "I love you." The words come out muffled and choppy from the emotion in her voice.

"I love you too, baby, more than *anything*. Remember that."

"You know this isn't over, right? Matt isn't going to let this go."

"I know, but I'll protect you, Charlotte. *Always*. No one is going to take you from me. That is a *promise*."

# Author's Note

This was the story that made me believe that I could do this. That I could be a writer. That I could have a vision and bring it to life. That other people could *see* that vision. I know I touched on sensitive topics and ones that may have disturbed or made you feel certain things. But I'm glad that you were able to appreciate this story for what it was—a love story that results in spite of inconvenient circumstances. A story that possessed me in a way that changed who I was as a writer and as a person.

For those of you that have been on this journey with me for quite some time, you know how much these characters mean to me. I hope I did them justice.

For the new readers, thank you for going on this ride with me and I hope you stick around for what's next. We're just getting started.

# Acknowledgments

They say it takes a village to raise a child. It takes one to write a book as well.

*Katherine and Carri*: the people that were forced to share a space with me while this came together. You guys deserve medals. Thank you for being so supportive of my dreams and for helping me achieve them. And most importantly, for knowing when I need silence and when I need wine.

*Carmel and Erica*: I'm fairly certain I sound like a broken record at this point when it comes to you two. There truly aren't enough words to thank you for everything that both of you have done. You inspire me every day and I wouldn't want to be on this ride with anyone else.

*Liz*: The first thing I see when I look at this book—my first paperback book is your work. You shared something with me that I'll never forget. I am so overwhelmed and in awe of what you did for me. Thank you for making my book so beautiful. All the love.

*Helen and Kristene:* The best betas a person could ask for. Truly. I hope you're not sick of me yet, because you two are stuck with me forever. Thank you for your thoughts and ideas. Thank you for knowing and loving my characters as well as I do.

*Meli, Suzan, Christelle, Alexis, Amanda, Jeanette, Kelly, Samantha, Kristina, Rachel, Harlipen, Paula, Leslie, Nani, Pat, Carol (x3), Kerri, Colleen, Gayle, Hope, Regina, Amber, Candice, Crissy, Aby, Kris, Karen (x2), Gloria, Julie (x2), Connie, Nichole, Tonya, Tatiane, Cindy, Lori, Shannon, Kim, Marie-Lyne and SO many more including Everyone in the Hive(s):* Thank you for your friendship. Thank you for your enthusiasm. Thank you for the laughs and the love. I always repeat the saying that sometimes "family" is the one you're born into and sometimes it's the one you make for yourself. Thank you for being that family. That tribe. That village.

# Also by
# Q.B. TYLER

*My Best Friend's Sister*
*Unconditional*
*Forget Me Not*
*Bittersweet Love*
*Love Unexpected*
*Unlawful* Coming Soon


## BITTERSWEET DUET
*Bittersweet Surrender*
*Bittersweet Addiction*


## CAMPUS TALES SERIES
*First Semester*
*Second Semester*
*Spring Semester*
*Summer Semester* Coming Soon

# ABOUT the Author

Hailing from the Nation's Capital, Q.B. Tyler, spends her days constructing her "happily ever afters" with a twist, featuring sassy heroines and the heroes that worship them. But most importantly the love story that develops despite *inconvenient* circumstances.

Sign up for her newsletter to stay in touch!
eepurl.com/doT8EL

Qbtyler03@gmail.com

Website:
www.authorqbtyler.com_

Facebook
www.facebook.com/author.qbtyler

Reader Group:
www.facebook.com/groups/784082448468154

Goodreads:
www.goodreads.com/author/show/17506935.Q_B_Tyler

Instagram;
www.instagram.com/qbtyler.author

Bookbub:
www.bookbub.com/profile/q-b-tyler

Twitter:
twitter.com/qbtyler

Printed in Great Britain
by Amazon